Forget this ever Happened

CASSANDRA ROSE CLARKE

"[A] trippy, twisty SF mystery...
Original and compelling." —*Booklist*

HOLIDAY HOUSE • NEW YORK

Copyright © 2020 by Cassandra Rose Clarke

All Rights Reserved

HOLIDAY HOUSE is registered in the U.S. Patent and Trademark Office.

Printed and bound in August 2020 at Maple Press, York, PA, USA

www.holidayhouse.com

First Edition

1 3 5 7 9 10 8 6 4 2

Library of Congress Cataloging-in-Publication Data

Names: Clarke, Cassandra Rose, 1983- author.

Title: Forget this ever happened / Cassandra Rose Clarke.

Description: First edition. | New York : Holiday House, [2020] | Audience: Ages 14 and
up. | Audience: Grades 7-9. | Summary: "Set in 1993, teenage Claire navigates the
eerie town of Indianola, Texas, where a fissure in time and space has made nothing
is as it seems"— Provided by publisher.

Identifiers: LCCN 2019052551 | ISBN 9780823446087 (hardcover)

Subjects: CYAC: Space and time—Fiction. | Family life—Fiction. | Lesbians—Fiction. |
Memory—Fiction. | Supernatural—Fiction. | Texas—History—20th century—Fiction. |
Texas—Fiction.

Classification: LCC PZ7.C55334 Fo 2020 | DDC [Fic]—dc23

LC record available at https://lccn.loc.gov/2019052551

ISBN: 978-0-8234-4608-7 (hardcover)

For Rozi Ayers, lover of the real-life Indianola

CLAIRE

Claire climbs out of the back seat of her parents' car and stands on a cracked driveway surrounded by brown grass. The air smells of oil refineries and dead fish. After a moment's hesitation, she shoulders her backpack like a soldier preparing for war.

Her mother has already pulled Claire's suitcase out of the trunk. She leans against the car and squints at the squat, pink brick house waiting at the end of the drive. "You'll have fun," she says. "Living on the beach."

"We're not on the beach."

"You're close enough." A pause. "Grammy says my old bike is still in the garage. It's only about a ten-minute ride."

Claire doesn't answer. She assumes time has distorted her mother's memory. There's nothing about this house, with its peeling shutters and straggly flowerbed and patches of bare soil, that suggests the beach.

Claire's mother walks up to the front door and rings the bell. In the shade of the porch, she pushes her sunglasses up on her forehead. Claire hangs back in the hot sun. Her mother doesn't look like she belongs here: She's too sleek, too polished, too fashionable. And yet

1

here is exactly where she grew up. Twenty years ago, Claire's mother bounded down that sidewalk and rode her bicycle through the shabby little town of Indianola and lived, in one way or another, an entire childhood and adolescence. Claire can hardly imagine it.

The door swings open. Behind the screen, Grammy's face appears, powdery with makeup. She still wears her hair like it's the sixties.

"You're late," she says.

"There was a wreck on the highway." Claire's mother taps her foot. "Could you let us in? It's sweltering out here."

Claire knows it won't be any cooler inside. The house was built before air-conditioning, and Grammy never bothered to install it because Grammy never bothers with anything that would bring her into 1993.

Grammy unlatches the screen and retreats into the potpourri-scented darkness. Claire's mother pushes her way in first, quick and impatient—Claire knows she gave up her Saturday to drive her down to Indianola, and she's probably thinking of all the household chores she needs to take care of, all the work she brought home with her from the real estate office. Claire follows her in, down the narrow hallway, into the living room. It's like stepping into a cave. The curtains are drawn tight over the windows and the air is hot, like Claire expected. Stuffy. A metal fan rotates in the corner, casting an arc of moving air that's not nearly wide enough to encompass the whole room.

"I'm going to put you up in the blue room." Grammy shuffles over to her chair and collapses into it. Her skin is pale beneath her makeup, and there are dark circles under her eyes that Claire has never seen before. "That was always your favorite, wasn't it?"

"Sure." Claire is lying; she's never had a favorite room. Her family usually stays at the Days Inn when they visit Grammy. It has air-conditioning.

"Let's drop off your things. I really want to get back on the road by two o'clock." Claire's mother bustles down the hallway. Grammy watches from her chair, her glasses reflecting the light of the floor lamp. She doesn't offer to help because she can't help. That's the entire reason Claire is here: Her grandmother is sick with some sort of chronic disease that leaves her constantly exhausted. She insisted that Claire stay with her this summer, even when Claire's mother offered to scrape together the money to hire a live-in nurse.

The door to the blue room is the only one open in the hallway, and the room itself looks as it always has. Dusty sheer blue curtains. A twin bed with a tattered blue quilt. A desk weighed down by an old-fashioned typewriter and stacks of ancient ledgers. A vanity with an arch of lightbulbs and a cloudy mirror. A framed photograph of a mansion on the wall, black-and-white, with a palm tree growing in the front yard. Inset in the frame is a metal label that reads *Sudek Mansion, 1890.* But the Sudek family, Claire's family, has never owned a mansion, as far as Claire knows. She asked Grammy about it once when she was younger and got yelled at for her trouble. Just another unpleasant Grammy memory.

Claire's mother opens up the closet, drags out the fan, plugs it in. It switches on immediately at high speed, stirring around the hot air. A trickle of sweat drops down Claire's spine. It's going to be a long, lonely summer.

"Do you need any help unpacking?" Claire's mother looks over at

Claire, her hands on her hips. Claire can tell by her expression that she expects the answer to be no.

Claire shakes her head.

"Good. I'm really going to have to hustle to get back."

Claire tosses her backpack on the bed, next to her suitcase.

"I wrote down all the numbers you might need." Claire's mother pulls a sheet of paper out of her purse, folded into a tight square. She hands it to Claire and Claire unfolds it. There they are, all the numbers.

"You've got her doctor, the local hospital, the closest neighbors—the Freytags, you remember them? Plus I wrote down the number for the grocery store. Maybe they do deliveries."

"I doubt they do deliveries," Claire says.

"Well, I'm sure Grammy will let you borrow the car."

Claire doubts that too, but she doesn't say anything.

Her mother taps her foot, frowning down at the list. "I don't think I'm forgetting anything. You can always call the house if something comes up. You have the credit card we gave you?"

Claire nods.

"*Only* for emergencies. Grammy agreed to pay you an allowance each week, so you spend that on yourself."

"I know, Mom."

Her mother draws her into a hug. The fan blows dust across them both. For a moment Claire thinks she can smell the sea.

"Have fun this summer," her mother says.

"Impossible," Claire says.

Claire expects her mother to chide her, but she only sighs again, and brushes Claire's hair away from her forehead.

"Nothing's impossible here," she says, and her voice is very far away.

Claire stays in her room after her mother leaves. She hangs up a few of her blouses but realizes she finds the prospect of unpacking too depressing. This isn't a weekend visit: It's an entire summer. She has to give up her life in Houston for three months. No one-dollar nights at the skating rink. No afternoons stretched out in the sun at the neighborhood swimming pool. No concerts. No trips to the mall. No late-night drives with Josh, the one boy who's ever given her the time of day.

All her freedom—gone. Wiped clean away. Sometimes she thinks her mother does these sorts of things on purpose, like she doesn't want to let Claire be a teenager, like Claire has to skip straight ahead to adulthood. Claire is pretty sure her mother just sees her as live-in staff and not a daughter at all. But Claire isn't a nurse, for God's sake! What if Grammy falls and can't get up, like the lady in the commercial? What if she has to go to the hospital? Worse, what if she *dies?*

Claire shudders. She barely remembers the CPR class she took a couple of summers ago. And yet here she is, having to care for a relative who may as well be a stranger, all because Grammy refused to let her mother hire a professional, and Claire's mother, who usually never lets anyone tell her what to do, actually went along with it.

Claire peers through the curtains, past the grime on the window, and out at the front yard. Everything looks dead. The fan hums in the background.

Sighing, she turns and pulls clothes out of her suitcase until she finds her Walkman. It still has the cassette that Josh gave her, with all those darkly dreamy gothic bands. She's been listening to it nonstop since the end of the school year, ever since she found the cassette waiting

5

for her in her locker, wrapped up in a sheet of notebook paper. *Lovely Claire* was written across the front in fancy looping script.

Claire sprawls out on the bed and stares up at the globe lamp hanging from the ceiling. Old-fashioned. Everything in this house is old-fashioned. She closes her eyes, loops on her earphones, and hits play. The music erupts mid-song. She can barely understand the lyrics, but maybe that's the point. The fan cools her skin. Maybe she can stay like this until August, trapped in a coma of music and heat.

A knock at the door.

Claire sits up and pulls off her earphones. Grammy walks in without waiting for permission.

"You aren't going to unpack?" Grammy asks, steadying herself against the doorframe.

"It's too hot."

Grammy snorts. "You'll get used to it."

Claire doesn't say anything.

"I thought I'd show you the kitchen. Your mother said you can cook?"

Claire shrugs. "I had to learn. She and Dad are never home."

"Well, that's more than she can say for herself at your age. Come along."

Claire tosses the Walkman aside and follows Grammy out into the hallway. It's like walking through water. The air fills her lungs and stays there.

The few times Claire has been to Grammy's house before, it was always Christmas. The house looks empty without strands of garland and a blinking tree shimmering with tinsel. Claire imagines she'll get used to seeing it this way. The thought depresses her.

The kitchen looks empty too. Claire isn't sure she's ever seen it when it isn't stacked with dishes and pots and pans, when her mother and aunt aren't bustling around getting dinner ready.

"Just wanted to show you where everything is, so there won't be any confusion later." Grammy opens up drawers and cupboards and points things out as she talks. Her movements are slow and shaky and weak. Claire feels a pang of sympathy despite her annoyance with this whole situation. It's not Grammy's fault she's sick, and it's not necessarily Grammy's fault that Claire doesn't know much about her either. Her mother certainly hasn't gone out of her way to make sure Claire ever had the chance to really speak with her own grandmother.

"Pans are here," Grammy says. "Dishes. Silverware. Pantry. The stove is gas, you have to light it with a match." She pulls a box of matches off the windowsill next to the sink. "Do you know how to do that? I'm sure your mother has the finest electric range in that tacky eyesore she calls a home up in Houston."

"Yes, I know how to do it." Claire shivers with annoyance.

"I don't want you burning the house down."

"I won't." The annoyance turns to rancor: How hopeless does Grammy think she is?

Grammy nods with satisfaction. "I like to eat dinner around five thirty. You can do what you'd like until then, assuming you've finished any chores. Watch out for the vermin. We've got rats out here and if you touch one you'll get a disease."

Claire doesn't answer. Grammy surveys the kitchen, wisps of hair falling into her eyes. She doesn't brush them away. "There are some things in the pantry," she says. "Mrs. Freytag got them for me. Let me know when you need to buy more groceries."

7

Claire nods.

"I've got to take my pills three times a day." Grammy points at a divided plastic pillbox sitting on the windowsill next to the matches. "One with each meal. Nasty things, but the doctor insists, and I want you to make sure I don't forget."

"Okay," Claire says.

"I'm not used to being sick." Grammy stares at a blank spot on the wall beside the refrigerator. "Not used to it one damn bit."

Claire doesn't know what to say. She waits for Grammy to elaborate, to give her some hint as to how she should respond, but instead Grammy turns and shuffles out of the kitchen. A minute or two later, the television switches on, flooding the house with the roar of applause from an afternoon game show. Claire opens up the pantry: cans of tuna and cream of mushroom soup, some noodles, some boxed cereal, a loaf of bread. Claire shuts the pantry. The TV jangles in the background. It's so hot, Claire can hardly think straight.

She doesn't want to be inside this house anymore.

There's a door next to the kitchen table that leads to the back patio. Claire slips out. A breeze blows in from the direction of the Gulf, cool and salty, and so it's actually cooler out here than in the house. It's probably even cooler on the beach.

Claire steps off the patio and walks over to the garage. It's not attached to the house; it must have been built later, thrown together with leftover parts. Claire heaves the door open. The air inside is hot and stifling and smells faintly toxic. Grammy's old Chrysler Cordoba lurks in the shadows. A string hangs down from the ceiling, and when Claire pulls it, the garage floods with yellow light. There's not much space to move around the car, since the garage is filled with stacks of boxes and rusting tool parts, but Claire picks her way around the perimeter as best she can, mindful of spiders and scorpions and diseased rats.

She's almost to the back of the garage when she spots the end of a handlebar poking out from behind a cardboard box of moldering books.

"My ride." Claire's voice bounces around strangely inside the garage.

She takes a deep breath and climbs up on the box of books, balancing herself as best she can. The bare lightbulb and the square of sunlight don't reach all the way back here. The shadows crawl over her feet. She imagines a rat sticking its pointy face out of the darkness and biting her.

Still, a bike is better than walking, especially in a Texas summer. So Claire grabs hold of the handlebars and lifts. For a moment nothing happens, but then the bike jars loose. One of the boxes crashes down and its contents scatter across the floor—all yellowed school papers covered in an unfamiliar scrawl. Claire tugs the bike all the way free and wheels it out of the garage. Then she goes back in and cleans up the papers, shoving them haphazardly into the box. Her aunt Susan's name is written across the top of them all. Claire doubts her own mother even keeps her report cards, even though she makes A's every semester.

The bike waits for her out in the sun, although it's so coated in dust it doesn't even gleam. Plus the tires are flat. Figures. Claire swipes the dust off the seat, and her hand comes back coated in a layer of gray grime. Maybe there's a bike pump buried somewhere in the garage, although given the way the summer's gone so far, she's not banking on it.

"Hello there!"

The voice comes out of nowhere, musical and bright like a wind chime. Claire jumps and looks over her shoulder.

A girl in a yellow sundress stands at the end of the driveway, a basket tucked in the crook of her elbow. She lifts her free arm and waves wildly, like she and Claire know each other.

"Are you Claire?" she calls out.

"Yes?"

"I'm Audrey." The girl has the same fresh-faced look as the pretty cheerleaders at Claire's school, all pink glossy lips and wavy blond hair. She strides forward and sticks out a hand. Claire takes it, aware suddenly of the sweat on her palm. But Audrey doesn't seem to mind. She just smiles more brightly and shoves the basket in Claire's direction.

"I live down the road. Your grandmother told my mom that you were going to be staying with her this summer, and I thought, wouldn't it be just *grand* if we became best friends? There's hardly *anyone* my age around here. We only have one hundred kids at the high school."

"Oh." Claire feels like she's under some kind of attack. She takes the basket gingerly on both sides. It's full of cookies wrapped in plastic Baggies.

"I made them myself. I'm in the Future Homemakers of America."

Claire is somehow both shocked and not surprised at all that such a club exists in Indianola.

Audrey smiles even wider. "What clubs are you in at your school?"

"Uh." Claire looks down at the cookies again. "I'm not really in any clubs." She hesitates for a moment. "I won second place in the science fair, though."

"Oh, that's great!"

Claire feels pathetic. Back in Houston she was proud of the fact that she didn't join any clubs. It made her one of the cool kids; Josh didn't join any clubs either. But it's clearly different here, and when faced with the prospect of this long, empty summer, she isn't willing to alienate Audrey with her non-joining ways.

"Anyway," Audrey continues. "I have a car, so if you ever need me to drive you anywhere, feel free to call. I stuck my number in the basket." She points. "It's on the welcome card. Oh, and I know you're probably busy with unpacking and everything, but I'd be so *happy* to give you a tour of Indianola if you'd like." She beams with pride. "I was the official tour guide when Governor Richards visited last year, so I've got practice."

"Oh, okay."

They stare at each other. The Gulf breeze stirs Audrey's hair around her bare shoulders.

"Is that your bike?" she asks.

Claire glances down at it. "Yeah, well, it was my mom's. I need to find an air pump—"

"I have one at my house. You can borrow it." Another bright grin. Claire feels both welcome and unnerved.

"Sure, that would be great." Claire shifts her weight. The basket of cookies is heavy. She looks down the driveway at Grammy's house, squat against the pale sky. The rest of the afternoon stretches out in front of her, and the idea of spending it inside that hot, stifling house is not remotely appealing.

"Hey," Claire says, and turns back to Audrey, who smiles at her again. "About that tour. We could do it now, if you like. I'm really not busy and I'd like to get to know the town and everything, since I'll have to take care of my grandma."

Audrey claps her hands together and lets out a delighted squeal. "Oh, I was *hoping* you'd say that."

Claire slides the cookie basket up her arm and pushes the bike back into the garage. Audrey stands on the driveway with her hands on her hips, watching her. Still unnerving.

"Let me just drop the cookies off," Claire says.

"Oh, I'll come with you!" Audrey says. "I'd love to say hello to Mrs. Sudek. She's such a sweet old lady."

Claire doesn't say anything. *Sweet* isn't the word she'd have used to describe her grandmother.

They go into the house. The room swims as Claire's eyes readjust to the darkness. She sets the cookies on the kitchen table. Audrey walks down the hallway like she's been here before.

"Mrs. Sudek!" she calls out. "It's Audrey Duchesne!"

Grammy's sitting in the living room chair, the TV blaring. She looks up at Audrey and blinks like she isn't sure what she's seeing. "Ah," she says. "Hello."

"Claire and I are going on a tour of the town." Audrey loops her arm through Claire's, startling her.

Grammy doesn't smile. "Very well. Be back by five." But she's look-ing at Audrey as she speaks, her eyes narrow and appraising. Claire can see the resemblance to her own mother, who's certainly turned that expression on Claire plenty of times. Especially in the last few years.

But Audrey either doesn't notice or doesn't care. She swings around, taking Claire with her, and leads her outside. Claire feels like she's caught up in a tornado that's whirling her away from Grammy's house. Audrey leads her down to the driveway to a little blue two-door, the glass in the windows coated with a layer of salt. Claire crawls into the passenger seat. The car is very clean. No sand, no crumpled receipts. It looks brand-new.

"Indianola's not very big." Audrey cranks the engine and the air-conditioning roars on with it, already set at full blast. "So this won't take *too* terribly long."

Claire nods. All Claire knows of Indianola is this neighborhood and the Days Inn on the highway and the convenience store where her father always stops to buy gas. They only come out here every other year at Christmas. Eight visits total, and even those visits were in and out, Claire's mother corralling them back to Houston as quickly as she could. The town itself, then, is a mystery, nothing more than a name on her grandmother's address.

Audrey weaves through the neighborhood. The houses are spaced out, isolated, as if each wants to pretend the others don't exist. They pass by a sprawling whitewashed suburban-style mansion and Audrey says, "That's my house. You can come by whenever you like."

Claire nods, although something niggles at the back of her thoughts. She swears she's never seen that house before—

The thought vanishes, replaced by a memory of a walk after Christmas dinner two years ago, Claire and her mom strolling past a house twice the size of all the others on the street.

Claire rubs her forehead.

A few minutes later, they're on the main road leading into town. No one's out; Claire doesn't blame them, not in this heat. They pass by a seafood shack and a shop selling cheap swimsuits and sunglasses.

"That road leads down to the public beach," Audrey says, pointing. "It's nice enough." They drive along, past a strip mall and the grocery store, which is smaller than Claire expected. There's a gas station,

Alvarez Quick-Mart, the same name as the one on the highway where her father stops for fuel. They pass another one a few moments later, with the same orange-and-white sign. This one is next door to an exterminator. A big sad-looking cockroach lights up, its neon washed out by the sunlight. *Alvarez Bros. Exterminators*, the sign says, then below it, in smaller letters: *All manner of vermin, no exceptions.*

"Is this the same Alvarez who owns the gas stations?" Claire asks.

Audrey glances at her. "Oh yeah, they own half the stuff in town." She turns down another side street. "They even opened up a video store last year, so we *finally* have a proper one. I used to have to rent videos from the grocery store. Does Mrs. Sudek own a VCR?"

"No way. It's weird enough she has a TV."

Audrey laughs. "Well, they rent them out. I can show you, if you like."

Claire shrugs. The road narrows. It's lined with old houses that have been converted to shops and restaurants. One of them has a painting of a pizza on the sign, and the word *Arcade* glowing in the window.

"Oh cool," Claire says. "An arcade."

Audrey glances at it and tosses her hair. "If you're into that sort of thing. Here, there's the video store."

It's attached to a motel, old-fashioned-looking, the *NO* in the vacancy sign switched on. The video store just says *Alvarez Video* and there's a poster for the *Twin Peaks* movie in the window.

"Wow, awesome," Claire says, and for the first time since her mother announced how she'd be spending her summer, she sparks with excitement. "They've got good stuff. The Blockbuster by my house just has popular crap. You know? Cartoons and rom-coms."

"The Alvarezes are very successful," Audrey says, a little primly. "Do you want to see the beach? It's just a little ways down the road."

"Sure."

They drive on, and Claire starts feeling better about her summer in Indianola—making the best of the situation, the way her mother told her to do on the boring drive down. There's an arcade and a beach and a cool-looking video store and Audrey, even if she is too perky. Maybe these three months won't be entirely wasted.

The beach appears suddenly, the road diving off into the dunes. Audrey parks the car so that it faces the water and they sit in the air-conditioning, watching the waves roll in.

"This summer's going to be wonderful," Audrey says. "Don't you think? The beach, the video store, the two of us! We'll have such fun."

"Yeah." Claire nods. The roar of the AC covers the roar of the Gulf. She can't shake the sudden feeling, stupid as it is, that Audrey was rooting around inside her head. "Totally."

CHAPTER

CLAIRE

Cicadas whine from their invisible hiding places in the trees. Claire repositions the standing fan so that it blows directly on her like a blast of static. She found the patio outlet this morning while she was sweeping grass off the cement, and now that's it the middle of the afternoon she's grateful. It really is noticeably cooler out here in the sea breeze than it is trapped inside Grammy's house.

Claire has been in town for three days. Audrey's driven her to the grocery store to buy a few toiletries she left at home, but Claire hasn't had time to go swimming at the beach with her or really hang out. The chores Grammy mentioned on the first day take a lot more time than Grammy led her to believe. Already Claire has cleaned the house from top to bottom, in addition to cooking Grammy's meals, helping her in and out of bed, and bringing her the little white pillbox three times a day. No wonder Grammy refused to hire a nurse. What she really wants is a maid.

At least Claire has this afternoon to herself. Finally.

She switches on her Walkman and arranges a sheet of stationery on the old encyclopedia she's using to write on. She found the stationery in her bedroom, buried deep in the desk. It's old, with swirls of blue flowers and a yellow tint to the paper. She thinks Josh will appreciate it. He likes old things.

Josh, she writes, leaving off the *Dear* because it sounds too girlfriend-y. *I've been listening to the tape you gave me. It's great! I really*

She stops and lifts her head and stares out at the empty backyard, keeping one hand pressed against the stationery so it doesn't blow away. The music doesn't quite cover up the hum of the fan. She doesn't know how to describe this music. She has to make it clear that she *appreciates* it, but not that she thinks it's too heavy or dark (which she kind of does).

She turns back to her letter.

like the fourth song ("Prelude to Agony"). The lyrics really speak to me.

She reads over what she wrote and feels revolted. She scratches out *speak to me,* digging the pen in so deep, the words completely disappear.

captures what it's like to

Claire sighs. She thought it would be easier to write to Josh, since then she could think about what she's going to say before she says it, but it turns out that she thinks too much. Maybe she ought to call him. But then Grammy would ask about the charges, and she'd probably tell Claire's mother about them, and it would be a whole big *thing* and just not worth it. Plus, what if Josh doesn't want her calling anyway? Definitely not worth it, then.

The wind picks up, smelling of the sea. Claire can't hear it over the music, but she can see it knocking the palm trees around. Something ripples in the grass—a shadow, a dark quick movement.

It stops.

That's when Claire knows that it's not some trick of her eye. She stays still, watching the dark spot in the grass. It's too big to be a rat. A rabbit, maybe? A little thrill of excitement goes up her spine. She never sees wild animals in Houston. Well, not anything interesting, just birds and maybe a nutria if she goes to the park.

The shadow twitches again. Claire reaches down and turns off the cassette. She pushes her earphones down so they loop around the back of her neck. The fan pushes her hair away from her face.

Out in the grass, the shadow lifts its head.

At first Claire isn't clear what she's seeing. The head is reptilian, gray scales glittering in the sun. But it's too big to be a lizard or a snake—

An alligator? Are there alligators around here?

She freezes. The excitement evaporates. She remembers a school trip she took last year, out to the Big Thicket, and how the guide warned them about alligators as they were racing down the banks to the river. "Don't get too close," he shouted over the shrieks and giggles of delight. "If you hear it hiss, you need to back away!"

Claire isn't sure if she's too close right now. Slowly, she gathers up the encyclopedia and her stationery and pen. Maybe she can dart inside and call animal control. Grammy probably won't want an alligator in her backyard.

She stands up, moving slowly, not taking her eyes off the alligator.

It hisses.

Claire drops the encyclopedia. Her letter to Josh flutters across the patio.

And then the alligator stands up.

Those are the only words Claire has for it—the alligator *stands up*, on two hind legs, like a person.

It's about two feet tall, its body covered in thick, glossy gray fur, the scales of its head scattering around its shoulders. A tail curls around its legs, flicking out at the end, catching the light of the sun.

A red scarf is draped around its neck.

Claire doesn't move. She considers the possibility that she's hallucinating. But then the creature lifts one hand, the fingers too long and curving in arthritically at the last joint. It points at Claire.

"Girl," it says, in a low hissing voice.

Claire screams. Blind with panic, she runs into the house, where she slams the door shut and jams the lock into place. The window beside the door is still open, the wind stirring the curtains. She can see the creature—the *monster*—staring at her through the mosquito screen.

She shrieks again and bangs the window shut. The monster still stares at her. She knows she has to close off the rest of the house, but her fear has her rooted in place.

"What's *going on* out here?" Grammy shambles into the kitchen, her hair mussed from her nap. "Screaming and carrying on—I need my rest."

"Look!" Claire shouts, jabbing her finger at the window. "*Look.*"

Grammy doesn't answer right away, and for one terrifying second Claire is certain that Grammy doesn't see it, that she's having a breakdown, that maybe this is the reason her parents shipped her out here, she's having a breakdown and they know and don't want to deal with it because it would interfere with their perfect, modern lives—

"Oh, hell," Grammy says. "They aren't supposed to get this close to town. You'll need to call the exterminator."

Silence.

"What?" says Claire.

Grammy inclines her head toward the window. "The monsters. Probably not the most accurate term, but it's what we call 'em. They're a nuisance around here. Not dangerous really, not unless you provoke them." Grammy narrows her eyes at Claire. "You didn't provoke it, did you?"

"I don't—I don't think so?"

Grammy peers out the window. "Oh, probably not. It's just staring at the house. Damn things. Call the exterminator, they'll come clear it out for us. The number's next to the phone. I'm going back to my nap. My joints are hurting too much for this excitement. Wake me up when you've got dinner ready." She moves to go back to her bedroom. Stops. Looks over her shoulder. In the sunlight her skin is chalky and pale. "You probably want to stay inside until the exterminator gets here. We try to keep our distance from the things."

"Planning on it," Claire says shakily.

Grammy nods and leaves the kitchen. Claire turns back to the window. The monster is where she left it, standing amidst the yellowed overgrown grass, swaying like it's being blown by the wind. She stares a few moments longer, waiting for something to change. Waiting for something to make sense. Nothing does.

She goes to the kitchen phone.

A list of phone numbers is written on a piece of paper with an oil company's logo plastered on the bottom, the handwriting faded and old. The exterminator is four numbers down.

Claire steals another glance at the monster. It's still there. Hasn't moved.

She dials. The phone rings two times.

"Hello, Alvarez Exterminators. How may I help you?" The woman on the other end sounds bored. Claire takes a deep breath.

"I have a, uh, a *monster*"—she cringes as she says it—"in my backyard and, uh, I was told to call—"

"How big is it?" the woman asks.

"What? Oh, I dunno, I—two feet, I guess?"

"Did it speak?"

"Um." Claire leans up against the wall. She wonders if she fell asleep out in the heat and this is all some weird nightmare. "Yes? It pointed at me and said *girl*."

The woman makes a clucking sound. "And the address?"

Claire tells her.

"Very well. I'll have someone out there in about ten minutes." She hangs up before Claire can say anything more.

For a moment, Claire listens to the dial tone, hoping it will wake her up. But it doesn't.

She sets the phone back in the receiver. Then she goes to the window, and her heart leaps: The monster's vanished. But no—after a second she sees that it's just crouched down in the grass again. Her letter to Josh is still out there, her pen and papers scattered across the patio. She'll have to start over. And figure out some way to tell him about the monsters that doesn't make her sound insane.

She digs her nails into her palms, even though she doesn't really think she's dreaming. Her dreams are never this vivid. They tend to happen in black-and-white.

Claire closes the blinds. Then she goes around to all the other doors in the house and locks them. She turns on the TV with the sound down low so that it won't disturb Grammy. There are only two stations out here, both local stations that crackle with static. Neither show anything interesting, but she leaves *The Golden Girls* on to have some noise in the house. Her head buzzes. She's come to this house every other Christmas for the past seventeen years and not once has she seen a monster. Not even heard someone *talk* about them.

She thinks about her mother during those trips, fussing in the car as her father drove the family down the highway. Her brother would turn on his Walkman right away, but Claire didn't always feel like listening to music, and sometimes she listened to her parents' conversation instead. *I hate going to this place*, her mother would always say, flipping through the magazine in her lap. *You know how it is.*

Her father grunted in reply.

You know how it is. Claire always took that to mean that Indianola was dull and backward, a time capsule stuck in the 1960s. Or that her mother hated the way Grammy insulted their life in Houston, complaining that Claire's mother had to be the breadwinner, that she didn't have time to maintain a proper home.

But maybe her mother meant something else. Maybe she meant monsters.

Monsters her mother didn't even bother to warn her about when she dropped Claire off. Although that would be like her, wouldn't it? She was probably too wrapped up in some client or other to mention it.

Claire kicks at the ottoman sitting in front of the chair and it skitters across the room, just as the doorbell rings.

She switches off the TV and goes to answer it. She expects a middle-aged man in coveralls, or maybe a priest, but instead she finds a girl her own age, tall and pretty and brown-skinned, with tangled black hair and dark liner around her eyes. She holds a big metal cage.

"You called about a monster?" she asks.

"You're the exterminator?" Claire blurts it out before she can stop herself.

"Yep. Julie Alvarez." She holds out her free hand. Claire shakes it. Julie grins at her. "Did you just move in or something? Isn't this Mrs. Sudek's house?"

"I'm her granddaughter. I'm helping her out this summer."

"Oh. Tight." Julie shifts the cage from one hand to the other. "So where is it? Out back, I guess? I didn't see anything when I drove up." She jerks her thumb over her shoulder, toward a big white van with a plastic sculpture of a cockroach perched on top.

"Yeah. Out back. You can come through the house." Claire holds the door open and Julie shrugs and walks in. She's not wearing a uniform, just hot-pink shorts and a Nirvana T-shirt knotted at the waist. Not what Claire expected at all.

Claire leads her through the house. When they get to the kitchen, Claire opens up the window blinds, her heart pounding. The monster's still out there, the scaly curve of its head poking out above the grass.

Julie sets the cage on the floor and presses one hand against the window, peering out. She gives a nod like this is all familiar to her. "And you said it spoke?" She reaches into her pocket and pulls out a notepad. "Says here it called you *girl*?"

"That's what I thought it sounded like..." Claire's voice trails off. The way everyone, from Grammy to the receptionist on the phone to this girl Julie, is treating the monster like a normal everyday thing just convinces Claire further that she's having a breakdown.

"No, that's good." Julie smiles at her again. It's a nice smile, genuine and warm. Not like Audrey's weird strained smile. *Audrey.* She didn't say anything about monsters either. "If it can talk to you, that means I can talk to it. Should have it cleared out within the next few minutes."

"It won't hurt you, will it?"

Julie looks up at her. "We've got an arrangement."

Claire doesn't know what that means: Julie has an arrangement? Or the town does? Is that why no one's ever said a word about the monsters to Claire before? But Julie doesn't explain, only opens the door. Heat rushes in. Through the window, Claire sees the monster stick its head up.

"Hey there," Julie calls out, swooping down to pick up the cage. She ambles outside and pulls the back door shut, but Claire can still hear her, her voice muffled and fuzzy. "You know you're not supposed…" And then Julie moves too far away from the house, and her words become too indistinct.

Claire leans up against the window, her chest tight. Julie drops the cage in the grass. Stands with her hands on her hips. The monster lifts its head a little higher and bares its teeth. Claire tenses, certain the monster's going to attack—but no, it's only speaking.

Julie gestures at the cage. The monster stares at her. She crosses her arms over her chest, hitches her shoulders. Points at the cage again. The monster doesn't move. She throws her hands up. Her voice raises, loud enough that certain tones seep through the window, but not so loud that Claire can make out what she's saying. Claire realizes that she's no longer frightened, exactly. She watches the window like she's watching TV, with a morbid, confused fascination. Julie's trying to negotiate with a monster, with some—*animal*. Claire doesn't think there's any way this can work, and yet it's clear that Julie has done this before.

Julie crouches down in the grass. The monster perks up its head

24

and tilts it at her. Julie slaps one hand down on the top of the cage. Points off into the distance. Shrugs.

And then, to Claire's amazement, the monster trundles into the cage.

Julie closes the latch without any rush. She picks the cage up with one hand and sets it down on the patio. The monster's curled up inside like a cat, head resting on its claw, staring forlornly off into the distance.

The door opens and Claire jumps away from the window.

"Christ, it's hot out there." Julie wipes her forehead. "Not much better in here, though. No offense."

"My grandma doesn't have air-conditioning."

"Aw, suck." Julie points her thumb toward outside. "Anyway, I got it. I'll haul it off to the power plant. I'm not sure why it was down here. They aren't supposed to come into town. Part of the deal, you know?" She shrugs.

Claire stares at her. She understands each individual word, but all strung together like that they become gibberish. Power plant? Deal?

Julie's staring at her and frowning. Heat rushes into Claire's cheeks. She looks down at her hands. Her heart's beating a little too fast, even though she's not scared anymore.

"You didn't know, did you?" Julie says.

"What?" Claire looks up at her.

"About the monsters? You said you're just here for the summer?" Julie shakes her head. "This stupid town. They expect everyone to just *know* when they pass the city limits." She rolls her eyes.

Claire stares at her. "No," she finally says. "No one ever told me anything. I mean, I'd been coming here for Christmas, and my mom grew up here—"

"Oh, well, it would've had to be Mrs. Sudek who tells you." Julie shifts her weight from foot to foot, looking antsy and uncomfortable. "The farther you go from town, the more you forget."

"Forget?" Claire stares at her.

"The monsters, yeah. I don't know how it works. Just that people who leave, when they come back—we have to remind them. And no one does because everyone in this town's an asshole." She sighs. "Basically, we've got these monsters that live out in an old power plant on the edge of town. They've been here since forever, pretty much. Way back in the day they made a deal with the townspeople to stay on their own spot of land."

"But—" Claire shakes her head, trying to piece everything together. "So they're *endemic*? Just in Indianola?"

"Dunno," Julie says. "Probably not, since they aren't anywhere else around here."

"So where did they *come* from? They had to come from somewhere!"

"Yeah, no one really knows. They've just sort of—always been here. That's what my dad told me. Anyway. They aren't supposed to come into town, but sometimes one of 'em disobeys. I'm authorized to round 'em up and take 'em back to the power plant."

"Power plant," Claire says slowly. "So…but…maybe *that's* where they came from?"

"Nah, they moved there in the thirties, I'm pretty sure." Julie shrugs. "No big deal. Makes it easy to stay away from them, you know?"

The world's been invaded by dream logic. Monsters living at a power plant, people losing their memories. Were there monsters back in Houston, and Claire can't remember them, now that she's come here?

She feels dizzy and sick. She wants to talk to Josh. He'd tell her the truth. He'd tell her if monsters were real or not.

"They shouldn't bother you again." Julie smiles. "And if they do, all you've got to do is give me a call."

Claire nods. She thinks she might throw up. The world's been uprooted. The rules are broken. She understands nothing.

JULIE

The girl living at Mrs. Sudek's place is pretty cute. Innocent-looking. Sweet. Like she spends all her time studying and worrying that she's not going to make straight A's on her report card. Julie wonders if she'll see her around again. Probably. It's a small town.

"I could pay one of you to hang out in her yard," she says to the monster. "Then I'll definitely get to see her again. What do you say to that?"

The monster's still curled up in its cage, which she strapped into the front seat. She's supposed to stash them in the back of the van, but sometimes she lets them ride shotgun. This one's not particularly chatty.

"Girl," it says, in that low hissing voice they all have.

"Yeah, yeah, I'm a girl, she's a girl." Julie pulls up to the blinking red stoplight at the edge of town. "Figures I'd have to take shit about it from y'all too." She guns the van forward, out toward the highway that leads back into civilization. Only one direction out of town, unless you have a boat.

"Girl," the monster says.

"Christ, learn a new word." The van's the only car out on the road. People don't drive this stretch of Highway 316 that often, since it takes you past the power plant where the monsters have made their home. Instead everybody takes Comal Road around the bayou, even though it adds about thirty minutes to the trip. "Is this some new trick?" she asks, glancing over at the monster's cage. "Learning one word so that you qualify for sentience and I have to waste time hauling you back to the power plant?"

"Girl," the monster says.

Julie sighs. Honestly, she still hasn't bothered to learn all the rules and bylaws governing the relationship between the good people of Indianola and the monsters who made this spot of Texas their home; no one else in town seems to care, and Julie has big plans to get the hell out of Indianola as soon as she graduates. What do you need to know about monsters once you leave the county limits? Nothing, that's what, because nothing is exactly what you'll remember about the stupid things anyway.

The monster turns around in the cage and settles its head down on its paws. Weird that it had gotten so far away from the power plant—the ones who can't talk usually stay close, since they're considered vermin and can be exterminated. *A threat to the human population*, that's what the official documents say. Julie doesn't like the idea of killing them, even though it was the monsters themselves who said it was okay, that it's like killing rats or deer. It almost never happens, and she's never had to, but still.

They drive on. The edges of Indianola disappear into the fields of pale grass, already turning yellow in the summer heat. The radio station crackles and then disappears, the way it always does—once you pass the power plant it'll kick up again, as strong as ever. Julie switches it off, though, because she knows from experience that sometimes you hear voices in the static.

The power plant materializes on the horizon.

Julie has seen it dozens of times, but it's always a surprise, and it always leaves her with an uneasy feeling in the pit of her stomach. It looks like a painting on the poster for a science fiction movie, a convoluted tangle of gray pipes, twisting and winding on top of one another. At night the pipes twinkle with amber lights. Julie's only seen that once. She knows you don't come out here at night.

There's smoke today, a thin trickle of it seeping out of the plant and flattening against the pale sky.

"So what do y'all got cooking in there?" Julie asks, trying to deflect her nervousness.

"Girl."

Julie shivers, her chest tightening. "Jesus, I hope not." She pulls up to the entrance gate. The *KEEP OUT* sign's still there, dotted with rust. It's not the sign that keeps people away. Not even dumbass football players try breaking in here. Everyone in town knows it's bad news.

And yet her father won't give her a job at the video store like she keeps asking, and so here she is, punching in the access code.

The gate screeches open. Julie eases in. The monster shuffles in its cage, trying to sit up.

"Almost got you home," she says, cruising down the narrow main road. The power plant rises up on both sides, hemming her in. Julie clenches the steering wheel tighter. The van and the smoke are the only things moving in the entire plant.

Finally, she makes it to the main building, where Aldraa spends his days. She parks in the usual spot, climbs out, heaves the monster's cage out with a grunt. It's hotter here than in town, the sun reflecting off all these acres of asphalt. When it catches the metal in the pipes, it throws off broken shards of white light.

Julie takes a deep breath, puts in her earplugs, tells herself nothing's going to happen, and then goes inside.

Being inside is even worse than being outside. The monsters have the buildings fixed up the way they like, warm and humid and crawling with strange dark green plants that look sort of like moss. Julie does her best not to look at those plants, because when you do, you see that they twitch and pulse like they're breathing.

"Julie Alvarez." Aldraa's voice booms through the room, rattling like thunder, reverberating across her eardrums. It hurts even with the earplugs. "You are here."

He always knows who it is. "Yes, I'm here." Julie sets the cage on a clear patch of floor, where she can see the speckled tile from when this used to be a place for humans, and peers into the thick, dingy dark. "One of your boys got out."

A pause. Julie's heart thuds. She wants to drop off the monster and leave, the way she's supposed to. Except today she's got some questions for Aldraa.

"I'd like to speak to you." Her blood rushes in her ears. "I need to ask you something."

Another pause. Aldraa's breathing somewhere in the recesses of the lobby. The monster rattles against its cage, and Julie kneels down and opens the latch. The monster shoots out, scurrying into a tangle of plants.

The floor shakes. Once, twice. Footsteps.

Julie straightens up. She braces herself.

Aldraa appears.

He's enormous, almost as tall as the high lobby roof, and shaped like a person but not quite. His proportions are off, his arms and torso too long and twisting, his head too small. Julie tries not to look straight at him, but still she feels the beginning throb of a migraine in her right temple.

"What do you want?" he says.

"You're in violation of the agreement," Julie says, keeping her eyes on a spot just above his left shoulder. There's something about him that makes her dizzy, like he's much more solid, much more *there*, than the things around him. And that includes her.

"I haven't left the power plant in forty-nine years."

The headache surges in time with the beat of his voice.

"I realize that. But the monster I just brought in was at an Indianola citizen's house. *In town*." She points off at the undulating vines, her hand shaking. "The only thing he could say was 'girl,' so he could have been exterminated."

"But you didn't exterminate him." Aldraa kneels down, the floor shuddering beneath him. He opens his mouth and reveals the rows of sharp gleaming teeth through which he makes a rattling noise that bores deep into Julie's brain. She cries out, digs the palm of her hand into her temple.

The monster from Mrs. Sudek's house slinks out of the plants and scurries up Aldraa's arm.

"Why did he say 'girl'?" Julie asks, drawing herself up, trying to eke out her bravery. She tells herself that she's protected, that no harm can come to her.

"Why do you assume there's a reason?" Aldraa does something with his mouth that's meant to be a smile; it's something he learned from humans but doesn't work with the muscles of his face. Seeing it sends a wave of nausea rushing through Julie's stomach and she has to take a deep breath to stop from throwing up.

"Because," Julie starts. The nausea worsens; her thoughts are becoming gummy and loose like melting candy, turning to slime in the room's humidity. He's doing this to her. Aldraa. "Because there's a girl there, a new girl—you aren't going to hurt her, are you?" She can't remember much about the new girl. Only a flash of green eyes, a gleam of pale skin. The phone call—Brittany saying *Got a monster down at Mrs. Sudek's.*

"Stop," she says. "Please, whatever you're doing with my head, just stop screwing around with me."

"I don't know what that means."

"Yes you do." Julie takes a deep breath and concentrates.

"Are you certain Lezir was in the town?" Aldraa strokes the monster's back with his long vine-like fingers. Gray fur ripples through them.

"Yes. Dammit, Aldraa, stop. Answer my question." Her voice sounds far away and muted. "You know you have to. It's part of the treaty, if I think something's wrong, or that someone's going to be hurt—"

"We are going to hurt no one!"

His voice lashes out like a thunderstorm, and Julie stumbles backward, clamping her hands over her ears. The monster from Mrs. Sudek's house dives off Aldraa's arm and disappears into the green darkness, and the plants rustle and sway around her, despite the absolute stillness of the air.

"We've done nothing wrong," Aldraa says, softer this time, even though she can still feel his voice inside her bones.

"I'll go to the mayor," Julie spits out.

"We've done nothing wrong," he says again, and Julie knows she can't be in the building with him much longer, that if she keeps hearing him and seeing him, her mind's going to shatter.

"You better not hurt her!" Julie says before she turns and bolts out of the power plant.

Outside, the air is as hot as it was inside, but the sea breeze is up, whistling forlornly through the pipes and smokestacks of the power plant. Julie collapses on the asphalt, sucking in deep breaths of air, trying to calm her racing heart. With trembling fingers she takes out the earplugs. Her eardrums ache, but being out in the bright sun, away from Aldraa, is already starting to soothe her migraine.

Her van's still in its parking place, the cockroach bobbing in the wind.

The power plant looks empty, but Julie knows she's not alone. The monsters are in the shadows; they're hiding up in the windows. Watching. Planning, maybe. She doesn't know what.

Julie climbs in the van and turns on the engine. The airconditioning blasts across her sweaty skin. *Girl*, the monster had said, in the yard of a house where a new girl lives. They're interested in her.

Aldraa may not have answered her questions, but Julie is determined to find answers anyway.

The sheriff's office is at the edge of town, a brown building emerging out of an empty field. Julie pulls into the lot and shuts off the van engine. She's still sticky from the power plant, and the smell of the place clings to her skin, that smoky burning-metal scent. But at least she's not there now.

Julie climbs out of the van and goes inside, the arctic air chilling her as she walks through the door. It's like crossing a force field. Inside, the office is as shabby and worn-out as always. The yellow fluorescent lights make everything look brown.

Lawrence is sitting at the front desk, scribbling notes in the margins of a textbook. He sighs when he sees her.

"What do you want?" he asks.

"Hey, cuz, that's no way to treat me."

"Don't call me that. I'm on duty."

Julie rolls her eyes. "Yeah, but it's from *Shakespeare*. It's in *Romeo and Juliet*, cuz."

"I don't care. I'm on duty and the only way you're supposed to address me is 'officer.' Or 'deputy.'"

"I'm not doing that." Julie grabs a chair from the waiting area and drags it over the floor so that she can sit across the counter from Lawrence. He sets his pen down and watches her, his brow drawn tight, the way it gets whenever he's angry. Lawrence never shows his anger in the usual ways. He doesn't yell or stomp around, just lets the anger seep through his skin and manifest as weird tics in his face. Julie knows it's because he's trying his hardest not to be like his father.

She arranges the chair to face him and sits down.

"I see you've got the van out there," Lawrence says. "I take it you're supposed to be working."

Julie shrugs. The truth is she doesn't want to go back to the exterminators, doesn't want to risk getting called out to trap another monster.

35

"So maybe camping out at the sheriff's office isn't the best way to spend your time right now? Uncle Victor isn't paying you to distract me."

"Distract you?" Julie asks. "You're reading a freaking book! I bet the sheriff's not paying you to do *that.*"

Lawrence scowls at her, an expression that makes him look pouty, like a child. It's hard to take him seriously. "I'm studying," he says. "Something you don't know anything about."

"Hey, I passed all my classes last year. Even got an A in history."

Lawrence folds up the book and sets it under the counter. Then he leans forward, steepling his fingers together like a villain in an old Bond movie.

"Do you have a *crime* to report?" he asks.

"Nope. But I do have a question for you—a real one," she adds, when he looks like he's about to start in on some first-class Lawrence nagging. "Related to you being sheriff's deputy." She pauses, trying to figure out the best way to ask it. Lawrence's obsession with rules makes him annoying sometimes, but it can come in handy too. She thinks now is one of those times. "I just picked up a monster at Mrs. Sudek's house…"

Lawrence rubs his forehead at the mention of Mrs. Sudek's name.

"Yeah, I know. I didn't actually have to talk to her, though, it was great. She's got her granddaughter staying there."

"So what's your question?" Lawrence asks.

"Didn't you hear me? I picked up at a monster! At Mrs. Sudek's house!" Julie sighs. "In *town.*"

"Oh."

"Yeah. Usually I'm driving out to those empty beach houses in hurricane alley to pick 'em up."

"Right." Lawrence frowns. "This still seems more like a matter for Uncle Victor."

Julie slouches down in her chair. "Dad'll just tell me not to get involved. You know how he is."

"He's trying to protect you." Lawrence sighs. "Everyone in town keeps our distance from them. It's the safest thing to do."

Julie rolls her eyes. It's true that most of the people in town do their best to pretend the monsters don't exist. Julie knows why: Because everyone's scared of them. Scared of the memory lapses, the eerie power plant, the possibility of what they might do to Indianola. But as an exterminator, she *has* to interact with them. It just sucks that no one will let her find out more about them.

"This town's full of rednecks. I don't know why you'd listen to them."

"They pay my salary."

"Whatever. Look." Julie leans onto the counter. "The whole thing was weird. I thought it might be related to Mrs. Sudek's granddaughter."

"Why? What would she have to do with it?"

"Because she's new!" Julie sighs. "You know how this town is. She didn't even know about the monsters. No one had told her! And then one shows up at her house—" Julie stops, startled by a new possibility. "Oh my God, is that why everybody wants to keep it a secret? Because otherwise the monsters will hurt strangers—"

"Stop right there." Lawrence lifts up the counter and joins Julie on the other side. He puts his hands on his hips and manages to fake a pretty convincing Stern Adult expression. "The treaties cover all humans within the boundaries of the town. They aren't coming after Mrs. Sudek's granddaughter. New or not, she's protected."

Julie glares at him. Figures he'd say that. He's nineteen now, and that makes him officially grown up. And the adults in this town are always doing this—saying you just shouldn't worry about the monsters, setting up treaties and exterminators to handle them and acting like it's all so normal.

"Larry, you are not being very helpful."

Lawrence scowls. "Don't call me Larry."

She knows he hates Larry; that's why she only uses it whenever he's pissing her off.

"I'm just worried about her, is all," Julie says, looking away from Lawrence, toward the door behind the counter that leads to the holding cells.

"You don't even know her." Lawrence puts a hand on Julie's shoulder, and she looks over at him. He's got that concerned expression because he knows her secret, knows the way she is. The two of them have been friends since she was four and he was six, running around together in Aunt Rosa's big backyard and looking for monsters hiding in the canna lilies. When they were older he found the girlie mags she stashed under her mattress. He didn't tell her parents. That's how she knows she can trust him completely.

And she hates that now he's dismissing her like some little kid.

"Yeah, do you know all the people you help?" she demands. "Isn't that why you decided to become a cop in the first place?"

"I'm a sheriff's deputy. And you're right, I don't know them. But nothing's going to happen to this girl, as long as she keeps her distance like everyone else." He smiles. "We have the treaties. Do you really think your dad would have you working at the exterminator's if he thought the monsters would break them?"

Yes, Julie thinks, but she doesn't say anything out loud.

CHAPTER

CLAIRE

Claire rides her bike to Audrey's house. They made plans to go to the beach yesterday, when Audrey called just as Claire was clearing up the dishes from dinner. The timing was perfect, and it gave Claire a cold, shuddery feeling, like Audrey had been waiting for that exact moment to call.

Which of course is *ridiculous.*

Claire doesn't have any cold, shuddery feelings right now, not in this heat. There are no clouds in the sky, just the bright, searing sun. It's a good day to go to the beach. Of course, Claire forgot to pack sunscreen. She can already feel her skin burning through her T-shirt.

Audrey's house materializes around the bend. It's big and sprawling, with a three-car garage and a flower garden in the front. The flower garden is filled with roses, the blossoms big and heavy. Claire doesn't think she's ever seen such lush roses in June before. They ought to be burned up by now.

Claire wheels her bike up the sidewalk and props it up out of the way. She rings the doorbell and waits, wiping her sweaty hands on her shorts. She has her swimsuit on under her clothes and it's just making her hotter.

Audrey answers.

"Claire!" she cries. "I'm so glad to see you. Come in, come in."

The house is cool and dark and has the same silent buzzing on the air that Claire always associates with museums. Audrey shuts the door and the house vibrates with its own quiet.

"You ready to go?" Audrey speaks in a normal voice, but Claire feels like they should whisper.

Claire starts to nod. "Oh no, wait," she says, and she hopes she isn't pitching her voice too low. "I didn't bring sunscreen with me and Grammy didn't have any—"

"Oh, you can borrow some of mine! No problem at all. It's upstairs." She gestures with one hand, and together they walk through the foyer and into the living room. It's decorated with black and white furniture. The only spot of color is a vase of red flowers and a red abstract painting hanging on the wall.

Claire blinks. It's not the sort of living room she would have expected to find in Indianola.

"Oh, is this your friend?" A woman breezes in. Her hair hangs in perfectly formed waves around her face. She wears a dress and an apron and pearls and high heels, exactly like a mom from an old television show.

"It is! Mother, this is Claire." Audrey gestures toward her and Claire forces out a smile.

"Oh, it's so lovely to meet you!" Mrs. Duchesne holds out one hand, her nails French-tipped and filed into expert ovals. Claire shakes it. "I'm so glad there's someone new to the neighborhood for Audrey to be friends with." She smiles so widely that Claire's mouth hurts. "Well, you two run along. I've got some baking to do."

That does not surprise Claire in the slightest.

"This way." Audrey leads Claire up the stairs, which open up into a landing done in the same black-and-white-and-red scheme as downstairs. It makes Claire's eyes hurt.

A little boy runs across the landing, whooshing out of one door and into another across the way, so quickly Claire isn't sure she saw him.

"My brother," Audrey says, but she doesn't elaborate.

They go into a bathroom. It's white: white tile, white shower curtain, white rugs on the floor. It looks incomplete somehow. Half-formed. And although the floor is stone tile, neither Audrey's nor Claire's shoes make any noise against it; sound in the bathroom is as muffled as it is in the rest of the house, with its plush white carpet. Claire feels vaguely uneasy.

Audrey pulls an orange bottle of sunscreen out of the cabinet, the color too bright against the white backdrop.

"Is this kind okay?" She holds it up to Claire. Claire nods. The orange feels like it's burning her eyes. She doesn't like being in this stark, silent house. The way it muffles sounds means her heartbeat is even louder, so loud it sounds like a drum.

"Great! Let's go, then."

Claire steps out of the bathroom immediately—then jumps. A little boy with blond hair and solemn blue eyes stands out in the hallway. He stares at Claire, unmoving like a statue.

"Oh, get out of here, Michael." Audrey flicks her wrist and the little boy scampers off, disappearing into a nearby room. The door slams shut. Claire is glad for that: She doesn't know why, but she has no desire to see what lies inside that room.

They go downstairs and don't see anyone else, although Claire hears a woman's humming coming from someplace in the back of the house. She doesn't recognize the melody, but it sounds old-fashioned. It makes her feel weird too, kind of empty and alone and hopeless.

When Claire steps outside again, it's like she's been holding her breath.

After the air-conditioned chill of Audrey's house, the sun is pleasantly warm instead of sweltering, and Claire is grateful to be outside in the natural light. She smells the sea and exhaust from the road and realizes with a jolt that she didn't actually *smell* anything in Audrey's house, which is strange. All houses have their particular scent, a residue from the people who live there. Not Audrey's.

"You want to put your sunscreen on now?" Audrey asks.

"I'll do it at the beach." Claire just wants out of here. Audrey shrugs and they climb into her car and zip off. The tree-lined road dead-ends into the main street leading into town. It's a street that Claire recognizes. The rest of the way through town is familiar—normal, even. Slowly, the weird chattery feeling from being inside Audrey's house subsides until it seems as intangible as a bad dream.

They pull up at a stoplight. The exterminator building is on the other side of the intersection. The neon cockroach sign flickers. Claire wishes cockroaches were all she had to worry about.

"I'm so glad we're becoming friends!" Audrey chirps suddenly, yanking Claire out of her own head. "You're so much more interesting than anyone else here in town."

"What? Oh, yeah, I'm glad too." Claire shifts around uncomfortably. Her bare legs stick to the car seats. "I was afraid I'd be stuck at Grammy's house all summer, bored."

The light changes. Audrey shoots out into the intersection, humming along to the Mariah Carey song playing on the radio. Claire watches the exterminator's building go by. She wants to ask about the monsters, but Audrey's so sickeningly normal, it seems wrong somehow to do so.

"Oh, no, I'm definitely not going to let you be bored this summer." Audrey shakes her head, her hair swishing around her shoulders. "Not one bit."

"That's good to hear. Although since we're friends, I hope you won't mind me asking—" Claire fumbles around for the words. "You know about the monsters, right?"

Silence. The song ends and the radio goes over to the frantic prattle of the DJ. Claire is clammy all over, certain she should never have asked.

"Of course I do," Audrey finally says. "Everyone does."

"No one told me." Claire stares out the window. Businesses zip by. "There was one in my backyard. I thought I was hallucinating."

"Oh, you poor thing! Mrs. Sudek didn't warn you?"

"Grammy doesn't tell me anything." Claire scowls. "It's like she just expected me to *know*."

"We're all so used to them," Audrey says. "We forget not everybody has them around. Plus"—she lowers her voice—"I think a lot of the older folks are *ashamed*, you know? Everyone thinks the monsters are the reason we don't have any tourists." She shrugs. "But wait'll you see the beach. It's not exactly a tropical paradise."

She turns down a side street, and the Gulf flashes between the gaps of buildings.

"Besides, people forget about the monsters when they cross the city limits. It's their way of hiding themselves, I guess. But when you leave town, you forget the monsters even exist."

Claire gets a clammy feeling in the pit of her stomach. Julie told her that too, but it still frightens her. She wonders, with a jolt, if she ever saw the monsters on her previous trips into Indianola, if those memories were washed away as her family barreled their way back to Houston.

"You don't need to worry. The monsters don't usually come into town."

"People keep saying that," Claire says, forcing away the strange reverse déjà vu of not remembering them. "But Grammy's house is in town."

"I'm sure it was just a fluke." Audrey glances over at her and smiles. "If you don't agitate them, they won't hurt you."

Claire shivers.

Audrey drives past a *Welcome to Indianola Beach!* sign. The beach isn't as crowded as Claire expects. A few families dot the sand, their brightly colored lawn chairs and towels spread out in front of the dunes. Audrey parks and they both climb out of the car. The wind blowing off the water is hot and damp.

"I don't think this is too bad," Claire says. "At least it's not too crowded."

"Yeah, that's one benefit of not having any tourists."

Claire slathers on her sunscreen while Audrey peels off her tank dress, revealing a neon-green bikini underneath. She stands with her hands on her hips, facing the water, not speaking. Her face is glazed over. She seems lost in thought.

The wind sweeps down the beach, blowing Claire's hair around so that it sticks to her sunscreen. Indianola Beach is like every beach Claire has been on, but it's also like none of them, although Claire can't exactly say why.

"Done," Claire says, because she isn't sure that Audrey will notice.

Audrey blinks. Her features come back to life. "Great! Do you want to wait before we get in the water? So the sunscreen soaks in?"

She sounds like a mom. Claire shakes her head. "Really, it's not a big deal."

Audrey shrugs and together they walk down to the shoreline. It's blocked by piles of prickly brown seaweed, and they pick their way through it, standing on tiptoes and giggling at the sliminess.

"I hate seaweed," Claire says. "It looks like something from another planet."

The first shock of cold water makes them shriek. The Gulf churns around them, the water frothy and greenish brown. They wade out until they're about waist-deep and the tiny waves buoy them up. Pieces of seaweed brush past Claire's legs, making her jump. She thinks of jellyfish.

"So this is Indianola Beach," Audrey says.

"Is there usually this much seaweed?"

"Sometimes. Better seaweed than jellyfish."

There it is again, that feeling that Audrey's dipped inside her head.

They swim for a while. Audrey mostly floats on her back, but Claire splashes around in the water and rides the waves toward the shore. The sun washes out the rest of the sky and tosses sparkles down onto the Gulf. It's fun, but Audrey's company is dull enough that Claire wishes she were here with someone else—with Josh, specifically, even though she can't imagine him on a beach. The bright sun doesn't suit him. But as she drifts up and down with the water she daydreams about

45

an afternoon on the beach with Josh anyway, her bare skin brushing against his under the water, the two of them sharing a blanket as the sun sets into the dunes.

Eventually, Claire's skin starts to feel hot and sore.

"You're burning," Audrey says. She's still floating on her back, moving to the rhythm of the waves. Her eyes are closed, and Claire wonders how she could possibly know; she'd actually started to think that Audrey was asleep. "You should have put the sunscreen on at my house. If you go in the water right away, it washes off."

"I just burn easily," Claire snaps back, annoyed at being lectured to like a little kid. "Although I should probably sit in the shade for a while."

Abruptly, Audrey rights herself, dropping her legs into the water. Her own skin is as evenly tanned as it was before, without a single hint of a burn. She wades over to Claire's side. "I'm sorry," she says, her voice swelling with sincerity. "I didn't mean—"

"It's fine." Claire is suddenly aware of the enormity of the ocean. Although she can see the beach, the dunes, Audrey's car, a family a few yards away, she feels as if she's trapped on the open sea, surrounded by nothing but water and sky and emptiness. "I feel like going in anyway. My arms are tired. And the seaweed's everywhere."

Audrey nods. "We can walk along Seaside Drive. And get something to eat, if you'd like."

"Fine." It's not really Audrey that's bothering her, Claire decides, it's the water itself. She can't shake that feeling of being mired in infinity.

A wave swells up behind her and Claire catches it and rides it halfway to shore. She wades the rest of the way in, picking through the seaweed and the sand back to the car. The sun is so bright that when Claire looks over at Audrey all she sees are rays of light.

Like the ocean, it makes her feel small.

Maybe she does need to eat something. She skipped breakfast and didn't have much lunch, so perhaps this woozy sense of being lost is just hunger.

"Seaside Drive's just over there," Audrey says, pointing to a spot past the dunes as they towel off and pull their clothes on over their bathing suits. "The pizza place is there, remember? With the arcade."

Claire nods. They walk across the sand to a boardwalk that takes them over the dunes. There's a sign warning them of rattlesnakes. Claire wonders if it really means to warn them about monsters.

She looks over the railing, but all she sees are vines and sand.

The boardwalk takes them over the seawall and drops them onto Seaside Drive, and as soon as Claire sees the town proper, the paved street and the salt-scrubbed storefronts and the old cars stopped at the light, she feels normal again.

She glances at Audrey, who looks over at her and smiles. "It's always nice walking in the sun after you've been in the water, don't you think?"

"Sure." Claire shrugs. She's just glad the world feels right.

It only takes five minutes to get to the pizza arcade. An *Open* sign blinks in the window, next to a flyer for something called the Stargazer's Masquerade Ball.

"Oh we *have* to go to that," Audrey says, tapping one finger against the flyer. "It's the biggest thing in Indianola. You'll still be here, right? In July?"

"A masquerade?" They go into the arcade. The sudden blast of air-conditioning sends ripples of goose bumps up Claire's legs. "And yeah, I'll still be here."

"There's some astronomy club or something that started it back in

47

the 1800s. Who knows why." Audrey seems bored by the origin. "But it's such fun! Now, what kind of pizza would you like?"

The arcade is dark. Most of the light comes from the arcade cabinets or the little red lamps sitting at each table. Like the beach, it's mostly empty.

"Pepperoni's fine." Claire looks around the arcade. The only other people here are a guy in a tan's sheriff's uniform sitting at one of the tables and a girl hunched over a *Ms. Pac-Man* game. After a few seconds, Claire recognizes her—she's the exterminator girl. What was her name? Julie.

Claire is oddly relieved to see her.

Audrey sashays up to the counter and places the order. Her voice, perky and bright and perfectly grating, carries over the blips and beeps of the video games. Julie glances up, looks over at the counter, and frowns. There's the ripply sound of Ms. Pac-Man dying.

"Crap!" Julie says, loud enough that Claire can hear. The sheriff glares at her. "Do you have a quarter?" she asks him.

"No." He speaks more softly than Julie, and Claire can't hear the rest of what he says, but it's enough to make Julie roll her eyes. She leans away from Ms. Pac-Man and looks out over the arcade and that's when her gaze falls on Claire.

Claire immediately looks away, her cheeks burning. She can't believe she's standing next to the salad bar just *staring* at some girl she doesn't even know—

"Hey, Mrs. Sudek's granddaughter!"

Claire jerks her head up, her face still warm. Julie ambles over. Her cut-off shorts barely peek out beneath the hem of an oversized T-shirt screen-printed with a scene from *Vertigo*.

48

"You found the Pirate's Den, huh? It's the only remotely cool place in town."

"Yeah." Claire smiles and Julie smiles back at her. Her smile's genuine in a way that feels welcome after spending the afternoon with Audrey. "I like your shirt. *Vertigo*'s one of my favorite movies."

"Really? Mine too!"

"I saw it at a special screening last year," Claire says, aware that she's probably babbling. "They had a film festival with a bunch of old movies."

"That's awesome," Julie says. "I saw it on TV when I was a little kid and got obsessed. When I got a VCR it was the first movie I tried to buy."

They look at each other in the dim light.

"So, did you come here by yourself? You can eat with me and my cousin, if you want. That's him over there." She points at the sheriff, watching them with his arms crossed over his chest. "Oh no, he's got his cop stare on." Julie laughs. "Don't worry, though, he's off duty."

"I wasn't worried."

Julie smiles. Claire wants to accept Julie's offer. Wants to sit at the table and watch her play old video games. But then Audrey walks over to their side, and Claire remembers she's not here alone.

"Sorry, it took *forever*. No one was at the counter, and— Oh! Hi, Julie!"

Claire's chest twinges in a weird way. It almost feels like jealousy: Audrey and Julie know each other? But of course they do, Audrey said the school only had one hundred students.

Julie blinks at Audrey. "Hi?" she says, her brow furrowed. "Do we— did I exterminate something at your house, or—"

Audrey laughs, twinkling and bright. "No, silly. We had Mrs. McClane's trig class together last year, don't you remember?" She wags one finger in false admonishment and puts a hand on her hip. "I know you skip out on the pep rallies, but you should still know your school's cheerleaders." Another laugh.

Claire always skips pep rallies at her school too. She and Josh go to Mr. Ramirez's room and work on their projects for art class—that was how they first started talking, all those months ago. And she doubts she could name even half the cheerleaders on the squad. They're all super friendly, but her school is so huge that she rarely crosses their paths.

If only Julie had been the one to bring her a gift basket her first day here, not Audrey.

"Yeah," Julie says, and she rubs at her head. "Yeah, I'm sorry. No, I remember. Mrs. McClane's class." She shrugs. "I liked that class. Guess I was paying more attention to the math than anything else."

"I *hate* math," Audrey says brightly. There's something insincere about her voice, though, like she doesn't really believe what she's saying.

"Sure." Julie looks around. "Y'all want to come eat with us? If either of you've got quarters, we can play *Ms. Pac-Man.*" She points at the game.

Audrey just stands there with her smile frozen into place. Claire digs three quarters out of her wallet. "I've got some quarters," she says, feeling stupid.

"We'd *love* to sit with you," Audrey gushes, finally.

Julie looks from Audrey to Claire. "Awesome," she says, but she looks at Claire when she says it. Claire hands her the quarters, feeling shy. "Let me introduce you to my cousin, Lawrence. He's the cop."

"I'm a sheriff's deputy," Lawrence calls out.

"Whatever." Julie leads Claire and Audrey over to the table. Audrey immediately sits down next to Lawrence and holds out her hand. "I don't believe we've met," she says.

"No." Lawrence takes her hand and shakes. "No, although—are you a cheerleader? I feel like I've seen you at the games—" He rubs his forehead and closes his eyes. "I'm almost certain—"

"I am!" Audrey chirps. "Made varsity last year."

"And you were a junior, like Julie? Pretty impressive."

Audrey beams. Beside Claire, Julie rolls her eyes. She leans in and whispers in Claire's ear, "No cheerleader would look twice at him when he was in high school, so now he's freaking out. Look at him."

Claire presses her hand over her mouth so she won't laugh out loud. Lawrence leans forward, nodding earnestly at Audrey's chatter. Julie snorts.

"It's gonna be a while before your pizza's ready. Wanna play a game? We can do two-player on something if you want."

"Sure." Claire shrugs. "We can play *Ms. Pac-Man*, that's fine with me."

Julie's eyes gleam. "It's the best one here. The arcade in Victoria has newer stuff, *Mortal Kombat* and *Samurai Shodown* the last time I was out there, but that's like an hour drive. My mom doesn't like me driving out there."

"I know *Mortal Kombat*!" Claire says, excited. "Me and my friend Josh play it together every day after school."

"Isn't it fun?" Julie grins. "So, are you into video games too? Not just Hitchcock movies?"

"Yeah." Claire glances over at Audrey, wondering if she ought to feel guilty about ignoring her, about *wanting* to ignore her, but Audrey's wrapped up in Lawrence. "I don't think I'm very good, though."

Julie swipes her hand dismissively. "I doubt that."

They walk over to the game and Claire slips in the quarters. "You can go first," Julie says with a smile. Claire smiles back, a warmth in her chest.

She hasn't played *Ms. Pac-Man* in years, but she manages to make it to the second level before she dies. When Julie takes her turn, her whole demeanor changes. She rests her fingers on the controls like a fighter pilot. Her eyes look straight forward, unblinking, and she straightens her shoulders. Ms. Pac-Man starts munching through the dots and Julie's fingers are a blur as she weaves around the maze. Claire leans up against the side of the cabinet and watches her, although she gets bored quickly and focuses on Julie herself instead. She's got that grunge girl style, her hair like she hasn't bothered to brush it since she woke up and her eyeliner dark and smudgy. Claire wonders how much a stick of dark eyeliner would cost at the Walmart on the edge of town.

Julie makes it to the fourth level before her turn ends. She nods in satisfaction and steps away from the game. They go back and forth, and when Claire pulls off a particularly tricky maneuver on her turn, Julie laughs and says, "*Awesome*," and Claire's cheeks burn.

It's fun, but when they're finished they don't have enough quarters for the both of them to play a second round.

"We should do this again," Julie says. "No one I know is really that into video games. It sucks too, because I got a Super Nintendo for Christmas last year."

"You have an SNES!" Claire cries. "That's awesome. My friend Josh

52

has one, well, his brother does, and he hardly ever lets us get on it. But I like it when we do have a chance to play." That would give her something to write about to Josh, wouldn't it? A letter detailing all her video game exploits. He'd think that was funny. She's pretty sure he would, anyway.

A dullness thumps at the back of her head. No, she was going to write him about the monsters. She'd even started the letter. Written a few lines and then abandoned it. She's not even sure where it is now.

"You should come over," Julie says. "I've got *Street Fighter II* and *Super Mario Kart* and a couple of others."

"I'd like that," Claire says, and she means it, not like when she says the same thing to Audrey.

"I've got tomorrow off. Here, I'll give you my number. Just call me whenever and you can come over."

Julie bounds over to the table and pulls a napkin out of the dispenser. Lawrence and Audrey don't even seem to notice her.

"Hey, Larry," Julie says. "You got a pen?"

Lawrence gives her a dark look. "Don't call me that."

"Do you?"

"No. Go ask Pete." He turns back to Audrey and says, "Sorry, what were you saying?"

"Wow, look at him." Julie's back at Claire's side. "Could he be any more obvious?"

Lawrence leans forward in his chair, nodding every few seconds. His eyes glow. Audrey gestures and swishes her hair back and forth as she talks. Claire has always wondered about girls like that, girls who can control boys—and not even a boy here, a *man*, a *sheriff's deputy*—with just their conversation.

"Is she always like that?" Claire asks in a low voice. "Just—anyone will listen to anything she says?"

Julie doesn't answer right away. When Claire looks over at her, she's frowning, her brow screwed up in concentration. She stares at Audrey.

"You know?" Julie says. "I really don't know. I can't remember."

Claire shivers. That ought to say something about Julie, but the truth is, it doesn't. It says something about Audrey.

Claire just doesn't know what.

CLAIRE

Julie agrees to pick Claire up the next afternoon. As Claire is changing out of her sloppy T-shirt and old shorts, the telephone rings, shattering the silence of the house. She bolts out of her room, half-dressed, since Grammy's taking her afternoon nap and she gets irritable whenever she's woken. "Hello?" Claire says breathlessly into the phone, before remembering to add, "Sudek residence."

"Claire? Is that you?"

"Mom?" Claire sighs and leans up against the wall. It's the first time her mother has called her since she dropped Claire off in Indianola a week ago.

"I can't talk long—I have a meeting scheduled in half an hour. But I saw that you'd called a couple of times and I wanted to make sure everything's all right." Her mother's voice is brisk and business-like. She might as well be returning a client's call.

"Everything's fine," Claire says. She pauses, her thoughts fuzzy. Why did she call again?

"Claire? Is everything all right?"

Claire glances up at the notepad beside the phone, sees the number for the exterminator. And then she remembers. "Monsters," she says. "I was calling about the monsters."

There's a long silence on the other end of the phone. The speaker buzzes in Claire's ear.

"I'd forgotten about those," her mother says, her voice distant and flat. Then: "Is everything all right with Grammy? Has she been taking her pills?"

Claire shivers and slumps farther down the wall. She thinks about what Audrey told her, how people forget about the monsters as soon as they pass the city limits. She wonders if that's what this is, or if it's her mother avoiding an awkward topic. The silence is heavy enough, though, that this time she doesn't think it's her mother's fault.

"Yeah, she's been taking her pills. Listen, Mom—"

"What is it, honey? I told you I can't talk long, so if you want to really chat we'll need to hold that off for some other time."

Claire's mother has never gone in for chats, and Claire has no idea why she'd want to start now. "Mom, it's not— There are *monsters* here, and I'm worried something really bad's going to happen to Grammy that I can't deal with—"

"We've had this conversation a hundred times already," Claire's mother snaps. "We're not having it again. Helping an old woman out with her chores isn't going to kill you, and she doesn't feel her disease is serious enough to warrant live-in help."

"What? I didn't say anything about the chores. I was—"

"No talking back, young lady. I know you're not happy about being in the country for the summer, but try to make the best of it." Her mother's tone softens then, the way it always does when she gets too harsh, as if she's finally heard herself. "There are plenty of fun things to do in Indianola. Have you been to the beach yet?"

Claire sighs. She's living in a town full of monsters and her mother's asking her about the beach. "Yes."

"Good. Oh! And of course you'll be in town for the Stargazer's Masquerade. That's in July, and I always had such fun at it. It's a costume party, you know. Ask Grammy about it."

"I already heard about it. Listen, Mom—"

"Sorry, dear, I really have to run. Call me if you need anything."

Her mother's favorite lie.

"Sure," Claire says, which is how she always responds. They say their goodbyes and Claire hangs up the phone. Her mother's voice rings in her ear, and for a moment Claire is homesick—not for her mother, necessarily, or even their messy house where the TV's always blaring in the background. But for Houston, for civilization itself. She misses Josh and her friends from school.

She misses living in a place where there aren't any *monsters*, for God's sake. A place where the city limits don't strip away your memory.

At least Julie's coming over today. Claire peels herself away from the wall and finishes buttoning up her plaid white-and-blue overall dress in the living room. Then she slips out onto the porch to wait.

Grammy acted weird when Claire mentioned she was visiting Julie as she helped walk Grammy into her room for her nap. "Not Audrey?" Grammy said, and when Claire shook her head, Grammy frowned like she didn't approve. Claire can't get the approval of anyone, it seems.

The sea breeze is up today, and it makes the shade of the porch almost pleasant. At two o'clock exactly, a bright red Mustang pulls into the driveway. Julie waves from the driver's seat, and Claire jumps up and runs over to the car.

"Hey!" Julie waves again as Claire climbs in. "Why were you waiting outside? It's so hot."

"It's hotter inside," Claire says. "Grammy doesn't have AC."

"Oh, that's right." Julie rolls her eyes and sets the car's air-conditioning to high. "There you go. So you're nice and cool."

Claire smiles and repositions the vents so that they're blowing on her face. She's glad to be out of Grammy's house and away from her mother's phone call. She hopes she can forget her family today, even if it's just for a little while.

Julie backs out of the driveway. Some riotous, angry music plays on the stereo. Claire doesn't recognize it, but she doesn't want to admit she doesn't recognize it.

"Thanks for picking me up," Claire says.

"It's all good. It's not like it's that far away." Julie turns down an unfamiliar street. Trees arch overhead like the ceiling of a cathedral.

"Oh, then I could have ridden my bike," Claire says.

"No way. It's too hot for that." Julie picks up speed and the trees zip by, concealing flashes of houses. She drums her fingers against the steering wheel, nodding to the beat of the music. Even though they aren't talking, the silence is companionable, and Claire feels more comfortable than she does with Audrey. Being in the car with Julie feels natural. It's not that way with Audrey.

"Here we are!" Julie slows down and pulls into a long driveway. The trees clear out, revealing a large, neatly manicured lawn. The house itself is huge, a hundred-year-old mansion with big gaping windows and stairs leading up to the door. A palm tree grows in front, and Claire feels a sudden rock of dizziness when she sees it. That palm tree is *familiar*.

No—the entire *house* is familiar.

"This is going to sound crazy," Claire says. "But I swear I've seen your house before."

"Really?" Julie pulls her car around to a detached garage. Claire cranes her neck around so she can keep looking at the house. Seeing it from the side, she doesn't get any flicker of recognition. It's only from the front, when she's looking at it head-on.

"Yeah. Like I've seen a photograph of it somewhere."

"Weird." Julie pulls into the garage and shuts off the engine. There are spaces for two other cars, although only one is full. Claire isn't sure what kind of car it is, but it's small and sleek and looks expensive.

"Yeah, I don't want to sound like some creepy stalker or something—"

"You don't." Julie laughs. "Maybe my house is famous and I just don't know it."

They climb out of the car. Claire squints down the driveway, sifting through her memories, trying to figure out where she's seen the house.

"It's just from the front," Claire says. "Isn't that weird?"

"Weirder things have happened," Julie says. "I have a summer job as a monster catcher."

And then Claire's thoughts click into place. She has seen the house as a photograph—a black-and-white photograph, hanging on her bedroom wall. *Sudek Mansion, 1890.*

Did this sprawling house used to belong to her family? If it did, it was well before even her grandmother's time.

"Come on, we can go in through the side," Julie says. "It leads into the kitchen, so we're guaranteed not to see my mom."

Claire follows Julie through a garden shriveled by the heat and up to a screen door. Julie unlocks it and they go inside, into the kitchen. All the lights are turned off. The house has a warm, lived-in quality, despite the luxuriance of the furniture and decorations. They head toward the stairs. Claire takes everything in, the framed artwork on the walls, the expensive-looking antique chairs, the chandelier hanging above the staircase.

"I know where I've seen your house before," Claire blurts out when she can't stand it anymore.

"What?" Julie glances over at her. They're on the second floor, walking on a Persian rug that runs the length of the hallway. "Where?"

"You promise you won't think I'm some crazed stalker?"

Julie laughs. "No! Here, we're going up into the attic." She grabs a cord dangling from the ceiling and pulls. Steps unfold like magic.

"There's a picture of it in my bedroom," Claire says. "My bedroom at Grammy's house, I mean. She's had it for years." She pauses. "It's labeled *Sudek Mansion*."

Julie locks the ladder in place and turns around to face her. Claire flushes with embarrassment, and for a moment she's certain Julie's going to kick her out, tell her she needs to go hang out with Audrey Duchesne, because Audrey Duchesne is the kind of freakishly normal friend that Claire deserves.

"That," Julie says, "is very odd."

"I'm sorry," Claire says.

"No, you're fine!" Julie grabs the railings of the ladder and pulls herself up two steps. She glances over her shoulder at Claire and grins. "I'm not going to hold you responsible for your grandma's creepiness."

"It's an old picture," Claire says. "Like, taken with one of those Victorian cameras where you have to stand still for a long time."

"Well, that was when the house was built, the Victorian era." She laughs. "You think your family used to live in my house? Like a hundred years ago?"

"I don't know. It would be weird, right?"

"Totally weird. Here, come on up! I promise I won't bite."

"Your room's in the attic?" Claire follows Julie up the ladder. It's a rickety thing, and it shakes with each step.

"Nah." Julie's already disappeared through the hatchway, and her voice floats down as if from heaven. "This is just my movie room."

"You have a *movie* room?" This is more impressive than a bedroom, even a bedroom in an attic. Claire scrambles the rest of the way up. When she pokes her head up out through of the attic's floor, she finds herself surrounded by treasure.

"Holy crap," she says, before she can stop herself.

Julie just laughs and reaches out a hand to help pull Claire up. The room is filled with *stuff*. Boxes and old dress forms, shelves of books and knickknacks, a three-foot-tall dollhouse that, Claire realizes, is a replica of Julie's house. Most of the old stuff has been cleared to the sides, though, making an empty space in the center of the room with a threadbare couch and a big-screen TV.

"I got that for Christmas along with the SNES," Julie says, pointing at the TV. "My dad likes to buy me stuff to make up for working all the time. Anyway, they meant for me to put it in my room so they could watch the news or whatever, but I put it up here instead." She grins. "I was already driving them crazy wanting to watch movies all the time."

"This is *awesome*," Claire says. She turns around in place, taking everything in. One of the old bookshelves has been dragged over next to the TV—Claire can see the trail left in the thin coating of dust on the floor—and a handful of VHS tapes are stacked on the top shelf along with a pile of game cartridges. "It's like my dream room. You could just watch movies all day and no one would bother you."

"Yeah, and the video store has some great stuff, too. Frank—he's the manager—he's got fantastic taste. We should go there sometime. Frank is the coolest person in town."

Cooler than you? Claire thinks, although she doesn't say it out loud. Way too embarrassing.

Julie pulls the game controllers off the shelf, unwinds the cords, and plugs them in. She hands one to Claire. "Which game do you want to play?"

Claire studies the games, then promptly answers "*Mortal Kombat*," since she's actually played it before, with Josh, and she doesn't think she sucks too badly at it.

The cords are just long enough to reach the couch, and Julie and Claire sit side by side and select their characters. Claire goes with Sonya Blade, the way she always does with Josh (she likes playing as a girl). Julie chooses Sub-Zero. The pounding of electronic drums, a digitized voice announcing *Fight!*, and the game begins. Playing takes most of Claire's concentration, and she winds up mashing the buttons down half the time, hoping for the best. Julie beats her in the second round with a flurry of ice.

"This is harder than I remember," Claire says. "I mean, I haven't played it much, so—"

"All I do is play it," Julie says, laughing. She saves their game and tucks herself in the corner of the couch so that she's facing Claire. "Honestly, I want to hear more about the Sudek Mansion."

"There's not much to say." Claire sets her controller down next to Julie's. "I mean, it's just a label on the picture. I have no idea why it's on there."

"Huh." Julie leans back in the couch, her expression thoughtful. "My dad always told me my great-whatever-grandfather built this place, but he could have been making it up."

"I asked my grandma about it once," Claire says. "When I was a little kid. The picture used to be kind of like the centerpiece of the living room—"

"Even weirder," Julie says. "I mean, no offense."

"No, it *is* weird! I remember asking her why she didn't live in *that* house anymore and she started yelling at me not to ask questions." Claire shakes her head. "That's Grammy, though."

Julie gives a crooked smile. "I guess we're connected, then. It was destiny for me to take the job at Mrs. Sudek's, and for you to come into the Pirate's Den when I was there with Lawrence."

"It was fate," Claire says gravely.

Julie laughs. "Exactly. Fate." She pauses. "Fated to become friends."

"Exactly."

Their conversation falls away, and this time the silence isn't quite so companionable, although Claire wouldn't call it awkward either. Julie looks down at her lap, her hair falling in dark tangles over her face.

Claire looks over at the shelf of movies. She sees *Alien, Reservoir Dogs, Evil Dead II,* and others she doesn't recognize.

"Why do you have so many tapes?" she asks, grateful for a question to fill the emptiness. "Isn't there a limit at your video store?"

Julie lifts her head, her eyes bright. "There is, but Frank lets me borrow anything for as long as I want. He's even given me a couple of movies out of the store's stock." She jumps off the couch and goes over to the shelf. "Like *Alien,* that was the first one I begged him for. I've been obsessed since I saw it on TV when I was nine."

"You got to watch *Alien* when you were a kid?" Claire's own mother enforces a strict PG-only rule, and as far as she knows, her dad gets no say in the matter.

"My parents didn't pay any attention. It doesn't have any sex, so they didn't care." She grins. "We can watch it if you want. It's pretty much my favorite movie of all time. I can just—relate to it, you know? What with the monsters in this town." She sighs. "Not that our monsters are that dangerous."

Claire squirms a little at the thought that someone might relate to a monster movie because they have real monsters in their backyard. She's still creeped out over the conversation with her mother, the way she just passed over any mention of the monsters. "I probably can't right now," Claire says. "I have to be back to my grandma's in an hour and a half." Julie looks so disappointed at this revelation that Claire says, "Maybe next time, though. I want to see it."

"Awesome!" They smile at each other across the room. Then Julie looks away. "We've still got time to kill, though."

Claire looks around, taking in the surroundings. "You've got a lot of cool stuff up here. Like that dollhouse."

"Oh God," Julie says. "The dollhouse."

"What's wrong with it?" Claire asks, smiling.

"Nothing, I guess, it's just creepy to have a copy of your house *inside* your house." She glances over at Claire. "To be honest, I didn't even know we had it until I moved my TV up here."

"Really?"

Julie nods. "Most of this stuff has been here for ages. I'm not sure my parents even packed it up. Might've been my grandparents."

Claire stands up and walks over to the dollhouse to investigate. She's read too many books with mysterious dollhouses to *not* do it.

"Ooh," Julie calls out from the couch. "Girl detective."

Claire blushes, glancing over at her. "I'm just curious."

"No, you're fine! I think it's adorable. I used to love reading the Nancy Drew books when I was younger."

Claire gets hung up on the word *adorable* for some reason.

"Let me know what you find," Julie says. "I haven't really looked at that thing at all."

Claire pushes away boxes so she can kneel in front of the dollhouse. Julie's right; it's very old, the wood distorted from damp or age. The whole thing is fuzzed over with a layer of dust. She peers into one of the miniature windows.

"See anything?" Julie calls, making her way across the attic.

"Not really." Claire feels around on the side of the dollhouse for a latch to open it. Julie crouches beside her, head cocked.

"I wonder who made it," she says.

Claire's fingers brush across the latch, but it won't open. She peers over at it. Rusted shut.

"Do you mind if I try to get this open?" she says.

"Go for it." Julie settles herself on top of a box labeled *Xmas Decorations* in thick black marker. "Maybe there'll be a thousand bucks in there or something."

Claire laughs and tugs at the lock with her finger. The metal crumbles into red powder and the latch springs up in a plume of dust. She yelps in surprise and scooches backward; Julie steadies her.

"Hey, careful," she says.

Claire coughs, waves the dust away. She pushes the dollhouse open the rest of the way.

It's full of shoeboxes.

"Okay, thank God," Julie says. "Because if it was a little miniature version of us in there, I was going to scream."

Claire laughs. "Nothing that exciting, I guess."

Julie pulls out one of the boxes and opens it, revealing stacks of loose photographs. Most of them look like they're from the fifties or sixties—lots of women in big bouffant hairdos, with ugly makeup and uglier clothes.

"Oh God, is that my *dad*?" Julie squeals and holds up a school picture of a dark-haired boy in thick horn-rimmed glasses, glowering at the camera. "It totally is!"

"He seems grumpy," Claire says.

"He *is* grumpy." Julie throws the photo back in the box. "I wonder why these got shoved in there." She pulls out a few more shoeboxes, all of them filled with similar pictures. Nothing as old as the Sudek Mansion picture, though.

It occurs to Claire that part of her thought the dollhouse might explain the picture. It seems old enough, its painted interiors faded with age, its miniature gas lamps dark. She isn't sure why she cares, but the insistence is there, gnawing at the edges of her thoughts, the way the monsters are always gnawing at the edges of her thoughts, hiding themselves in her periphery. There's a connection somewhere in this room—between Grammy and this house, her family and Julie's family, even between her and Julie. She can almost feel it, a faint pulse on the air, dragging her away from the room's center.

Julie's still digging through the pictures of her family, laughing softly to herself. Claire pulls out another box—not a shoebox, something older and half-decayed, the brittle cardboard splitting at the seams.

That pulse on the air surges. Claire feels the atoms in her body jumping around. Just for a second, and then it's gone, and Claire is sure it's her imagination.

She pulls out the old box. It's full of documents as thin as dead leaves, neat typewritten letters marching across the page. A date across the top: *December 12, 1920.* Isn't that the year Grammy was born? But the documents don't say anything about the Sudeks. Claire sets the box aside, peers deeper inside the dollhouse.

Her blood rushes in her ears, and she thinks she hears a ringing in the distance, a low constant tone like a phone that's been left off the hook. There's one last box inside the dollhouse's dusty shadows. The ringing grows louder. It's all she can hear.

Her fingers graze something slick and cool, like polished wood.

The ringing stops. Claire can breathe again.

She tugs on the box, but it doesn't move; it seems to be wedged into the lower floor of the dollhouse. She pulls harder. There's a pause, a moment of held breath, and then the container lurches free and Claire goes toppling backward over the attic floor. A stack of cardboard boxes tips and crashes, stirring up a cloud of dust.

"Oh my God, are you okay?" Julie drops the photographs she was studying and kneels at Claire's side. "Wow, that was inside the dollhouse?"

"Apparently." Claire looks down at her prize, a simple rectangle carved out of a rich dark wood, shining in the lights. Now that it's out in the open, Claire can't imagine how it fit.

"Well, open it up!" Julie sits back and crosses her legs.

Claire takes a deep breath. Her fingers tingle when she touches the box, little bursts of static electricity shooting up her arms. She lifts up the lid.

At first, she doesn't know what she's seeing. It looks like a storm cloud has been caught and stuffed inside a coffin. But then, slowly, details emerge: seams and piping and ribbons. It's a dress.

Claire lifts the dress out of the box. The fabric fans out with a whisper, gray and gauzy. Pale ribbons drape around the neckline, and dark green embroidery creeps up from the hem, fanning out in strange, eerie patterns that remind Claire of the wildness of the sea.

"Wow, Mom would freak if she knew this was up here."

Julie's voice drags Claire back to the attic room. She blinks, shakes her head. "It is really pretty."

"Mom's super into old clothes and stuff." Julie stands up. "Here, let's see how it'll look on you."

Claire laughs. "I doubt this would even fit over my leg."

Julie rolls her eyes. "At least hold it up. There's a mirror over in the corner somewhere."

Claire stands up, bringing the dress with her. The waist is corset-narrow, and when she presses it up against herself she can still see her body on each side.

"Yeah, I won't be wearing this anytime soon," she mutters.

"Over here!" Julie calls out. "Just to see."

Claire turns, the dress swirling around her feet. Julie drags a swinging full-length mirror out next to the TV, and Claire walks over to her, still holding the dress up, trying not to stumble over the hem. When she looks at her reflection she just sees herself, holding up a long drape of gray fabric.

"Doesn't look like much."

"I bet it would look great on you," Julie says.

"Yeah, if you could take it out about ten inches."

Julie just shakes her head, smiling a little, watching Claire as she poses in the mirror. The dress sweeps across the floor.

"I wonder whose it was," Claire says.

"Maybe there's something in the box."

Claire lets the dress drop. "Maybe." She loops the dress over her arms a couple of times and walks back over to the box. Julie picks up the lid, flips it over. Shakes her head. Then she picks up the box proper. When she turns it upside down, her eyes go wide.

"What is it?" Claire asks.

"Check it out." Julie upturns the box. A name is carved into the wood, in looping script.

Abigail Sudek

Julie lets out a low whistle. "Maybe your great-great-great-grandma did used to live in this house."

Claire considers this. "I think you might be right," she finally says. "Isn't that weird? That our families shared a house."

Julie glances at her. "Not weird," she says. "Just cool."

And at that, Claire smiles.

JULIE

Julie kicks her feet up on the desk, narrowly dodging a stack of mimeographed forms Brittany asked her to file. Julie has no intention of doing it. Filing's Brittany's job, and she loves passing along work to Julie ever since Julie's dad told Brittany she's in charge—of Julie, anyway—whenever he or the manager, Eric, aren't around. Which is most of the time.

Julie leans back in her chair, her hands resting behind her head. The phone hasn't rung once since she got here, and Forrest has already laid claim to all the bug jobs. He always comes in thirty minutes early for that exact purpose. Julie swears he and Brittany are conspiring together to make this job even more miserable than it already is. *Alien* might be her favorite movie, but the reality of hunting monsters is a dreary experience all in all.

The AC kicks on, rustling the papers on the desk. Julie tips an ugly marble paperweight over with her foot so it'll trap the papers in place. Then she checks her watch. Only 1:27. She's been here for two hours and already she's going out of her mind with boredom. She wishes she could call up Claire, although she doesn't want to come across as pushy. They had a good time the other day, playing *Mortal Kombat* and excavating that old dollhouse. The dress Claire found is hanging from the mirror in the attic, set up next to the TV. Julie likes glancing over at it whenever she's watching a movie. It's like a little piece of Claire left behind.

Julie is aware of how creepy that would sound if she ever admitted it to anymore.

The knob on the office door rattles. Julie immediately swings her feet down to the floor and starts riffling through a stack of forms, trying to pretend she's doing work. Brittany's liable to tattle on her to her dad. The forms are all monster requisitions from the last few days, when Julie's been off. Most of them were down on hurricane alley, right where they're supposed to be. Nothing in town.

The door slams open. It's not Brittany. It's Julie's dad.

"Damn thing's still sticking," he mutters. "I'll have to say something to Brittany."

Julie suppresses a grin. Brittany will hate that, getting called to repair doors like a janitor.

"Hey, Dad," Julie calls out. Her dad glances up at her and squints through his thick glasses.

"You're working today?" He shakes his head. "No, of course, I knew that. Don't want you lazing around the house too much. It's good to keep a young mind occupied over the summer."

As if lazing around the exterminator's office is such an improvement on Julie's productivity.

"Not really working," she starts. "There's no—"

"Well, whose fault is that?" Her dad shoos her out of the seat, and Julie obeys, grudgingly, moving to perch on the edge of the windowsill instead. The hot sun warms her back.

"Forrest," she says. "He took all the bug jobs."

Her dad pulls open one of the drawers and extracts a thick black address book. He tosses it to the desk with a thump.

"You know you aren't supposed to be doing bug jobs anyway." He flips through the address book, running his finger down the letter tabs sticking out at the sides.

"Bug jobs are safer." She's parroting a line she heard from her mom at dinner; Julie's mom has been a semi-ally in the fight to get Julie a job at the video store, one of the few things her mom has ever sided with her on. "I bet I'd work a lot harder at the video store."

"Frank doesn't need anyone." Her dad stops on one of the address book's pages, its lines filled with his incomprehensible dark scribble. "Aha! I knew I had Georgia's number somewhere."

"Who's Georgia?" Julie asks.

Her dad doesn't answer, only grabs the phone and begins dialing. He glances over at her. Julie can hear the faint ring of the line. "And you know where I stand on the video store. We talked about this. Working at the exterminator's is giving you skills you're going to need— Georgia? Oh, I've been trying to get a hold of you! How are those Coke shipments?"

Julie leans back against the window, not caring that she's smashing the plastic blinds. She and her father have gone over this a hundred times already, ever since he informed her that she needed to pay her own way in the world, just like he did. A lie, of course—money has been in the Alvarez family for years, and Julie knows for a fact that her dad

72

spent his youth zipping around the highways in a Chrysler 300 gifted to him on his sixteenth birthday. Her grandpa told her all about it.

Still, her dad persists with the argument that Julie needs to learn how to protect herself against the monsters, that she needs to learn how they think and how they react in different situations. Julie's pretty sure her dad expects her to come back to Indianola after college and take over his business empire, which would include sitting on the committee that signs treaties with the monsters. But Julie's got other plans. Her eyes are on Austin. Frank's already showed her some of the experimental films that have been coming out of there, and she wants in on it. She just has to finish high school first. And survive working at the exterminator's office.

"Yeah, mm-hmm, that sounds great. Thanks, Georgia." Her dad laughs, big and hearty and fake. "You too! Watch out for those scamps."

Julie wonders when her father started saying the word *scamps*.

Her dad's still chatting with Georgia when the button for the second line lights up. Julie's heart clenches. She hopes it's not a job, hopes it's just someone calling to complain that Forrest is running late.

Her dad sees the light too, and he looks at her and points at it and points at the door. *Go check with Brittany.* She doesn't need him to say it out loud. The lines in his forehead do the talking.

She sighs and pushes away from the window. Leaves him laughing in his chair. Out in the lobby, Brittany has the phone tucked between her shoulder and ear as she scribbles down notes. It looks like the job book. Dammit.

"We'll send someone over right way, Mrs. Sudek," she says.

Julie's heart leaps. A job at Mrs. Sudek's means a chance to see

Claire again, and this time totally at random. Maybe it really is fate for the two of them to be friends.

Or more than friends.

Julie shoves the thought aside. Dwelling on it'll just make her heartsick.

"Got a job for you," Brittany says, hanging up the phone.

"Yeah, I heard. It's at Mrs. Sudek's?" Julie holds her breath. She hopes she didn't mis-hear.

"Yep. Another talking monster. You're going to want to note on the report that this is the second one in a week. The committee'll need to hear about it."

"I know how to do my job," Julie snaps.

Brittany rolls her eyes and blows a bubble with her gum. Her glittery butterfly clips flash in her perfectly straightened hair.

"Here's all the information," she says, tearing the sheet out of the job book and handing it to Julie. "Nothing too unusual. She said it was tall, though, so you'll want to make sure to take the big cage."

Julie doesn't say anything, just shoves the information sheet into her pocket and bounds out of the office. Her heart thrums with excitement—well, excitement and nervousness both—but at the same time she feels a cold twist of dread. Not because of Claire, but because another monster has gone to Mrs. Sudek's.

Julie wonders if the committee will actually do anything about it. They don't do much—no one in town does, really. Everyone just keeps their distance.

She climbs into the van and roars off down the street. It doesn't take her long to get to Mrs. Sudek's house, especially since she goes faster than she should and runs a couple of yellow lights. She pulls into the driveway and parks. The house is closed up tight, like a birthday present waiting to be opened. Julie takes a deep breath. She checks her reflection in the rearview mirror. Her eyeliner's still looking good. Not that it matters, right? Claire isn't going to notice her that way.

Besides, she's got a monster to deal with.

She hops out of the van and opens up the back doors so she can drag out the big cage. It comes with little wheels to make transport easier, but they always get stuck if you take them off pavement, so Julie leaves the cage sitting on the driveway. She'll come back and grab it when she can.

Julie rings the doorbell.

At first there's only silence. But then footsteps whisper on the other side of the door. It swings open. Claire steps up to the screen, sunlight falling in tiny squares across her face.

"Oh, Julie!" she says. "I was hoping they'd send you."

Julie's heart swells. "Well, you know, I heard the name Sudek, and apparently we've got a house in common—" She shrugs. Claire laughs, a sweet twinkling sound that chimes around in Julie's head. "It's out back again, isn't it? I didn't see anything when I drove up."

"Yeah, in the same place as before." Claire pushes open the screen and Julie steps into the foyer. She's never liked Mrs. Sudek's house. It's too stuffy, too closed-in, and breathing the air feels like choking on the past. But it's a lot more tolerable with Claire standing at her side, her bare arms crossed over her chest, her pale skin almost glowing in the dusty gloom.

"What did it say?" Julie asks. "Brittany said it was a talking one."

"Yeah." Claire rubs her arms and looks down. "I didn't really—it was talking about astronauts."

75

"Astronauts?" Julie frowns and looks down the hallway. Blue TV light flickers in the living room. "Really?"

"Yeah. It kept asking me if I'd seen the astronaut, and—"

"It asked you questions?"

Claire nods. For the first time Julie is really aware of the glint of fear in her eyes. It's faint, but she should have seen it earlier.

"It didn't make sense," Claire says.

Julie takes a deep breath. "I'm going to go talk to it. Do you—" She hesitates. "Do you mind coming out there with me? Since it was talking to you, it might be here—" She doesn't want to finish her thought. *Might be here for you.* Claire looks away. Strands of hair stick to her neck and the side of her face, and her skin gleams with sweat.

"Are you going to keep yammering in there or are you going to get this creature out of my yard?"

Claire jumps at the sound of Mrs. Sudek's voice. Then she looks up at Julie and mouths an apology.

"Don't worry about it," Julie whispers. Then, louder, she calls out, "I'm here, Mrs. Sudek! We'll get you cleared out in no time."

Julie remembers the way to the back door. Claire walks alongside her. They pass through the living room, where Mrs. Sudek stares at her TV, her face ghostly and thin in the light.

At the back door, Julie puts her hand on the knob and turns to Claire. TV noises trickle in from the living room, and Julie pitches her voice low, and says something she's always wanted to say to a girl:

"Don't worry. I'll keep us safe."

Claire smiles, a crooked, gorgeous smile, and Julie pushes the door open.

Sunlight pours in, bright against the darkness of the Sudek house. Julie and Claire step out into the heat.

The monster stands in the yard.

It's tall, long and thin like it's been stretched out. Julie's definitely going to need the large cage. But its height isn't the only alarming thing about it: Its arms are too long for the rest of its body, and its fingers are too long for its arms. It looks like an aloe vera plant, fleshy spikes jutting out of the ground. Its face is narrow and pointed, and its eyes glint greenish in the sunlight.

Julie feels a wash of nausea, looking at it.

"What are you doing in town?" she asks.

The monster doesn't answer.

Julie walks right up to the edge of the patio. "My friend here said you can talk," she says. "But if you don't prove it to me, you know the treaties give me the right to exterminate you."

The monster's mouth splits open, revealing rows of teeth, like a shark. Julie starts backward, her pulse pounding. A hand touches the top of her back. Claire, steadying her. Julie draws up all her bravery.

Maybe that was supposed to be a smile.

"You're correct," the monster says, and its voice is like steam and cold dark machinery. "I can speak. Truly speak, not like the *xenade* who wandered too far into town five days ago."

Xenade. Julie's heard that word before. It's the monsters' name for themselves.

"So why are you here?" Julie asks.

The monster moves, sliding forward on one of its clawed feet. Claire shrieks and grabs Julie's arm, her nails digging into Julie's skin.

The monster stops and looks past Julie at Claire. Julie tenses. The monster looks back to Julie. Back to Claire.

Even in the patio shade, Julie feels like she's drowning in the sun's heat.

And then the monster sniffs. It lifts up its nose—its snout?—and sniffs the air, once, twice. Claire's grip tightens on Julie's arm.

"Are you going to get the hell out of here or not?" Julie asks. It's all she wants, for the monster to leave so she doesn't have to ride with it back to the power plant. "I've got a cage. You know you'll have to get in if you don't go."

"Interesting," the monster says. "Very interesting." It lurches forward over the dead grass, moving closer to the house. The monster's movements are strange and jerky, like it's not used to walking, and it takes a long time to get across the yard.

But then one of its feet steps onto the porch. And then the other.

Claire sputters out a gurgled, frightened sound, and Julie turns to her and puts a hand on her arm and Claire looks at her, their faces so close they could kiss.

"It's going to be okay," Julie whispers. "They really aren't dangerous."

The monster sniffs again. Julie whips her head back around to face it. "What are you doing?" she says. "You can't come this close to the house."

The monster turns its green eyes on Claire.

"Leave her alone!" Julie steps in front of Claire, trying to block the monster's line of sight. "What in God's name is wrong with you things? You know the treaties. You aren't supposed to be here."

"I came to warn the Sudek about the astronaut," the monster says.

"What the hell does *that* mean?" Julie shouts. Claire presses close to her, her breath hot against Julie's shoulder. "An astronaut?"

The monster retreats back into the yard. Those fleshy tendrils roil around, and Julie stands trembling, thinking how out of place it looks, like something that shouldn't even exist in this world. Maybe that's why it wants to talk about astronauts.

"I merely find it interesting," the monster says, "to see an Alvarez and a Sudek, standing side by side."

Silence floods the yard.

Julie fumbles around for her voice. "Now why would you say a thing like that? How do you even know our names?"

"I can smell it on you. The Alvarez line." It directs one tendril at Julie. "And the Sudek line." Another at Claire. "It's an interesting combination, cosmically speaking."

Julie glances at Claire, afraid that Claire will somehow interpret the monster's nonsense for the truth. But Claire isn't even looking at her, just staring out at the monster with wide, frightened eyes.

"I still don't know what you're talking about," Julie says. "Now, are you going to leave or not? I can get my cage." She pauses. "Or the Taser. You know I'm authorized to use it if I deem it necessary." Which she doesn't want to do.

The monster makes a strange crackling noise that reminds Julie of electricity. "Aldraa won't like that."

"Aldraa knows you're not supposed to be here."

"What we are and are not supposed to do—" The monster's voice fades away for a moment. More like a radio flickering in and out rather than a lost train of thought. Julie doesn't like it. "Things are changing.

Every *azojin* things will change, but they should not change like this. It is unnatural."

It's hard for Julie to hold on to the word that he says, the *a*-word. She thinks *Agosín*, the last name of a girl at school. But no, that's not right either. The word catches on her thoughts like a half-remembered song.

"And that's why you're coming into town?" Julie says, her voice trembling. "Because things are changing?"

The monster looks at her. "Yes."

The yard goes silent. Not just Claire and Julie and the monster, but everything: the wind, the rustle of plants, the droning of cicadas and grasshoppers.

This isn't good, the monsters breaking the treaties. Not good at all. A slow trickle of dread seeps into Julie's stomach.

"I'll return to our allotted space," the monster says. "There's no need to use your Taser or your cage on me. But as the *azojin* approaches, the treaties will disintegrate. Remember that, Alvarez and Sudek." It sniffs the air again. "That's an interesting scent, really. The two of you together. You could bring about much change in this world if you found access to the timelines."

"Oh, for the love of—" Julie throws her hands up, trying to pretend that she's not afraid the monster *knows* somehow. "Will you just leave? Stop babbling nonsense!"

Somehow, though, Julie doesn't think it's nonsense. He said the word again, the word that buzzes around her thoughts. It makes her bloodstream spark.

The monster backs away. Julie and Claire press close together. Julie has never felt this unnerved about a monster before. Not even

Aldraa and the weird way he distorts reality ever made her feel so out of sorts.

"Keep going!" Julie calls out as the monster moves across the yard. "If I have to show up at another house for you, I'm getting out the Taser for sure!" She speaks with an authority she doesn't feel, but at least the monster disappears around the side of the house.

Claire lets out a long sigh of relief and slumps against the brick. Julie feels the same way: shaky, like she's just run the mile in her PE class at school.

"You can do that?" Claire asks, after a moment. "Just let it walk away?"

Julie sighs. "Yeah. We're supposed to take a hands-off approach as much as possible."

"Is it going to hurt someone?"

"I don't think so. They don't really hurt people." But Julie isn't convinced of that herself, and she can tell by Claire's expression that she isn't either. "It hasn't happened since before I was born. The treaties and all."

"But it has happened before." Claire's eyes shimmer. Julie's afraid she might start crying. "Do you think they'll hurt me? Is that why they're coming here?"

"No," Julie says quickly, wanting to do anything she can to make Claire feel safe. "No, it's super rare. The guy I heard about who got hurt, they say he was hassling them, maybe even hurting them. One of the rumors said he was trying to hunt them like deer." Julie takes a deep breath. "And besides, he got hurt at the power plant. Nowhere near town."

Claire trembles.

"But I mean—I'll ask my dad. I'll make sure you're okay." She smiles, and Claire returns it, thin and wavering.

"I didn't know what it was talking about," she says. "Astronauts and everything."

"They're always like that." Even though Julie's never heard them refer to someone by their family name. "They don't think like we do, you know?"

Julie moves toward the back door, wanting to be in the safety of inside, even if it is Mrs. Sudek's house. But Claire says, "There was a word."

Julie stops, her hand on the doorknob. "What?"

"The monster—it said a word. I can't remember—"

Agosín, Julie thinks, but she knows that isn't it.

"I heard it too," Julie says, frowning. "But I don't know—I lost it."

"Is that dangerous?"

"I don't know." Julie meets Claire's eye. The sunlight splashes against Claire's brown hair, making it shine golden. Julie wishes this moment and this closeness didn't have anything to do with monsters.

"I just think it's funny that I can't remember it. Not in a ha-ha way, but—" Claire hesitates. "That happens a lot with the monsters. If I think about them too much, then it's harder to concentrate on them—I guess it's not that funny."

Julie nods. The word keeps slipping further and further away, like a dream. She's pretty sure it started with *A*—

"I should go ask Mrs. Sudek for her payment," Julie says. "Maybe you can come over in a couple of days, and we can get something from the video store. I'll be off on Saturday."

Claire nods. "I'd like that."

Julie pulls the door open.

Her head buzzes. She can't stop thinking about herself and Claire, intertwined together, like their scents.

⌒

Julie's hands are shaking as she drives through town. She doesn't want to go back to the office yet, doesn't want to learn there's another monster waiting to be collected down in hurricane alley somewhere. The last thing she wants right now is to deal with monsters.

The word is gone completely. She can feel its absence, like a black hole, but even that is starting to fade. When she tries to remember the word, memories of Claire come in instead. Claire smiling in the sunlight. Claire's hand brushing against hers. Claire kissing her on the beach, the waves rolling in around their feet. Sure, Julie would rather think about Claire, but the monsters and this missing word leave her with a queasy feeling in the pit of her stomach.

Something's wrong.

After seventeen years Julie's grown used to the ways the monsters slip into the edge of things. Claire is right: You can't think on them too much. If you try, they just pull further away, like a particularly tricky math problem. But Julie has never lost an entire memory like this, not without leaving town. She just—doesn't like it.

The exterminator office appears up ahead, the neon cockroach waving its antennae back and forth. Julie slows down. Her heart thuds in her chest. The lost word is a whisper in the dark crevices of her memory.

She drives past.

Julie takes a deep breath and loosens her grip on the steering wheel. Lawrence. She just needs to talk to Lawrence. Maybe this has happened to him before—maybe she's overreacting. Lawrence is good for telling you that you're being illogical.

She pulls the van into the Texaco station—not the one owned by her father, thank God—and parks next to the pair of pay phones on the side of the building. She digs around in the cup holder for a quarter and then climbs out into the heat. The sun bounces off the gas pumps, throwing squares of light into her eyes. She shakes her head and scurries over to the phone. Drops in the quarter. Punches in Lawrence's number.

The phone rings twice before Aunt Rosa answers, her voice whispery and dry, the way it always is these days.

"Aunt Rosa?" Julie says. "It's me. Julie. Is Lawrence at work?" Lawrence always answers the phone when he's at home, since Aunt Rosa has trouble moving around. And Julie expected him to be home today—she thought she remembered him mentioning that he had today off, that he needed to study for a test or something.

"Oh, Julie, dear. Hello. No, he's not at work."

"School? I thought his classes were at night."

Aunt Rosa laughs. "He's out." She lowers her voice a little. "With a *girl*. I think he's on a date, although of course he denies it." She laughs again, and a jolt of confusion shoots through Julie's chest. Lawrence?

On a *date*?

"Oh," she says. "Okay. Well—let him know I called, okay? I'm working today."

"Of course."

Julie hangs up the phone and sags against the phone booth. This can't be right. It has to be some kind of study date or something.

Lawrence is too busy trying to become a detective to mess with girls right now. Most of the girls in Indianola aren't into him anyway.

Julie trudges over to the van. She still doesn't want to go back to the exterminator's. She thinks about Brittany's shrill voice, the phone jangling in its receiver, calling her out to capture some other monster—no thank you.

She starts the engine and sits there for a moment, listening to it idle. If Lawrence is on a date, there are only a few places in town he could be. The K&L Root Beer Drive-in is the only restaurant worth talking about. Or the Pirate's Den. Which is more date-y, anyway.

Julie throws the van into reverse and pulls out of the parking lot. She'll swing by the arcade. Just to see. If he's there, she can ask him about the monsters, the missing scrap of her memory. If he's not, she'll go back to the exterminator's and deal with it.

It only takes five minutes for Julie to get to the arcade. No one's out. She doesn't see Lawrence's car in the parking lot, and she almost turns and drives off. But maybe he didn't drive. Maybe his date drove. Lawrence is down with that sort of thing. A modern man.

Julie parks and climbs out and walks across the simmering parking lot. Sweat beads up on her forehead. The signs blink in the arcade windows. A flyer for the Stargazer's Masquerade is plastered to the front door, the ink not yet faded from the sunlight. They use the same stupid design every year, cheesy little figures looking up at the stars. It was probably drawn back in the seventies.

Julie pushes the door open, the air-conditioning cooling her sweat. At first she thinks the arcade's empty. There's nobody even standing behind the counter. But then, over the chirps and beeps of the video games, she hears Lawrence's voice.

"Thank God," she mutters to herself. She plunges into the arcade and follows the sound of it. "Hey, Larr—"

She freezes. Lawrence is here all right. And he's with Audrey Duchesne.

They're sitting together in one of the far corner booths, the date booths, the ones with the red-tinted lamps hanging above the tables. Both of them are turned away from her—Lawrence is squeezed into the booth beside Audrey, his arm thrown around her shoulder, his nose pressed into her hair.

Julie stares at them. Blood rushes in her ears. Lawrence says something to Audrey that makes her laugh, and her laughter floats out into the arcade, trilling like the machines.

Julie slinks away. Her heart pounds. She can't even remember why she wanted to talk to him in the first place. Only that it seemed so important, and now the only important thing is getting out of here. Her face is hot. She can't believe she drove to find him. Can't believe she didn't trust that Lawrence actually was on a date, an honest-to-God date. And with Audrey Duchesne, the cheerleader. The sort of girl who wouldn't have given him the time of day in high school.

Julie dives out of the arcade. The cicadas buzz up in the trees, and the sun pours bright and hot over the asphalt. Julie's dizziness clears. She glances back at the arcade. Lawrence on a date. No big deal. Good for him.

She just wishes it wasn't with Audrey Duchesne.

CHAPTER

Seven

CLAIRE

The day after the monster came to Grammy's yard, Claire is still think-ing about it. She can't stop thinking about it. Not just the monster—the memory of which is, in the way of monsters, pulling apart at the seams—but about Julie.

She lies on her bed with her Tori Amos tape blasting through her earphones and keeps replaying the encounter with the monster. *An Alvarez and a Sudek.* Claire isn't technically a Sudek—her last name's Whitmore—but she doesn't think the monster cares about that.

She wonders what her and Julie's intertwined scents smell like to the monster. A friend back in Houston had a perfume-making kit, and they used to tap the essential oils onto strips of paper and mix the scents together that way. Maybe it's something like that. Individually, she and Julie are one way, but together, they become something new.

Claire kind of likes the idea. Even if the thought of it coming from a monster leaves her unsettled.

After lunch, Julie calls. Grammy answers the phone and shouts for Claire to come take it, and when Claire comes slinking into the kitchen, Grammy gives her a dark look.

"You know I don't like you seeing that girl," she says in a low voice, the phone pressed against her chest.

Claire feels a swell of irritation. "We're friends," she says.

"You better not be making plans with her for today," Grammy says. "You're going to visit with Audrey."

Claire hasn't heard anything about this. "What?" she says. "Audrey?"

"You made plans last week." Grammy shoves the phone at Claire. "Remember?"

Claire shakes her head. Why would she make plans to hang out with Audrey so far in advance? She presses the phone to her ear, still confused.

"Julie?" she says.

"Hey, I was just seeing if we're still on for going to the video store tomorrow."

"Sure."

"Excellent. By the way, I saw something *crazy* yesterday. After the— you know. The monster."

"Oh?"

Grammy hasn't left the kitchen. She stands next to the stove with her thin arms crossed over her chest. She wobbles in place, as if yelling at Claire to answer the phone was enough to exhaust her. She looks pale, her skin thin and almost transparent. Sometimes Claire hears her coughing in the middle of the night.

"Yeah. Definitely. It's about Lawrence. I'll tell you tomorrow, though—I want to see what else I can find out about it."

Claire can't concentrate on Julie's gossip about Lawrence. Grammy's still staring at her. When Claire catches her eye, she mouths, *Audrey*, and Claire blinks. Julie has moved on to chattering about the general awesomeness of Frank, the video store manager, and Claire catches a fragment of a memory, Audrey calling, asking if she wants to go to the beach.

"I'll see you tomorrow, then," Claire says to Julie, and then she hangs up the phone.

Grammy stares at her.

"See?" she says. "I didn't make plans for today."

"Audrey will be here soon," Grammy says. "If I recall correctly."

Claire rubs her forehead. She feels like she just stepped off of a roller coaster. Yes, Audrey did call. It was a lot like Julie calling right now. Claire had been listening to music in her room; Grammy called her into the kitchen.

"I'm going to go get ready," she mutters. She leaves the kitchen and heads into her bedroom. Sunlight streams in through the blinds, illuminating flecks of dust. It's already so hot in here Claire can hardly think straight. She switches on the fan.

"I want you to know I'm not happy about you making plans with the Alvarez girl."

Claire jumps and whirls around. "It's for tomorrow," she says, startled. She didn't hear Grammy coming. "I'm still going to see Audrey. And I'll make sure I get all my chores done too."

"This isn't about the chores." Grammy steps into Claire's room and Claire goes still, like a wild animal has just crossed her path. Or a monster.

Grammy glances at her bed—made this morning, as always—and at the basket of dirty clothes in the corner, at the stack of cassettes sitting on top of the vanity. "I just don't want you seeing that girl so much."

"Why not?" Tension coils up inside Claire. She sits down at her vanity and pretends to rummage around in the makeup drawer. "She's nice."

Grammy stops a few paces away. Claire watches her in the vanity's mirror.

"She's a bad influence," Grammy says.

Claire shoves the drawer shut and turns around. "Is that *really* the problem with her?" Claire suspects it's not. She suspects the problem lies more with Julie's brown skin.

Grammy's eyes narrow. "Of course it is. She got caught drinking at a party last summer. Do you think your mother would want you hanging around that kind of girl?"

Claire doubts her mother would care. She also can't imagine Julie at a high school drinking party.

"In fact, I better not hear that's what you're doing with her tomorrow," Grammy says. "Getting drunk out behind Griff's. Don't think I don't know what you kids do."

Claire has no idea what Grammy is talking about. "I'm just going over to her house," she says. "Her mom will be there. They have a nice house, you know." She jabs her finger at the photograph hanging on the wall. "I mean, you certainly like it well enough."

Grammy's face darkens, and she pulls the photograph down so quickly that she starts coughing. Claire tenses. But then Grammy looks up and wipes her mouth and says, "I'm quite aware, thank you. And this is *not* the Alvarez house. This photograph was taken before they owned it."

"It's their house now," Claire says. "This is the nineties. Deal with it."

Grammy glares at her, but she doesn't say anything more, only stalks out of Claire's bedroom. Claire sighs and turns back to her mirror. Her reflection seems slanted at an angle.

The doorbell rings, startling Claire. She doesn't move from her vanity. A picture of her and Josh from a show at Numbers last winter is tucked into the frame. She's so used to looking at it that she hardly sees it anymore, but now she reaches over and plucks it off the mirror. Josh scowls at the camera. She's been saving her weekly allowance from Grammy—she should call him. He's always willing to talk to her, even if it's just about random stuff, arcade games and music and the weird philosophy books he's always reading. Maybe, since he's never been to Indianola, she can even tell him about the monsters.

God, she misses when conversations with Josh were the strangest part of her life.

"Claire!" Audrey storms into the room, bringing with her the scent of hairspray and Calvin Klein perfume. She plops down on the bed like she owns it. "What are you looking at?"

"What? Oh." Claire shakes her head, trying to clear her thoughts. Ten minutes ago she didn't even know she was supposed to see Audrey today. "Just a picture of a friend."

"A friend, huh?" Audrey grins. "From Houston?"

"Yeah." Claire drops the photograph onto her vanity and stands up. She doesn't want to talk about Josh with Audrey. She doesn't want to talk about *anything* with Audrey.

"I thought we'd go to Surfway Beach," Audrey says. "It's outside of town, but it's not so good for swimming, so it won't be as crowded."

"You don't want to go swimming?" Had they talked about this when they made their plans? Claire can't remember.

Audrey shakes her head. "I've got something *way* better. It's this new game. I've got it out in my car."

"A game?"

The world tilts.

"Yeah, like an arcade game. You like arcade games, right?"

"Sure." Claire shakes her head, trying to get rid of that weird dizzy feeling. "But why don't we just go to the arcade? How can you have an arcade game on the beach?"

"You'll see." Audrey grabs her hand and everything settles back into its usual place. Claire lets Audrey tug her toward the door. "It'll be *soooo* much fun, I promise!"

Claire nods, thinking, *If you say so.*

"I'll have her back before dinner, Mrs. Sudek!" Audrey shouts as they stumble out the front door and into the blazing sunlight.

Grammy doesn't answer.

They climb into Audrey's car. A big gym bag patchworked in neon colors lies across the back seat.

"That's the game," Audrey says, and starts the engine.

They drive down to the beach. Audrey switches on the radio and sings along to a country station, all songs that Claire doesn't know. No one's out on the street, but it's the middle of the day, and it's hot. So that's not such a surprise.

Surfway Beach is farther away than the main city beach, far enough that they pass a *Thanks for visiting Indianola!* sign in order to get to it. The road narrows and twists into a subdivision of candy-colored beach houses. Everything's faded from the salt. Claire catches glimpses of the Gulf of Mexico in the distance, glinting between the houses.

And then the houses end, replaced by a long stretch of road surrounded by sand dunes and sea grass.

Claire gets an uneasy feeling. She stares out the window at the dunes, imagining that they're full of rattlesnakes and monsters. She isn't sure she wants to face down a monster without Julie's help.

"Here we are!" Audrey pulls off the road. An old wooden sign says *Surfway Beach* in plain white letters, the paint peeling off in strips. The car bounces through the dunes and the wheels grind against the sand. The beach is completely empty. Not even an old man taking his dog for a walk.

"See?" Audrey says. "Much better than Indianola Beach. We get some privacy."

"Are you sure we're allowed to be here?" That uneasy feeling hasn't gone away.

"Of course! I wouldn't get you in trouble. Come on." Audrey bounds out of the car and grabs the bag. Claire follows her, but once she's out of the car, she hesitates, looking at the water.

Nothing seems right. It's not like it was back at the house, where the world was tilted. Here, the world doesn't seem like—the *world*.

Audrey turns to her, the wind blowing her hair across her face. She looks like a girl in a perfume ad. "Come on!" she says again. "I promise this'll be fun! Plus, I brought snacks!"

The wind buffets against Claire, and the sea roars in the background. She picks her way across the sand until she's at Audrey's side. Audrey grins at her; her yellow silk sundress, covered in screen-printed sunflowers, shimmers in the sun.

"Isn't this *fun*? Like we're explorers."

Claire doesn't mention that they passed a cluster of houses not five minutes ago. Of course, she can't see any trace of the houses from the beach—staring down the shore, she only sees sand and water and creeping dune vines.

Audrey spreads a blanket on the sand and sits down. She pulls things out of the bag, one at a time, and lines them up in neat rows. Claire expected a Gameboy, but she's never seen what Audrey has here. In fact, she's not sure she's even seen anything that's even *like* it, not in any arcade or mail-order catalog or on TV or anything. It's a series of little plastic buttons, all different sizes, attached to slim metal squares. Audrey doesn't set them up in any particular order, at least not that Claire can see.

"Sit!" Audrey says, and pats the blanket beside her. "You're making me nervous, hovering over me like that."

Claire sits down, but she doesn't look away from those buttons. It's as if they're spiders or cockroaches, and if she looks away, they'll scuttle up her arm.

Audrey pulls out another metal square, this time with no buttons, only a flat smooth surface. Then she pulls out a trio of Tupperware containers, red, yellow, orange, and lines them up along the edge of the blanket.

"There we are!" she says. "Oh, wait, I forgot." She pulls the lids off the Tupperware, revealing Cheetos, carrot sticks, and slices of Cheddar cheese.

"Wow," says Claire. "All the snacks are orange."

Audrey's grin stays plastered on her face. "Of course! Isn't that how you do it?"

Claire isn't sure how to answer.

Audrey's grin deepens. She grabs one of the carrot sticks. "Okay," she says. "The game. It's super fun." She holds up the blank metal square. "This is the controller. You use it to make the buttons light up." She gestures at the rest of the equipment. "They'll also create a tone."

This isn't like any arcade game Claire has ever played. She's not even sure how it's a game at all, really.

"Why don't you go first," Claire says. "And show me how it works." The row of buttons makes her nervous. She keeps glancing over her shoulder, certain she's going to see a monster creep out of the sand dunes. But there's nothing.

"Oh, of course!" Audrey straightens up her spine and sets the controller in her lap. She touches the top left corner, and one of the medium-sized buttons lights up bright electric blue and lets off a long, sighing hum. Not even a *tone*—that would suggest something electronic, something created by a machine. But this sounds entirely organic. A siren's song.

"How is it doing that?" Claire asks. "It's not even connected."

"It works like a TV remote." Audrey slides her fingers down the controller and more of the buttons light up, all that same unnatural blue. Each one adds a different note to the song.

Song—it's not the right word, but it's the only word Claire has to describe it. The notes layer on top of each other, haunting and strange, and the music drifts over the beach, catching on the wind. Claire wonders how far it can carry, if it will go all the way across the Gulf to Florida, to Mexico, to the Caribbean.

The music stops abruptly. Claire is jerked back down to earth. Audrey stares at her, smiling.

"You want to try?" she says.

Claire looks at the square of metal in Audrey's lap. She does want to try, desperately. She's never wanted to do anything more than she wants to do this, right now.

"Sure." She tries to be nonchalant. But Audrey smiles like she knows better.

Audrey hands over the controller. When Claire touches it, energy zaps into her fingers. Her heart rate surges. She takes a deep breath, settles the controller in her lap the way Audrey did.

"I just touch it?" she asks. "Do I press in—" She lays her fingers on the controller and notes erupt into the air like a fountain, discordant and wild. She snatches her hand away. "Oh, that wasn't right."

Audrey's eyes glitter. "It's okay. You have to get the hang of it, is all. Try using one finger."

Claire taps her index finger against the top of the controller. This time there's only one note, long and drawn out. She lifts her hand. The note stops.

"Good." Audrey nods with satisfaction. "Now try moving your finger around."

Claire does. She slides her finger down in a straight line, and the notes ripple out across the beach. She traces a circle and she taps the controller at different intervals. The music is out in the wind and it's inside her head, an extension of her thoughts. She's aware of Audrey sitting there, watching her with a strange teacher-like intensity, but it doesn't bother her. The heat from the sun, the rough scatter of sand across her face—none of this bothers her either. She can see now why Audrey called this an arcade game. It's certainly as absorbing as one.

Claire goes through all the shapes she knows, listening to the music they create. She tries abstract squiggles and the dots and dashes of Morse code. Each shape creates a different melody, some beautiful and some sad and some frightening. And then, distantly, she remembers the monster in her backyard, the one who said that she and Julie created a scent. Maybe it's not like the perfume strips after all. Maybe monsters don't use the right words for things. She and Julie aren't an interesting scent, they're an interesting melody. This game has showed her a truth: All the things in the world create music, and as we move through the universe, that music runs into other music and overlaps. Everyone in the town overlaps with everyone else, and together they create the music of Indianola.

Claire spells out her name in looping swirls of cursive on the controller. The music it creates is music she has always known, and it shudders deep down inside of her like an echo.

Audrey says something, her voice far way. It sounds like *You're getting it.* Or maybe *She's getting it.*

With a burst of excitement Claire spells out Julie's name, and she pictures Julie as she does so, imagines that it's Julie sitting across from her on the blanket, her tangled black hair shining dark gold in the sunlight. And that music is unlike anything Claire has ever heard, complex and rich and haunting, minor-keyed. It chimes with the music that's inside her, *her* music, *Claire's* music, this cosmic mystery she's coming so close to understanding—

"I think that's enough for now, don't you?"

This time, Audrey's voice cuts through Claire's thoughts like a sword.

Claire snatches her hand away from the controller and the music evaporates, replaced by the rush of waves against the shore. Slowly, the world starts to come back to her, in fits and starts, spangles of sunlight and bursts of hot wind.

"I think you were enjoying yourself a *little* too much," Audrey says in a sly, knowing way.

Claire blushes. She tosses the controller at Audrey and mumbles, "It was all right. Wasn't much like a video game."

"It's a new kind." Audrey smiles and tucks the controller back into her bag. "You did a good job with it, though. Took to it like a natural."

Claire looks out at the ocean. Her head is fuzzy, like she's been sitting in front of the TV for hours, rather than playing with Audrey's game for five minutes. The waves lift up, white-crested. Gulls circle around through the pale sky, squawking at one another. The wind tosses Claire's hair to the side.

High up against the clouds, something glints.

Claire's heart skips a beat. It's just a flash of light, flickering, catching on the sun, but it's up too high to be a boat, and she doesn't hear the roar of an airplane. She stares at the light. It flashes like a camera and then disappears.

"Did you see that?" she asks Audrey.

"See what?" Audrey gazes back at her with a lucid, unwavering expression. "I didn't see anything."

⌐

Audrey pulls into Claire's driveway. The house looks faded and unfamiliar against the yellow grass. Claire shivers. She's still out of sorts from playing that game on the beach.

"We'll need to get together soon," Audrey says, fixing her hair in the rearview mirror.

"What?" Claire glances over at her. "What for?"

"The Stargazer's Masquerade, *duh.*" Audrey drops her gaze from the mirror. "Do you know what costume you're going to wear?"

"I'm not even sure I'm going." Claire's head throbs. What she really wants is to go lie down in front of the fan in her room.

"Oh, but you have to go! It's the most exciting thing that happens in Indianola all year, and you're going to be here for it!" Audrey twists around in her seat and faces her.

"I don't have a costume," Claire says.

"I'm sure we can think of something." Audrey leans back against the car door and looks at Claire appraisingly. "You have an elegant face, has anyone ever told you that?"

"No." Claire looks over at the house again. "Maybe we can talk about this later? I'm really feeling pretty—"

"Absolutely not."

Audrey's voice sounds magnified and transmitted, like it's coming in over the radio. The pounding in Claire's head swells, and she jerks her gaze back over to Audrey, who's smiling sweetly in the patch of sunlight shining through the window.

"What did you say?" Claire says.

"That you have an elegant face."

"No, you didn't, you—" The memory seeps away from Claire until there's nothing to grasp on to. "We were talking about the dance."

"Yes, exactly." Audrey gushes like a teacher praising a student. "And your costume."

Claire shakes her head. "I don't have anything to wear."

Audrey looks at her. She's smiling as if she has a secret. The pain in Claire's head jars for a moment. It feels like something's come loose.

Then Audrey reaches over and takes Claire's hand. Claire looks up at her in surprise, and then she freezes, not sure what she's seeing.

Audrey's eyes are *glowing*. They're the same color as the moon. Claire can't look away.

"A costume," Audrey says, and her voice has that crackling radio quality again. "A gray dress. Silk. You found it in Julie's attic."

"It won't fit me." The words sound far away, like someone else is speaking them.

"Oh, but it will. I've seen to that. After all, what do you think that game was doing?"

And then Audrey blinks, and Claire reels backward, the headache so bad, she sees spots of light dancing across her vision. Silver. Silver light.

"Oh, you're not looking so good," Audrey says.

Claire glances up at her, expecting something to be wrong with her eyes, but they're the way they always are, wide and bright blue.

"I told you I wanted to go lie down." Had she, though? She can't remember.

"You should do that." Audrey smiles. "I'll see you later. We can talk about your costume then."

Claire stumbles out of the car. She presses against both of her temples, hoping the pressure will relieve the pain. It doesn't. She keeps her head down because the sun is too bright, and stepping into Grammy's dark house is a relief. The TV's on, commercials blaring, but Grammy's not in her chair. The sound bores into Claire's skull. She reaches over and twists the dial until the image evaporates. Silence. Another relief.

She goes into her room, shuts the door. Turns the fan on high and sprawls out on her bed with her eyes closed. In the whine of the fan, she hears Audrey's voice: *a costume, a gray dress, silk*. Over and over, each oscillation of the fan the start of a new word.

A costume.

A gray dress.

Silk.

Claire opens her eyes. A water stain spreads across the ceiling, and in the dusty light it's the same color as the dress she found in Julie's attic.

A gray dress. Silk. A costume for the Stargazer's Masquerade.

It's the greatest idea she's ever had.

~

"Okay, this place is amazing."

Claire stands in the doorway of Alvarez Video, taking in the labyrinth of six-foot-tall shelves, all stuffed to the brim with VHS tapes. The headache that's been pulsing at her temple since hanging out with Audrey subsides at the sight of them.

"I know, right?" Julie steps up beside her and lets the door slam shut, the bell in the entryway jangling. "Not bad for a crappy town in the middle of nowhere."

"Not *bad*?" Claire swoops her gaze over the shelves. They're marked with hand-lettered signs indicating the genre: *Horror* here, *Westerns* there. She thinks about the Blockbuster in the strip mall by her house in Houston, how *empty* it feels in comparison. "I've never seen so many movies in one place!"

"Told you, Frank's the best." Julie pushes forward and vanishes into the space between the *Foreign: Japan* shelf and the *Science Fiction* shelf. "Frank!" she bellows, her voice muffled by the video cases. "It's your favorite customer!"

Claire follows behind her, trailing her fingers along the battered VHS cases. She recognizes some of the names from the film magazines she used to flip through at the Waldenbooks in the mall: *Akira, My Neighbor Totoro, Hiruko the Goblin*. She stops on that last one, her heart rising into her throat. The title is hand-lettered in black marker, the box the plain black-and-white sort you buy at the dollar store. "Oh my God," she says. "This never got a US release!"

"It did if you know the right people." A heavyset guy with long curly hair sticks his head around the corner. "I'm guessing you're in the Japanese section, huh? Great stuff. Turn around and look at the French section, too—I just got *Last Year at Marienbad* and *All the Mornings of the World*. Everyone should see those before they die."

Claire turns and pulls out a box. There's nothing on it but a handwritten title: *The Beautiful Troublemaker*. "I think I've heard of this! *La Belle Noiseuse*!"

"Oh God, you found his pride and joy. All these copied movies." Julie materializes behind Claire and moves up close to her. "He's not even supposed to *have* these."

"Well, yeah, but foreign films don't really get released much. *Somebody* needs to make them available." Claire looks up at Frank, who's grinning at her. "Do you really rent these out?"

"Of course! But only to the right people," he says. "And if you're a friend of Julie, you're the right people."

Claire slides out *Hiruko the Goblin* and gazes up at Julie. "Do you know this one?" she asks, trying not to sound too eager. "I hear it's like *The Fly*—"

"I've *seen* it," Julie says, her eyes sparkling, and Claire feels a jolt of excitement. "It's buck wild. We can totally rent it if you want. And watch it at my place."

Claire nods. "Double feature with *Aliens*, right? I still need to see it."

Julie shakes her head and presses her hand to her heart. "An absolute travesty. We have to fix that." Then she pulls on Claire's wrist, drawing her deeper into the store. "Come on, let me show you what else he's got."

They weave through the shelves, the air dim and cool and filled with dust. Frank is settled back behind the checkout counter, flipping through an issue of *Fangoria*. "You let your friend pick!" he calls out as they glide past him. "She's obviously got better taste!"

"Shut up!" Julie yells back, dodging a cardboard standee of Bill and Ted.

They wind up in a narrow back room. *Classic*, says the hand-lettered sign, and there's a small shelf that just says *Hitchcock!* in big block letters.

"Oh, man!" Claire cries out.

"I remember you liked my *Vertigo* shirt," Julie says, looking sideways at Claire. "Frank's got everything, even the hard-to-find ones."

Clare kneels down in front of the shelf, sweeping her gaze over the titles. Julie's right: There are movies here that would never in a million years show up on the shelves of Blockbuster. *Under Capricorn, Jamaica Inn,* even *The Ring*—some of these look like bootlegs too, but Claire's pretty sure Hitchcock's entire oeuvre is represented.

"Pretty righteous, huh?" Julie leans against the shelf. Claire looks up at her, grinning.

"I can't believe all these movies are here," she says. "In Indianola! Of all places."

"I know!"

Claire stands up. She's never met anyone who knows as much about movies—not even Josh, although he pretends to.

Julie pushes a hand through her messy hair, her hip jutted out at an angle. Her black nail polish is already flaking off her nails. And she's grinning at Claire like they're best friends.

She really is the coolest person Claire has ever met.

CHAPTER

Eight

JULIE

At the end of her shift on Friday, Julie calls up Mr. Vickery, the man in charge of the committee that deals with the monsters and the treaties. She put her report in about what had happened at Claire's house a few days ago and never heard anything back. She knows they can be slow, but someone's life could be in danger here. Claire's life, in particular. They've been talking pretty much every day since they hung out watching movies at Julie's place, and Julie has dreams of playing the hero, sweeping Claire off her feet like in those romance novels Julie's mom is always reading. Not that a phone call is nearly so exciting.

The line rings a couple of times and then Mr. Vickery himself picks up—Julie stole his direct number out of her dad's address book.

"Mr. Vickery?" she says, hoping she sounds like an adult.

"Yes? Who is this?"

"My name is Julie Alvarez. I'm Victor Alvarez's daughter."

"Ahhh." His voice softens. "Yes, little Julie."

Julie scowls at that.

"How's your mother?"

"She's fine. I was calling about the report—"

"Yes, I received it. Troublesome stuff." He doesn't sound troubled. "Have there been any other issues? Any—" Papers shuffle on the other side of the line. "Have there been any deaths or injuries since you filed it?"

"No." Julie twines the phone cord around her finger, irritated and impatient. "I just wanted to see what you were going to *do* about it. Before someone gets hurt."

More shuffling. It sounds like static.

"Well, Julie, the committee's looking into it. These things take time."

"Take time! The monsters are violating the treaties and coming into town."

"I realize that. But unless there's proof of a serious, immediate threat to a human, we prefer to keep our distance. I'm sure you're aware of the delicacy of our situation here in Indianola. There aren't really any precedents for things like this, you know. And we've found that keeping *us* separate from *them* is the wisest course of action."

Julie glowers. She's heard this tone of voice before—from her father. It's his politician's voice, the one he uses when he's trying to let her down gently. So she knows what Mr. Vickery is saying. They aren't going to do a damn thing.

She thanks him and hangs up the phone. The clock on the wall clicks over to six o'clock. Quitting time. Julie sighs. Claire can't hang out today and she doesn't feel like going home, doesn't feel like sitting up in the attic staring at a TV screen and marinating in her own thoughts. Maybe Lawrence is home. He doesn't usually work in the evenings, and she's been meaning to talk to him anyway. She wants to know what the hell's going on with Audrey.

Julie leaps out of her chair, not bothering to tidy the scatter of papers strewn across the desk. She goes across the hall to the break room and clocks out. Out front Forrest is leaning over Brittany's desk, trying to flirt. Julie ignores both of them and steps out into the hot, steamy evening.

She picks up a hamburger for herself and a blended Coke float for Lawrence—it's his favorite and a tried-and-true bribery item—at the K&L Root Beer Drive-in. Then she speeds through town so her food doesn't get cold.

Since Lawrence still lives with his mom, his house doesn't look like he belongs there, with its pale blue siding and the rosemary and jasmine growing along the porch. But Julie knows that Lawrence sticks around because Aunt Rosa has a lot of health problems, and he doesn't want her to be alone. His dad fled the picture years ago, and when his mom reverted to her maiden name, Reyes, Lawrence changed his last name to match.

Julie rings the doorbell. The porch looks the same as it has since she was a little girl and used to come over here on Sunday afternoons. She hopes Lawrence is actually home, and not out on some creepy date.

Footsteps shuffle around inside the house, and then the door opens. Lawrence peers out through the screen.

"What are you doing here?" he asks in a whisper.

Julie holds up the blended float. "Wanna hang out?"

"Is that from K&L?"

"Sure is."

Lawrence slides the screen door open. "Mom's sleeping," he says. "So you need to be quiet."

"I'm always quiet," Julie whispers. "Besides, I don't want to stay in the house. I thought we could go shoot targets out back, like we did when we were kids." She pauses, grinning. "Unless you had other *plans*."

Lawrence rubs at his forehead. He seems a lot older than nineteen. "Why would I have other plans?" He's trying to play it cool and failing.

Julie just shrugs, though, and steps past him, handing him the blended float. The house is quiet and neat like always. Lawrence keeps it clean. She plops down at the kitchen table and eats her hamburger while Lawrence lurks over by the refrigerator, slurping at his float.

"Haven't seen much of you lately," he says.

"Haven't seen much of *you* lately."

Lawrence doesn't meet her eye. "I've been working."

"That what the kids call it these days?"

"You'd know. You're the kid."

Julie shoots him an irritated look, then takes a bite out of her hamburger. "Fine. I'll go first. I've been hanging out with Mrs. Sudek's granddaughter. Claire."

"Mmm." He pauses. "Be careful."

"Be careful with what? We're just friends." She doesn't look at him, though. "You're the one that needs to be careful, if you're seeing Audrey."

"I just don't want you to get all heartbroken again."

Julie takes another bite of her hamburger. He certainly knows how to weasel out of a conversation. She knows he's thinking about what happened with Kimberly Diaz last year. To be fair, it was an emotional disaster of epic proportions. But Julie's managed to get over it, mostly, and besides, Claire is different. She's from the big city.

"It's your turn," Julie says. "What's been keeping you busy?"

Lawrence shrugs "Pretty sure you know."

"Oh come on! Since when do we keep secrets from each other?" Julie tosses a wayward tomato onto the burger wrapping. "Audrey Duchesne? Really?"

Lawrence scowls. "Yes, really. Why's it so surprising?"

"Because you're a nerd and she's a cheerleader."

Lawrence rolls his eyes.

"Seriously, what's going on? Did you ask her out?"

Lawrence hesitates. Takes a drink from his float. Then he sighs and sits down at the table with her. "She asked me out, actually. The day after we saw her at the arcade. Just—called me up, out of the blue."

A chill crawls down Julie's spine. "How'd she get your number?"

"Same way anyone else would. It's listed." He leans back in his chair. "Are you jealous or something?"

Julie makes a gagging noise. "Of you? Hell no. Audrey is—she creeps me out, is all."

"The grunge girl hates the cheerleader. You're such a cliché."

"Don't call me a cliché. And I didn't say I hate her. I said she creeps me out."

"And why exactly does she creep you out?"

Julie falls silent. She chews her hamburger. Lawrence stares at her from across the table. It's true, she can't say why; only that something seems, well, *wrong* with her.

"I think she's just trying to play you," Julie finally says. "So you won't bust her drinking at the Stargazer's Masquerade this year."

Lawrence laughs and shakes his head. "I can take care of myself, Julie." He swirls his float with his straw. "So how's work?"

There he goes, changing the subject. She lets him, though. She doesn't want to talk about Audrey anymore.

"Another monster came by Claire's house." She pauses to grab a couple of fries. "I really think something's going on. The committee's not doing anything about it, though. *Typical.*"

"The monsters don't hurt people unprovoked," Lawrence says. "There's no reason they'd start now."

Julie finishes up her hamburger and wipes the grease from her fingers. "Yeah, yeah, I know." She looks up at Lawrence. "So, target practice? I bet you need it, for cop school."

Lawrence keeps sitting there, looking annoyed.

"It'll be fun," Julie says. She doesn't add that she thinks the concentration will help distract her from thinking about Audrey, or about the monsters, or about Claire and the idea that their scents intertwine in a cosmically interesting way. What the hell does that even mean?

"I don't want to wake Mom up."

"What? Because of the gunshots? You know it's like a ten-minute hike down to the target spot."

"Fine." Lawrence gives a sigh of defeat. Just like an old man. Yeah, Audrey's definitely using him for boozing purposes.

Julie grins. "Excellent! Go get the guns. I'll meet you round back." She balls up the wrapping from her hamburger and tosses it in the garbage. Lawrence disappears into the mysterious fathoms of the house and Julie goes out onto the back porch. Even though it's late in the day, the sun hasn't set, which means the air is still hot. At least the target spot is shady.

She plops down on the wooden swing that Aunt Rosa keeps out on the porch as she waits for Lawrence. Another relic from her childhood. She used to try to flip over the top when she was a little girl, but Lawrence always hated that swing. His father made it for his mom during one of his sober periods, and Julie understands now that Lawrence dismisses it as a bribe. Which it probably was.

The back door opens. Lawrence steps out with a rifle and a box of bullets and two pairs of safety goggles. His cop gun is tucked into the holster he wears with his uniform. Dork.

"Can I shoot your pistol?" Julie asks immediately.

"Absolutely not." Lawrence hands her the rifle. "You're familiar with this one. I don't want any accidents."

Julie pretends to be annoyed, making a big show of hemming and hawing. But really, it's part of the tradition of target practice. Lawrence always has to stick to the rules. It's comforting that even if he's dating Audrey, that much hasn't changed.

They step off the porch and head to the back of Lawrence's property. This house has been in his family for ages, on his father's side, and so even though Aunt Rosa raised Lawrence here more or less by herself, really the house and land and everything belong to Lawrence. Which is kind of weird, because even though he gave up the deed, Lawrence's dad is still alive. Uncle Randy. Julie doesn't know him, just has a vague memory of a tall, rangy white guy smoking cigarettes on the back porch, the silver glint of a beer can always within arm's reach.

She's pretty sure Lawrence's obsession with rules is part of his quest to become an inverted image of his father: His father's the negative, he's the photograph.

A breeze picks up and rustles around the trees. The path leading down to the target is really just a strip of worn-away grass, nothing official. Julie's been coming down here as long as she can remember. It's her one concession to growing up in a redneck town like Indianola. She might refuse to do stock shows or wear cowboy boots, but she'll shoot a gun at an empty Coke can.

"Do you really think the committee's not going to do anything about that monster coming into town?"

Julie glances over at Lawrence in surprise. "You're the one who says not to worry."

Lawrence shrugs. "I don't think the monsters are going to hurt anyone. But I don't like the committee just sitting on their hands either. We can't just let a treaty violation slide."

It's nice to know that Lawrence agrees with her on something for once, even if it probably *is* just because he loves rules.

They keep walking until the trees clear out and reveal the big dirt backstop Lawrence installed during one of his fits of safety obsession. Julie remembers him backing his truck up to the tree line and piling dirt into a wheelbarrow to cart it over. It seemed like a lot of work, but she knew he did it so stray bullets wouldn't vanish into the woods.

The big metal box of targets sits in its usual place in front of the backstop. It's been there long enough that grass has grown around it so that it look like an extension of the woods. Bits of broken glass sparkle in the sunlight. They've never kept real targets out here, just old glass bottles and aluminum cans that Lawrence rinses out and stores in plastic bags in his garage.

"I'll set them up." Julie leans her rifle up against a tree and bounds over to the box. The latch is nearly rusted away. She flips it open, pulls out five Coke bottles, closes the box, and lines them up in a row. When she turns around, Lawrence is loading his gun, the muzzle pointed toward the trees. She goes over beside him.

"I haven't been out here in a long time," Lawrence says. "They have an actual shooting range down at the station."

"Oh yeah? Has your aim gotten any better?"

Lawrence gives her an annoyed look. "Actually, yes, it has."

Julie grins. "You go first, then. Let's see what you got."

"Put on your eye protection."

Julie makes a face at him, but she does as he asks, and when he hands her a pair of earplugs, she puts those in too. She knows from experience it's not worth arguing with him about it.

Lawrence lines up his gun and fires off five shots, one after another. Three of the bottles explode, shimmering in the sunlight.

"Damn," Lawrence says.

"Ha! Brutal. I bet I can get them." Julie grabs the rifle and loads it and lines up her shot. It's been forever since she'd last come out here, but the motions come to her like a sense memory. She pulls back the bolt and squeezes the trigger. The rifle's explosion sets her ears to ringing, but at least the bottle's nothing but bits of fragmented sunlight in the grass.

"Got it!" she shouts.

"Yeah, I can see that." Lawrence doesn't sound too impressed.

Julie lines up and takes her next shot. The last bottle tips off the chest and rolls a few feet before stopping, unharmed.

"That counts." Julie straightens up.

"Hardly. Set your gun down."

Julie smirks at him but does as he says. Lawrence walks up to the box and picks up the bottle Julie missed as well as an assortment of Coke cans and lines them all up. Over the muffle of her earplugs Julie can make out the chattering whine of cicadas up in the trees and the distant buzzing of grasshoppers. The sounds of heat, the sounds she's always associated with this place.

"So tell me more about this thing with Claire."

Julie goes still. "There's no thing," she says. "We're friends."

Lawrence pulls his gun out of its holster and looks over at her. "You said that. I was asking about the thing with the monsters."

He fires off three shots and three Coke cans go flying off into the dirt.

"Aren't you going to shoot at the rest of those?"

"Figured I'd leave them for you."

Julie picks up her rifle and peers through the scope. "They keep showing up at her house. Twice now, like I said." *Bang*. She misses completely. "The last one, it was saying something about astronauts."

"Astronauts?"

Julie looks through the scope again. The Coke cans loom distorted and huge in front of her, glittering in the sunlight. Everything feels distorted lately. "And it said me and Claire are cosmically interesting."

Bang. She fires before she's ready, so she has a few deafening seconds to prepare for Lawrence's reaction to that statement. Figures that she actually gets that last bottle. Glass sparkles everywhere. She puts her rifle down, staring straight ahead.

"Cosmically interesting," Lawrence says.

"Yeah." She keeps squinting out at the dappled sunlight. It's peaceful out here, quiet when the guns aren't going off, and Julie remembers how Lawrence called it a sanctuary once, a place where he could escape his father. Maybe that's why she works up the nerve to tell him the whole story. "We also found a dress that probably belonged to one of her relatives in the attic."

"How could you possibly know that?" Lawrence asks.

Julie looks over at him. "There was a name on the box," she says. "Abigail Sudek."

He stares at her with his annoying cop's intensity and she looks away, her cheeks burning.

"Sounds like a mystery," he says at last.

"Yeah, you'd like that, wouldn't you?" She glances over at him again. "What with wanting to be a detective and all?"

Lawrence doesn't say anything, just hoists his gun and fires off a couple of shots. Both of the remaining Coke cans fly up into the air. One of them disappears into the trees.

"Nice," Julie says. She slips on her rifle's safety and leans it up against a nearby tree. The cicadas whine louder, their chattering song rising and falling. "It's just weird," she says, "that we seem to have this connection."

"You think it's some kind of sign of true love?" Lawrence pretends to inspect his gun.

"Don't make fun of me. Not when you're taking freaking Audrey Duchesne out for pizza." Julie sighs. "Apparently Mrs. Sudek claims the Sudeks used to own my house. Like a hundred years ago or something. Which is weird. I thought our family built it."

Lawrence looks up at her, his brow creased. "Yeah, okay, that is a little weird. But you know you can probably research this, if the family names go back this far."

"What are you talking about?"

Lawrence shakes his head. "Surprise. I say the word *research* and you completely shut down."

"Shut up."

"I *mean* that your parents have enough crap shoved in the attic, there are probably some old deeds up there. If the Sudeks really did own the house back in the day, that would prove it." He shrugs. "Dunno why your parents would lie about it, though."

"Maybe they had a feud." Julie grins. "You know, Lawrence, sometimes you don't have terrible ideas."

"If you want to dig around in old boxes, have fun."

Julie hardly hears him, though. A feud would make sense. Maybe that's why she and Claire are cosmically interesting.

She can't wait to call Claire with her latest hypothesis.

Julie calls Claire as soon as she gets back home, her heart thrumming. But when the phone clicks on, it's Mrs. Sudek's voice on the other end.

"Oh," Julie says. "Hello. I'm calling for Claire."

The line goes quiet save for the weird crackle that you hear on all Indianola phones.

"Who is this?" Mrs. Sudek snaps. "Audrey, that's not you, is it?"

Audrey? "Um, no, it's Julie, from the—"

"Claire can't go out," Mrs. Sudek says. "She's doing chores."

And then the line goes dead. Julie groans and tosses the phone on her bed. She was so excited to have another reason to see Claire—and one that had nothing to do with monsters. Now she doesn't know what to do with herself.

She flings herself back on her bed, beside her phone. She hates her bedroom, with all its pretentious Victorian furniture, all picked out by her mom's decorator. The only place she was allowed to *add her own touch*, as the decorator put it, was inside the closet, and Julie lined the walls with posters from her favorite bands, X and Bikini Kill and Heavens to Betsy. A little bit of the twentieth century hidden away behind closed doors.

She suspects the decoration issue was part of the reason her parents gave her free run of the attic, even if they said it was because they didn't want her hogging the TV. She'll give them credit for that much.

The attic is Julie's space through and through, and that's why she goes up there now even though she's not in the mood to play SNES or watch movies. She can't think in her bedroom. In the attic, she can. It's like being inside her own head, instead of her mother's.

She switches on the light, grabs a Coke out of the mini-fridge tucked in the corner, and sprawls across her couch. A distorted version of her reflection appears in the blank TV, her chin swelling out to hideous proportions. No wonder Claire doesn't like her except as a friend.

Julie sighs and settles down into the couch's worn cushions. She drops her head over the armrest so she can look at the attic upside down, something she used to do as a kid. From here she's got a perfect view of the mirror, the gray dress still obscuring the reflection.

So Mrs. Sudek is being a jerk. That doesn't mean Claire doesn't want to see Julie. Still, doubt worms its way into Julie's thoughts. Why did Mrs. Sudek think she was Audrey? Claire doesn't even seem to like Audrey that much—

Enough. Julie knows she needs to distract herself. She can find the deeds herself, see if there's anything to Mrs. Sudek's claims.

She swings down from the couch and goes over to the old dollhouse, still hanging open from when they found the box with the dress. She stands with her weight on one foot, drinking her Coke, appraising the stacks of old junk. Even though Julie claimed the attic as her own, she never really went through any of the stuff that gathers dust up here. She just shoved it out of the way so she could set up her TV. All she knows is that this is stuff that's been here since forever—most of her family's Christmas decorations and other seasonal things are stored out in the shed.

She has no idea where to start.

Finally, Julie closes her eyes, spins around twice, and jabs her finger out at the stacks. When she opens her eyes, she decides she's pointing at the third box in a stack half-hidden behind an old wooden chest.

It takes her a few minutes to drag the box out of the mess, and by the time she's through, she's coughing and hacking in the clouds of dust. She drops the box on the floor and something clanks inside it. Julie cringes and hopes she didn't break anything.

She kneels down and slides the lid away, half holding her breath— but inside there's only a tangle of candlesticks and silverware, all black with tarnish. Julie extracts a fork and rubs it against her shirt. She manages to clear a bit of the tarnish away, enough to see the silver underneath. Real silver, she supposes, since it tarnished.

She slides the box aside and selects another. This one is full of old clothes, dresses and blouses and things from the thirties. The next box is so heavy that Julie almost collapses under its weight; she lets it drop and then pushes it over to the investigation spot. Inside, she finds several thick leather-bound books. They look old. A hundred years old, even.

Her heart skips a beat.

She pulls one out and opens it. The page is filled with rows of writing, all in the same spidery, old-fashioned script. Across the top someone has written *Register of Mr. Javier Alvarez, the Alvarez Motel.*

The Alvarez Motel. The first stake in the Alvarez empire. She's heard this story before, about how her great-great-grandfather bought the Alvarez Motel with his last fifty dollars. Her father told her when she was a little girl, trying to get her interested in the family business.

She runs her finger down the columns of text. Dates, numbers, names, amounts. Financial records. These are financial records of the Alvarez Hotel, all dated back to June 1901.

"Getting closer," she murmurs.

Julie quickly flips through the four remaining ledgers, checking first the dates, then the names, to see if she can find any clues. All the dates are for the first few years of the twentieth century, and there's no mention of the Sudeks.

Then, in the last ledger, as she's flipping through the pages, a photograph falls out.

Julie stops for a moment, still clutching the book. The photograph fell facedown, and there's something written across the back, in the same spidery handwriting as the ledger.

Abigail, 1892.

Julie glances over at the dress. The same Abigail?

Slowly, she turns the photograph over. It shows a young woman with fair hair and large dark eyes, a corseted waist, and a high-necked dress. She's standing outside, beneath a palm tree, a house filling up the background.

Julie's house.

Julie flips the photo back over. It still reads *Abigail, 1892.*

Hardly proof that the Sudeks used to own the house, though.

She looks at the woman again, studying her features closely, trying to find some hint of Claire in them. There is something about the shape of the woman's mouth, the upward slope of her eyes, that suggests Claire, suggests that the two could be related.

Julie sets the photograph aside and riffles through the ledgers, trying to find something she missed. There's nothing. She stacks them back in their box and goes over to where she found them originally, and picks up the two closest boxes. One contains some broken china and a crumple of silk handkerchiefs. The other contains little decoupage boxes, a jar of perfume, and knickknacks wrapped up in strips of muslin. Julie lifts each item out and lines them up on the floor.

At the very bottom of the box, tucked underneath a larger piece of that patterned muslin, is a bundle of letters.

Julie picks it up at the edges. The paper is old and thin and yellowed, and the writing on the front is faded, although not so much that Julie can't read it.

The top letter is addressed to Javier Alvarez.

She flips through the stack. All of the letters are addressed to Javier, and all in the same slanted, neat handwriting, although none of them list an address or include a stamp. Julie pulls one of the letters out of its envelope. It's addressed formally, *Dear Mr. Alvarez*. Julie skips to the name at the bottom.

Abigail Sudek.

⌒

Julie parks her car two houses down from Mrs. Sudek's. It's almost midnight, and she doesn't want to take any unnecessary risks.

She drags out her backpack, stuffed with the letters, the photograph, and a flashlight, and slings it across one shoulder. Claire's street is quiet and empty, the sea wind whistling forlornly through the trees.

It's late enough that the day's heat has evaporated a little, and it's almost pleasant out here in the silvery starlight.

She walks over to Claire's house. All the lights are off, and the house looks like it's been abandoned to the shadows. This is going to be the hard part. Julie's not entirely sure which window is Claire's. Fortunately, she's been in houses in this neighborhood that have the same layout, and she's pretty sure the master bedroom—Mrs. Sudek's—is in the back.

Pretty sure.

Julie goes up to the first window and taps lightly on the screen, then jumps out of the way, pressing herself against the wall and peering over to the side to get a glimpse of whoever looks out. No one does. She knocks on the screen again. Same thing.

She takes a deep breath and goes over to the next window and tries the same thing, although she knocks a little harder, enough that the screen rattles in the frame. This time, a light switches on, and Julie's heart starts thumping against her chest. She presses against the brick and waits.

Nothing happens. The light's still on, a little bright spot behind the blinds.

Julie knocks again.

A second passes. The blinds split open. Julie sees a flash of Claire's eye.

She leaps in front of the window and waves.

Claire blinks, then pulls up the blinds. Julie waves again, her breath in her throat.

Claire smiles and waves back. Her hair is mussed from sleep and she has on an old tank top with her pajama bottoms. She looks completely adorable. Julie's heart sighs.

Claire pulls up the window a couple of inches and bends down to speak through the crack. "What are you doing here?" she whispers.

"I tried to call," Julie whispers back. "But your grandmother said you were busy. I figured—"

"She was lying?" Claire smiles. "She totally was, I've been bored all day." Then she glances over her shoulder. "I'm not sure it's the best idea—"

"I found something." Julie holds up her backpack. She doesn't want to say goodbye to Claire, not right now. "Letters from Abigail Sudek."

Claire's eyes go wide. "The same name as the dress!" she whispers.

"Yep. She wrote them to someone named"—Julie pauses dramatically—"Javier Alvarez. Who I know for a fact is my great-great-grandfather."

"Oh, wow, really?" She glances around her room, then back at Julie. "Wait there. I'll be out in a minute."

Julie nods. Claire closes the window and the blinds and Julie sits down in the grass beside the house, the backpack resting on top of her knees. The night sings around her. It's all very romantic.

She knows she shouldn't think that way.

A few minutes later, Claire skitters around the side of the house. She's changed out of her pajamas and into a fluorescent pink tank top and a pair of shorts, although she's barefoot.

"Where's your car?" she asks, still whispering.

"Down the street. I didn't want her to hear me in the driveway. Where's a good place to talk?"

"That side of the house. It's the complete opposite end from where her bedroom is." Claire points in the direction she appeared. "And no one can see us from the street."

Julie's not particularly worried about random passersby spotting them outside, but she figures it's better to be safe than sorry. She stands up and follows Claire over to the side of the house. Claire keeps glancing back over her shoulder, and smiling, and looking like she's having the greatest time.

A warmth spreads through Julie's stomach, up into her chest.

The side of the house is lined with big oleander bushes, but they find a clean spot of grass where Julie can lay out all her discoveries. She pulls everything out and lines it up on the backpack, then switches on the flashlight and holds it on her shoulder.

"So what'd you find?" Claire asks. She picks up the photograph. "Oh my God, is this her?"

"That's what it says on the back. I mean, I'm assuming it's the same Abigail."

Claire nods, transfixed.

"But the really cool thing is the letters," Julie says, spreading them out on the grass. "So these are definitely from Abigail Sudek, you can see on the envelopes. But some of them say Abigail *Garner* on the return address, which is"—she shuffles through the letters until she finds one—"the same address as my house. Look!"

Claire picks up the envelope and squints down at it.

"The only thing I can't figure out is why your family name has been Sudek instead of Garner, if this really is your relative."

"Oh, I think I know the answer to that," Claire says. "My mom, when she took my dad's last name, caused this big scandal in my family. Supposedly the women in my family never took their husband's name."

"That's kind of badass, actually."

"I guess. But it looks like it didn't start with Abigail." She pauses for a moment. "So Abigail must have gotten married and moved into your old house. But she didn't marry Javier. I thought the house was always in your family?"

"That's what my parents said, but this was all happening a hundred years ago," Julie says. "Check out the dates."

"Eighteen ninety-three," Claire reads.

"Right. So the house was definitely in my family by the twenties, because that's when my grandmother was born, and she grew up there. But before?" Julie shrugs. "Anyway, none of this is even the interesting part."

"What do you mean?" Claire leans in close to Julie, her features elongated in the glow of the flashlight.

"So I didn't get to read through all of the letters," Julie says. "I thought we could do that now. But I think Abigail and Javier were having an affair."

Claire's eyes widen. "Are you serious?"

Julie nods, grinning a little.

"What did they say? Like, was it a torrid affair—"

The excitement in Claire's voice sends a thrill racing up Julie's spine. "I didn't get super far. You want to help me read?"

"Absolutely!"

"Okay, awesome." Julie sets down the flashlight and divides the letters into two stacks. "Let's divide and conquer."

Claire grins. Then she scoots over beside Julie, so close their knees touch. Julie goes rigid all the way through, but Claire just opens up her first letter. "So we can share the light," she says.

"Oh yeah. Of course." Julie smiles, tries to act nonchalant. She holds the flashlight beam between them and Claire leans in close with her eyes on the letter, the light spangling in her eyes.

They read.

It's peaceful, being out here in the balmy night, the only sounds the distant chirping of insects in the trees, and the rustle of century-old paper, and the quiet exhalation of Claire's breath. Whenever they finish a letter, they set it in a neat stack on top of Julie's backpack.

In the letters that Julie reads, it becomes clear that Abigail and Javier knew each other well. Somehow, they met. On the beach, at the grocer's in town: It's not clear from the letters. But one did woo the other, and Abigail began to write to Javier. The third letter explains that much. *I told you I would write, and write I shall.*

What Julie is able to glean from her reading is this: They were both living in Indianola at the time, Abigail in Julie's house, Javier in the old row houses that used to be where the fish supply shop is now. In her letters, she tells him of her daily activities, how she lunched with Rose on Wednesday and saw Marjory's new baby at Mass. At the end of every letter she answers questions he posed to her, and so Julie is left only with answers, flowery and obscure.

"You have to look at this," Claire says, breaking the silence. "I think you're totally right about the two of them having an affair."

"Really?" Julie takes the letter from Claire.

"It's at the bottom," Claire says, "The second-to-last paragraph."

Julie skims down, and then begins to read.

Marriage is an act of aggression. It's war for a more civilized time. I don't wish you to make the mistake of thinking I have any say in the matter of my impending marriage to Gregory Garner. It was a decision made by my parents, a stratagem to save the Sudek family that has nothing to do with love. I've come to understand love—that sort of love, the love between a man and a woman—only recently. As you know.

"You see?" Claire says. "The Sudek family? You're totally right, the dress must have been hers before she married. And then this: Only come to understand love recently? *As you know.* She's totally talking about Javier!"

"Yeah." Julie stares down at the words. She can't believe that her pet theory, born out of her own desire to be with a member of the Sudek family, actually has some weight.

"I'm going to set that one aside," Claire says.

They go back to reading. The silence settles around them again, soft and romantic.

And then Julie reads the first letter with a return address from Abigail Garner, not Sudek.

I simply can't not write to you, I'm afraid. I understand if you choose not to respond, but I assure you that Gregory will not be reading your missives. He's simply too busy in the oilfields—why, he's barely here most days! If I could have a letter from you, it would fill my hours with the warm memories of our time together.

It's a risk that pays off—Javier clearly keeps writing to her. They don't exchange declarations of love, but she does continue to tell him of her day-to-day life. Eventually, Julie notices a recurring name: Emmert.

I'm afraid Gregory has hired Mr. Emmert against my protestations. Yesterday he began work in our gardens, and I went out to ask him about the bougainvillea and the hibiscus, as a sort of test; don't worry, I remembered your warning! He was quite knowledgeable, but I must say, I don't care for him. He's rather vulgar in dress and mannerisms and I find him untrustworthy—unsettling, really. I told Mr. Hemshaw to keep close watch on the silver whenever he was working. Only said it was a bit of women's intuition, at which point Mr. Hemshaw nodded gravely and admitted he would never ignore such a thing. Amusing!

From what Julie can infer, Emmert was some sort of hired hand whom Javier knew and didn't trust, although Abigail never says explicitly why that might be. She mentions him in passing, usually as a complaint—that he makes her uncomfortable, that she wishes Gregory would get rid of him, but that he hasn't done anything yet that would justify having him dismissed.

Suddenly, Claire lets out a shout of delight, then immediately slaps her hand over her mouth.

"What is it?" Julie looks up at her, surprised.

"Oh my God," Claire says. "Oh my God, *listen* to this." She starts to read: "*Whenever I hold Charlotte in my arms, I feel a deep, pervasive sadness. I love my daughter dearly, with all my heart, and yet I cannot bring myself to love Gregory as I should. My heart belongs to her, of course, but I must confess it also belongs to you, my dear Javier.*"

"Are you kidding me?" Julie snatches the letter from Claire, scans over it wildly. "Dude!" she says. "This is like a soap opera."

"I know! And check this out. It's another letter, from about a month later." Claire clears her throat. *"My darling, your last missive brought me such joy. I could never abandon my daughter."* Julie watches Claire reading; her eyes are bright and glossy in the flashlight. *"To know you would never ask that of me—my heart is overflowing with love for you."* She stops and sighs dreamily, pressing the letter to her chest. "So romantic."

Julie smiles at her, tries not to think about her own forbidden feelings. "I can't disagree," she says, her heart tight.

They keep reading, the night silken around them. Julie keeps glancing up at Claire, thinking about her great-great-grandfather Javier, and what he did for Claire's great-great-grandmother Abigail, and what it could say about the two of them, sitting here in the damp grass, a hundred years later.

Then Julie finds an entire letter about Emmert.

The most dreadful thing just happened, Abigail wrote.

Oh, I wish Gregory could see Emmert for what he is! I have asked the morning girl to keep the windows open, as the heat has been unbearable these last few weeks. The wind from the ocean is quite blustery and always stirs up the curtains. I've never thought much of it, as my bedroom faces away from the garden, securing my privacy. But this morning, as I was dressing, I was horrified to find a narrow, leering face watching me: It was Mr. Emmert! I let out a horrified shriek and he scurried away, but when I took my concerns to Gregory, he once again utterly dismissed my complaints!

I do not understand why he consistently refuses to see Mr. Emmert for the scoundrel he is. His presence has always discomfited me—I've told you about his persistent stares anytime I take Charlotte into the garden. But for him to peer through my window, so brazenly—it's beyond comprehension! And Gregory simply will not listen to me!

"Are you seeing the name Emmert?" Julie asks Claire. "He's like a handyman or something for Abigail after she marries Gregory. She keeps talking about him. He sounds like a total creep."

Claire looks up from her letter. "Yeah, I've seen a few mentions. He sounds scary."

And then Julie comes to the final letter in her stack. It's very short, and written in a scrawled, frantic hand:

My darling, the final preparations are ready. I know we shouldn't trust him; I know he's an absolute cretin. But he's the only one who can make the arrangements, especially with Charlotte so young. Soon, we'll all be together. Soon, our lives will begin.

"Claire." Julie's heart thumps. "I found something."

"What is it?" Claire leans over Julie's shoulder, her breath a spot of warmth on Julie's skin. "Does it talk more about their affair?"

Julie only points to the letter. She rereads the lines along with Claire, her heart hammering the whole time, not only because of the discovery but because of Claire's closeness.

"She was going to meet Javier," Claire says, pulling away a little. "They were going to run off together, with Charlotte!"

"Damn," Julie says. "And in the 1890s? I mean, *damn*." She shakes her head. "But they didn't. I mean, obviously."

She glances at Claire out of the corner of her eye. Still two separate families.

"Maybe her husband found out," Claire says. "Or—it looks like there was someone else involved, someone who was making the arrangements—" She taps the letter.

"I think that's Mr. Emmert," Julie says. "Maybe? It's someone she doesn't trust but someone she and Javier both know. And he definitely sounds like he was a cretin. I wish there was more about him in the letters."

"You said you know for sure Javier's your great-great-grandfather," Claire says. "Are you sure Abigail's not your great-great-grandmother?"

"Totally sure. Her name was Constancia. There's a picture of her in the motel." She slumps back. "See, the story as I've always heard it is that my great-great-grandfather saved up his money to buy the Indianola Motel. He changed the name to the Alvarez Motel around the turn of the century, and then he married my great-great-grandmother. There's a picture of both of them hanging in the lobby."

"So he definitely didn't run off with Abigail and Charlotte," Claire says. "What happened, do you think?"

Julie shakes her head. She feels flushed, wild with the possibility that at one point in history Claire's ancestor and Julie's ancestor were in love with each other. She wonders idly if she and Claire could have the happy ending that Javier and Abigail didn't get.

No. Don't think like that.

Claire looks down at the letter in her lap, and her hair falls into her face. It shines in the moonlight like gold.

"It's dated," she says. "The letter. See? July 18, 1893."

"Okay," Julie says.

Claire smiles. "There's a library here, right? They've probably got old newspapers or something. We can look the date up, see if anything crazy happened around then. Maybe they just got caught. Or maybe something happened to stop them. It's worth checking out, don't you think?"

"They keep old newspapers at the library?"

"Yeah," Claire says, laughing a little. "I know, I'm a nerd."

"I don't think you're a nerd," Julie says softly.

Clare ducks her head, smiling a little. Then she reaches over and plucks up the photograph of Abigail Garner. She holds it under the pool of light.

"I want to know what happened," Claire says. "She's so pretty."

Silence. The night feels like it's breathing.

"You look like her," Julie says, and then her throat dries out.

Claire laughs. "You think I'm pretty?" She sounds pleased, maybe a little breathless.

"Sure," Julie says, and tells herself that straight girls do this all the time, they always compliment each other this way. It's *normal*.

"I find it hard to believe, is all." Claire sets the picture down with the two set-aside letters. "Boys never like me."

And there it is, that fatal stab. *Boys.*

But when Julie looks up at Claire, Claire is watching her with an unreadable expression. She doesn't seem disgusted or put off. More—hopeful.

"Boys are idiots," Julie says. "You're pretty."

Claire smiles. In that moment, in the honeyed nighttime, everything is all right.

CLAIRE

It's nearly four in the morning—Claire and Julie spent hours reading through the letters and working up their theory. Claire stretches out on her bed, on top of her blankets, and stares up at the ceiling, working backward through the night's events.

The most exciting moment had been when Julie knocked on her window. Claire thought she'd dreamed the noise at first, but she kept hearing that scratching along the screen. When she pulled apart the blinds she was afraid she would see a monster. Instead she'd seen Julie, and her fear had fizzled and transformed into delight.

But Julie's gone now, and Claire rolls over to her side, closes her eyes, wonders what her dreams will be like.

Banging shatters through her thoughts.

"Claire! Get up!"

She lifts her pillow just enough to see the clock on the bedside table. A quarter after eight. She must have fallen right asleep. Usually she sleeps later than that, and Grammy never complains, as long as her cereal box and bowl are set out the night before, along with her morning pills.

Claire hopes Grammy didn't catch her out last night with Julie.

"Is something wrong?" Claire sits up and rubs her eyes. Sunlight streams in through the blinds, bright and already hot. "Are you all right?"

Grammy slams open the door and comes into Claire's bedroom. She's wearing her blue housedress, her hair pinned up away from her face. She doesn't look all right, but then, she rarely does. Her skin is pale, like always, and her steps are shaky.

"You don't have plans today, do you?"

A chill ripples through Claire. She thinks about the afternoon on the beach with Audrey, that weird, haunting game. "I was thinking of calling Julie," she says carefully. Really, last night she and Julie made plans to go the library, but she doesn't want Grammy to know that.

Grammy's face darkens. "That girl is a bad influence. I told you about the drinking, didn't I?"

"And I told you, all we do is play video games and watch movies."

Grammy snorts. "Video games. That right there is bad enough. Well, you'll just have to cancel your plans. I think it's time for some spring-cleaning."

Claire resists the urge to point out that it's summer.

"I haven't had a chance to do a thorough cleaning since I got sick," Grammy says. "And I know I won't be able to manage on my own, not in my condition."

Claire sighs and slumps back against the headboard. Cleaning. It's better than being forced to spend the afternoon with Audrey.

Still, Claire has to wonder how dirty the house really is. She did clean the place when she first arrived, although that wasn't a true *deep* cleaning. She wonders if this isn't some ploy to get her away from

Julie. Or if Grammy did see her last night, and this is some sort of passive-aggressive punishment.

"I'd like it done today," Grammy says, and whisks out of the room.

Claire sighs, but she rolls out of bed, combs a few fingers through her hair, pulls on some ratty old shorts and a T-shirt. She wonders what would happen if she refused. If she snuck out her window and rode her bike down to Julie's house, to the beach, to the Pirate's Den. Anywhere but here.

She doesn't, though. Instead she goes into the bathroom and brushes her teeth. Then she grabs her Walkman and her R.E.M. tape and strides into the living room, where Grammy has already settled down for a day of rest and watching TV. Claire misses watching TV—she'd give anything to catch an episode of *Star Trek: The Next Generation* or *The Simpsons*, but Grammy never leaves her chair or her game shows.

"Where do you want me to start?" Claire asks.

Grammy glances over at her. "The bedrooms would be nice," she says. "Especially the closets. I've got so much crammed into them I forget what's there. If you could just do some sorting—we can take things down to the church charity once you're done." She turns back to her game show.

Claire sighs. She doubts those bedrooms have been properly cleaned out since the seventies. This is definitely about keeping her away from Julie. At least when she cleans the house at home, it's for her own benefit. Her mother doesn't keep up with the housework, and when Claire can't stand the sight of the kitchen counter piled high with food-covered pans, she'll scrub at them and put them away. Same thing with the bathroom. Not that her mother ever thanks her for it.

Claire loops on her earphones, starts up her music, grabs a banana out of the kitchen, and trudges to the second bedroom, the one done up in shades of yellow. She'll start there, move over to Grammy's, save her own room for last.

This is going to take forever.

The yellow bedroom is fairly empty, at least compared to her own room, with just a twin bed, a chest of drawers, and a big metal standing fan. Claire pulls open the top drawer. The sharp scent of mothballs drifts up in the air. The drawer is full of ugly sixties schoolgirl clothes. Claire lifts up the top item, a navy skirt sized for a little girl. Probably belonged to her mom or aunt at some point.

She works steadily through the morning, tossing everything she finds into categorized piles—girls' clothes, women's clothes, jewelry, holiday decorations, photo albums, weird inspirational books with pictures of tall grass and sunlight on the covers. She finishes the yellow room around the same time R.E.M. plays their last song on the tape. Claire swaps them out for Melissa Etheridge, although she's played that tape so much the songs are too gratingly familiar. She really needs some new music. Maybe she could ask Julie to make her a tape of the bands that she's always playing in her car. Claire isn't totally sure she likes that music, but it's so wild and intense that it reminds her of a thunderstorm, and she's always liked thunderstorms. The music reminds her of Julie too.

But, since Grammy has Claire cleaning out her junk rather than calling up Julie, Claire has to make do with Melissa.

Grammy's room is decorated in green, and the way the light filters through the gauzy green curtains makes Claire feel like she's underwater. There's a sickly sweet gardenia scent that isn't in the rest of the house. The music whines in her ear, and she turns it down, then shuts it off completely. The quiet hums. She loops her earphones around the back of her neck. It feels like trespassing, being in here.

"Here we go," Claire mutters. She opens up the closet.

Grammy's clothes hang in neat rows, her shoes lined up beneath them, the hat shelf above them full of boxes. Claire pulls one down. Dust explodes in a thick cloud, and Claire drops the box, coughing. The lid slides off.

Photographs.

Claire kneels and riffles through them. They're old, all people Claire has never seen before. She flips one over and it's dated 1935. She digs around a little deeper and pulls out a photograph of a woman in an elegant Victorian gown, her light hair piled up on her head in a series of impressive architectural whorls.

It's the same woman as the one in the picture Julie brought over last night.

It's Abigail.

The air suddenly seems taut. Claire flips the photograph over, but there's no writing on it, no scrawled name. She turns it over again and studies the soft lines of Abigail's face.

You look like her.

Claire flushes with a strange heat. She slips the photograph into her pocket, shoves the box back into the closet.

She goes into the narrow bathroom attached to Grammy's room. It's green too, green tile and green-and-white wallpaper, and the scent of gardenias is even stronger. Claire fills the toothbrush cup with water and takes a sip. She leans up against the wall, next to the window. Her heart is pounding and she can't say why.

Outside, the wind picks up, rattling the window's glass. Claire finishes her water and sets the cup back on the counter. She glances at herself in the mirror. The greenish light makes her look sick.

She turns toward the door, and as she does she catches sight of something in the trash can. A brilliant strip of color. She bends down and picks it up: It's a label, the sort that goes on an aspirin bottle. Weird. Who would pull the label off an aspirin bottle?

Grammy, apparently.

Claire tosses the label back into the trash and pulls open the medicine cabinet. It's mostly empty save for toothpaste and floss—and a bottle of aspirin. This one has its label on.

Claire takes a step back. Her heart's pounding again, even though she knows it's stupid. All she found was a *label*, it doesn't mean anything.

But Claire can't shake the feeling that it does.

She kneels down and opens the cabinet under the sink. A plunger lies on its side. A ball of crumpled paper towels lurks in the far corner. And, hiding behind the pipe, is a white, label-less bottle with a childproof cap.

Claire pulls it out and shakes it once, listening to the rattle of pills inside. She opens it up and dumps a few into her palm. Small, white, round. They look familiar.

Claire opens the medicine cabinet again and pulls out the aspirin bottle. Her heart thumps. It's the same size and shape as the bottle under the sink. She opens the aspirin bottle, dumps out the pills.

They're the exact same.

She lines the two bottles up on the cabinet, side by side. Why would Grammy keep a bottle of aspirin in her medicine cabinet, and another, without the label, underneath the sink?

Claire opens up the label-less bottle again and takes out one of the pills. She holds it up to the light. She's *certain* she's seen it before—

And then Claire's stomach knots in on itself. The pill drops out of her fingers and bounces across the tile.

She knows where she's seen that pill.

Her heart racing, Claire falls to her knees and scoops the pill up again. She closes it in her fist and strides out of the bedroom, taking the long way around to the kitchen, through the sitting room, so she won't have to walk by Grammy watching TV. The house is dark and stuffy and she feels like the walls are closing in on her, but she keeps walking, taking deep gulping breaths, until she comes to the kitchen.

Grammy's pillbox sits where it always does, on the shelf in the kitchen window.

Claire stares at it for a few moments. The TV chatters in the distance. It sounds like some kind of talk show. The pill slips against her sweaty palm. A round of applause erupts in the living room, and Claire darts forward, grabs the pillbox.

Opens it.

In each compartment lie three identical pills. Small, white, round. Claire remembers her first day here, Grammy saying she'd already gotten her pills together, that Claire only has to make sure she remembers to take them.

Trembling, Claire opens up her clenched fist. What she finds isn't a surprise, not really.

The pill from the stripped-off aspirin bottle is the same as the pills Grammy has been taking three times a day since Claire arrived.

Claire rides her bike to Julie's house, the hot wind blustering across her face. She can hardly breathe, hardly think. Grammy's been taking aspirin all this time. Her super-important three-times-a-day pills, the ones she could never afford to miss—they're *aspirin*.

Claire blows through the stop sign at the end of the street, whipping the bike hard to make her turn. Her feet pedal furiously, but really it's the confusion and anger that propel her forward. She knows she can't stop to think. She just has to ride until she sees the tall pine trees marking the entrance to Julie's driveway. It's all she can do.

As soon as Claire saw the pillboxes, she dropped the aspirin down the sink and walked out of Grammy's house. She can't think about that. She'll be punished somehow. Grounded. Forced to hang out with Audrey, which is worse.

Indianola flashes by. The air smells of salt water and fish, but even that's a better smell than the gardenias in Grammy's bathroom.

It takes Claire less time to get to Julie's house than she expects, but by the time she arrives she's drenched in sweat and panting hard. It's only as she's winding her way up the long driveway that she realizes Julie might be working.

She leans her bike up against a palm tree and takes a moment to catch her breath. She doesn't want to think about how she must look, red-faced and exhausted and dressed in cleaning clothes.

She hopes Julie won't mind.

Claire takes one last deep breath and goes up to the front door and rings the bell. No one answers. Claire closes her eyes. Maybe she should go back. This was a stupid idea. What if Grammy calls the cops?

The door opens.

It's a tiny woman with long honey-colored hair, teased up high around the crown of her head.

"Can I help you?" she says, in a voice that suggests she wants to do nothing of the kind.

"Is Julie home?" Claire is hot not just with exertion but with embarrassment.

The woman accepts this, though, and she opens the door a little wider and steps back. "She's up in her fun room. Are you that new friend of hers? Chloe?"

"Claire."

"Ah, yes." The woman looks like she doesn't care. "I'm her mother. Come on in, then. You know the room I'm talking about, right? The one where she plays her games?"

"In the attic, right?"

"Mmm." Julie's mother shuts the door, and Claire basks for a moment in the frigid AC pouring down the hallway. "Did you run here?"

"I rode my bike."

"You look like you're about to die." Julie's mom holds up one mani-cured hand. "Let me get you a drink of water. Wait here."

Claire doesn't protest. Her mouth is parched. When Julie's mom comes back, Claire gulps the water down and shoves the glass back at her. "Thanks!" she says, and then she heads toward the stairs before she changes her mind and decides to go back home.

The attic ladder is down. Claire can hear the *Mortal Kombat* music.

She climbs halfway up before shouting Julie's name. The music goes silent. Julie's face appears in the hatchway

"Claire?" she says. "What are you doing here? I thought you had to clean!"

Claire clambers up the rest of the ladder. "I couldn't stay in that house with her," she says. "Grammy's been *lying* to me."

"What do you mean?" Julie helps Claire up the last few rungs of the ladder, not seeming to mind the sweat. Claire collapses down on the floor in front of the couch. Julie's character in the game is frozen mid-leap, halfway between the ground and the sky.

"She has these pills," Claire says, her voice shaking. "My first day here, she told me I needed to make sure she takes them every day. She acted like it was a matter of *life and death,* her taking these pills. And today, she had me cleaning her room, I think she was trying to—" Claire stops, not wanting to tell Julie that Grammy probably hates her. "I mean, she just likes giving me busy work, you know? And I found the pills she's been taking. They're *aspirin*. She's been making a big deal about aspirin." Claire covers her face with her hands and curls her knees up against her chest, trying to draw away from the outside world. For a moment she has a flickering thought that her mother set this whole thing up to get rid of her for the summer, the way she ships Claire's brother off to sports camp ever year. She wonders if Grammy's in on it, willing to play along so Claire's mother can have her freedom. Except Grammy does look sick, always so pale and shaking. But she's only taking *aspirin*.

Claire feels a touch on her shoulder. She drops her hands away and Julie's sitting right beside her.

"It's probably nothing," Julie says gently. "I mean, maybe her doctor told her to take aspirin for her heart or something."

Claire hugs her knees in closer. "But that's not life or death, you know? And why did she put them in a pillbox? Why'd she keep it a secret?"

"Who knows why Mrs. Sudek does what she does? No offense," Julie adds quickly.

Claire doesn't say anything. She knows Julie's trying to make her feel better, and as much as she wants it to work, it doesn't.

"Did you ask her about it?" Julie says softly.

Claire shakes her head.

"I don't blame you. She's scary." Julie grins, trying to make it into a joke. Claire doesn't feel like laughing. "But I bet it's nothing, I really do. Just an old woman being particular."

"Maybe." Claire still isn't convinced. In a way, she knows Julie is right, that she could ask Grammy about it—Grammy's her *grandmother*, her flesh and blood, it ought to not be a big deal. But it is. Claire tries to imagine herself sitting down with Grammy, showing her the aspirin bottle and the pillbox, and she can't do it. Her mind goes blank at the thought. "I mean, she's just so clearly *sick*. She can barely get around the house some days. But it just—it feels *wrong*."

As soon as she speaks, Claire regrets it. Julie frowns at her. "What feels wrong?"

"Everything. Grammy's pills. Her illness." Claire stands up. Her head swoons, but she wants to walk around. She thinks it'll regulate her thoughts. "I can't put it into words."

Julie frowns from her place over by the couch. Claire traces a slow circle around the perimeter of the attic. With each step the discovery in Grammy's kitchen recedes further away from her. They're just *pills*.

But forgetting about it feels wrong too.

Claire passes in front of the full-length mirror and catches a glimpse of her reflection. She's still sweaty and pink-cheeked from the bike ride through the heat, and she reaches up to smooth down her hair.

A ghost floats beside her.

No, not a ghost—the gray dress. Abigail's dress. It snags on Claire's thoughts, dragging her away from her reflection and her whole reason for being here.

A gray dress. Silk. You found it in Julie's attic.

She shakes her head. Her reflection moves with her, but then, just for a second, her reflection's eyes flit off to the side, toward the dress.

Claire takes a step back. So does her reflection.

"Claire?" Julie appears behind her in the mirror, still frowning. "Are you okay?"

"I'm fine, I just had a weird—" Claire rubs her forehead and turns around, away from the mirror. "This is going to sound crazy, but can I borrow the dress?"

Julie goes quiet for a moment. Then: "Abigail's dress?"

"Yeah. Just—I won't do anything to it, I just—" She doesn't want to tell Julie that she's thinking about wearing it to the Stargazer's Masquerade. Julie'll laugh at her, because there's no way that dress is going to fit.

"Uh, sure." Julie shrugs, then reaches over and lifts the dress off the mirror. "Just bring it back when you're done, okay?"

Claire nods. Her head's clearing a little.

"Look, I think we ought to do something to distract you from this whole thing with your grandma." Julie drapes the dress, hanger and all, across the top of the couch. Claire watches her, not wanting to take her eyes off the dress. "We can watch a movie; I checked some out the other day. We had so much fun watching *Hiruki* and *Alien*, remember? And that reminds me, they're bringing *Aliens* back for a one-night showing in a week, which we are *definitely* going to."

Claire's cheeks warm at that. It's the first emotion she's felt all afternoon that really seems to belong to her.

"I don't feel like watching a movie," she hears herself say. "Maybe some other time. Really, I just—" She puts her hand in her pocket. Abigail's photograph is still there, crumpled a little from the ride over. Warmth floods up her fingers, and her thoughts firm. "No. Wait. Do you want to go to the library? Like we talked about last night?"

Julie's staring at her with her head tilted, her eyes squinting a little. For a moment Claire think she's going to ask again if she's feeling okay. She isn't sure how she'll answer.

"Yeah," Julie says. "Yeah, we can do that."

CHAPTER

JULIE

Julie hasn't been to the library in ages, not since she was a little girl and her mother brought her here for story time. The building looks the same as she remembers, a brown-brick cube surrounded by pecan trees, although there's a new sign hanging next to the drive: *Indianola Public Library*, painted over a scene of the beach.

"Wow, it's pretty small," Claire says as Julie parks.

"Yeah, it probably isn't much compared to the one in Houston."

They get out of the car. Claire leads the way up to the doors as if she's been here before. When they go in Julie is swamped with a rush of decade-old memories: her mother holding her hand and leading her to the little room in the back, a scratchy record player warbling out children's songs, the librarian with her straight skirt and her teased-up hair holding a picture book face out, reciting it instead of reading.

Julie shakes her head. Memory is a weird thing. Ten years and the library's been lurking in the back of her mind, waiting. She didn't even know it was there.

"So now what?" she asks Claire.

"We need to see if they have old newspapers." Claire definitely seems to know what she's doing. She walks over to a desk in the center of the lobby. A sign reading *Reference* is propped up in one corner.

"Excuse me," Claire says. "We're interested in looking at old issues of the Indianola newspaper."

The librarian at the desk is different from the one who did story time. She's older, her long black hair streaked with gray, an ugly enamel parrot pin on her big-shouldered jacket. "Well, you're in luck," she says, smiling. "We have all issues of the *Indianola Advocate* dating back to its founding in the 1860s. Do you know what date you need?"

Claire glances over at Julie, her eyes aglow with excitement. It's all a little nerdy by Julie's standards, but she's just glad Claire's distracted from that weird discovery about Mrs. Sudek's pills.

"July 18, 1893," Claire says. The date of Abigail's last letter: *My darling, the final preparations are ready.* "And then maybe, say, a month after that."

"Wonderful. Now, it's all on microfilm. I can show you how to use the machines."

"Oh, I already know!" Claire says brightly. "I've had to use them for school projects before."

The librarian beams. Claire's manner with her is easy, like she's used to dealing with adults. It's a side of her that Julie hasn't seen before.

"It's all in the reading room." The librarian stands up, pushing her chair away. "I'll need to pull the microfilm for you. If you go on in, I can meet you there."

The librarian bustles away from her desk. Claire looks over at Julie. "I hope there's something in the paper about Abigail and Javier. Don't you? I don't know what we'll do if there isn't." She smiles, wistfully. "What happened to them would just be an unsolved mystery, I guess."

"I do love that show," Julie says.

Claire laughs and an old man reading magazines at a nearby table glares at them. Claire's cheeks turn pink and Julie glares back, wanting to defend Claire's honor.

"Come on," Julie says. Claire nods, and they take off, weaving through the stacks until they reach the reading room in the back. When they go in, Julie realizes it's the same place she went for story time, but it looks different now. There are no bright puppets on the shelves or posters on the walls. The colorful carpets are gone. Everything's been replaced with boxy beige machines that sort of look like TV sets.

She feels weirdly empty, seeing this.

Claire sits down at one of the machines just as the librarian joins them. She has a cardboard box pressed up against her chest.

"Here you go," she says. "A month of the *Indianola Advocate* starting July 18, 1893." Claire takes the box and thanks the librarian, who smiles and leaves them alone. Four rolls of film are lined up side by side in the box.

"Let's see what we can find," Julie says. "I'll let you do the honors."

Claire smiles and feeds the film into the machine. Julie holds her breath, wondering what they're going to see.

Down on the Farm, says the first headline. The story is about the recent good fortune of someone named Howard Dunaway and his flock of one hundred hens.

"I guess that was important enough news back then," Julie says wryly.

"It was their livelihood, wasn't it?"

"Well, okay. Good point. And it's not like the newspaper nowadays is much better." Julie laughs, and Claire smiles along with her.

"Anyway, we didn't expect anything for July eighteenth," Claire says. "It would be something after—something to keep them from meeting."

Julie nods, and Claire starts zipping through her microfilm. Her profile lights up with the caramel light of the microfilm's projection and her hair turns golden, like a halo.

Warmth flushes through Julie's bloodstream.

She watches as tiny, hundred-year-old headlines flash on the screen and then vanish. None of them explain why Abigail and Javier weren't able to run away together. Julie wonders if they'll even find anything.

But then Claire makes a confused noise in her throat, moves the film backward.

"Look at this," she says. "The dates skip."

"What? What do you mean?"

Claire gestures at the screen. The date on the newspaper reads *July 20*. But when she rolls over to the next screen, it's a date marker, *July 24, 1893* scrawled in black ink.

"Maybe it's a mistake," Julie says.

Claire clicks past the date marker to the newspaper itself. Unlike the past issues, there is one huge word stretching across the front page: *HURRICANE*. Then, below it, in small letters: *Deaths est. at 10.*

"Whoa," Julie says. "A hurricane? We get them, but…this sounds huge."

"You didn't know about it?" Claire's eyes flick across the screen.

Julie reads over her shoulder, squinting at the bright screen. The fuzzy letters of the newspaper swim and blur.

Recovery in Indianola has been swift after the sudden appearance of a cyclone three days ago. Despite being felled by trees, the telegram towers have been repaired by an unknown benefactor, and the road appears to be clear.

The *Indianola Advocate* mourns the dead who were lost amid the storm's wind and waves.

Beyond these basics, though, the article isn't clear on what happened. It's mostly about damages.

"Weird," Julie says. "It's like the reporter didn't know what was going on. He's so vague. Wasn't he *there*?"

Claire slides over to the next page. Julie grabs her chair and pulls it right beside her. Their knees touch.

"This would explain what happened to Javier and Abigail, though," Claire says, still reading the newspaper. "Maybe they were supposed to meet and then the hurricane hit."

"Maybe." Julie feels a flush of disappointment. She was hoping for something more dramatic than a storm, like a midnight duel between Garner and Javier.

Claire is transfixed, though, leaning close to the screen, reading, Julie can only assume, every word of the paper's front page. Julie skims instead. Everything is about the hurricane—the landscape was ripped to shreds, but nearly all of the town's houses were still standing afterward, which strikes her as just kind of…odd. A farmer on the outskirts of town was upset that his cotton crops had been flooded, but most people seemed grateful that the town had survived. Even the reporter snuck in some editorializing: *Praise be to God that we emerged through the storm unharmed. Truly a miracle happened here.*

There are drawings of the damage, fallen trees and a flooded beach. Someone wrote an article about the experience of hearing the storm roll in from the confines of his dining room, that slow dawning dread.

And then the name *Javier* jumps out at Julie.

"Wait." Julie puts her hand on Claire's arm. "I just saw—oh my God, I did! Look, there!"

She points at a column headed *Goings-on.* Halfway down the column is a paragraph about a Mr. Javier Alvarez and a Mrs. G. Garner. Julie stars to read it out loud:

"Friends of Mrs. G. Garner will be delighted to know she is recovering nicely from her ordeal during last week's storm. When we spoke to her, she credited Mr. Javier Alvarez"—Julie nudges Claire, grinning—*"a Mexican national, with saving her from what would certainly have been a gruesome death. Instead, it was her kidnapper—"* Julie's eyes go wide. "Kidnapper!" she cries.

"Look!" Claire jabs at the screen. "Look who it was." She picks up reading, her words breathless. *"—Mr. Henry Emmert, who met his end in a watery grave, drowned in the very same cabin in which he had shackled Mrs. Garner in the hours before the arrival of the storm."*

Claire twists to look at Julie, her eyes wide. For a moment, the only sound is the humming of the light from the machines.

"That's him, wasn't it?" she said. "The guy who was staring at her in the letters?"

"Yes!" Julie shakes her head. "I guess Abigail was right not to trust that loser." She laughs. "Also, they put that under 'Goings-on'? Look, the next item is about Methodist ladies knitting socks for the hurricane survivors."

"Yeah. Who knows." Claire squints at the screen. "But this still

150

doesn't make sense to me. Why wasn't Charlotte there? The newspaper doesn't say anything about her."

"I don't know. Maybe Abigail decided not to take her?"

"Maybe." Claire frowns. "But even if she did, why didn't Javier save Abigail from Emmert and *then* run away with her? If they couldn't get out then because of the storm, why not do it later?"

Julie reads through the article again, trying to piece together the clues. "Maybe she changed her mind?" she says. "I mean, she didn't have her kid with her."

"She was willing to do it before!"

Claire's right—something doesn't quite add up. And Julie thinks it's because of Mr. Emmert.

"The story says Emmert kidnapped her," Julie says slowly. "In the letters, though, they had hired him to help them rendezvous. I mean, that's what I got out of it." She looks over at Claire, and Claire nods in agreement. "So I think Emmert backstabbed them. He said he was going to help and then he just kidnapped Abigail instead—to ransom her, I guess. Probably he did it before she was supposed to leave, so he didn't take Charlotte. I don't know. But that might be why they couldn't leave together, like they planned."

Claire considers this, her gaze unwavering as she stares at the glowing screen. "Maybe," she says. "I mean, this story makes Javier look like the hero, so I don't think anyone knew about the affair. And Emmert's dead, so he can't tell on them." She pauses, tilting her head. "Maybe they just decided not to push their luck. That's kind of sad, really."

"Yeah." Julie thinks about the picture of her great-great-grandparents hanging in the lobby of the Alvarez Motel. It was taken when they were in their forties, and both Javier and Constancia look dark and serious. In that picture, he doesn't look like a man who would run off with a married woman. And maybe that's why. Because he tried, and it was almost a total disaster.

Almost.

Julie looks over at Claire. "Maybe I'll save your life sometime."

"Maybe I'll save yours," Claire says. "Return the balance."

Julie laughs.

Claire turns back to the screen. "I don't know," she says. "I still feel like something's missing. I just don't know what, though."

"I'm not sure how we could find out. I don't think my parents even know this story."

Claire hits the print button on the side. "There," she says. "Now we have a copy, just in case."

"What? Where?"

"Up at the front. They'll hold it for us until we're done."

"Oh, cool, I didn't know you could do that." Julie smiles. "You're good at this."

Claire's cheeks pinken. "Only thing I'm good at."

"Oh, I don't know about that." Julie feels breathless; the story about her great-great-grandfather risking his life to save the woman he loved has her wanting to take her own risks. "I mean, you're pretty good at making my summer interesting."

Claire smiles a little. Then she says, "Let's see if there's anything else," and moves to the next section of the newspaper. It has more information about the storm, but nothing terribly interesting, and nothing more about Abigail Garner's rescue from a kidnapper. The next day's paper continues on with information about the hurricane too. A family was uncovered, scared but unharmed, from a collapsed boat, bringing the estimated deaths down to twenty. The mayor was interviewed, saying that the repairs needed for the town were nowhere near as extensive as feared.

The next day is more of the same, as is the fourth. *Hurricane Repairs Continue.*

"No more gaps," Julie says. "Did you notice that?"

"They probably had to stop printing because of the storm."

"Yeah." Julie feels strangely unconvinced, though. Like the gap in reporting means more than is obvious.

And that's when she sees it. A flash of a word. *Creature.*

"Stop stop stop!" Julie says.

"I have!"

The huddle close together. It's a little item, another paragraph under *Goings-on.*

Miss Hattie Luce was visited this morning (Tuesday) by an unusual creature, similar in shape to an alligator but covered in fine silver fur. It bit several of her father's prized hogs before Mr. M. Horn attacked the creature with his pistol, shooting it dead. We are uncertain of the creature's origins, but we advise all residents of Indianola to watch their livestock and children as the matter is investigated further.

"This *has* to be referring to the monsters," Claire says. "But they're acting like they've never seen them before!"

"Oh my God. I guess they arrived around the turn of the century."

Julie says, thinking for a moment. "But it's never been clear where they came from…or how they got here. I wonder if they have something to do with the hurricane?"

"Maybe." Claire looks over at the screen, at the little warning in the bottom corner. "It would make sense, don't you think? There's a really big, weird hurricane, and then right after it, we see mention of the monsters?"

A little shock of frisson ripples down Julie's spine. "I'm *sure* they're related."

Claire hits the print button and spins forward through the film.

"What are you looking for?" Julie leans forward.

"Anything else about the monsters." Claire's eyes are shining. "This is so interesting, to see them talked about in the paper like this." She looks at Julie. "Does the paper mention them now?"

"Are you kidding?" Julie laughs. "And leave a record? Hell, no!"

"That's what I thought." Claire pauses, gaze skimming across the screen. "Oh, my God, Julie! Look at this."

Julie leans forward. Claire points at a column near the top of the page. *NOTICE*, reads the deceptively simple headline. But then:

Mr. Javier Alvarez has bravely led the charge in organizing arrangements with our town's unwanted residents. He, along with the Rev. George Bray, invites all interested parties to bear witness at the signing ceremony this Monday, July 27, at the First Baptist Church on Avenue C. The treaties developed by Mr. Alvarez and Rev. Bray will serve as protection against the strange and troublesome creatures.

Julie falls back against her chair. "Holy crap!" she says. "So it's true." She shakes her head, thinking about all the times she teased her father for insisting that it had been her great-whatever-grandfather who first set up the treaties with the monsters.

"You knew about this?" Claire glances at Julie.

"I'd heard stories," Julie says. "But I don't know, I wasn't sure I totally believed them. I mean, my parents also said the house had always been in our family, and that turned out to not be true."

"I feel like we're stumbling onto something," Claire says, and Julie nods. She just doesn't know what yet.

CHAPTER

Eleven

CLAIRE

Claire can't sleep. It's nearly five in the morning and her thoughts are spinning with everything she's learned in the last few days: the letters, the thwarted kidnapping, the first appearance of the monsters. Plus Grammy's reaction when she finally came home yesterday, after running out on her chores. She was grounded for a week.

So that's another worry, the knowledge that she has to spend the rest of the week trapped in a house with Grammy and her lies about her medication.

Claire rolls over on her side, staring at the wall. The picture of Julie's house is still gone—she wonders where Grammy put it. Grammy has to know about all this history. Maybe it's the real reason for her opposition to Julie.

Maybe Grammy can even fill in the blanks.

Claire doesn't sleep, she just lets the mystery of Abigail and Javier and the monsters roll around in her brain as she listens to the humming of the fan. Sometimes she thinks about Julie too, the way they sat so close together to see the microfilm screen, and that moment the other night when Julie told Claire she was pretty, how there was the slightest tremor in her voice—

The memories give Claire a shuddery feeling that isn't entirely unpleasant. It kind of reminds her of how she feels—used to feel?—about Josh. The longer she lies there, the more her thoughts seem to elongate away from her until they become their own independent entities. She sees herself taking Julie's hand. She sees Julie brushing her hair away, and then kissing her, once on the cheek, once on the forehead, once on the mouth.

Claire flops over again. She feels embarrassed, as if Julie might read her thoughts across town. Julie's her friend, and she's not supposed to think about friends that way. Especially not if they're girls.

⌐⌐

When the sun starts to peek through the blinds, Claire is still awake.

She watches the room brighten. At 7:30, she finally gets up for lack of anything better to do. When she looks at herself in her vanity mirror, she sees that her eyes are ringed in dark circles.

Claire dresses, pulling on a long, light dress that ties in the back, and trudges into the kitchen. Grammy is already awake, eating the cereal Claire prepared the night before.

"Did you take your pill?" Claire asks automatically. The question jars her, and she looks away from Grammy, toward the refrigerator.

"I did, thank you." The pillbox isn't sitting on the windowsill. Claire glances over her shoulder, sees it on the table beside Grammy's cereal.

"I take it you're ready for a day of cleaning," Grammy says.

Julie pulls a grapefruit out of the refrigerator in response.

"Oh, don't pull this attitude with me. Your mother did the same thing and it was never becoming on her either. And look where it got her, having to work for a living."

"I told you I was sorry," Claire murmurs. She sits down at the kitchen table, as far from Grammy as possible. As she slices her grapefruit into halves, she can feel Grammy staring at her. The air sparks.

"It just doesn't seem like you," Grammy said. "Running away like that. I told you that Alvarez girl is a bad influence."

Claire looks up. The sunlight pours in through the windows and lights up Grammy's white hair so that it look like a halo. The light reveals all the shadows in Grammy's face too, and the sharp lines of her cheekbones and collarbones jutting out of her skin. It's not that she looks old but that she looks sickly, and for the millionth time Claire wonders why she isn't taking real medication.

"Her name's Julie," Claire says.

Grammy turns back to the newspaper. "I know what her name is." She lifts up one corner and reads. Claire stares at the headline on the back—something about baseball.

"She's not a bad influence."

"Then why did you run out on your chores?"

"I was tired. I needed a break." Claire digs her spoon into her grapefruit, but she doesn't have much appetite. "I think the real reason you don't like her is because the Alvarez family bought their house from ours a long time ago."

Claire can't believe she just said that. It's like her words have separated out from her the way her thoughts did earlier.

The refrigerator's hum seems too loud.

Grammy turns a page of the newspaper. Takes a bite of her cereal.

"Now where would you get an idea like that?"

She doesn't look at Claire, but her voice is cold and sharp-edged. It's not the same sort of sharpness it had when Claire came home yesterday afternoon, sheepish for running away. This seems—dangerous.

"I read about it somewhere."

Grammy looks up. Her eyes glitter. She doesn't seem like herself.

"You're right," she said. "They did buy our house out from under us. From under your great-great-grandmother Abigail Sudek."

The name rings in Claire's ears. "Don't you mean Abigail Garner?" she says. "Because I read about her too."

"What sort of things have you been reading, Claire?" The question is like a gunshot going off.

"I read that she and Javier Alvarez were in love, even though she had to marry someone else. Then Javier bought the—"

Grammy flings the newspaper toward Claire. It erupts in mid-air, pages scattering like birds. Claire freezes. The pages drift slowly to the table, to the floor; one covers Claire's grapefruit. On the other side of the pages sits Grammy, her expression furious and filled with something Claire has never seen face-to-face before. She thinks it's hatred.

"Don't you dare talk about Javier Alvarez," she hisses. "That man brought shame upon Abigail. Brought shame upon the entire family. He seduced her, put ideas in her head—she almost abandoned her family because of him, did you know that? She had a child!"

Claire doesn't answer. *She was going to take her too.*

"And then *Javier* drew up those dreadful treaties, which forced your great-great-grandfather to give up a portion of his oilfields to accommodate the monsters. Meanwhile, Alvarez is rewarded by the city governance, given a big fat check for those treaties. Ten years later, my grandfather's fortune had dried up without the oil. They had to sell Abigail's house—yes, it was *hers*, built by her father when he moved here from Poland. Everything is Javier's fault."

"What?" Claire snaps. "It's not Javier's fault that Garner had to give up some of his oilfields! If anything, it's the monsters'!"

"Exactly!" Grammy's voice is shrill and Claire shrinks away. "There are forces in this world you can't even begin to understand, and Javier exploited them!"

Grammy leans back in her chair. She's even more drawn and worn-out-looking than she was a few moments ago. She smooths one hand over her hair.

"I'm sorry," she says, not looking at Claire. "I didn't mean to lose my temper like that. But it's a sore spot in our family, you must understand."

Such a sore spot, Claire thinks, that this is the first she's hearing of it.

"It's the reason the women in our family give their children the name Sudek—and the reason we prefer to keep it ourselves." Grammy smiles bitterly. "Except for your mother, of course. But your aunt, she kept the tradition, at least." Grammy sighs and drops her head back, her gaze wandering up to the ceiling. Claire doesn't dare move. "Abigail reverted back to her maiden name, Sudek, when Gregory Garner died. She said the name was all she had. There were no sons, you see. And Abigail's daughter, my mother, Charlotte, saw that if you give away your name, you give away everything else too. So she kept it, and it's all we have left now."

Grammy looks at Claire then, and she seems almost grandmotherly again. "You understand, don't you? The Alvarez family was our ruin."

Claire doesn't know how to respond. She looks at the newspaper pages scattered across the kitchen table. "I should clean these up," she says, and she pushes her chair away and stands.

Grammy doesn't say anything, only turns her gaze toward the window. Claire gathers the papers on the table, uncovering the white pillbox. Seeing it gives her a sick feeling in her stomach. It's all just aspirin. Grammy looks like she's dying, and all she's taking for it is aspirin.

"Oh dear God," Grammy says. "I didn't need this so early in the morning."

Claire thinks that she's talking about their conversation—but then she looks up, out the window, through the slats in the blinds, into the backyard.

She drops the papers and they scatter anew.

A monster stands on the back patio.

It doesn't look like the others she's seen—it's closer to animal than to human, crouched on all fours, its hind legs bending high over its back like the legs of a grasshopper. It has a long, thin face and eyes that glitter like gray stones, and it's staring at Claire through the window.

She totters to the side, dizzy. Grammy pushes away from the table with a sigh and goes to the phone.

The monster leaps forward and slams against the window. The glass cracks.

Claire screams and falls backward. Grammy whirls around, dropping the phone so that it clatters to the tile. The monster presses its face against the window, its breath forming a perfect circle of fog on the glass. Claire stares at it in horror.

The monster opens its mouth, long tongue lolling. Saliva drips down the pane.

"Get away, Claire!" Grammy shrieks. "Back into the bathroom! Away from the wind—"

"The astronaaaaaaut," the monster says, dragging the word out into a long, low hiss. "The astronaaaaaaut is heeeeere. Avoooooooid."

Claire scuttles back a few paces, but she makes no move to leave the room. The monster rears its head back and slams up against the window again. Grammy screams. Claire can hear her fumbling around for the phone, but she keeps her own eyes fixed firmly on the window, on the long, dripping tunnel of the monster's open mouth.

"The astronaaaaaaaaut," it says. "Coooooming for yoooooou, Suuuuuuuuudek."

Sudek. Her grandmother's name. Abigail's name. It bounces around inside of Claire's head like electricity.

The monster lifts up one of its hind legs and rams it against the window. Tiny fractal cracks blossom farther out along the glass.

"Yoooooooou muuuuuuust goooooooooo. It is heeeeeeeere."

"This is Mrs. Sudek down on Magnolia Road. I've got another one—"

Claire hears Grammy's voice through a constant buzzing. A buzzing, she realizes, distantly, that comes from the monster pressing so close to the glass. She can almost see the atoms in the air, churning up the space around it.

The monster drags its tongue up the glass and the sight of its dark throat makes Claire's stomach lurch, like she's looking at a dead thing.

"Get someone out here right away, it's trying to break in—"

"Astronaaaaaaaaaut," the monster says. Its eyes flash.

"But *don't* send the Alvarez girl—"

"What?" Claire whips her head around to Grammy. But then

162

there's another sound of cracking glass and Claire turns back to the monster again. It's pressed its other back foot against the window, its body twisted around itself, foot-face-foot. Claire's stomach roils again. This is not natural.

"Suuuuuuudek," the monster hisses. "Yoooooou—"

Grammy digs her fingers into Claire's shoulder and jerks her to her feet. The monster tilts its head, and it tilts it too far, to an unnatural angle.

"We've got to get away from here," Grammy says, pulling on Claire's arm with a strength that doesn't suit her frail, shuffling body. "Into the bathroom. The exterminator will be here soon."

"Why'd you tell them not to send Julie!?"

Grammy drags Claire out of the kitchen, into the living room. The monster watches them go, but only for a second—then pushes itself away from the window with enough force that the cracks deepen. Its shadow darkens the living room window.

"Because she's just a girl!" Grammy pulls Claire into the hallway. Claire stumbles after her, afraid the monster will break in someplace.

The hallway bathroom door hangs open, and Grammy shoves Claire in first and then follows, switching on the humming fluorescent light and locking the door.

"Get in the tub," she says.

"It's not a tornado!"

"Dammit, Claire, now's not the time to fight with me. Do as I say."

Claire steps over the tub's edge. Her whole body is shaking, and she's struck with a sudden wave of dizziness: The monster must be on the other side of the wall. There's no window here, but Claire can feel it anyway, in the way the air jumps around.

Grammy joins her in the bathtub and puts one arm around her shoulder and pulls her in close. Claire shivers against her frail, bony frame. The tub feels claustrophobic and at the same time full of echoes, as if it is an enormous place. Claire's breath bounces off the tiles.

"Don't worry," Grammy says in a bedtime-story voice, a voice that's almost soothing. "They'll be here soon. And we'll be safe."

But Claire doesn't feel safe. Not at all.

⌐

That afternoon, Claire nails flat pieces of wood over the kitchen window to protect the cracked glass until the repairman can come out to fix it.

Grammy sits on the porch with an iced tea in one hand, watching Claire work. Her presence puts Claire on edge, but at the same time Claire doesn't want to be out here alone.

The broken window isn't the only evidence of the monster. The colocasia plants growing up next to the house are trampled, the soil ripped up: an unsettling sight that Claire tries to ignore. There's also the lingering scent of metal, sharp and burning and tickling at the back of Claire's throat.

"When you're finished with this," Grammy says, "I want you to call up Audrey."

Claire pauses, her hammer poised to strike. She looks at Grammy over her shoulder. "What?"

"Audrey Duchesne. I want you to call her up when you're finished." Grammy sips her tea and settles back into her chair. "You haven't seen her in a few days and you know I'd rather you spend your time with her than with that Julie Alvarez."

Claire hammers the nail into place, remembering the man who'd shown up at the house. He'd gone around back, but the monster had already vanished. That's another reason why they're boarding up the window. Just in case the monster comes back.

"I thought I was grounded." Claire steps away from the window and plucks another nail out of the old coffee can. The wood's in place; at this point she's just fortifying it. She doesn't ever want to see that monster's face peering at her between its own clawed feet again.

"I figured you've been punished enough," Grammy says. "And besides, I'm sure Audrey'll want to see you. It's summer and she doesn't have to work. Give her a call."

It sounds not like a suggestion but a demand. Grammy uses the same tone of voice as when she informed Claire that Claire would be covering the window.

"Are you sure it's safe for me to be out?"

"You'll be safe," Grammy says.

Claire sighs and hammers in another nail. She doesn't want to see Audrey Duchesne. She wants to see Julie. After the monster attack, and cowering in the bathtub for nearly an hour, Julie's the only who will make her feel protected.

"Call her," Grammy says.

Claire sighs and admits defeat. "Fine." She picks up another nail.

"I think it's secure enough," Grammy says. "Go on in, give Audrey a call."

Audrey, Audrey, Audrey. Claire'll be happy if she never hears that name again. She tosses the nail back into the coffee can and then gathers up her tools and goes inside. Grammy doesn't follow, only stays in her spot on the porch, staring out at the empty yard.

The kitchen is darker than usual with the board across the window. Claire puts the tools back in the cabinet and then goes over to the phone. Might as well get it over with.

Audrey's number is written on a Post-it note and stuck on the wall next to all the numbers that Claire's mother left behind. It's written in a girlish, loopy handwriting that Claire doesn't recognize. It must belong to Audrey. Feeling pliant from the heat, she dials in the numbers, listening to the *click-whir* of the rotary. Grammy really is stuck in the 1960s.

The phone only rings once before Audrey answers.

"Duchesne residence," she says in her cheerful voice. "Audrey speaking."

Claire shivers despite the muggy heat inside the house.

"Hey Audrey," Claire says, "it's—"

"Claire! I know, I recognized your voice. I feel like I haven't seen you in *forever*. I'm afraid I might have gotten a bit caught up in seeing Lawrence Reyes." She giggles, a grating sound. "Sorry I've been such a bad friend! A girl should never give up her friends for a boy, that's what I always say, and yet look at me now."

"Yeah, well—" Claire doesn't want to think about Audrey dating Lawrence Reyes. She feels a prickle on the back of her neck, as if someone's watching her. But the window's boarded over, and Grammy's still outside.

Suddenly all Claire wants is to be out of that house, away from the place where the monster attacked.

"Can I come over now?" Claire says. "I don't have anything to do."

"Of course! I'll totally make up for neglecting you. I've got another game we can play, what do you think?"

166

Claire feels a dull emptiness in the back of her head. "Sure, whatever. I'll ride my bike over to your place."

"Wonderful! I'll see you then."

Claire hangs up. The kitchen door scrapes open, and Grammy steps inside. "Did you call her?" she asks.

Claire nods.

"Good. It's nice to see you spending time with someone more—"

"White?" Claire says.

"That is absolutely not what I was going to say." Grammy shuffles past her and sets her empty glass in the sink. "Really, Claire, you ought to know better."

Claire feels that emptiness in her head again. Her thoughts seem to swell. Grammy never clarifies exactly what Audrey is more of.

"I'll be back for dinner," Claire says.

"All right. Have fun!"

No mention of monsters, no mention of danger. She wishes Grammy would do more than call an exterminator.

But she won't. So Claire needs to ring Julie and tell her what happened. Maybe she can call from Audrey's house.

Claire doesn't bother changing or rinsing off. It's just Audrey. She goes into the garage and pulls out her mother's bike, swiping away the cobwebs—she rode it yesterday to Julie's house, but weirdly the webs have already returned—and wheels it out to the driveway. Fluffy white clouds line the sky. A hot breeze pretends to be cool. Claire rides to Audrey's house through the muggy air and the hum of cicadas, her hands tight on the handlebars. She expects a monster to leap out of the shrubbery, but the streets remain empty.

The house is as neat and well-manicured as Claire remembers. The rosebushes are still offering heavy pink blossoms beside the front door. The grass is greener here than in any of the yards Claire passed.

She rings the doorbell. Audrey answers, dressed in one of her pretty sundresses, this one a honey-colored silk shift. Her hair shimmers in the sunlight.

"Claire!" she cries. "*So* good to see you! I'm sorry again about neglecting—"

"I'm fine," Claire says. "I've been hanging out with Julie." The AC trickles outside, cool against Claire's sweaty brow.

"Julie Alvarez? That's nice." She says this in a vague way, as if to suggest she's trying not to have an opinion. "Why don't you come in?"

Stepping into Audrey's house is like stepping into a television show. No messes, no stains on the white furniture. The contrast between colors is too bright. It's more real than real.

"Well, hello there!" Audrey's mother materializes in the hallway with a tray of cookies. "Audrey told me you were coming over. Would you like a snack?"

She brandishes the cookies. They're big and fluffy, chocolate melting in the crevices. And they smell amazing.

"I just *love* baking," Audrey's mom says.

"These look awesome." Claire takes a cookie, hoping that means Audrey's mom will disappear back into the cavern of the kitchen. The cookie is still warm.

Audrey's mom beams. Audrey stands off to the side, watching this exchange with a bland, unreadable expression.

"Wonderful!" Audrey's mom swirls around on the heel of her stiletto—stilettos? Weird. Not even Julie's mom, with her stylish, expensive clothes, wears stilettos inside. "You girls have fun."

She walks back through the living room. Claire looks down at her cookie, then takes a bite. Soft and chewy and chocolaty. Perfect.

"Let's go up to my room," Audrey says. "I think you'll really like this game."

"Okay." Claire nibbles on her cookie as they walk up the stairs. The house is as quiet as a museum. Claire feels like she shouldn't be eating here. A thought niggles at the back of her head—

"Oh," she says. "Wait."

Audrey stops and looks over at her.

Claire's head swims. "Your phone," she says. "Can I borrow your phone?"

"My phone?"

Claire nods. "I need to call someone. Just real quick. I—forgot to call them at my house."

"Oh," says Audrey. "Of course. The phone's back downstairs. In the hallway. I can show you if you like—"

"No, I can find it." Claire scurries back down the stairs. She can't believe she almost forgot to call Julie. This town gets in your head and changes things.

The phone sits in a little alcove at the base of the stairs. Claire grabs it and dials Julie's number. She hopes Julie's not at work, since she doesn't have the exterminator number memorized.

"Hello?"

"Julie!" Claire breathes a sign of relief. "Oh God, I need to talk to you—"

"Claire! It's about the monster, isn't it? The one at your house this morning? I heard from Brittany. Are you okay?"

"Yeah, I'm fine." Claire glances up at the stairs; Audrey's standing

169

at the top of them, her hands on her hips. "Just rattled. I can't talk long. I just—I wanted to tell you what happened. Grammy's acting like it was no big deal, but I just—isn't there something we can do?"

"Forrest said the monster had taken off by the time he'd gotten there."

"Yeah, but—" Claire glances up at Audrey again. Despite the blasting AC, she's starting to sweat. "Maybe you can talk to your cousin?" She doesn't want to say Lawrence's name in front of Audrey. "See if he can help?"

"I can try." Julie sounds doubtful. "I can talk to Mr. Vickery too, the guy in charge of the monster committee. He wasn't useful before, but since the thing basically *attacked* you—"

"That would be great," Claire says. "Listen, I really can't talk now— I'll try to call you tonight, okay? Just—see if you can figure out something." She hesitates. "It would really mean a lot to me."

There's a pause on the other end, a rush of static. "Sure thing."

"Claire?" calls out Audrey. "Are you almost done?"

"Gotta go," Claire hisses into the phone, and then she hangs up. "Yep!" she calls out. "Thanks."

"Oh, it's no problem." Audrey smiles beatifically. Claire bounds up the stairs, her heart hammering. *Julie will do something. She'll figure out a way to stop the monsters.*

Audrey's room is at the end of the hall. Claire expects it to be white and black and red, like the rest of the house, but when Audrey opens the door, Claire is met with a wash of pink: pink walls, a frilly pink bedspread, pale pink carpet.

Claire isn't sure what to say, so she takes another bite of cookie.

"It's like the other game," Audrey says, breezing through her room. Claire follows her cautiously. The light is different in here because of the pink curtains, filtered and hazy. Claire feels a moment of dizziness, but when she sits down on the edge of the bed, it disappears.

Audrey rummages around in her closet. All her clothes are arranged according to color, and the top shelf is lined with neat plastic boxes. She really is perfect.

"So did you ever get the dress for the Stargazer's Masquerade?" Audrey calls out over her shoulder.

"Oh." Claire has forgotten about the dance. She and Julie never talk about it. But she pictures the dress hanging from the back of her closet door and nods. "Yes. I haven't tried it on yet. I don't think it's going to fit."

Audrey emerges with a thin cardboard box. Claire's heart jumps: It's probably just a normal board game, Monopoly or Clue, but it makes her feel weird.

"It'll fit," Audrey says. "I'm *so* excited. The dance is the most fantastic thing that happens in Indianola. The event of the season."

She does not appear to be saying this ironically.

"You'll get to meet all the kids from the school," she adds.

"Well, I'm just here for the summer." Claire's heart kind of twists at that, though—she'll miss Julie back in Houston.

"I know." Audrey flounces over to the bed. "But it still might be good to meet some new people, don't you think?" She balances the game on top of one of her pillows and sprawls out. Claire looks down at the name on the box: Fallow.

"I've never played this before," Claire says. The truth is she's never even heard of it. The box looks old-fashioned too, illustrated with 1960s children sitting around a table. Something about it gives Claire the creeps.

"Oh really?" Audrey doesn't sound surprised. "It's super fun. Here, let me show you." She opens the box and dumps it upside down. Playing pieces spill across the bedspread, and then the playing board drops out. Audrey unfolds it. A multicolored track winds around in a circular, complex labyrinth. Claire can't tell where it begins or ends.

"What color?" Audrey asks.

"Green," Claire says. Audrey hands her a green triangle.

"Start in the center," Audrey says. "You're trying to work your way out."

"So it's just a maze?"

"Sort of." Audrey sets her own piece, yellow, at the labyrinth's center. Claire does the same, and for a moment she feels swoony, like she's been out in the heat too long.

"You roll the die," Audrey says, "and that tells you how long you get." She pulls out six hourglasses and lines them up, one next to the other, on the bedside table. "One minute to six minutes," she says, sweeping her hand across the hourglasses. "You have however long to try and work your way out of the maze. Once your time is up, the next person gets to go."

Claire stares down at the board. The game seems stupid. They're just working a maze. Kid's stuff.

When she looks at the labyrinth it seems to wriggle and squirm in front of her.

"Are you ready?" Audrey says.

Claire nods and picks up the die and tosses it on the bed. Two. Audrey flips the two-minute hourglass. "Go!" she says.

Claire picks up her pyramid. Ten paths lead out of the labyrinth's center, and all of them knot up together the farther out they go. Claire chooses one path at random and slides her piece over the board, following its twists and turns—until it twists and turns in on itself in an endless loop. Claire's eyes water. She goes back to the beginning, chooses another path, begins to follow it.

"Time's up," Audrey announces.

"Really?" Claire sets her piece down. It feels like thirty seconds have passed, not two minutes. But sure enough, the sand has all spilled to the bottom of the hourglass.

Audrey rolls a five. Claire is certain that Audrey will solve the labyrinth immediately—this seems like one of those games that the owner always wins, like Trivial Pursuit, because they can memorize the board. But Audrey hesitates and starts and stops just like Claire did. And this five minutes actually feels like five minutes. By the time the hourglass runs out, Audrey's only a bit farther into the board than Claire.

They continue on like that, taking turns rolling the die. Audrey flips the hourglasses. Claire inches forward through the labyrinth, constantly turning back and retracing her steps. She has a difficult time looking away from the board, and the labyrinth looms larger in front of her until it seems to take over the entire room.

The die falls with a soft thump on the bed that echoes over and over in Claire's mind; it's amplified, a million times louder. Three minutes. Audrey turns the hourglass, and the movement of her arm is too slow, like she's moving through honey. Claire is certain she can hear each individual grain of sand as it slips through the hourglass. Three minutes. She turns back to the board. The labyrinth swirls into itself. She touches the green pyramid. The labyrinth writhes, resettles. She gasps: No, she realizes, this is normal. This is the labyrinth.

She slides her piece forward. The scraping of wood against cardboard is loud and shrill inside her head. She reaches a dead end.

"Time."

It's Julie's voice. Claire knocks the pyramid over in surprise and looks up and sure enough Julie sits on the other side of the bed, her long legs folded and her shoulders bare, skin gleaming in the weird pink light of the room. She smiles and Claire feels a fluttering deep inside herself she's only ever let herself associate with boys.

"Julie?" she whispers.

Julie's smile brightens, and when she smiles her face changes and she's Audrey again, Audrey in short shorts and a spaghetti-strap tank top. And then she's just Audrey in her sundress.

"Six minutes," Audrey says, and turns the hourglass.

Claire blinks, rubs at her eyes. Julie's not here. Julie's at home, talking to Lawrence, trying to stop the monsters from attacking again.

Julie does smile like that, though. Sometimes.

The fluttering returns. Claire tries to shove it away, confused. Audrey slides her piece around the board like she's dancing a ballet, gliding one direction, stopping, gliding the other. Claire wonders if they're ever going to finish the game.

The hourglass empties. "Time," Claire says, although she feels like some other force is speaking through her. What does she care if it's time? She'd be just as happy giving up, doing something else. It's only a game. Games don't have to finish.

174

But still she reaches for the die, rolls it across the bed.

Six minutes.

She's nervous as she goes to move the pyramid, nervous and a little excited, although it's a cold-sweat kind of excitement, excitement that almost feels like dread. She keeps glancing up at Audrey to see if she's become Julie again. But it's always Audrey who stares back at her.

Claire moves the opposite direction. She doesn't concentrate as hard on the board as she did before, not with her constant checking for Julie, and she doesn't move very far in those six minutes.

"Time," Audrey says.

Back and forth they go. It ought to be boring, but it's not. The maze is such a confusing tangle that looking at it makes Claire feel tired, the way she does whenever she sits for tests at school. Her brain aches like a sore muscle.

Part of her wonders if this game is a test, if all of Audrey's games are tests. But why would Audrey test her? She's just a pretty cheerleader on summer vacation.

Claire rolls a four.

Audrey rolls a two.

Six.

One.

Three.

Two.

Two.

Four.

Back and forth, back and forth. Sometimes it's Julie sitting across the bed, sprawled out in skimpy clothes, tangled hair falling around her shoulders. Sometimes it's Audrey. And even though Claire understands, on a subconscious level, that Audrey is real and Julie is not, Claire realizes that she feels safer when she sees Julie on the bed. *Hallucination*, she thinks when it's not her turn, when the fake Julie is hunched over the board, moving her yellow piece through the labyrinth. The word gives her a little chill of fright. She's hallucinating. But if you know you're hallucinating, is it really a hallucination? Or is it something else?

The fake Julie looks up from the board and smiles. Claire's heart squeezes. It doesn't matter if this is the real Julie or not, she will keep Claire safe from whatever it is Claire fears—not just monsters but the strange fear creeping around the edge of the room, faint but insistent. It's like walking down a hall by yourself, late at night. You know there's nothing there, but you still feel eyes staring at you out of the shadows.

Only Claire feels eyes staring at her out of the maze.

She waits until the fake Julie has been replaced by the real Audrey. Waits for the hallucination to disappear, along with that warm sense of safety. Audrey rolls a five. As she reaches to turn over the hourglass, Claire says, "Wait."

It takes a tremendous amount of effort to say that, more than Claire expects. Even she's startled by the word when it bounds around the room, sounding like a trumpet.

Audrey looks over at her, fingers on the hourglass.

"Why don't we do something else?"

The words are like molasses, sticky and slow. Like the way time gets whenever it's Claire's turn to play. But asking that question makes her head feel clearer than it has all afternoon.

"Something else?" Audrey frowns. "Do you not like playing?" Her lower lip juts out in a childish pout and Claire is struck with an overwhelming wash of grief.

"No, it's fine, it's just—" Claire flounders for the words. "I'm a little tired of sitting here, you know? I didn't realize it would take so long."

"We're almost done." Audrey's expression brightens. "Look how far from the center we are."

Claire looks even though she knows the exact location of her piece. She *is* far from the center, crawling her way around the edge. But it's a maze. Just because you're far from the center doesn't mean you're close to the exit.

"It really shouldn't be that much longer," Audrey says. "I promise."

"I really don't care if I win or not—you can say you did. I mean, I'll just forfeit."

"Forfeit? This isn't football." Audrey giggles. "Why don't we see it through to the end? It's important to finish things."

That last sentence bangs around in Claire's head. Yes. It is important to finish things. Hasn't she been taught as much all her life, by her mother and father and teachers at school? It makes sense to her even as she knows her will is weakening.

"Especially this," Audrey says, although she speaks in Julie's voice. "If we stop early, then the obfuscation won't be finished."

Claire jerks her head up. Audrey is Julie again, and Julie is stretched out on her side, one hand draped over her hip.

"The obfuscation?" Claire says.

But Audrey-Julie ignores the question. "Come on," she says, "it'll be fun. You'll feel so satisfied once you get out."

That's too much. Claire doesn't want to say no to Julie. So she nods, and on her next turn, she rolls a three.

Two.

Six.

Six.

One.

Two.

Four.

On it goes. There's a rhythm to the game—the thump of the die on the bed, the click of the turned hourglass, the whisper of falling sand. Sometimes when Claire looks up, Julie's staring back at her with an expression that reminds Claire of the covers of certain magazines, and her stomach flip-flops around and it's difficult to concentrate on the maze.

Claire is distantly aware of the light changing in the room, the glow of pink sunlight fading until there's only the harsh, sharp light from the ceiling fan. She's distantly aware that this isn't a good thing. But at the same time, as she inches forward on the maze, she's struck with a shivering thrill—*I'm almost out, I'm almost out*—and so they keep playing.

Claire rolls a six. The hourglass flips. When she looks at the maze she can't exactly see her way out, but she can sense it, a light at the end of a tunnel that exists only in her head. She picks up her pyramid and slides it along the board. The way clicks into place. Left turn, right turn, loop back around.

The sand falls.

The pyramid moves across the board.

And Claire sees it, the exit. It's so obvious now that she's at the end, the way it snakes and threads through itself.

Claire pushes her piece out of the maze.

Audrey bursts into applause. "You won!" she cried. The hour-glass runs out, but it doesn't matter; the game's over. "See, wasn't that worth it?"

Claire rubs her forehead. She feels like she's waking up from a fit-ful sleep.

Those thoughts that had been in the back of her consciousness come rushing forward. "My God, what time is it?"

"What?" Audrey frowns. "Oh, did you need to be home by a certain time?"

"Yes! Five o'clock." Claire twists around, trying to find a clock in the frilly decorations of Audrey's room. She finally spots one on the dresser drawer, an old-fashioned alarm clock beside a neat stack of *Seventeen* issues. It takes her a moment to decode the jumble of lines and numbers.

Nine thirty-five.

It's *nine thirty-five.*

"Oh my God!" Claire jumps up from the bed, knocking over the board. The two pyramids and the die go rolling across the floor. "Oh my God, Grammy's going to kill me!" The strangeness of the game has been forgotten; she only has a vague memory of seeing Julie in Audrey's place, and of Julie's voice saying *the obfuscation.*

An SAT word. Claire learned it last year in English. *Obfuscate. Verb. To render obscure or unclear.*

None of that seems real now. The only real thing is Grammy's fury. "I have to go. Why didn't you tell me?" She glares at Audrey, who sits primly on the bed, her hands folded in her lap.

"I didn't know," she says.

179

Claire glowers and runs out of her room, out into the black and white of the rest of the house. All the lights are on. Audrey's little brother sits watching an old TV show, *Father Knows Best*, in the upstairs landing. He looks at her when she rushes past, the TV light shining across his face, his eyes blank.

A chill ripples through her.

She bolts down the stairs. There's a strange smell down here, like sugar burning. When Claire goes through the living room a man is reading the newspaper in a sweater and house slippers. Smoke twists up from a pipe.

He sets the paper in his lap and looks at her with the same empty expression as Audrey's brother.

For a moment Claire is frozen, like his eyes have caught her. Why didn't Audrey come downstairs with her? Isn't that the normal thing to do? But then, she rushed out of the room so quickly.

The man lifts his paper again.

Claire turns around. Her heart's beating too fast. The house hems her in. The rooms and hallways remind her of the maze on the board game. Like she has to roll a die to find her way out.

No. It's just a house. The foyer is attached to the living room, like most houses.

She leaves the living room without saying anything to the man, who she assumes is Audrey's dad. She doesn't see Audrey's mom. But she makes it to the front door. It looks the same as when she arrived. Claire turns the lock and pulls it open and she has a moment of terror that she's not going to see Indianola.

But of course she does: There's the neat front yard, the weird rosebushes, Audrey's car parked in the driveway. Her bike leans up against the garage.

It's full dark.

Shaking, Claire leaves the house and picks up her bike. The day's heat lingers on the air, a reminder that it's not *too* late. But she's probably going to get grounded again.

She climbs on her bike and rides home.

⌒

The porch light is on at Grammy's house, glowing a sickly yellow. June bugs flit around it and cast pale shadows against the wall. Claire wheels the bike into the garage.

She starts formulating stories, excuses: We went to the beach and Audrey's car broke down. No, better: Someone sideswiped her and we had to deal with the insurance claims. Her parents took us to dinner and I didn't want to be rude. Her little brother got sick and we had to take him to the hospital—

Claire takes a deep breath. None of these sound believable; all of them could be checked on. Maybe she should just tell the truth. We played a game and lost track of time.

She goes inside.

The TV's blaring. It doesn't sound like the ten o'clock news. *Northern Exposure*, maybe. Claire creeps in, easing the door shut. The kitchen lights are off.

"Claire?"

Grammy doesn't sound angry. She doesn't sound worried either.

"I'm so sorry," Claire starts, moving into the living room. "We lost track of time—"

"It's all right." Grammy mutes the TV. Claire stops short. This is the last answer she expected.

"I didn't fix your dinner—" she starts.

"Oh, don't worry about that. I asked Carol Chase to bring me something from Munro's." Grammy twists around in her chair. "There are leftovers in the fridge, if you're hungry. Did Audrey feed you?"

Claire stares at Grammy. She has no idea what to think. Grammy gives her a pleasant smile.

"Well, I hope you had fun at least." She turns back around in her chair and picks up her remote. "Oh, and that Alvarez girl called. You know I don't like her."

She sounds angrier about Julie calling than about Claire coming home late. Claire backs out of the living room, into the kitchen. The refrigerator hums. Claire realizes she's starving. She hasn't eaten all day. They were playing that *game*. She can barely remember it now, only that it took a long time. Monopoly? It must have been Monopoly.

Claire opens the refrigerator. A little foam box sits on the shelf next to the bread and the pitcher of tea. She takes it out, dumps its contents on a plate—some kind of meatloaf, it looks like—and sticks it in the microwave. When it's done she takes the plate and a Coke and a fork into her bedroom. She wants to be away from Grammy and the constant chatter of the TV.

She's got a hollow feeling that stems from more than hunger, a sense that something's been carved out of her. That it's been hidden away, tucked out of sight. Obfuscated.

She puts on her music as she eats, that mix tape from Josh. Josh. God, she's hardly thought about him all summer. Funny how he was all she could think about in the spring.

When Claire finishes eating she doesn't feel satisfied, but she doesn't think food's going to help her. She thumps the plate on her desk and lies back on her bed and listens to the music swirling around the room. The lyrics seem nonsensical to her, the music discordant. She switches it off. The house is silent; no TV noise. Claire pushes off the bed and steps out into the hallway. All the lights are out. Grammy must have gone to bed.

She creeps into the kitchen and picks up the phone and dials Julie's number.

It rings twice. Julie picks up.

"Hey," Claire says. "I'm sorry about calling so late—"

"Not a big deal. We're all still up."

Julie's voice is like a favorite blanket. Claire slumps back against the wall, feeling relieved.

"I'm sorry about calling you earlier like that. My grandma wouldn't let me get to the phone and then she made me go hang out with Audrey."

"Oh God. I can't escape that girl, between you and Lawrence."

"It's not me!" Claire says in a fierce whisper. The last thing she wants is for Julie to think she actually *likes* Audrey. "It's Grammy. She keeps pushing us together!" She sighs. "Anyway, did you find anything out?"

"I talked to Mr. Vickery. The committee's big thing is that they can't intervene unless a monster actually hurts someone. But since there was property damage he said he'd look at the report."

Claire is struck with a kind of desperate hopelessness. "But that's his job, isn't it? To deal with renegade monsters?"

"Theoretically."

"What about the police? Or Lawrence? Did you talk to Lawrence?"

"The police don't handle the monsters. Out of their jurisdiction— human bad guys only."

Claire sinks back on her bed. "Are you sure we can't call, like, the National Guard?"

"Wouldn't work. If you try to talk about the monsters to someone who's not in town they just act like they didn't hear you."

This is basically what Audrey said, weeks ago, when Claire first learned about the monsters. She sighs.

"But I'll see if I can get Lawrence to help. I couldn't talk to him today, he was working and then studying, but I'll try to find out something tomorrow. And my dad's out of town right now, but when he gets home, I'll talk to him too."

Claire closes her eyes. "Thank you," she says softly.

"It's nothing, really. I don't like the idea of monsters messing with you."

Claire looks up at the ceiling. She feels warm. Flushed.

"Anyway," Julie says. "Do you still want to see *Aliens* next week? At the theater?"

"What? Aliens?" The word clangs in her head for a moment like a warning bell. Then she remembers. The first one was Julie's favorite movie. Monsters—fake monsters—stalking through a spaceship. They'd watched it together. It was good.

"Sure. I know it sounds nuts, but movies with made-up monsters always make me feel better about the real thing. It's like—if you make a movie about monsters, you can control what they do, y'know?"

"I guess." Claire rubs at her forehead. "But yeah, I'll go see it. Is there really a movie theater here?"

"Yeah. It's pretty crap and only has one screen, but they like to show old movies every now and then, and we are super lucky to get *Aliens*."

"Cool."

"I know! Friday night only. Do you want to come with me?"

"Sure," Claire says, and then her brain fills in, *It'll be like a date*. She blinks. Why did she think that?

"Awesome. I've already taken some time off work. I promise seeing this movie will make you feel better. It always does me. Works like a charm."

Claire isn't sure about that, but she still likes the idea of spending an evening out with Julie. It's a little glimmer of light in today's darkness. "I'll just have to butter up Grammy a bit. Do plenty of chores. But she did unground me, so I should be all right."

"Excellent."

They chat for a few minutes more, mostly about the movie and all of Julie's favorite parts. But then the conversation shifts, away from monsters entirely. They wind up talking for another hour. When Claire finally hangs up the phone, she no longer feels empty.

JULIE

Julie goes over to Lawrence's house as soon as she gets off work the next day. It's the middle of the afternoon, the sun blazing in the sky, heat radiating off the street in waves. She knocks on the door and waits. She called the sheriff's office before she left the exterminator's, and a gruff old man told her Lawrence isn't working today. She hopes he's home and not out on a date.

The door swings open. Lawrence stands on the other side. He looks pale and drawn, like he hasn't been sleeping. His hair is mussed too, which isn't like him.

"You okay?" Julie says.

"What? Yeah, I'm fine." Lawrence smooths his hair back. "What's up? I don't have time to really hang out—Audrey's coming over in a little bit."

Julie makes a face at the mention of Audrey's name.

"Don't be like that."

"Whatever. Look, I need to talk to you. It shouldn't take that long." Julie slides through Lawrence's door without waiting for an invitation. "How's Aunt Rosa?"

"She's doing well. Reading in her room."

Julie nods and moves into the living room. Lawrence switches on the standing lamp, and it floods the room with dim, golden light. "Is everything okay with you?"

"Everything's okay with *me*." Julie turns to look at him. "A monster attacked Claire two days ago."

Lawrence stares at her from his place next to the lamp. He crosses his arms over his chest. "Is she hurt?"

"No." Julie collapses down on the couch and scowls.

"Did you—*want* her to get hurt?"

"No! God. It's just—since no one got hurt, Mr. Vickery won't do anything about it. But the monster flung itself at her window! It broke the glass! That's got to be outside the treaties." She looks over at Lawrence. He's still staring at her, still has his arms crossed over his chest. "That's why I'm here."

Lawrence sighs.

"Come on, man! Serve and protect, right?"

Lawrence drops his hands to his sides and walks over to the couch. Sits down beside her. "Yes," he says. "But the monsters are outside our jurisdiction. You know that."

Frustration wells up inside Julie. Of course she knows it. Everyone in Indianola knows you don't call the cops when you see a monster. You call the exterminator.

"Please." Julie looks up at him, pleading. "This isn't normal monster stuff. They're targeting her. They know her *name*. Well, her grandma's name. But they're coming for her."

Lawrence frowns, a line forming down the middle of his brow. "How do you know that?"

"Because I've seen it!" Julie throws her hands up in frustration. "And I keep trying to tell Mr. Vickery, but he doesn't listen, and *Dad's* been out of town for the last two days, and you're my last hope." She shakes her head. "I even went to Aldraa back when they first started—"

"Who? Aldraa?"

"The head monster. I went to him and—"

"You talked to the *head monster?*"

"I was dropping off another monster that I'd picked up. I've talked to him before. It's really not that big a deal." Julie glares at Lawrence. "But he didn't make any sense—big surprise there. I'm *sure* something terrible's going to happen to Claire and no one cares and I can't get any answers."

"Calm down," Lawrence says, holding up his hands. "Back up. How do you know something terrible is going to happen to Claire?"

"I *told* you, a monster attacked her house yesterday morning. It broke her window. Forrest went out there to check it out but the monster was gone by then, but he still told me about the damage. And apparently the monster said something about astronauts, and that the astronaut was coming for her." Julie fixes Lawrence with a firm gaze. "It was a threat."

"It might have been a threat," says Lawrence thoughtfully. "Or it might have just been monster nonsense. Why would she be in danger from an astronaut?" He gestures out with his hands. "You see any astronauts around here?"

"You're not listening," Julie says. "I want you to do what cops do and investigate. Find out what the monsters want. The exterminator's not set up to deal with that kind of crap because we're just exterminators. No one thinks the monsters are anything more than a nuisance. But what if there's something else going on?"

188

"So that's why you want the sheriff's office involved," Lawrence says. "Because you think something else is going on?"

"Yes!" Julie pulls at her hair. "I mean, I don't know. Claire is scared, and I promised I'd help her. And the committee won't do crap, and I'm not going to Aldraa because he could be the one sending them, and that just leaves you." She juts her thumb at him. "You, or the sheriff's office, or whatever."

For a moment Lawrence looks at her. Then he says, "I think you're overreacting here. No one was hurt. If the monster could break the glass, then it could easily have hurt Claire or her grandmother. But it didn't."

"But—"

Lawrence holds up one hand. "You're only upset about this because you've got a thing for this Claire girl."

Julie's cheeks flush hot with anger and embarrassment. "That is *not* the only reas—"

The doorbell chimes, rippling through the house. Julie starts at the sound of it.

"That'll be Audrey," Lawrence says. "You're going to need to skedaddle."

"Who the hell says *skedaddle*?" Julie snaps.

Lawrence rolls his eyes and then gets up to answer the door. Julie sits on the couch, marinating in her anger. She knew this would happen. Lawrence is an adult now. He's content to sweep the monsters under the rug like the rest of the adults in town. Keep his distance. Let the treaties do all the work. He doesn't care that Claire's life could be in danger.

It's not just because I like her, Julie thinks. *It's not.*

Lawrence steps back into the living room, his arm wrapped around Audrey's waist. Julie glares at them, but Audrey just smiles back.

"Hi Julie," she says. "I hope you're doing well."

"She was having a minor emergency," Lawrence says. "But we've got it sorted now, don't we?"

"I had a wonderful time with Claire yesterday," Audrey says. "Absolutely wonderful. We played a game."

"Good for you," Julie says. And even though she knows Claire was only at Audrey's house because her grandmother made her go, part of her still stings with jealousy. "And no, Lawrence, we don't have my *minor* emergency sorted. No one's doing a damn thing to help—"

But Lawrence isn't listening. Audrey has wound her arms around his shoulders and is standing up on her tiptoes so she can nibble at his ear. Lawrence laughs softly, his face turning toward her.

"Dammit," Julie mutters. Audrey kisses Lawrence on the neck, and his cheeks turn pink as he glances over at Julie and then glances just as quickly away.

"I can see you're busy," Julie says, with as much ice as she can muster.

"I told you, Julie, I'd help you if I could, but it's outside my jurisdiction. Talk to your dad."

"Dad won't help." Julie stands up. Audrey's still kissing Lawrence, but Julie can see her glancing Julie's way too, her eyes bright and mischievous. Julie hates this. She hates that she's going to have go call up Claire and say there' s not a single force in town that will help her.

Not a single damn one.

⌐

Claire says she'll be able to get away from her grandmother's house for a few hours. She tells Julie to wait for her at the beach, and Julie does, sitting up on the gazebo that was built and dedicated to the bird watchers of Indianola. The only birds she can see are seagulls.

"Hey! Julie!"

Julie jumps at the sound of Claire's voice, then twists around to find her wheeling her bike across the sand. The wind whips her hair away from her eyes, and her legs and shoulders are bare, her skin gleaming in the blazing sunlight. She squints up at Julie and then props her bike against the side of the gazebo.

"You haven't been waiting long, have you?"

Julie shakes her head.

"I told Grammy I wanted to go out and get some exercise. She didn't question it." Claire hops up onto the gazebo. She looks so hopeful that Julie doesn't want to tell her the bad news. "So, did you find out anything? About that—that monster?"

Julie turns back out to the sea. The waves roll into the shore. "No," she says. "No one'll help us."

"What?" Claire sits down beside her, close enough that Julie can feel the warmth of her body. "Why not? Isn't that their jobs?"

"That's what I said." Julie slumps forward on her knees. "The committee won't do anything because no one was hurt—"

"My window broke!"

"Yeah, apparently they don't get bent out of shape about property damage. I went to Lawrence too."

"The sheriff's office," says Claire with a sigh of relief. "They *have* to do something."

Julie glances over at her. Claire's eyes are big and trusting and Julie hates every adult in Indianola for letting her down.

"They don't, actually." Julie sighs. "*Not within their jurisdiction.*" She says it in a high-pitched, mocking voice, and she thinks about Lawrence letting Audrey climb all over him. Figures that he'd turn out to be a typical guy after all.

"Not within their—" Claire is gaping at her. "But the monster *attacked* me. It came *straight at* me. I just—I can't believe this! What sort of cop doesn't care about that?"

All of them, Julie thinks. She looks out at the ocean again. "It's the adults in this town," she says. "They get used to the monsters. They don't imagine anything could change."

Claire makes a frustrated noise in her throat. "We should call the FBI or something."

"I told you, that won't work." Julie shakes her head. "I think the monsters do something to us. Like, not just to our memory." She frowns, turns back to Claire. "You can feel it, can't you, the way you just want to *accept* everything?"

Claire hesitates. Then she nods. Her cheeks are pink—from the sun or from exertion, Julie can't tell. They make her look like a girl in a magazine. "My thoughts go fuzzy, if I think about the monsters too much…"

"Exactly." Julie hesitates. Claire is still watching her, still looking hopeful. "We can't depend on the adults."

"Then what are we supposed to do?"

Julie thinks about this. The wind blows in off the sea, salty and cool. Claire is still looking up at her, like she expects Julie to have all the answers. Julie takes a deep breath.

Then she throws her arm around Claire's shoulders. Her heart hammers, and she can't believe she's doing this. But Claire only leans against her, and Julie can feel her bare skin against hers and it makes her brave.

"We'll just have to figure things out for ourselves," she says. "That's all."

The waves crash up against the shore. Claire doesn't say anything, but she doesn't pull away either.

CHAPTER

CLAIRE

Claire takes her time riding her bike back from the beach. Her thoughts ricochet around inside her head.

She thinks about the day of the monster attack, after the exterminator left. She wanted to call the police. Grammy told her not to bother, that the police didn't deal with the monsters. That as few people as possible are supposed to deal with the monsters.

Claire never did call, but she always assumed that had been one of Grammy's lies. And now Julie's confirmed it.

The police don't care.

The monster committee doesn't care.

And who else is there? Grammy seemed as unsettled by the monster attack as Claire was, but she hasn't mentioned it since it happened; in the end, she doesn't care either. Claire knows what will happen if she calls her mom: The monster's strange magic will work on her, and she'll ignore any comments about them and chastise Claire for not caring about her own grandmother, for being lazy and not wanting to work. She'll tell Claire this summer's good for her and then she'll say she's got a house viewing and that'll be it. And Claire knows Julie's right about

194

calling for outside help: She's seen for herself what happens when she brings the monsters up to someone outside the city.

Claire pulls up to Grammy's house. She stops in the driveway. The cicadas rattle in the trees, and the sound makes her tense, because it's a sound she's come to associate with the monsters. But the yard is empty. She hops off her bike and wheels it into the garage.

She goes inside. The house is dark and quiet. No chatter of voices from the TV. Claire slips into the hall and checks on Grammy's door— closed, and Claire can make out the soft hum of the fan behind it. Grammy's taking her afternoon nap, sleeping through the hottest part of the day.

Claire walks into the kitchen and checks the pillbox. The little white aspirins are still there, just like they were at lunchtime. Claire shoves the pillbox back on the windowsill. Another thing that makes no sense. Grammy doesn't look *well*. Most days, her skin is almost translucent, the dark shadows under her eyes deep. She barely moves from the TV to the bedroom to the kitchen table. She's practically a ghost.

Claire knows she can't keep feeding Grammy aspirin when she's so obviously sick.

She looks over at the phone numbers listed beside the phone. Her heart thumps. She wants there to be someone in Indianola who can help her, who can do what they're supposed to do.

Grammy's doctor's name and phone number stare at her, written out in her mother's neat handwriting.

Claire takes a deep breath. And then she walks across the kitchen and dials the number.

A woman answers on the third ring, voice bright and perky. "Dr. Byrne's office, how may I help you?"

"I'm calling about my grandmother," Claire says. "Myrtle Sudek? She was diagnosed with a wasting disease a couple of months ago and I'm her caretaker. My name's Claire Whitmore."

"Myrtle Sudek?"

"Yes. She was supposed to give permission for me to access her medical files." Claire's mother had insisted. "I'm really worried about her. She's not taking her medication."

The woman gives a sympathetic hum. "You poor thing. Let me check the records. Please hold."

The phone clicks over to tinny elevator music before Claire can respond. She leans up against the wall, her heart hammering, one ear listening to the music and the other listening for Grammy in the hall-way. But why feel nervous about Grammy? Claire is just trying to check up on her.

The music clicks away. "You said your name was Claire Whitmore?"

"Yes."

"Well, she did give you permission for her files, but other than that—there's nothing here. She hasn't been into the office in nearly eight months."

A heavy thud falls to the bottom of Claire's stomach. "What?"

"That's what it says. It looks like she gave you permission a few months ago, but she hasn't come in, and Dr. Byrne hasn't written a pre-scription for her. What'd you say she was diagnosed with again?"

"A wasting disease," Claire says, but the words are mealy against her tongue.

"You mean she's losing weight? There's really no such thing as a 'wasting disease'—you'll need to have her come in to see Dr. Byrne if you want to know—"

"I don't think she'll do that," Claire says. She doesn't want to be on the phone any longer. Her head is spinning. Grammy was diagnosed right at the end of the school year. She remembers the phone call, her mother sitting down at the dining room table, nails tapping as she nodded her head with the phone pressed against her ear. "Thank you."

Claire hangs up.

For a moment, she can only stand there, trying to breathe. Then she turns around until she can see the white pillbox sitting on the counter.

Maybe Grammy isn't sick. Maybe she is.

But either way, she's lying.

Julie was right, Claire thinks. They really are on their own.

The movie theater is small and shabby and smells like half a century's worth of stale popcorn, but the movie's full. Claire and Julie sit up in the balcony. It's the first time Claire has been out of Grammy's house since she rode her bike to the beach, and there's something comforting about being here, with Julie, surrounded by people.

"I'm gonna try and talk to my dad tomorrow," Julie says while they wait for the movie to start. "He's supposed to get back in tonight."

"Do you think he'll help?" Claire asks.

Julie sighs. "Honestly? Probably not, not if the committee said no. But I might be able to get some advice out of him." She brushes her hair out of her eyes and then looks over at Claire. "We're going to come up with something, I promise."

"I'll let you know if anything—shows up." Claire shivers. "But so far, nothing."

"There's hasn't been much at the exterminator's either. Just the ones that can't talk, and they haven't been coming into town, just wandering around by the beach houses."

Claire is sure that Julie means this as a comfort, but it only puts Claire further on edge, like the monsters are planning something.

Julie glances over at her. "Hey," she says. "Don't worry. It's going to be okay. And I promise the movie will cheer you up."

Claire smiles, doubtful.

"I'm serious," Julie says. "The best way to forget about monsters is to watch a monster movie. You'll see."

The lights dim then, and the audience falls into a quiet hush. When the movie starts, Claire stares at it, half comprehending, waiting for it to make her feel better.

Julie, though, leans forward through the entire thing, half draped over the railing, transfixed. When the movie gets too scary, the aliens gliding across the screen with slashing tails, Claire watches Julie instead, although she tries to be surreptitious about it, glancing at Julie out of the corner of her eye, at the light flickering across her face.

When the final alien is killed and the movie ends, scattered applause ripples through the theater. Julie pounds her hands together enthusiastically.

"That was awesome!" she says. "What'd you think?"

"It was good."

"Did it make you feel better about everything?"

Claire considers this question. She has to admit there is something soothing about movie monsters, about the idea that monsters can be controlled at all.

"Yeah, it really did."

"Perfect. I'm so glad."

I'm so glad. Claire smiles at that.

The crowd shuffles out of the theater as the credits roll, but Claire and Julie stay seated, waiting for the path to clear.

"Do you have to go home right away?" Julie asks.

Claire checks her watch. It's almost ten. "I wasn't sure how long the movie would be, so I told Grammy midnight."

Julie grins. "Sneaky."

Claire pretends to preen.

"So we've got two hours to tear up the town."

"Better make it good," Claire says. Up on the screen, film company logos rotate by.

"The Pirate's Den closes at ten," Julie says. "We could go back to my place, but I don't really feel like going home either."

"We're definitely not going back to my house."

Julie laughs. "No way. We could always go to the beach."

Claire doesn't answer. The lights come up in the theater.

"Indianola Beach is closed," Julie says, "but we can go down to the private beach along hurricane alley. My uncle has a house there and he's cool with us hanging out."

"Hurricane alley?" Claire looks over at her. "Isn't that where you're always catching monsters?"

"They haven't been going to the south end." Julie pushes back her hair. "I dunno, I just feel like being outside tonight. But we can go back to my house if you want."

Claire thinks about the beach at night, the crashing waves and the moon-lined shadows. She wonders if they'll see monsters, if those monsters will attack them. She's surprised when the idea gives her a thrill of excitement along with a shiver of fear. Maybe the movie *did* help her, more than she realized.

"Let's do it," she says.

They leave the theater. Julie chatters about the film, reliving all her favorite parts. Claire listens, nodding her head like she agrees.

They climb into Julie's car. Julie starts the engine.

"Lawrence always teases me about liking *Aliens*," Julie says. "He says we get enough aliens in Indianola."

Claire's heart skips like a record. "You think they're aliens too?"

Julie laughs. "I don't know what the hell they are. Another side effect of no one ever talking about the stupid things." They cruise down the empty street. Half the lamps are burned out, and the car creates long sliding shadows across the fronts of the shops. "When you're a kid, you ask questions about them: Are they aliens? Dinosaurs? What? But no adults will give you a straight answer." She frowns, staring ahead at the dark road. "And then one day it's like a switch turns off, and you just give up. Like we were talking about the other day."

Claire looks over at her. Every now and then the color from the traffic lights floods through the car, staining Julie like an Impressionist painting. She sighs, and her breasts swell beneath her tank top. Claire looks away, cheeks hot, wondering why she noticed something like that.

"You're really the only person who talks about the monsters with me," she says, because right now the monsters feel like a safer topic. "Everyone else acts like I should just ignore them."

"That's how they are." Julie nods. "They pretend it's totally normal. Even when new people move to town, after a while they just *accept* everything. Like, oh, it's too hot to go outside during the summer, and we're due for a hurricane this year, and monsters will creep through your backyard sometimes. Whatever causes it, I think it's the same thing that makes people forget when they leave the city limits."

Claire stares past her reflection in the window, out to the darkened town. She thinks about all the adults who have dismissed her concerns. Maybe accepting the monsters is a part of growing up. She's not sure what that means about growing up, though.

Julie turns off the main road, into a neighborhood of beach houses lined up on stilts. The world feels empty, and Claire shivers.

Julie parks at a house on the corner. The porch light is on, sallow yellow, and an old Buick from the 1970s sits lopsidedly among the weeds.

"Is this your uncle's house?" Claire asks.

"Sure is. He's probably asleep by now, but he won't mind if we park here. He knows my car."

They get out. The wind sweeps through the neighborhood, stronger than it had been down at the theater. It's late enough that the night's already starting to cool down, and the air's balmy and almost pleasant. Julie loops her arm in Claire's. The touch is startling.

"This way!" Julie says, pointing off toward the sand dunes. They lope forward with their arms entangled. Claire feels light, as if the wind could blow her away. It's not like the dizziness she gets when she sees the monsters. It's more like the dizziness she got whenever she saw Josh.

They creep through the dunes, Julie whispering that they need to watch out for rattlesnakes.

"Rattlesnakes and aliens," Claire says, but the wind whips her voice away. She can already hear the waves rushing along the shore. They sound louder at night than they do during the day.

She and Julie step out of the sand dunes. The water glitters silver in the moonlight, and the waves are high and frothy, the closest Texas comes to surfing waves.

"Wow," Claire whispers.

"I know, it's beautiful out here at night." Julie stares out at the sea, her hair rippling around her shoulders. "One of my favorite places in town. Even though technically we're trespassing, you know."

"But you said your uncle didn't care!"

"He doesn't." Julie laughs. "C'mon, let's go down to the water."

The sand looks silver in the shadows, as if they're walking across the surface of the moon. When they come to the waterline, Julie kicks off her shoes and splashes into the shallow film of water. She stomps around in it, laughing.

"I haven't been out here in forever," she says. "My mom would bring me to visit Uncle Michael, and she and him would sit out on his porch smoking while I came down to the water." She looks up at Claire, the wind whipping her hair around. "I used to pretend to be a monster-hunter."

Claire smiles, imagines a younger Julie creeping through the dunes, looking for clues. "Now you actually *are* a monster-hunter."

"Yeah, and it sucks." Julie grins. "Way more fun to pretend. Hey, which character from the movie are you?"

"What?"

"From the movie—regular ol' monster-hunting sucks, but what about hunting *super*-monsters?"

Claire laughs. The salt-tinged air makes her woozy, the way she felt when she had wine at a wedding two years ago. "You want to pretend we're in the movie?"

"Well, yeah. It's what I always did when I was kid to make me feel better about living in a monster-infested town." Julie grins. "What do you say? Want to try it out?"

Claire nods. "I guess."

"I call Vasquez. You want to be Ripley?"

"The main character?"

"Yep." Julie turns back to the dunes. "This is what I used to do when I went fake monster-hunting. Any dune without vines on it, that's a monster. You have to try and destroy it."

"How do you destroy a dune?"

"Kick at it and stuff."

Claire shakes her head. She feels silly and self-conscious, but there's something freeing about it too, being out here alone in the dark, under threat of monster attack, and instead of acting scared you just act brave.

Julie's already making her way across the beach. Her steps leave hollow trails in the sand. She tosses her shoes off to the side and then turns around at the start of the dunes.

"You coming?" she shouts.

"Is that how you talk to Ripley?"

Julie's laughter echoes down the beach. It makes Claire feel like they're the only people in the world. She runs over to Julie's side, the wind damp and cool against her skin. She never wants the sun to come up.

Together they survey the dunes.

"Nothing but vines," Claire says.

"Nothing but empty *hallways*," Julie corrects.

"Corridors. Isn't it *corridors* on a spaceship?"

"That was a planetary colony."

"Whatever."

Julie steps into the dunes themselves, and Claire follows, cautious. In the moonlight the dunes do sort of look like monsters, even the vine-covered ones—hulking and eerie, lying in wait. They rise up around Julie and Claire like a fence. At least they don't say anything about astronauts. At least looking at them doesn't make Claire feel like the world is leaning at a tilt.

Claire trips over a loose patch of sand and bumps up against Julie, her hand brushing the back of Julie's hand.

Julie intertwines her fingers with Claire's.

The movement is as natural as the wind, and although Claire is startled, she doesn't pull her hand away. She doesn't want to.

"There's one!" Julie shouts, pointing with her free hand.

"Get it!" Claire shouts, and they run forward, still holding hands, and kick at it.

Sand showers over their feet, glittering like diamonds. And there is one bright flash of a moment when the dune really is a monster, when it represents that constant miasma of anxiety that's been a part of Claire's summer since that first monster rose out of the grass and called her *girl*. When she looks at the dune, she sees the monster that launched itself at her window, that hissed *astronaut* and tried to crawl inside. She lets go of Julie and plunges her hands into the sand and flings it out onto the surrounding dunes. She's not just tearing apart a monster, she's tearing apart her fear. Anything that frightens her, she flings into the night air.

The sand makes a whispering sound as it falls, and that sound, that whisper, pulls Claire away from the beach. She's standing in Audrey's bedroom, a maze stretching out in front of her.

"Don't let its blood get on you!" Julie shrieks delightedly.

The vision evaporates and then Claire doesn't even remember

having it, only a vague sense that she stepped out of herself for a moment. She kicks at the dune, hopping around on one foot.

Claire and Julie have created a large, shapeless indentation into the side of the dune when they give up, collapsing down on their backs. To Claire it feels like being in their own world together, a place made out of soft moonlight and the sound of the ocean.

"Well, that was silly," Claire says.

"What, you don't want to be a kid again?"

Claire drops her head to the side and finds Julie looking at her. A dune vine is twisted against her cheek and tangled up in her hair, and it reminds Claire of a picture of nymphs she saw in her Latin textbook at school.

"I don't know," Claire says. "Seems there are some perks to being a grown-up."

Julie grins, and her whole face lights up and it's beautiful. "Yeah, I guess you get to do whatever you want. But you've already seen how worthless the adults are around here. They just go with whatever the town wants from them."

"Whatever the monsters want from them?" Claire says, her uneasiness about being out at night returning. She thinks of Audrey's house again. Why does she keep thinking of Audrey? She doesn't want to.

"Maybe." Julie falls silent, still watching Claire, and then she sits up. Claire's skin prickles. Her breath feels short. The night is perfect.

Julie leans forward. She puts her hand in Claire's hair. Claire doesn't understand what's happening.

And then Julie kisses her.

For half a second, Claire kisses back, and there's a flash of light behind her eyes like a supernova.

But then panic floods through her. *This isn't right this is wrong this is unnatural.* She squirms away, tearing through the dune vines. Julie sits back and she doesn't look angry or sad or disappointed, only resigned.

"I'm sorry," she says. "I shouldn't have done that. I thought you —"

"I-It's okay," Claire stammers. She hears an ocean inside her head. *I thought you wanted me to,* was that what Julie was going to say? "I'm not mad or anything, I just—I like boys."

She remembers the supernova flash behind her eyes. She thinks about Julie's bare shoulders and bare legs and tangled hair. The curve of her breasts beneath her shirt.

But Claire *does* like boys, she's certain of it, she's been pining over Josh since last year.

Julie stands up and dusts the sand off her shorts. Even now, even with embarrassment churning up her stomach, Claire doesn't want to look away, her movements are so graceful and lovely. But that's a normal thing, to admire another girl. It doesn't mean she *likes* her.

Julie tucks a piece of hair behind her ears, crossing her arms over her chest. "I'll take you home," she mutters, not looking Claire in the eye. "I'm really sorry."

She leaves, picking her way through the dunes. The sun didn't have to rise for the night to come to an end.

But Claire doesn't follow her right away. Instead, she sits there in the vines and thinks, *I'm straight, I like Josh, I'm straight,* while at the same time replaying the kiss in her head, that half second when she kissed back, when it was everything a kiss should be.

JULIE

Julie drives through a red light at the intersection on Main Street. She has her music turned up too loud, Exene howling about how the world's a mess. Julie gets it.

Stupid. Stupid stupid stupid.

Julie tears around the corner. Her stomach feels like it's falling into pieces. The movie, the beach—everything had been so romantic and perfect and Julie ruined it by taking a chance that she had never dared to take before. She doesn't blame Claire. It's Julie's fault. She knew better. She's known all her life that this is the way things are in Indianola. Like the monsters, like the treaties. Girls don't kiss girls here. In Austin they do. But not here.

Julie thinks about all the girls she's liked, all the way back to Mary McNally in second grade, which was when Julie figured it out. They used to walk around the playground together after lunch, running through the circuit of slides and jungle gyms and seesaws. They always ended up at the merry-go-round, which was Mary's favorite. On Valentine's Day Julie gave Mary a card she made out of construction paper and lace; Mary gave her one too that said *Best Friends*, and Julie, even at eight years old, understood that *Best Friends* wasn't exactly how she felt about Mary, although she didn't know any other way to put it into words.

Later, when she figured those words out, she still didn't say them. Not in this town, where the Pentecostal preacher shouts his sermons so loudly you can hear them from Julie's backyard on Sunday mornings. And her father, being a pillar of the community like he is—that's how Julie's mom put it when she found the *Hustler* in Julie's room last fall. Lawrence had kept the magazines secret for years, which made Julie lazy about hiding them. "Your father's a pillar of the community and you wouldn't want anything to disrupt that, would you?" She had the magazine rolled up so you couldn't see the woman on the cover. "This sort of thing—it's not what we want getting out. It could be very troublesome for our family."

That was all her mother had said about it. She didn't even seem angry. But it was clear she expected Julie to keep it a secret. Even Lawrence has told her she ought to keep it to herself until she goes to college.

Julie speeds through Indianola. It's like a maze she's been walking through for the last seventeen years and still not found the exit. Even the moonlight can't make these streets exciting.

She pulls onto Lawrence's street.

It's almost eleven o'clock, and her curfew on weekends isn't until one. She doesn't feel like going home, and Lawrence is the only person she knows who isn't judgmental about stuff that doesn't involve breaking the law. Out of all the people in Indianola, he's the only one who Julie actually wants to see right now. She just hopes he's not out with Audrey.

Only one of the windows in his house is lit up, the big one in the living room. Julie parks in his driveway and goes around to the back door. She lifts the big flowerpot of Mexican heather up from its usual spot, plucks up the key, dusts off the dirt. But when she sticks the key in the keyhole the door swings open, unlatched, revealing the dark, humming kitchen. A TV mutters in the background. Julie eases the door shut and sets the key on the counter and follows the glow of the TV.

Julie creeps into the living room. She knows she should have knocked at the front door like a civilized person, but right now she wants to feel like she belongs somewhere. The TV is switched to the news, droning on about President Clinton and denuclearization and NATO, and Aunt Rosa looks asleep, her head lolled at an angle. Lawrence sits in the other recliner, flipping through a textbook. Thank God Audrey didn't drag him away tonight.

"Boo," Julie says.

Lawrence jumps and the book slides off his lap and lands with a thud on the floor. Aunt Rosa jerks awake.

"What is it, Lawrence?" she gasps.

"It's just me," Julie says, and she sweeps in and kisses Aunt Rosa on the forehead.

"Should you be out this late?" Aunt Rosa reaches for a remote and changes the station to some late-night show.

"Curfew's till one. Felt like saying hi to my dear cousin Lawrence."

Aunt Rosa shakes her head, but she's smiling. She's used to Julie.

"What are you doing here?" Lawrence asks. "Is there a problem?"

Julie looks over the TV. The audience laughs at something the celebrity guest says. "Not exactly," she says.

"Do you want something to eat?" Aunt Rosa asks.

"Oh, no thanks."

Lawrence plucks his book off the floor and tosses it onto the coffee table. *Introducing Psychology.*

"Studying on a Friday night, eh?" Julie asks.

"Some of us are responsible. C'mon, let's go out back. Mom'll be going to bed soon."

Aunt Rosa waves her hand dismissively, her gaze fixed on the TV. Julie trails after Lawrence, feeling listless and unhappy. Normally Lawrence's house is enough to cheer her up. Not today.

Lawrence grabs the key off the counter as they go out the back door. The porch is narrow and crowded with Aunt Rosa's planters, so Julie kicks off her shoes and walks out into the backyard, her toes sinking into the grass. It reminds her of being out on the beach with Claire.

"Seriously," Lawrence says, "what's wrong? You haven't been bugging me the last few days."

"Yeah, because you keep disappearing with Audrey." Julie glances at him over her shoulder. "She okay with you studying on a Friday? Or did you two break up?"

"No, we didn't break up. She had plans." He walks over to her and they stand in his backyard, looking out toward the woods. Most of the stars are blocked by the trees. It'd be a good time to go shoot at targets, if it wasn't nighttime, if it wasn't dark. Or maybe the darkness is what makes it perfect. Julie's feeling reckless. That was the whole reason she suggested they go to the beach in the first place.

"Well, good for you," she says coldly.

Lawrence is staring at her, waiting for her to tell him what's wrong. God, he's really got that authority figure thing down.

"You're going to be the best cop," she tells him, finally. "I saw what you were studying in there. Psychology? You'll be inside the bad guys' *minds*."

"I'm already a cop," he says. "I'll be the best *detective*."

Julie smiles at that.

"Now tell me what's going on," he says. "Is it something with the monsters?"

"No. It's nothing. Just—teenager trouble. You don't want to hear about it."

Lawrence doesn't say anything, although she can sense his disapproval in the darkness. She wraps her arms around herself and steps up to the edge of the trees. She keeps replaying the kiss in her mind. The soft dry brush of Claire's lips against her own. The sweet fruity scent of Claire's shampoo. The barest hint of pressure when Claire actually *kissed back*—

That was Julie's first kiss. First kiss with a girl, anyway. First kiss that matters.

And Claire hated it.

Julie's eyes are wet, and she wipes at them like she can get the tears to evaporate before they fall. Lawrence's shoes crinkle against the grass, but Julie walks farther into the woods, like she can avoid him. It's stupid, going out here barefoot. She doesn't care.

"Julie!" Lawrence shouts, just as Julie hears a long, low hissing.

She freezes. The hissing sounds mechanical, like steam releasing from a valve. It comes from everywhere. She whips her head around and sees nothing but dark underbrush.

Another rush of hissing.

And then, through the trees, a glint of silver eyes.

"Can you talk?" she asks. It's an automatic response, the first thing she was taught to say when she joined up with the exterminators.

"Can you?" It's not so much a voice as it is a modulation in the hissing. Julie glances over at Lawrence and finds him half crouched, as if he's about to leap.

Julie turns back to the eyes. They jerk to the right, then steady themselves, floating in the darkness.

"It appears I can," she says flatly.

The monster moves into a fragment of moonlight. At first all Julie sees is oily gray skin, undulating like a giant slug. She takes a step back.

"You're not supposed to be out here," she says.

"I was looking for you." The monster rears up. Branches snap and shredded leaves shower around it, this mass of gray skin offset only by those silver lamplight eyes.

Lawrence bounds over to her side, holds his fists out in a fighting stance. The monster ignores him and looks straight at Julie.

"Why?" Lawrence says in his cop voice. "Why were you looking for her? She's an exterminator, it's spelled out in the city codes—"

"I'm not going to speak to him," the monster says to Julie. "I'm going to speak to you."

Julie's whole body is sick with fear. This monster is demanding, self-possessed, terrifying.

God, why didn't the committee *listen*?

The monster lurches closer to her, oozing over the ground, revealing itself in patches of moonlight. She doesn't dare look away as it slithers forward, its tail sluicing over dirt and dead fallen leaves. It fixes its glowing eyes on her and Julie takes a deep breath, trying to steady herself, to keep from passing out. If she can just make it through this, then her dad and the committee will have to listen. They'll have to.

The monster stops.

"She's been hidden from us," the monster says.

Julie blinks, trying to find a place on the monster's flat, slimy face she can actually look. She settles on the spot between its eyes and the narrow slit of its mouth.

"W-Who has?" she stammers out.

"The Sudek," the monster says.

Julie's heart jumps around inside her chest. "The Sudek? You mean Claire?" Saying her name feels painful, even with the monster bearing down on her. *Stupid.*

"The one to save us from the astronaut. She's been hidden away. We suspect the astronaut, the astronaut's maze. The astronaut knows that we know, that we are getting too close."

"The astronaut!" Julie shrieks. "What is with this freaking astronaut?"

Her voice echoes around the trees, melting into silence. She's rooted to the ground, her only movement the rise and fall of her chest. She cannot catch her breath. She's not sure she ever will again.

The monster shudders all over like an enormous, revolting Jell-O. "*Da zsa ful zsu sho,*" it says. "That is our word for it. Is that easier for you to understand?"

"No," Julie says. "And what do you mean Claire has been hidden away? I just—" She stops, her head swimming. "I just *saw* her. Did something happen—did you do something—"

The monster's mouth drops open and it lets out a long hiss. Julie jumps backward. The air takes on a stale, cold smell. Metallic.

"She is still here," the monster says. "That is good. But she's been hidden from us. We can't *see* her. Which means we can't help her."

Julie senses movement off to her side—Lawrence? But when she looks over at him, he's frozen, watching them carefully. She whips her head back toward the monster. Its mouth has sealed back up again. Its eyes glow.

"I don't understand," she says. "What do you want with Claire? Help her with what?"

"She is the key."

And then the darkness moves. Something slimy and hot slaps against Julie's bare leg and knocks her to her back. Her head slams hard against the ground and she stares up at the stars in a daze. They twinkle with the far-off light of other suns.

"Let her go!" Lawrence shouts. "I'm a deputy with the sheriff's—"

"You don't understand," the monster tells her, "but I can show you."

"What?" Julie looks up just as she's dragged forward over the ground. The monster's tail is wrapped around her ankles, a thick, disgusting coil. Julie screams. She hears Lawrence shouting her name, but his voice is far away, on the other side of a wall. The stars blur together into lines.

"I'll show you," the monster repeats.

Julie blinks.

Julie blinks, and she's not in Lawrence's backyard anymore.

The stars are still overhead, still streaked into lines across the sky, tangled and twisted up like knotted yarn. But she's lying on her back in thick mulchy soil, and the air is thick and humid and hot, the inside of a sauna.

Something wriggles over her bare ankle.

Julie shrieks and kicks it off. She sits up, her head spinning. Walls rise up on all sides, coated in thick, ropy vines, flashes of yellow and silver eyes blinking at her from the shadows.

She's in the power plant. The roof is gone, but she's in the power plant.

"What— How did you—" She struggles to her feet and immediately swoons, the strange air of the power plant going straight to her head. The monster stands a few paces away from her. It oozes over the soft ground, and its eyes flash, overly bright in the darkness.

"Take me back!" Julie shouts. "You aren't allowed to do this! It's against the treaty!"

"It's against the treaty to harm you," the monster says in its hissing-steam voice. "And I am not going to harm you. Only show you. Look up."

Julie doesn't move. It's her only act of defiance.

The monster slumps down. It almost looks as if it's sighing. "I had to bring you here," it says. "I could not stay in the outside for long. The air isn't right for me." It pulls its head back, flesh rippling all the way down its body. Julie shudders. "But I can show you the timelines."

This time, Julie looks up, compelled by curiosity. The roof is still gone, and the stars streak across the sky.

"Look," the monster says.

"I am!" Julie clutches at her stomach, trying to soothe her quaking fear.

"Look at the timelines."

"The timelines," Julie whispers. She squints up at the streaking stars. *Timelines.*

Desperation tugs at the edges of her thoughts. "I don't understand," she says. "Just freaking explain it and let me go!"

"Look."

"I'm looking!"

And then Julie sees it. One of the lines of light brightens and jerks up, tracing a new path through the ink of the sky.

"A change in the timeline," the monster says. "In this room only, you can see them, shifting and eroding. A timeline brought us here, and it must remain stable, unchanged."

The brightened line drops back to its original position.

"Like that," the monster says. "It must stay like that."

The monster falls silent. The glow in the starline disappears, and then that line fades in with all the others. *Timelines,* Julie thinks, and she has a sudden image of her life and Claire's life as two lines of light intersecting in the summer of 1993. A moment was changed that day she went to Mrs. Sudek's to capture a monster. Julie has never thought of her life in those terms before—she always dreams of the future, not the present and certainly not the past. But now she understands that the future and the past are part of the same line. They cannot be separated.

"The astronaut came here to re-create the past with cosmic magic," the monster says. "And in so doing, the timelines will be knotted and confused. The past will become the present, the present the past. And both will change."

"*What?*" Julie says.

"We do not know why the astronaut wishes to do this. We tried to warn the Sudek but we could never get close enough to her to show her all this."

Julie looks up at the sky again, the tangle of starlight. Timelines.

"So you're warning me," Julie says. A shiver works up her spine. "Is Claire in danger? The Sudek?"

"We do not know." The monster inches forward over the thick ground. "We only know that things must happen as they did. If the timelines are disrupted this town will no longer exist. The astronaut must not understand that. But we do."

Julie shakes her head. "You want me to *save the town*? Why do you care?"

"For us—if the town vanishes, our own history changes. We came here to escape annihilation and if the past is changed we will be annihilated for certain. And you will be annihilated too. Surely that distresses you."

"Of course it distresses me! I just don't understand what you're asking me to do!"

"Stop the astronaut. You are cosmically linked, you and the Sudek."

"I don't know what that means!" Julie cries. "Can I talk to Aldraa? Can he help?"

"Aldraa is no expert," the monster says. "He's merely a politician."

"What?" Julie's momentarily slammed by that particular revelation—they have politicians?

"I'm sending you back now," the monster says. "You've seen the timeline. You know it must stay unchanged, lest we die and you disappear."

"What? No!" Julie lunges toward the monster, ignoring her fear, her quiver of disgust. "You didn't explain anything! I have no idea what's going on—"

The monster stares at her with its silver eyes.

She trips on a slick patch on the ground, stumbles, catches herself before she falls. But when she looks up, she's no longer in the swampy heat of the power plant. She's in Lawrence's backyard, the air cool against her skin, the trees rustling in the breeze.

She looks up, and the stars are fixed points of light in the distance. "Julie?"

It's Lawrence. Julie whirls around to find him rushing toward her.

"Are you all right?" He speaks in the brisk, even tones Julie's always associated with TV cops, but she can see the wild light of fear in his eyes. "It looked like you disappeared. I thought—"

"It took me to the power plant," Julie says.

"What!? Are you hurt? We need to call Uncle Victor right now—"

"I'm fine. I was only there a few minutes. It just—talked to me. About nonsense." Except Julie doesn't think it's nonsense. She thinks she just doesn't understand it.

And the town might be in trouble. And Claire—Claire too—

"That's not even possible." Lawrence pinches the bridge of his nose. "I only lost sight of you for a few seconds. There's no way it could have dragged you all the way to the power plant."

"I don't know. I'm just saying what happened. I'm fine, though."

"You still need to tell Uncle Victor," Lawrence says. He's back in his no-nonsense cop's voice. "He should be back in town by now, right? And we'll need to file a report about it, I'm sure." He pauses. "With this happening, and me seeing it—I might be able to help you, like you were asking."

Julie nods. She shakes with leftover adrenaline. The memory of the timelines is starting to fade. It feels like a dream. Not a nightmare. The nightmare was the moment Claire pushed away from her.

"I'm taking you home," Lawrence says.

"Dad'll be in bed. I can tell him tomorrow. I was already planning on talking to him anyway."

"I realize that. But you don't need to drive home by yourself so late.

Come on." He jerks his head back toward the house. Julie doesn't protest. The monster's dry hiss of a voice keeps going around in her head like a fragment of a melody. Whenever she closes her eyes she sees the trace of the timelines.

She stays close to Lawrence as he hurries back into the house. They step into the yellow pool of the porch light, and she's grateful she isn't alone.

⌐

Julie wakes up the next morning feeling blurred, as if she's a painting someone spritzed with turpentine. Her alarm is clanging on her bedside table, and she turns it off and then rolls onto her side and shoves her pillow over her head. Pink light still filters through.

She thinks of the timelines.

She thinks of the monster dragging her to the power plant.

She thinks of Claire, pulling away from their kiss, stuttering apologies, scrambling backward over the sand.

Julie throws the pillow on the floor. Sunlight floods her room. She wonders if she ought to feel angry at Claire. She doesn't. It's just an intense, drowning sadness, the sort of thing that can't be cured. Only the symptoms can be treated. Like the flu.

But on top of that, there's the same worry from before that Claire is in danger, that the monster wasn't sputtering nonsense. *She's hidden from us.* But she's not hidden from Julie. What was it they said hid her away—the astronaut's maze? Julie doesn't know of any mazes around here.

Julie pushes herself out of bed. She set her alarm so she could catch her dad before he disappears off to work. She's in no condition to go driving around town trying to find him; she shouldn't have driven last night. Her heart's broken. And you can't operate heavy machinery with a broken heart.

She goes downstairs, following the scent of breakfast, and finds her dad at the table, the newspaper scattered in front of him. His customary cup of coffee—black—steams at his side. He takes a drink without looking up from the paper.

Julie raps on the doorframe to get his attention.

"Morning, Dad," she says. "You have a good trip?"

He keeps reading for another couple of seconds—*Senate Okays Space Station, Microsoft Previews New Windows OS*—before glancing up at her. "I did, although it seems my daughter was replaced while I was gone. Not used to seeing you so early."

"I didn't sleep well." Julie doesn't expand on that, shivering at the thought that she could be replaced. She definitely doesn't mention the unsettling dream she had about an astronaut walking across the beach, hand in hand with Claire. Claire had peered over her shoulder, the wind blowing her hair into her eyes. She was beautiful, and Julie woke up, and that was the last of the sleep she was going to get.

"Mmm," her dad says, returning to his paper.

"I've been needing to talk to you for the last few days," Julie says.

Her dad peers at over the top of his glasses. He doesn't like it when you dance around the subject; his time, he says, is valuable, even with his family. "What is it?"

"It involves the monsters." She's certainly not going to tell him about what happened with Claire.

"Monsters? Was there an issue? Did you follow the procedure for when I'm away? Let Brittany know?"

"It's not like that," Julie says, cutting him off before he starts in on

220

one of his procedure rants. Her fear is too sharp to deal with it this morning.

Her dad frowns. He's already got on his suit and tie, and that makes him intimidating, not comforting. "What exactly happened, Julie?"

Julie presses up against the doorframe. She takes a deep breath. "My friend Claire—Claire Whitmore, Mrs. Sudek's granddaughter—was attacked by a monster a few days ago. Well, not quite attacked—I mean, it attacked her house, not her. Forrest went out there, couldn't find the monster. He filed a report, but Mr. Vickery doesn't care because no humans were hurt."

Her father watches her. "Well, yes. He's bound by the statutes of the treaties." He sighs. "Really, Julie, you should know this by now. You'll be taking over my spot on the committee someday."

Julie bites back the urge to argue and instead tries to steady her breathing. "Look, I do know, okay? But then...last night...something else happened."

His brow furrows. "Go on."

"I was at Lawrence's," she says. "And a monster came out of the woods, and it—it dragged me to the power plant. I think it was the power plant. I'm pretty sure."

"What?" he says sharply. "It *dragged* you?"

"That's not exactly right," Julie says. "It didn't, like, drag me, it *took* me—just for a few seconds—"

Her dad holds up one hand. "No. Stop. *That* may be a treaty violation." He frowns. "It didn't hurt you, though?"

Julie shakes her head.

"And you said it *didn't* do the same thing to your friend? That it just attacked her house?"

"Yeah, but Claire is pretty sure it was trying to get to her, it just couldn't. It cracked her window."

"Okay, I'll look at the report when I go into the office today. Now, this monster, when it dragged you off—what the hell did it want? Did you let it know you're an exterminator?"

"Yes! I know how to deal with the monsters when they're acting normal!" Julie's voice pitches forward in a panicked whine. "It wasn't about me. I told you, it had to do with Claire. The monster kept talking about an *astronaut* and how Claire's been hidden."

"Hidden?" Her dad looks up at Julie with concern. "Has she gone missing?"

"I just saw her last night. I think she's okay." Julie looks down at her lap. "I don't know. I should call her—" She moves toward the phone, but her dad stops her, one hand laid across her arm.

"In a second," he says. "Your mother's going to kill me when she hears about all this. Were you supposed to go into work today?"

Julie shakes her head. She'd taken off because of the movie last night—because she knew she'd be spending the evening with Claire. That's what she gets for being optimistic.

"Good. I'll let Eric know you're not going to be working there for the time being." Her dad drops his hand away and slumps back in his chair. "Dammit, I didn't need this today. We'll file a complaint and have Forrest look into it."

It takes Julie a moment to register what her dad just said. She won't be working at the exterminator's anymore. That's all it took, a semi-kidnapping and a few moments of terror. All her dad's talk about setting up her future in town and how monster-catching was teaching her more useful skills than college ever would didn't amount to much when she was actually put in danger.

She wonders what this means, if he and the rest of the committee will actually do something now about keeping Claire safe.

"We'll put you on at the hotel," her dad says, almost distractedly.

"What?" Julie says, although she should have known she wouldn't get the rest of the summer off. Not that she wants to, not after what happened with Claire.

"Or the video store, would you like that better?"

Julie's heart gives a leap despite everything. "You know I would."

Her dad snorts. "This wasn't supposed to be dangerous. You know that. But if something is changing—" He shakes his head. "Hopefully we can get this sorted out, get you back at the exterminator's in no time. It's important."

Julie doesn't respond.

"Let me finish my coffee," her dad says. "Then we'll file the complaint and make sure the committee hears about this. And I'll call Frank and have him get your paperwork started." He looks up at her. His eyes are hard, steely, the eyes of a businessman. "Don't think you're getting out of learning the family business, though. You're an Alvarez. Dealing with the monsters is what we *do*."

Then he picks up the newspaper again. Nothing disrupts his morning routine. Not even monsters dragging his daughter away or trying to attack her friend.

"I'm going to get dressed," she says.

"Good." Her dad flips a page of the newspaper. "Don't dawdle. We need to get this taken care of."

Julie doesn't mention that he's the one reading the newspaper and sipping at his coffee. Instead, she goes up to her room and picks up the phone and dials Claire's number from memory. She could have called from the kitchen, but she doesn't want her dad eavesdropping on the conversation.

Her heart riots inside her chest, and every time the phone rings on the other end it's like nails scratching down a chalkboard. Then the line clicks. Someone's answered.

"Hello?"

It's Mrs. Sudek, her voice raspy-rough. Julie is stunned into silence.

"Hello? Anybody there? I don't have ti—"

"Mrs. Sudek," Julie says, to fill the space. "It's Julie Alvarez. I really need to speak with Claire—"

"Claire is busy right now. I'll tell her you called."

Julie is struck hard in the chest with a peculiar mixture of relief, that Claire is not missing, and misery, that she can't speak to her. Can't try to apologize for her actions last night.

"Okay, then—"

Mrs. Sudek hangs up.

Julie sighs and replaces the receiver. Her head feels fuzzy. She wonders if Claire told her grandmother what happened. Her parents will kill her if the whole town finds out her secret.

The room feels like it has lost all of its oxygen, but still Julie drifts over to the closet, to get dressed to face the day.

CHAPTER

CLAIRE

The next morning stretches out long and empty.

Claire doesn't tell Grammy what happened with Julie. It's not any of Grammy's business. It's no one's business but hers.

Anytime the memory starts to resurface, Claire pushes it away and thinks about Josh instead. It's hard to think about him, though. It's been so long since she's seen him that his face is half-blurred in her mind, and she can't remember what his voice sounds like. She used to get warm whenever she thought of him. Now she doesn't. His memory is flat and pleasant and completely unremarkable.

Julie keeps trickling back into Claire's thoughts. She thinks about Julie's movie room, and playing SNES, and going to the beach, and eating pizza at the Pirate's Den. She thinks about the first time she and Julie played *Ms. Pac-Man* together. When one memory gets in, the others follow, like a flood.

That afternoon, during the hottest part of the day, Claire goes outside and turns the sprinkler on and stretches out underneath its spray of water in her bathing suit. It's the only thing she can think to do in the heat. She stares up at the bleached sky and listens to the cicadas as the water falls in rhythmic bursts across her skin. The grass prickles against the back of her body. She thinks about the kiss.

It wasn't Claire's first kiss—that honor belongs to Ethan Cosgrove, a boy who asked her to homecoming two years ago. Their lips brushed across each other in the front seat of the station wagon his parents let him borrow for the evening. The kiss had made Claire's whole body light up, but at the same time she felt like she was taking part in some complicated rite of passage, and everything about the evening—the awkward swaying beneath Christmas lights, the itchy fabric of her dress, the unfamiliar shellac of hairspray in her hair—had all been elements of that rite, a lead-up to the kiss.

The kiss with Julie was different.

The kiss with Julie was like the beach last night, dark and laced with shimmers of danger and moonlight. The kiss with Julie was something pure, something Claire isn't sure she understands.

Because she's straight. She can't love a girl.

Can she?

The sprinkler *tch-tch-tchs* its way across Claire. The drops of water catch in the sunlight and form rainbows that flicker in and out of existence like images on a breaking-down projector. Those rainbows feel like Julie's kiss. They're beautiful and strange and Claire can't quite grasp on to them.

It doesn't matter anyway. Claire shoved Julie away in her confusion, and now she hasn't heard from her. Every time she passes the phone she wills it to ring, even though she hasn't decided what she's going to say to Julie.

Another cascade of water from the sprinkler. It's warm as bathwater from the sun, but when the sea breeze kicks in Claire almost feels cool. She settles deeper into the grass, lets the haze of heat overtake her. There's no point in thinking about Julie. There's no point in thinking about anything.

"Oh my God, what are you doing?"

It takes Claire a moment to place the voice.

"Audrey?" She pushes herself up on her elbows and cranes her head back. Audrey stands on the patio and waves.

"Haven't seen you in a while!" she calls out. "Thought I'd say hi."

"Yeah." Claire slumps back down on the lawn. The sprinkler makes another pass in her direction. The thought of dealing with Audrey Duchesne right now exhausts her.

"Anyway, what is this? A sprinkler?" Audrey walks across the yard. Claire drops her head and watches her approach sideways.

"Yeah," she says. "I was hot."

"Right, no AC." Audrey laughs. Her hair glints in the sun. It hurts Claire's eyes. "I came over to talk about the Stargazer's Masquerade. When I called, Mrs. Sudek said you were available to chat."

The cicadas' rattle swells when Audrey says *Stargazer's Masquerade*. Claire forces herself to sit up. "Yeah," she says. "I'm not sure I want to go."

Audrey's face darkens like a storm cloud. "What? Why not?"

"I don't know, I just—" Claire watches the water from the sprinkler. *I just don't want to go without Julie.* Why is she thinking that way? "Aren't you going to go with Lawrence Reyes anyway?"

Audrey laughs. "Well, of course, but I still want you to come with us! A double date."

"I don't have a date."

"I'll get you one."

Claire closes her eyes. "I'm just not sure I want to go, okay?"

"Did you not get Abigail Sudek's dress?"

Audrey's voice is close, right in Claire's ear. But Audrey herself is still several feet away, out of range of the sprinkler.

"The dress," Claire says, feeling dazed.

"Your costume," Audrey says brightly.

"It won't fit."

"Have you tried it on?"

Claire shakes her head. The dress is hanging on the back of her closet door. Every morning it swishes past her as she pulls out her day's clothes.

"We should do that right now."

Claire doesn't say anything. She really doesn't want to go through the humiliation of not even being able to pull the dress over her hips.

"Come *on*," Audrey says, and she actually stamps her foot in the grass. "You can't just lie outside all day."

"Pretty sure I can," Claire says.

The sprinkler tosses water over her again.

"But it's the Stargazer's Masquerade," Audrey says, and her voice has a strange, reverberating timbre to it. "You need to try on that dress."

Claire's thoughts blur. The water on her skin feels too cold, despite the sun blazing overhead.

"Fine," she says. "But it's not going to fit."

"We'll see," Audrey says in a singsong.

Claire sighs and pushes herself up. She shakes out her hair and brushes the flecks of grass off her skin. The cicadas buzz, and for a wild, stupid moment Claire wishes a monster would come ambling through the yard, so she could have the excuse of calling up the exterminator. Of calling up Julie.

But the yard remains empty.

"I'm so excited to see how it's going to look on you," Audrey says.

"You're going to be disappointed." Claire hops up onto the patio, drops of water trailing after her. "Nothing made for a hundred-pound woman in a corset is going to fit me."

Audrey just smiles at that, and something in her smile gives Claire a chill.

When they go inside, Grammy's awake from her afternoon nap and has the TV on—Claire recognizes *As the World Turns*. Grammy glances up as Claire and Audrey traipse through the living room.

"Hello, Audrey," she says, her voice flat and measured.

"Hey, Mrs. Sudek!" Audrey throws her arm around Claire's shoulder and Claire has to resist the urge to shrug it off. "We're trying on Claire's costume for the Stargazer's Masquerade."

"Ah yes. Well, have fun." Grammy turns back to the TV. She doesn't ask about the costume itself. Maybe she saw the dress hanging in the closet.

Claire grabs a towel out of the bathroom before going into her bedroom. Audrey plops down on her bed, making herself at home. The sight of it rubs Claire raw.

"So where is it?" Audrey asks.

"In my closet." Claire rubs the water out of her hair and then pulls the closet door open. The dress flutters.

Audrey breaks into a huge grin. "It's just beautiful, isn't it! Oh, that color will go *perfectly* with your skin tone."

"Right." Claire pulls the dress off the hanger and holds it up to her body. The dress is tiny. She smooths it down against her stomach.

"Put it on!" Audrey cries.

"Over my swimsuit?" Claire stiffens with irritation. She feels like Audrey's trying to embarrass her. She has to see that there's no way the dress is going to fit.

"Yeah, just to see how it'll look. Then we can start talking about hair and makeup."

It bothers Claire that Audrey's talking about the dance as if Claire has agreed to go—which she *hasn't*—but she sighs and tosses the dress onto the bed.

"Help me undo the buttons," she says. Attempting to try it on is probably the only way to get Audrey to shut up.

"Awesome!" Audrey hunches over the dress. Together they undo the dozens of tiny buttons running in a line down the back of the dress. Then Claire picks it up and pulls it over her head. She expects it to catch on her boobs so that she's left standing with a mass of century-old silk draped over her head. But to her surprise the dress slides down over her waist and hips, settling into place with a sigh.

"What the—" Claire turns in place, trying to make sense of this miraculous fit.

"Told you!" Audrey jumps up from the bed and grabs Claire by the shoulders and sets her into place. "Let's do up the buttons. Just to get a sense."

"There is no way—"

"It's totally fitting."

And it is. Audrey's fingers brush against Claire's back as she slips each one into place.

"This is impossible," Claire says. "You saw when I held it up to me. It was half my size!"

"It must have just looked small," Audrey says.

Claire doesn't answer, only stares over at her vanity as Audrey finishes up the buttons. She knows it didn't just look too small. It *was* too small.

"There!" Audrey steps back. "I didn't button up all of them, but this should be enough to give you a general idea."

Claire lifts up her skirts and walks over to the vanity mirror. She can only see part of herself, her waist and hips. The dress skims over her silhouette, not too tight and not too big.

"You look *amazing*," Audrey says, her voice gushing with delight. "You'll have the best costume there! I'm thinking of going as a hippie, so we can be like, young ladies through the ages."

Claire bends down, trying to catch more of a glimpse of herself in the mirror. The bodice of the dress fits as well as the rest of it, and the fabric shimmers as if threaded through with silver. Despite her damp hair and the nights of fitful sleep and her current lack of makeup, in the dress Claire's skin seems to glow. She gathers up her hair and piles it on top of her head and for a moment she doesn't even recognize herself.

"This is going to be so much fun!" Audrey's face appears alongside Claire's in the mirror. The illusion shatters, and Claire drops her hair. "Now we'll just have to get you a date! Don't worry, though, I have a plan."

"What?" Claire straightens up and looks at Audrey. "No, that's really not necessary."

"Don't be silly." Audrey claps her hands together. "He's a trainee with the sheriff's office named Christopher. He's *dreamy*, although not as dreamy as Lawrence, of course." She giggles. "I'm planning to meet up with him and Lawrence later tonight, if you want to come."

"I still haven't decided if I want to go to the dance at all."

"Of course you want to go!" Audrey takes Claire's hand and twirls her around. The dress flares out at the waist, the fabric stirring up a soft breeze in the hot room. "Look at you! When else will you have an opportunity to wear a dress like this?"

Claire doesn't have an answer to that. Audrey lets go of her hand and Claire sits down in front of her vanity. Claire stares at the glass, then lifts one shoulder as coquettishly as she can. A pretty dress and a date with a boy. Her thoughts are fuzzy with the promise of normalcy.

"I'll go with you tonight," Claire says. "And meet this guy. And then I'll let you know."

Audrey floats in the mirror behind her, and when Claire says that, Andrey's whole face erupts into a dazzling smile.

⌐

Audrey promised to pick Claire up around ten o'clock. Grammy usually goes to bed long before then, but tonight she stays up, the glow from the TV casting long, eerie shadows across the living room. She's thin enough that Claire thinks she can see her skull beneath her skin.

"I hope you girls have fun," she says when *Scattergories* goes to commercial break.

Claire looks over at her. "You're not worried about me going out drinking? It's so late."

"You'll be with Audrey."

Claire sighs. They sit in silence until the doorbell rings. Claire jumps up to answer it, aware of Grammy leaning out of her chair to peer into the foyer.

Audrey stands outside, bathed in yellow porch light, dressed in a lime-green minidress, body shimmer sparkling on her collarbone. Claire smiles at her, but really she's thinking about the night that Julie knocked on her window and they stayed up late reading the letters Abigail had written Javier.

She shouldn't think about Julie. Audrey's taking her to meet a boy, a perfect way to prove to herself that she's completely normal, and that the daydreams about the kiss are just an ordinary part of growing up.

"Ready to go?" Audrey asks.

Claire nods, even if she isn't so sure.

"Have fun!" Grammy calls out from the living room.

"We will!" Audrey calls back.

Claire feels like plans are being made over her head.

She and Audrey go outside and climb into Audrey's car. Claire isn't sure where they're going exactly, only that they're meeting Julie's cousin, Lawrence. She really hopes Julie hasn't told him what happened.

"You'll love Christopher," Audrey says as she starts the engine. "He's such a sweetheart." She glances at Claire. "He just graduated this past May, so, you know, he'll be more mature than a high school boy."

Claire gazes out the window as Audrey pulls onto the road. The streetlights flicker across her face. She wonders if Christopher will be anything like Josh, with his skinny build and long, dyed-black hair. She knows he'll be nothing like Julie.

Why should he be like Julie?

Claire wraps her arms around her stomach and focuses her attention on the roar of the engine. Lawrence and Christopher. That's totally normal, right? Two girls staying out late so they can meet up with guys. One hundred percent normal.

They drive for about ten minutes, and then Audrey pulls up to a playground next to a church. All the church lights are off except for a big spotlight focused on a cross, but a pickup truck is parked in the square lot, with two guys sitting in the back. One's drinking from a can. The other's Lawrence, his lanky frame familiar even in the darkness. So that's how normal this is going to get, Claire and Audrey meeting boys to drink beer. And Grammy was worried about *Julie* getting Claire drunk. All she and Julie ever did was watch movies and play video games and go to the library, for God's sake, speeding through microfilm to read about their ancestors.

And Claire looked forward to those days far more than she's looking forward to this. Her eyes are on Lawrence. It's only been a day. Julie probably hasn't told him.

Audrey parks next to the pickup truck. Christopher looks nothing like Lawrence, although he is closer to Claire's idea of a cop. He has muscular shoulders beneath his tight T-shirt, and heavily gelled hair and bland features. He lifts his can. "How's it going?" he calls out, his voice muffled through the closed windows of Audrey's car.

"Look at Lawrence," Audrey says with a sigh. He's slouched down in the bed of the truck, looking uncomfortable. He doesn't wave at them like Christopher does. It seems odd to Claire that Lawrence is sitting in that truck while an underage trainee drinks a beer. It doesn't fit with what Julie told her about him.

Then again, he hasn't bothered to help with the monster attack, so maybe he isn't the person Julie thinks he is.

Audrey bounds out of the car. Claire waits a moment, watching Audrey run up to the truck, laughter trailing out behind her. She turns to Claire and gestures for her to join them. Claire knows she can't sit in the car forever.

She steps out into the warm night. Christopher reaches into the bed of the truck and extracts a couple of cans from some hidden cooler. He tosses them to Audrey, who catches them effortlessly. She hands one to Claire without asking if Claire wants one. Claire stares down at the can. The red-and-gold Lone Star logo stares back. Her face goes red; she feels like Audrey and Christopher are staring at her, so she pulls back the tab and takes a polite sip and manages not to make a face. But when she looks up, it's Lawrence who's watching her. She can't read his expression.

"Hey, babe." Audrey swings herself up onto the truck bed and throws her arms around Lawrence's shoulders. He turns away from Claire and buries his face in Audrey's neck.

"Get a room, you two." Christopher jumps out of the truck and lands, cat-like, a few feet from Claire.

"Shut up, Christopher!" Audrey shouts back, and then she's kissing Lawrence, her hands running down his chest. Claire looks away.

"Hey," Christopher says. "You Claire?"

Claire turns to him and smiles, feeling like an idiot. "I am."

"Cool." Christopher doesn't seem to mean this. He drains the last of his beer and tosses the can into the back of the truck. It bounces and hits Audrey in the leg.

"Hey!" she shouts, extracting herself from Lawrence. In the icy light of the cross his expression looks glazed over. Possessed. Claire feels a nervous twinge in her stomach before remembering that his glazed expression has nothing to do with ghosts or demons.

Probably.

"Stop making out," Christopher says.

"I'll do what I want," Audrey says. "Isn't that right, Lawrence?"

"Whatever you say." Lawrence gazes at her. He doesn't seem to be aware that Claire and Christopher are even there.

Still, Audrey threads her arm around Lawrence's waist and then pulls him over to the edge of the truck bed. He jumps off first and helps her down, and then together they stumble over to the swing set. Christopher looks at Claire. For a moment Claire is afraid he wants her to squeeze his waist like that, but he just sips at his beer and says, "You going to that dance thing?"

"What? Oh. Yeah, probably." Did she decide to go to the dance after trying on the dress? Claire can't remember. It's frustrating how fuzzy her memory has been this summer.

"You should come. They'll be there." He gestures with his beer can at Lawrence, who has settled into one of the swings. "Lawrence is a cool guy, even if Audrey's got him whipped." Another drink. Claire doesn't know how to respond, but she doesn't have to. Christopher ambles over to the swing set without waiting for a reply.

Claire surreptitiously sets her beer can next to the truck's tire and follows him.

Audrey swings back and forth, her hair streaking out behind her. Lawrence gives up on the swing and leans up against the structural pole instead, watching Audrey. It's weird to think that this is the guy Julie claimed was so dependable, the guy she said would help them with the monsters. He seems so ordinary to Claire. So *typical*. Nothing like Julie.

His expression's still glazed, and with a start Claire is reminded of

236

a hypnotist show she saw on TV once. The audience volunteer had the same expression.

It's a weird way of thinking about it, but it's the only one that works: He's hypnotized by Audrey sliding back and forth like a comet through the gloomy night air. Even Christopher watches her with that same softened expression. It's like they aren't really here at all.

Audrey leaps off the swing. She lands in a crouch in the grass, and Lawrence gives a whoop and a holler and a round of applause. She stands up with her arms over her head like an Olympic gymnast. Claire feels like she's watching some sort of mating ritual that she doesn't understand.

Josh and his mix tapes, that made sense to her. Julie kissing her in the dunes—that made sense too.

She shakes her head to make the thought go away. It doesn't. She had expected her summer to be more like this, and been pleased that it hadn't—that she'd met Julie instead. And now she's trapped in her own expectation.

She feels a jolt of understanding. That's why this whole thing feels so off: It's exactly what she imagined Indianola teenagers to be like. Drinking, pickup trucks, blandly handsome older boys. It's all here. And Audrey is acting like she's already drunk, even though Claire knows she's only had one beer.

Despite the lingering heat, Claire shivers. She wants to go home. This just doesn't feel right.

"Claire! Come swing with me!" Audrey materializes at Claire's side and drags her over to the swing set. Claire feels dizzy. Christopher and Lawrence stand next to each other. Lawrence still isn't drinking, but

Christopher moves with mechanical precision. An arm lifts, an arm drops.

"No." Claire pulls away, shaking her head. Audrey tilts her head at her.

"What's wrong?" she says. "Isn't this what you wanted to do?"

A chill ripples down Claire's spine. She shakes her head again. "No, I don't really—my grandma's going to be so angry if I'm home late."

"You know she doesn't mind! Not as long as you're with me." Audrey grabs for Claire's hand again, but Claire snatches it away at the last moment.

"I'm tired," she says. "It's been a long day."

Audrey doesn't move. Her expression hardens into a cold, stiff mask. It's just the moonlight, Claire tells herself. She just looks like that in the moonlight.

"Everyone okay?" Lawrence shouts.

"Fine." Audrey drags out the word. She blinks and her whole face changes and she's back to being the bubbly, pretty cheerleader. "Every-thing's fine. Claire is kind of tired, so I'm going to take her home."

"Aw, too bad," says Christopher. "You just got here."

It doesn't sound like he really means it. Claire doesn't care. She's not sure Christopher or Lawrence care about anything.

Audrey walks over to the car. Her hair *swish-swishes* against her back and it's the loudest sound in the playground and Claire doesn't know why. Lawrence lifts his hand in a wave and then Christopher does the same. She can't stand to look at them.

"See you at the dance," Christopher says.

"Sure." She keeps her head down. Audrey's car engine turns on and headlights flood across the parking lot. Her escape.

JULIE

Julie starts her new job at the video store. It should be a condolence: Frank knows more about movies than anyone she's ever met—except maybe for Claire, whom she tries not to think about. And it's nice working for someone who actually likes her for once. But she just can't conjure up any excitement. Instead, she sits at the front counter and stares at the rows of VHS tapes and thinks about the starlines tracing across the sky. *Timelines.* An intersection here, a divergence there. She and Claire have diverged.

But she also knows that just because she screwed everything up with that kiss, it doesn't change the fact that Claire is still in danger, from monsters or from astronauts or from both. Her dad said he'd talk to the committee, but she hasn't heard anything from him, and she doesn't trust the adults to do anything anyway.

As much as Julie has always wanted to work in the video store, she hates that she's stuck here now, unable to do anything to unravel the mystery and save Claire. Just like a freaking grown-up.

At lunch, she walks down to the convenience store at the end of the street. The air is a little cooler than it has been—something about a thunderstorm working its way along the coastline. The sky is overcast, and the sea breeze is soft against her skin. At the store, she buys a rotisserie hot dog and a Slurpee while Billy Ray Cyrus blasts tinnily from the speakers overhead.

"You sure your mother wants you eating that?" asks the guy behind the counter.

Julie gives him a dark look. "You're the one selling them."

He shrugs. "Just saying."

She slides her cash across the counter and goes outside. After being cooped up, she's glad for the mild, salty air. It helps clear her head so she can think about the monsters and the timelines and the threat to Claire.

Claire, who doesn't even want to kiss me.

She follows the street down to the empty field between the Ruizes' house and the Locketts' property and plops down beneath a sprawling oak tree. The hot dog is hot, greasy nirvana. Julie's been craving junk food ever since Claire broke her heart, like the cholesterol can glue it back together.

Julie finishes her hot dog and folds its cardboard carton over on itself. The sea breeze rustles through the field, stirring up the leaves of the oak tree. The clouds move against the sky. Julie leans back in the grass and stares up at them, looking for shapes and seeing nothing. The air's heavy. It's definitely going to rain.

The wind gusts and the tree branches knock around and clatter like bones. An odd smell floats in on the wind, a chemistry classroom smell. Vaguely chemical. Vaguely metallic.

Monsters.

Julie sits up, her heart thudding. She doubts they're stalking her because they want to rent *Wayne's World.*

The field is empty. The grass ripples like the sea. She twists, looking behind the tree. Nothing.

When she turns back around a monster stands a few paces away.

Julie shrieks and jumps to her feet, kicking the crumpled hot-dog container into the grass. The monster blinks at her. It's almost human-sized, with a large bulbous head and too-skinny arms and translucent skin beneath which Julie can see the pulsing lines of veins, the blood so dark, it's almost black.

"Alvarez," the monster says in a voice that bleeds in with the wind.

Julie presses up against the tree, her vision blurring. It's happening again. This isn't some monster wandering in from the power plant. It wants *her*. Just like the slug monster. Just like the monster that attacked Claire.

"You aren't supposed to be here," Julie says, fumbling for her voice. "You're too far into town."

"Looking." The monster sways in place, as if it's so light, the wind can blow it around. "Aldraa sent."

"Aldraa sent you?"

The monster nods, looking like dandelion fluff on a stem. Julie's almost afraid its head will fall off from the effort, since the movement is clearly not a natural one. "Thought you rather speak me."

Julie stares at the monster, not sure how to respond. Instead of the slug monster? Aldraa must have found out how badly that visit went.

"More human, yes?" The monster lifts one of its skinny arms, and something clicks in Julie's head. The monster looks closer to human than the slug. *That's* why Aldraa sent it.

"What does Aldraa want?" she asks. "Is this about the astronaut? About Claire?"

"Da zsa ful zsu sho."

"I don't know what that means!"

"Astronaut."

Julie digs her nails into her palms. She flicks her eyes around, looking for the slug monster, for anything that could lash out and drag her away. "I said that."

"Yes. Astronaut." The monster blinks its huge, round eyes. *More human.* Only on a technicality. Really, the distortion in its arms and head makes it painful to look at.

"I didn't understand before," Julie says, "and I don't understand now. What astronaut are you talking about?"

The monster takes a moment to consider this. Watching it think, Julie realizes that, somehow, she isn't as afraid anymore.

"Is this why y'all have been coming into town?" she asks slowly. "Because of this astronaut?"

The monster shakes its head, and this movement seems as unnatural and contorted as nodding. "Timeline," it says. "Because. But *da zsa ful zsu sho* concern yes."

Julie slumps against the tree trunk. "This is pointless," she mutters to herself. Then, louder: "You aren't telling me anything new. Aldraa should know by now he's got to send someone who can *explain.*" She stoops down and picks up her Slurpee, which is already starting to melt down into syrup. She stirs it around with her straw. "The last one, it said Aldraa didn't know anything. But Aldraa sent you to me."

"Desperate."

"Who is? You? Aldraa? The sl—the monster from three nights ago?"

The monster pauses. Julie sips on her Slurpee. She doesn't feel fear, exactly, but her hands still shake. She hopes this time the monsters will tell her something practical, something she can *use*.

"All," the monster finally says.

Julie frowns. "All?"

"All." It gestures with one arm and then the other, sweeping out in wide circles. The grass ripples around them, and Julie feels cold.

"All the monsters?" she says. "You're all desperate?"

The monster nods. Its expression is blank and doll-like—it's those huge shining eyes—but for a moment Julie thinks she sees a tremor of something else, something like fear. She's seen it before on monsters' faces, when she was first learning the ropes of the exterminators—she'd been out there with Forrest and he insisted it was her imagination. But she'd never been convinced.

"You're desperate to do something about this *da zsa—da zsa ful zsu sho*—this astronaut?"

"Yes."

"Because of the timelines?"

"Yes."

Julie takes a long drink of her melted Slurpee. The same thing over and over. Astronaut. Timelines.

"What do you need me to do?" She squares her shoulders, hoping the answer is something she can actually manage.

The monster lifts its face to the sky, and its transparent skin glows in the humid gray sunlight. The dark veins pulse all over its body. It's thinking hard, Julie realizes. Concentrating.

The monster looks at her. Julie goes still. She's holding her breath.

"You have to stop the astronaut," the monster says, and its shoulders slump, as if speaking a full sentence is too much weight to bear.

Julie guns the engine on her car, pushing sixty-five on the highway leading out to the power plant. After her conversation with the monster, she told Frank she got her period so he would let her go early. If Aldraa has answers, Julie wants to hear them.

The highway is empty. The clouds press down low in the sky, a dark smudge growing out of the southeast, over the Gulf. That storm coming in.

Julie drives on.

The power plant appears, lights twinkling in the thin daylight. Julie presses down on the gas. The speedometer needle inches up to seventy, to seventy-five. She's not even through the gates and already her head feels thick and heavy. But Aldraa's going to answer her questions.

She'll make him if she has to. Somehow.

Julie pulls into the drive. Wind whistles through her car windows. It's a lot stronger here in the power plant, strong enough that her car shakes.

She slams into the parking lot in front of the main building, not bothering to park between the lines. When she pushes her door open the wind catches it and almost slams it shut on her. She intercepts the door with her foot, kicks it back open, climbs out. Her hair billows into her face. The smell of rain is everywhere, and layered over that is the chemical scent of the power plant.

Julie stomps into the main building, choking back her fear.

The air inside is unmoving. When the door slams shut, Julie can't even hear the wind howling outside. She pushes her hair away from her face and scans across the thick, tropical crush of plants.

"Aldraa!" she says. "I need to speak with you!"

Her courage falters now that she's inside, now that she's in this still-as-death air, surrounded by dense growing things. She realizes she forgot her earplugs. Still, she forces herself to march deeper into the building, deeper into the emerald gloom. The humidity sinks into her lungs, and already sweat beads on her skin.

It's hotter inside than it is out.

"*Aldraa!*" she shouts. "Will you please tell me what's going on?"

Branches snap, leaves rustle. Julie whips her head around. Off in the left-hand corner the plants ripple. She watches that place, her hands curled into fists, her heart racing.

Aldraa's clawed foot appears, and then his leg, and then the rest of him. Julie's vision immediately blurs. She shakes her head, looks off to the side.

"You've been sending monsters to me," she says, staring at a fan spray of some primeval fern. "One of them even kidnapped me and brought me here. All of them keep talking about astronauts and time-lines and I want to know what the hell is going on."

Her voice is sharp in the thick stillness of the building. Aldraa rumbles forward over the plants, moving slowly, swaying from side to side. The building tremors and shakes.

"Yes," he said.

His voice is so loud that she claps her hands over her ears.

"Why?" She forces herself to look at him directly. Her head spins. The room tilts. It's been too long since she's talked to him.

"Our town is in danger."

Our town. As if the monsters live here too.

They do, whispers a scratchy little voice inside Julie's head.

"What sort of danger?" Julie says. "From an astronaut? Do you even know what an astronaut is?"

"A starway traveler," Aldraa says. "One who travels alone, usually. There's no exact translation in your language—*astronaut* is the closest we could come."

"We?" She takes one step closer to him: a mistake. The room swings around. She drops her gaze and takes a deep breath. Her ears ring. "Who else is in on this? Why are you sending messengers to me? Why not my dad? Or *any* freaking adult. You do know what an adult is, right?"

Aldraa's long-nailed fingers tap against his thigh, one after another. It's a parody of human impatience, and it doesn't suit him. He's not human.

"Because you're already involved," he says. "We thought it would be easier."

"We!" Julie shrieks. "Who!"

"The council."

Something curls up inside of Julie. A council. She's never heard of this, not from her dad, not from anybody. They've only ever interacted with Aldraa.

"Another word that doesn't translate exactly," Aldraa says. "But that's all I will tell you about our ways. It's not important. The only important thing now is to find the astronaut and stop her."

"The astronaut is a her. A woman."

"She looks like a woman, yes."

Julie closes her eyes. A migraine is forming at her left temple. She won't be able to stay much longer.

"You need to give me something else to go on."

"We can't." Aldraa stoops down and leans close to Julie, closer than he's ever been before. Even in the dim light she can see a faint spiderweb of veins across his gray skin. Bile rises up in her throat, but she pushes it down. "She's hiding herself from us, from everyone in the town." It's like standing next to speaker at a rock concert. "She is in a"—he stops for a moment—"*la shul te tsaa*. A place where you can't see unless you look straight-on."

"A blind spot," Julie says. At this point, she can barely hear herself speak. Then, her thoughts wild: "Is that where Claire is too? Is that what the monster meant, about her being hidden?"

"Yes, I like that. A spot of blindness in the world." Aldraa's long arms ripple. "And you speak of the Sudek, yes? That is where she is. Hidden away from us by the astronaut. The Emmert, he's there too. She uses mazes to hide herself and her victims. We've seen it before."

"But not from me," Julie says, a statement that makes her chest hurt, because Claire is hidden away not by some monster's magic but by the bad luck of sexual orientation.

"No, she cannot hide her victims from any of your kind. Her technology isn't suited. But we asked for your help, no one else's, because it'll be easier for you—you are far more embroiled in the timeline. You are part of it, part of the history, and we are only guests."

"What are you talking about!" Julie can barely keep his words in order. Her migraine pounds against her skull. "Just tell me what's going to happen to Indianola! Or to Claire, or to me, or—"

Aldraa looks at her and Julie looks him straight in the eye, and like that, she's caught. Her vision floods with pale light, and she totters backward, puts one hand down hard on thick, lush moss that sucks her fingers in.

She can't move.

"I am telling you what's happening," he says, his voice booming deep inside her head. The pale light pulses in time with his words "But the vocabulary is different. Your language is hard for us. It doesn't suit our way of thinking."

Distantly, Julie hears a whisper of alien voices, of syllables not formed by human tongues.

"We came to this place not through the starway, but through the timeway. It's faster, yes, to travel through time. But risky. Dangerous to the travelers. And it disrupts things. We tried to ensure that our arrival would not affect this new place, but of course it was an impossible dream. Things changed here."

A coldness creeps over Julie. The light dims, and she wriggles the fingers of her trapped hand. *Moss, it's just moss.* "Things changed here? What sort of things?"

"The trajectory of the town, of course. It was meant to be one way, but our arrival sent your lives in a different direction."

Julie gapes up at him, shaking. Her life would have been different? In what way? Is there some version of the world where she isn't a giant freak at school, where she's had a girlfriend? Lots of girlfriends? Where her father never made her work at the exterminator's?

And then Aldraa turns away, and the spell he held over her breaks. The light disappears; the migraine recedes. Julie snaps her hand out of the wet, pulling moss and rubs at it. She takes deep breaths and reorganizes her thoughts as best she can.

"You came through a hundred years ago, didn't you?" she gasps. "With that hurricane?"

"Yes." She can feel Aldraa moving off to her side, feel the reverberation of his footsteps through the ground, but she only watches him in the periphery of her vision, so that he's nothing but a gray blur. "That hurricane meant the end of this town one hundred years ago.

We intended to inhabit its shell. But there were miscalculations…we arrived too soon…and the timeline was changed, to our dismay. Indianola came back to life. We cannot move elsewhere, because traveling through the timeway again would destroy us. It wreaks havoc on living organisms. Now the astronaut wishes to change things *again*—to shape the past so that the present will be transformed. That must not be allowed to happen."

Julie slumps back. The thick air crawls over her skin. *The gaps in reporting in the newspaper.* Maybe Indianola had died, for a few days. And then the monsters revived it.

She realizes she was thinking far too small when Aldraa said her life would have changed. Maybe it isn't a question of change at all. Maybe she would never have existed.

The thought leaves a dull ache inside of her. She thinks of the time she was swept out on a riptide and held underwater for a few seconds. Afterward, she sat gasping on the beach and considered the possibility that the sea could have been stronger, that she could have drowned. This was the same feeling now. The feeling of almost-dying-but-not.

"I don't know why the astronaut wants to change the timeline," Aldraa says, his raspy voice dragging her back into the present. "But it's imperative that you find her. She will erase all of us."

Julie shakes her head. "But you can't give me any way of finding her! I don't know what you want me to do!"

She forces herself to look at Aldraa's face, at a point on his cheek that she knows is safe. Her migraine swells, a sharp stab of pain, but she chokes it back and keeps looking at him. There is nothing human about his features, but for a glimmer of a second she thinks she sees a flash of terror. It shoots an arrow through her heart.

"One hundred years have passed today," Aldraa says. "When the astronaut does something, it will be tonight. That is the nature of her technology. Things must be re-created as they once were. The same place, the same people."

"Anyone from a hundred years ago is dead," Julie mutters. She feels numb.

"Their ancestors live on in this town."

A Sudek and an Alvarez. A cosmically interesting combination.

"Tonight doesn't give me very much time." Something catches on Julie's vision, and she looks away from Aldraa in time to see movement through the shadows, long and thin. She closes her eyes to combat a sudden wave of dizziness.

"We started visiting the Sudek weeks ago."

"But you didn't explain anything! I was scared! I thought—"

"Yes. You went to the committee. But they don't understand these things."

"I don't understand either!"

"I have explained to the best of my ability. Please, you must help us now." Aldraa drags himself over to her, and the light pushes in, and her head throbs with pain. "We are desperate."

Desperate. Julie stares down at Aldraa's clawed feet. She's always thought of the monsters as monsters, as enemies. But maybe they aren't the enemy here. They've never hurt her, only asked her to find an astronaut, an astronaut who will do something tonight—

Julie jerks her head up. Aldraa's looking down at her, watching her. In the gloomy shadows beyond him, Julie thinks she sees Audrey Duchesne.

Her migraine swells, and Audrey disappears, but the idea has already been planted. Audrey Duchesne. Tonight.

Tonight's the Stargazer's Masquerade.

Julie has forgotten about it. She'd never been interested in the masquerade. But Claire might be going. She borrowed Abigail's dress. Maybe she means to wear it as a costume.

"You sense something." Aldraa's voice booms through the darkness. "You sense the hidden ones."

"Don't talk!" Julie says, clamping her hands over her ears. Something splinters inside of her. Something that looks like Audrey Duchesne.

But what could Audrey have to do with all this? She *knows* Audrey Duchesne, has known her all her life. They moved together through the three schools lined up on Scarrow Street: Indianola Elementary, Indianola Junior High, Indianola High School. She remembers seeing Audrey Duchesne sitting on the swing set in a bright blue pinafore dress; she remembers her singing "Leader of the Pack" in the talent show; she remembers her cheering on the sidelines of the handful of football games Julie's ever bothered to attend.

She *remembers*.

"What is it?" Aldraa lurches forward. The air around him refracts and distorts, and Julie presses up against the moss-covered wall, trying to shut out his rumbling voice. She remembers Audrey Duchesne, but doesn't she also remember Sara Hassani in that pinafore dress? Swinging back and forth, shouting "Leader of the Pack" at the top of her lungs?

The two memories layer on top of each other, the images bleeding together. Audrey's face becomes Sara's face and back again. The pain in Julie's head is almost unbearable. She presses her thumb into her temple and white light flares in the back of her skull, and then all she sees is Audrey Duchesne, swinging back and forth, sunlight streaming through her golden hair.

She screams in pain and slides down the wall. Audrey keeps swinging inside her head. Julie forces her eyes open. Aldraa stares down at her. She looks at his mouth, at his rows of teeth.

"I can feel it," he hisses. "A disruption. She's been changing things already."

And then he lashes out one arm and seals his hand against the side of Julie's head. Julie struggles to pull away, but it does no good. The bones of his fingers sink into her flesh, into her mind.

"Let go of me!" she screams.

Aldraa whispers to himself, a low susurration of sound, someone saying *shhh shhh shhh* over and over.

"Aldraa!" Julie screams. She jerks her head violently, hoping to tear away from him, but it only sends pain tearing up through her skull.

"A disruption in the timeline!" Aldraa slides his hand away and Julie falls to the ground, landing in a thick mat of gray-green leaves, damp with humidity. She crawls away from him. Moss spores and dirt ooze between her fingers.

"Your memories have been disrupted," he says. "It is unnatural."

She stops. The plants creep around her hands and knees, oozing like oil over her skin.

"What did you do to me?" she whispers, staring straight ahead, at the little patch of white light that is the window in the door leading outside.

"Nothing. It was the astronaut."

Audrey Duchesne swings on the playground, back and forth, back and forth.

Julie stands up, her legs shaking. Aldraa stares at her. One of his hands hangs limp at his side, glowing.

Julie's anxiety for Claire has returned, a force stronger than the migraine, stronger than her fear. And Lawrence—Lawrence has been dating Audrey, letting her hold him and kiss him—

"I have to go," she says. "I'll tell you if I find anything."

And she races out of the building, out into the gray windswept world.

CHAPTER

Seventeen

JULIE

Julie drives straight to Claire's house. She knows that the responsible thing would be to go to her father or to track down Mr. Vickery and alert the committee to what happened. But she doesn't trust the committee to do anything about it other than file a report. Besides, it might be nothing. It might just be the ranting of monsters.

Or it might be everything. Julie wants to make sure Claire is all right.

She pulls into Claire's driveway and climbs out of her car. The wind billows and gusts and roars through the trees. Still no rain, though there's a distant rumble of thunder, a flicker of lightning.

A hurricane a hundred years ago almost wiped out the town. Is this another hurricane, making its slow way across the Gulf? No, of course not, it would have been on the news, and Julie's mom would have forced her to spend the afternoon hammering plywood boards onto the windows.

Julie takes a deep breath and walks up to the front door. Her blood rushes through her ears. She's more nervous right now, pressing her thumb against Claire's doorbell, than she ever was standing in front of Aldraa.

The doorbell echoes through the house. Julie shifts her weight, wipes her sweaty palms on the back of her shorts.

No one answers.

Dread tightens inside her chest. She rings the doorbell again. Something's wrong. She's sure of it.

She's about to leave the porch to try knocking on Claire's window when she hears footsteps on the other side of the door. She freezes in place. The door creaks open. Wind pushes against the screen door, making it rattle in its frame.

Mrs. Sudek peers out at her. Julie shrinks back, startled by the gauntness of Mrs. Sudek's features. She didn't look that bad the last time Julie was here.

"What do you want?" Mrs. Sudek barks.

"Is Claire here?" Julie asks. "I need to speak—"

"No." Her voice cuts through Julie like a knife. "She doesn't want to speak with you."

Julie almost falls apart right there on Mrs. Sudek's porch. But she squares her shoulders and forces back her sorrow and says, "I thought you said she isn't here."

Mrs. Sudek glares at her, eyes glittering.

"Which is it?" Julie asks, fortified by her own boldness. "Is she not here or does she not want to speak with me?"

The air crackles.

Mrs. Sudek's face slides in and out of the shadows. "She's not here," she says. "She's with Audrey Duchesne. She doesn't want to see you anymore."

The door slams shut. Julie slumps against the bricks, taking deep gasping breaths, trying not to cry.

She doesn't want to see you anymore.

She's with Audrey Duchesne.

Julie stiffens. Does she really believe Audrey Duchesne is a danger? That she's anything more than a pretty cheerleader leading a pretty, perfect life?

Her thoughts swirl around, thick and indistinct. She suddenly has the refrain to "Leader of the Pack" stuck in her head.

This isn't about Claire not wanting her. This is about Claire being in danger. And maybe Lawrence too, if Audrey's been toying with him. At least Lawrence knows how to shoot a gun.

Julie gets into her car and roars backward down the driveway. Claire's house stands sentinel against the bruised sky as she drives down the street, the wind rocking against her car. She hopes she can remember the way to Audrey's house—Claire pointed it out to her when she and Claire drove by it one afternoon, on their way to the beach, and Claire said, "Oh, that's where Audrey lives." It's close by, Julie remembers that.

She drives for five minutes, leaning close over the steering wheel. Her music slams around inside her head, and she hits EJECT on the tape player, although the silence isn't any better. It feels pounding and hollow, like the inside of a cave.

She turns down a side street, thinking the arch of trees looks familiar.

And then she sees it. Audrey's house.

She drives past it, slowing to take in the whole thing. It's a nice house, new, built of white brick, with a big porch and a basketball hoop in the driveway. The most normal house in the world.

She parks in front of the neighbors' house, behind an ugly tan pickup. She climbs out and closes the door and leans against the car hood, squinting across at Audrey's perfectly mown lawn. It's the brilliant green of Astroturf, striking against the crackling yellow grass of the neighbors.

Julie takes a deep breath and walks away from her car. She clutches her keys tight in one hand, the metal edges digging into her palm. The damp wind whips her hair into her eyes.

She hopes there's nothing here—that nothing is wrong with Audrey, period, that she's *normal*. But she doesn't think she is.

Julie steps onto the porch. Brilliant pink roses grow along the railing, and the cloying scent of them makes her dizzy. She takes a deep breath and presses her thumb against the doorbell.

No one answers.

Julie waits, listening to the howling of the wind. She rings the doorbell three more times. Nothing. Not even the sound of footsteps inside.

She knows she ought to leave. Just walk back down the sidewalk and climb into her car and drive away. Go to her dad, tell him what Aldraa said, let the adults deal with it. She can even feel something tugging at her, drawing her away from the house. A sort of magnetic field.

She turns around and goes down the first step. The pecan tree in the front yard shimmers from the wind.

But Julie wants *answers*. She wants more than the sound of a doorbell echoing through an empty house.

She walks around the side of the house, her heart hammering up near her throat. The neighbors' house is shrouded in overgrown shrubs—she can't see their windows, so she figures she can't be seen either. And if anyone *does* see her, and they ask her why she's sneaking around—she'll say she's on monster-hunting business.

Technically, she is.

Julie finds a gate, part of a big wooden privacy fence, leading into Audrey's backyard. She undoes the latch, and the wind catches the gate and slams it open, revealing a huge yard lined around the edges with tropical flowers.

She eases in, slides the door shut. Stops. Listens.

All she hears is the wind.

She creeps forward, past a greenhouse built into the side of the house proper. The backyard is lush and well-manicured. A vegetable garden sits in the corner, thick with green beans and tomato plants and squash. The sight of it makes Julie shudder—it's wrong, almost *impossible*. Most gardens have gone to seed this late in the summer. It's too hot for them.

A picture window looks out at the garden. Inside the house, the lights are switched off. A few feet away from the window a wooden door bangs in its frame. There's no lock. Julie goes up to it and cracks it open: It leads into a garage.

An empty garage.

She nudges the door open a bit farther. The air in the garage is stale and musty, like the doors haven't been open for a long time. Julie steps inside. No car out front, no cars in here—

No one's home.

She's about to turn around and leave, give up, when she notices an arrow of light running along the cement. The lights points to a door.

A door hanging slightly open.

Julie stares at it for a long time. The door leads inside the house.

No one's home.

She knows she shouldn't do this. She knows it's illegal, and not in the way that going seventy-five on the highway is illegal, either. But she's not going to steal anything. And the door's hanging open. If she gets caught, she can just say that she came by looking for Claire.

The narrow triangle of light beckons her closer. Her curiosity bubbles up, shot through with a sick sense of dread. She wants to see inside that house the way you want to see what's going to happen next in a horror movie.

With her toe, Julie pushes the door open.

It swings out, revealing a kitchen decorated in black and white. The light is on, bright and garish.

"Hello?" Julie calls out. "Is anyone home?"

She steps inside. It's freezing in here, that unnatural cold that can only be produced by an AC. She shuts the door and looks around. The kitchen doesn't seem as if it's ever been used. The white tiles gleam in the light; the floor doesn't even have streaks from a mop.

She moves forward, into the living room. More black and white. "Hello!" she calls out. Her voice almost echoes. "I didn't mean to just *come in.*"

Although of course she did. Not that it matters—her words are met with a weird, vibrating silence.

She slips off her shoes before walking onto the carpet; it's pure white, and she figures she's already tracked mud into the kitchen. Her feet pad softly as she paces forward, past the couch and the big TV. Yesterday's newspaper sits folded on the coffee table, angled just so, the way you'd expect to see in a furniture ad.

Carefully, she walks down a hallway. The lights are off, and even though there are no windows, it seems darker than it ought to. She follows it until she comes to the foyer, which doubles as a landing for the stairs.

"Hello?" she says, although she doesn't expect an answer.

Her heart's pounding. She knows she ought to go back, but she wants to see Audrey's bedroom. She wants to find proof that Audrey has always been here, that she swung on the swing set and sang at the talent show and hopped around on the sidelines for the football team. Julie wants proof that Andrey's not an *astronaut*.

This is insane. Julie knows that. But she goes up the stairs anyway. They creak beneath her weight. She realizes she's holding her breath and lets out a long exhalation when she reaches the top landing.

The ceiling is holed with skylights; it's much brighter than downstairs. Julie closes her eyes, tries to steady her heartbeat.

There. A door at the end of the hallway hangs open, revealing a room painted pink. She can only assume it belongs to Audrey.

She moves toward it. But as she does, she passes another open door. And she sees something out of the corner of her eye and her heart jolts and she looks—

And she screams.

The silence after her scream echoes around the house. Julie stares into the room, unable to move, her thoughts swooning.

Bodies.

There are *bodies* in there.

Claire, Julie thinks, and that's enough. She rushes forward, horror calcifying inside her. The bodies lie in a heap at the center of the room, tossed aside like dolls. There's no blood and no sign of a struggle: In fact, this is a playroom, and all the toys in the room are lined up neatly on shelves, not a single one out of place.

Julie falls to her knees beside the bodies. They're just a tangle of limbs and hair and clothes, and Julie can't tell where anyone starts or ends. She hears a strange rhythmic gasping and realizes that it's her, that she's hyperventilating. The room starts to spin. She throws out one hand to steady herself and accidentally hits the bodies. One of them tumbles over onto its back. Julie screams and scrabbles backward, hands over feet.

It's not Claire.

It's not Audrey either, but an older woman, with hair styled like the mom from an old fifties TV show. Her eyes are open, but it takes Julie a moment, in her panic, to realize there's something wrong with them—they have no irises, no pupils. They're just white. Blank.

Trembling, Julie reaches forward and lets two fingers hover over the woman's neck. She doesn't want to touch her. But she has to know—

She sets her fingers under the woman's jawline, feeling for a pulse.

And she snatches her fingers away.

It's *there*. The woman's heart is still beating.

Julie takes a deep breath, tries again. She makes sure she has her fingers arranged properly, so that she doesn't mistake her own pulse for this woman's. But no, it's definitely coming from the woman: a rhythm beating against the thin skin of her neck. Something's off about it, though. It's strong and sure but not the steady drumbeat she expects to feel. It's a vibration, not a beat, a lilting, musical purr that rises and falls like winter winds.

Julie drags her hand away. She stares at the bodies, her horror slowly giving way to confusion. The other two bodies are a man and a boy, and they both look like they're from the fifties as well, with old-fashioned haircuts and clean-cut looks.

261

Except for their eyes. Nothing but white.

She checks their pulses too. They each have one. Strong. Sure. Strangely musical.

Julie crawls back over the lush carpet until she bumps up against one of the shelves of toys. Action figures shower down around her, but she hardly notices: Her eyes are still pinned on the family tangled up in the center of the room.

Julie stares at the bodies, terrified, with no idea what to do next.

Audrey never swung on that swing set. Inside this house, with those bodies lying in a pile like dolls—Julie's sure of it. This is Audrey's family, isn't it? A fake family. Pod people for parents.

Julie inches up to standing, running her hands over the shelf, not caring when she knocks over more action figures. The bodies don't move at all. Julie isn't sure she even sees their chests rising and falling.

Aldraa's voice echoes inside her head: *Our town is in danger. Stop the astronaut.*

Julie takes a deep breath. She has to find Claire. Lawrence too.

Then she runs down the stairs, through the living room, out of the house.

CHAPTER
Eighteen

CLAIRE

Claire and Audrey spill into Grammy's house, carrying bags of makeup and costume jewelry from their trip to the drugstore in downtown Indianola. The Stargazer's Masquerade is in just a few hours, and Claire still isn't sure she wants to go. The sky is heavy and threatening rain, as it has been all afternoon. She hopes the storm will be bad enough to give her an excuse.

She switches on the foyer light in Grammy's house, trying to drown out the darkness from the upcoming storm.

"We're back!" Audrey calls out. "You don't mind if we get ready here, do you?"

Claire rankles at the way Audrey makes herself at home so easily. She doesn't like feeling as if Audrey's her best friend here, instead of Julie.

Is Julie my best friend here? Anymore?

She shoves the thought aside.

In the living room, the TV clicks off, and a few moments later, Grammy comes around the corner. She takes in Claire and Audrey and their stacks of packages.

"Looks like you found everything you need," she says.

Audrey beams at her. "Everything!"

Claire presses up against the wall, trying to squeeze past Grammy to get to her bedroom. "We need to get dressed," she says.

"Oh, of course, of course." Grammy claps her hands together and gazes down at Claire with a melancholy, faraway expression. "I do hope you have fun tonight. Your mother always enjoyed the Stargazer's Masquerade. I did too, when I was your age."

"It'll be a delight," Audrey says.

Claire nods. She just wants to get into her room, get dressed, go to the dance, get this whole night over with. She shouldn't have agreed to go. The fact that Abigail's dress miraculously fit isn't a good enough reason.

Grammy steps aside to let Audrey pass. Claire can feel her watching as she and Audrey make their way into her room. She shuts the door, imagining that she's shutting out Grammy's prying eyes too.

Audrey tosses the packages on the bed and puts her hands on her hips. "Where to start?" she says.

Claire shrugs.

"I usually do hair and makeup first."

"That's fine." Normally, Claire loves makeup, but she can't conjure an ounce of enthusiasm.

"Great!" Audrey goes over to the window and twists open the blinds. "Natural light is the best light," she explains, even though the light seeping through the window is an unusual, sickly green-yellow. It must be from the storm. "Here, I'll do you first. Sit, sit!"

Claire perches on the vanity seat. Audrey rustles around in their bags. When they were at the drugstore, Audrey bought three different shades of foundation, claiming she needed to blend them so as to match Claire's exact skin tone. The foundations were paid for with a handful of twenty-dollar bills that Grammy slipped into Claire's hand on the way out the door. Another oddity about today.

Audrey kneels down beside Claire and spreads out a pile of their purchased makeup—not only the foundations, but the powder and the brushes and the blusher and the eye shadow too. All of it. She grabs Claire's hand and flips it over so she can dab a bit of foundation on Claire's wrist.

"Mmmm, not quite. Let's see what happens when I—" She doesn't finish her sentence, only squeezes out a line from the paler foundation. She rubs the two together. "That's better, don't you think?"

Claire nods, although she can't tell the difference between this and her usual makeup. Her head feels foggy. The lights in the vanity dim and glow brighter like the beat of a heart—but only when she's not looking at them head-on. It's probably just her imagination.

"Here, turn this way so I can see you." Audrey tilts Claire's face away from the mirror. The room swims. "You're going to look *beautiful.*"

Audrey sweeps Claire's hair back and holds it in place with a clip. She streaks makeup across Claire's face. It's cold against Claire's skin.

I miss Julie, Claire thinks.

It's the clearest thing in her head right now. Last night she thought about the kiss on the beach, the damp wind and the roar of the waves and the dunes rising up around them like a fortress. Julie's lips brushing against hers and that brief half moment when she kissed back.

I kissed back.

Of course she kissed back. It's what she wanted, all this time. To kiss Julie.

Heat rises up in Claire's cheeks. Fortunately Audrey is turned away, selecting a powder compact from the collection on the counter. Claire looks out the window. The clouds are crowding in, thick and dark and heavy.

"Here, I think this color will work." Audrey brushes powder all over Claire's face. There's something hypnotizing about her movement, something hypnotizing about the vanity lights and the encroaching storm outside. Somnolence washes over Claire. Complacency. Audrey steps back and smiles, admiring her work.

"*Perfect*," she says.

The rest of the dance preparations go by in a blur. Claire leans up against the vanity as Audrey applies blush and lipstick and eyeliner, her movements quick and practiced. When she finishes the makeup, Claire tries to peek in the mirror, but Audrey shrieks and covers it with one hand.

"Not yet!" she says. "I need to do your hair! Here, let's go sit at the desk."

Claire obeys, standing up by rote. She catches a glimpse of herself in the mirror and isn't sure what she sees.

Audrey plugs in a curling iron and rests it on the desk. Claire takes a seat, and Audrey spins the chair around until Claire is facing the exact place where the picture of Julie's house used to be. Claire stares at the pale rectangle on the wall, the photo's ghost, as Audrey tugs and brushes and teases out her hair. The hot iron singes her scalp, and bobby pins prick like tiny, dulled needles. Hairspray fogs up the air. Heat. Pain at the temples. The strangest sense that Claire is being remolded.

She lets it all happen. It's become an obligation, like being here in Indianola in the first place. She *has* to.

"All done!" Audrey chirps. "You ready to see?"

Claire looks over her shoulder at her. Audrey beams. Claire's head feels heavy.

"I guess," she says.

Audrey grabs Claire's hand and pulls her to her feet and leads her over to the vanity mirror with a flourish.

"The new and improved Claire!" she cries.

Claire does not recognize herself.

The makeup has softened her features, plumping out her cheeks and smoothing over her jawline. Her eyes look bigger, brighter; her mouth is a perfect round bow. She doesn't look *bad*, she just doesn't look the way she's used to looking. She looks—

Old-fashioned. That's the word. Like a Victorian photograph.

Something niggles at the back of Claire's mind, something about Victorian photographs, but she can't catch on to it, and it disappears.

It's her hair too. Audrey has piled it up on Claire's head in a wispy, Victorian-style bun, a few tendrils of hair curling around her jawline.

"This is such a fantastic costume," Audrey says. "Now, put on the dress so we can see the finished product!"

"Right." Claire watches that unfamiliar mouth speak with her voice. "I'll do that."

"I'll start getting myself ready while you do."

Claire nods, still staring at the reflection in the mirror. It's so disconcerting, seeing this stranger stare back at her. She jerks her gaze away and glances at Audrey, who has moved over by the window. Behind her, the clouds have grown thicker.

"It's going to rain soon," Claire says. "Hopefully we make it to the dance okay."

"Nothing to worry about." Audrey gives a big grin. "Try on the dress! I want to see everything."

Claire nods and drags herself over to her closet. Audrey settles into the vanity chair, leans forward, tugs at the skin around her eyes. She selects a bottle of foundation and begins the makeup process for herself.

Claire pulls the dress from its place in the closet and turns around, facing the window, to change. She steps out of her clothes and pulls on the dress, careful not to smear makeup on the fabric or mess up her hair. In the darkness of the storm, she can make out the ghost of her reflection in the window's glass.

"Oh, you need me to do up the buttons, don't you?"

Claire twists around. Audrey's smiling at her from the vanity, one of her eyes made up, the other painfully bare.

"Yeah." Claire nods.

Audrey leaps up and runs over and does up the buttons. Claire stares at the window. Her heart pounds. She presses her hands against her stomach, feeling herself underneath the cool gray silk of the dress.

"There, all done!" Audrey gasps with delight. "You look *amazing*. Christopher is going to *love* it." She reaches over and adjusts the neckline. "Perfect," she says. She looks around the bedroom. "Don't you have a full-length mirror?"

"There's one in the bathroom."

"Oh my God, you have to look at yourself. Go, go!" Audrey makes shooing motions with her hands, and Claire obliges, slipping out into the dark hallway. The air crackles with electricity, and the hairs on Claire's arm stand straight up. She ducks into the bathroom and switches on the light.

Her reflection stares back at her.

She looks like a stranger. In the dress, she could be a person from another place, another time. Claire turns to the side, looking at her silhouette. Her waist cinches, wasp-like, as if she's wearing a corset. God, it just *isn't her.*

A perfect dress for a masquerade, then. But that doesn't mean Claire wants to look in any more mirrors.

Claire goes back to the bedroom, not wanting to be alone with her reflection. Audrey's teasing up her hair and spraying it with hairspray. She's finished her makeup, too, smoky eyes and wine-colored lipstick. Very modern. Claire wonders how she got it on so quickly.

"You look nice," Claire says. She picks her way over to the bed so she can avoid the mirror.

Audrey blasts her hair with one last burst of spray. "Almost done!" she says. "Then I can change and we can head out." She claps her hands together. "I'm so excited!"

She looks at Claire like she expects a response. "Me too," Claire says, even though she doesn't feel it. To try and make up for her lack of enthusiasm, she adds, "So what are you dressing up as?"

"What? Oh, Cindy Crawford." She points at a dark spot near her lip. "See? It's the mole."

Claire frowns. "Weren't you going as a hippie? So we could be girls through the ages?"

Audrey's eyes are as big as saucers. "No," she says. "Maybe you talked about doing something like that with Julie?"

Julie. Her name echoes in Claire's head.

"Yeah. Maybe."

Audrey walks over to the bed and digs around in the bags, pulling out a slinky, sequin-covered black dress that flashes in the lights. Claire sits down at the vanity, her skirts pooling around her feet.

When Audrey pulls off her top, Claire immediately looks the other way, her face hot. Julie's face flashes in her mind, and Julie's bare shoulders and tanned legs. Claire squeezes her eyes shut. Julie's laugh. Julie's tangled hair blowing in the wind. Julie sing-shouting along to the songs on her cassette tapes.

Julie.

"All done!" Audrey's voice rings out like a bell. Claire turns around and Audrey poses for her, lifting her hands over her head. She doesn't look so much like Cindy Crawford as she does the black storm clouds amassing outside.

"Okay, where's that full-length mirror?" Audrey asks. "I want us to look at ourselves."

Looking at herself is the last thing that Claire wants, but she leads Audrey into the bathroom anyway. The fluorescent light buzzes. The bathroom feels small and claustrophobic. Audrey flings her arm around Claire's shoulder and they stand side by side, each of them partially cut off by the mirrors' sides.

"Best friends," Audrey says.

A jolt goes through Claire. No. They are not best friends. If Julie had said that—

That wouldn't be true either, not really. Julie isn't a best friend. She's more than that. She's something Claire can't put into words.

"You ready to go?" Audrey pulls away and goes out into the hallway. "I'd like to get out of here before the rain starts."

"Fine with me." Definitely fine by Claire. The sooner they get to the dance, the sooner she can leave. This whole thing has been a huge mistake.

"Awesome!" Another dazzling smile. "I'm *so* excited."

They go back into Claire's room and slip into their shoes and grab their purses. The sky has darkened so much that it almost looks like nighttime. As Claire peers out the window, a crack of lightning slices the horizon in half. For a heartbeat the clouds are illuminated, and Clare thinks she sees faces in them.

"You girls be careful."

Claire whirls around, caught unawares by Grammy's voice, the faces in the clouds fading from her memory.

"Oh, we *will*," says Audrey.

Grammy glances at her, takes in the formfitting dress, the billowing hair, and says nothing. She looks back at Claire.

"You look lovely, my dear," she says.

It's perhaps the kindest thing Grammy has said all summer. Claire feels herself hardening up, and she wraps her arms around herself like a shield.

"I hope you have a wonderful time," Grammy says. She holds up a clunky old Polaroid, her sickly fingers crawling over it like a spider. "Let me get your picture."

"Ooh, a picture!" Audrey bounds over beside Claire and wraps her arm around Claire's waist. Claire feels caught in a riptide. Grammy holds the camera up. *Flash-click-whir.* A photo shoots out of the slot at the bottom, and Grammy grabs it and waves it back and forth.

"To remember this day," she says, her voice old and worn.

She slips the photograph inside her dress pocket without letting Claire or Audrey see the result.

Outside, the hot wind sweeps in violent gray gusts across the front yard. The trees slope and twist and the clouds press down on the land-scape as if to smother the entire town. Claire smells rain in the distance. Normally she likes the scent of rain, but tonight it's tinged with some-thing harsh and astringent.

"Hurry up, before the wind messes up your hair!" Audrey's already running to her car. Claire takes a deep breath and follows, diving into the passenger seat. The wind slams the door shut for her.

"Wow!" Audrey says. "That's going to be quite the storm." She starts the engine. Claire arranges the fabric of her skirt, piling it on top of her lap. *Quite the storm.* Who talks like that?

"Are you sure the dance is still happening?" Claire asks. "I mean, this storm seems pretty bad—"

Audrey pulls out of the driveway. The car shakes from the wind. "I'm sure it's fine," she says. "It hasn't even started raining yet."

An uneasy feeling has followed Claire out of the house, and she pulls on her skirts, trying to calm herself. The silk no longer feels slick and cool, but hot and constricting. The lace at the neckline itches her skin.

Something hangs on the air. Something is woven through that storm.

They cruise along the neighborhood and turn onto the main street. Audrey switches on the radio. They get a Victoria station, the music crackling with static. "That's the Way Love Goes." All summer long Claire has heard this song, Janet Jackson's whispered chorus ringing in her head. Especially when she thinks about Julie.

Audrey sings along, drumming her hands on the steering wheel. "C'mon!" she says. "Sing with me."

Claire looks out the window, into the storm-cloud darkness of the town. Audrey has pulled into a neighborhood lined with oak trees, their branches shaking ominously overhead. A few windows are lit up, little yellow squares floating in the distance.

"Stay here," she says, turning into the driveway of one of the houses and putting the car in park. "I'm gonna go grab Lawrence."

The porch light flicks on. Lawrence steps out of the house. Claire doesn't quite recognize him. He's wearing a suit and a long black cape, and he swings a cane around as Audrey drags him out to the car.

He crawls into the back seat. Claire twists around to look at him. He looks uncomfortable in his black suit.

"What are you?" she asks.

"A vampire," he answers.

"Don't you just love his costume?" Audrey gushes. "The cane's a nice touch, don't you think? It's been in his family for *years*."

"My father gave it to me." Lawrence stares out the car window. The brake lights turn his face crimson.

Claire shivers, balling her hands up in the fabric of her dress. A cane from his family, a dress from hers.

Claire sees a flash of Julie, smiling at her in the bright sunlight, her hair blowing across her face.

"Are we going to pick up Christopher?" Claire asks quickly, and tries to imagine his face instead. She can't.

"Oh, didn't I tell you?" Audrey looks over at her. "He's meeting us there."

"You didn't tell me that," Claire says. She glances back at Lawrence. He's still staring out the window.

"I'm sure I did." Audrey pulls out of the neighborhood. Claire isn't convinced, but she lets it drop. She doesn't feel like arguing with Audrey.

They drive down the main street of town. The streetlights cast great yellow spheres across the asphalt, and the signs in the shop windows glow. They pass Alvarez Video, then the Pirate's Den. Audrey turns the radio up, but this time Claire doesn't recognize the song. Audrey starts singing again, louder than before they picked up Lawrence, her voice sweet and clear, until Claire can't hear the radio anymore. Just Audrey's voice.

Then, with a jolt, she realizes where they are.

"We're going to the beach," she says.

Audrey falls silent. The song kicks back in, a faint whine in the background.

Claire looks over at her. "The signs all say it's at the VFW hall," she says. "Is that on the beach?"

A half second of hesitation. Then Audrey says, "Of course it is. Right, Lawrence?"

His voice from the back of the car is small and far away. "Yeah. The beach."

The radio DJ comes on, yammering about a flash flood warning.

"Are you *sure* the dance is still going on?" Claire gestures at the radio. "It's probably not safe to be on the beach—"

274

Audrey switches the radio off. "I'm sure."

"I really don't mind heading home. I mean, I'm kind of tired anyway, it's not a big deal. You two can still go out." She gestures back at Lawrence. "Probably don't want me intruding on your date anyway."

"I'm *sure*." Audrey swings the car violently off the road and they bounce along the sandy road, through the dunes. The car's headlights illuminate patches of sand and dune vines, leeching them of their color.

And then they're at the shore. Audrey puts the car in park, and the headlights shine across the water. The waves are huge, towering, like walls of glass.

Claire feels light-headed. She clutches the door handle, a sick feeling rolling around in her stomach. "What are we doing here?" she asks. "This isn't safe, this storm is going to wash us *away*—"

Audrey shuts off the engine and climbs out of the car. The wind sweeping in through the open door smells like rain and the sea and something burning.

"What are you doing?" Claire asks. She turns back to Lawrence. "What is she doing?"

Lawrence looks at her. His eyes are glassy in the darkness. "I don't know."

The back passenger door flies open. "Lawrence, sweetie," says Audrey. "I need you for a minute." She leans in and drapes her arms over his shoulders and kisses him, a kiss so intense that Claire has to turn away, flushing. A rustle of clothes from the back seat.

"Don't forget your cane!" calls out Audrey in a singsong voice.

The door slams again. Claire twists around in time to see Audrey and Lawrence walking toward the dunes.

"Hey!" she shouts. "What the hell!?" And then, because the confusion is too much, "This isn't the VFW hall!"

Claire fumbles for the latch to open the door. Her fingers close on it, and she tugs, but nothing happens. She tugs again, over and over. The door doesn't open. She double-checks, but the lock is up.

The door is unlocked, but it won't open.

"Audrey!" Claire screams. "Come back!" She leans across the driver's seat. There's a safety lock in these kind of cars, isn't there? To keep children from opening the door? Where is it?

"You can stop that now."

Claire jolts at the sound of Audrey's voice. She lifts her head, her hand hovering over the driver's-side door handle. Audrey looms outside.

"What do you mean?" Behind Audrey, all Claire can see is darkness. "Where's Lawrence?"

"Exactly where he needs to be." Audrey stares through the window. The wind blows her hair around like a flame. Her face is almost unrecognizable. Eyes too big, teeth too sharp, her features like they're carved out of bone.

She almost looks like a monster.

"Audrey! What are you doing?" Panic sharpens the edges of Claire's voice. "Why aren't we at the dance?"

Lightning flashes out on the Gulf, and in the sudden flare of the light Claire swears she can see Audrey's skeleton. It doesn't look like a human skeleton at all. Too long, too distorted.

"It's nothing personal," Audrey says. "Sorry."

Claire pulls on the driver's door handle, but the door won't budge. How is that possible? There are no safety locks on the driver's door!

A cold panic shudders through her.

"What's going on!" She bangs on the window, her vision blurring. Tears streak down her cheeks. "What the *hell*! Let me out, Audrey! I don't know how you have the doors locked, but this isn't funny anymore!" She wonders if Lawrence is in on this, if he's laughing up in the dunes. "I thought we were friends! Audrey!"

"I told you," Audrey says. "It's nothing personal."

She turns away from the car. Lightning flickers again, and through the windshield Claire can see the storm clouds, illuminated: But they're *not* clouds—they're inky black swirls, galaxies collapsing in on themselves.

Claire screams and slaps her hands against the windows as Audrey walks away, her dress flapping around her ankles and her pumps dangling from one hand. Claire yanks on the door handles again, snapping them up and down. She tries to roll down the windows. Nothing.

Audrey doesn't turn around. Just strides off into the dunes, disappearing into the darkness. Lawrence is nowhere to be seen.

Claire chokes back a sob. The wind shrieks as it blows around the car. Her thoughts a wild, anxious blur, she pulls off one of her shoes and bangs it against the window. It makes a soft, hollow sound, and she hurls it against the windshield in frustration. Nothing happens. She tries the door again, then crawls into the back seat, her dress tangling up around her legs, and tries the back doors and the back windows. Nothing.

Somehow, Audrey has sealed the car shut.

Claire slumps down. Her skirt pushes up around her waist. The car is hot and airless. The waves roar out in the Gulf, and every time lightning flashes she sees them surging, white-tipped and terrifying beneath that eerie, ink-soaked sky. Seawater sprays across the front windshield every minute or two, a fine, faint mist that leaves a dull feeling in Claire's stomach.

She sits in the back seat of Audrey's car, in her stupid costume, weeping. When the first raindrops dot the windows, she screams and yanks on the door handles again—but nothing happens. Because this isn't just a car, this isn't just a storm.

As Claire listens to the pinging sound of rain on the car roof, she thinks of a hundred-year-old hurricane, of her ancestor who'd been out on the middle of the beach as it rolled into shore.

The ancestor whose dress she is wearing, in the present.

JULIE

Julie careens through Lawrence's neighborhood, her heart banging around inside her chest. The sky roils with thick black clouds. It hasn't started raining yet, but it's so dark, the storm might as well be a hurricane, even though the radio hasn't reported anything but thunderstorms.

But Julie doesn't care what the radio does or doesn't say. It's the anniversary of the hurricane and a storm's blowing in and Claire is with Audrey and something terrible is going to happen.

Something terrible's going to happen, and Julie has to stop it.

She hurtles around the corner. Lawrence's house sits in the darkness, the windows barely illuminated. Julie presses her foot on the gas and lurches forward. She hunches over the steering wheel, her arms shaking from gripping it so tightly.

Thunder rumbles in the distance.

She pulls into the driveway and tumbles out of the car. Then she races up to the front door and rips it open. She has to catch him before he leaves for the Stargazer's Masquerade.

Aunt Rosa appears, her hair piled on top of her head. "Julie?" she asks. "You're not going to the dance?"

Julie's thoughts are wild. "Is Lawrence here?"

Aunt Rosa shakes her head. "You just missed him, sweetie. They left about five minutes ago. You might have even passed them on your way here."

"*Them?* Was Claire with him?"

"Claire?"

"My friend," Julie says hopelessly. "Mrs. Sudek's granddaughter."

"Oh, no." Aunt Rosa frowns. "I didn't see anyone else—Audrey picked him up. Sweet girl, don't you think?"

Julie's ears buzz. "Aunt Rosa, I really don't think Audrey is who she says she is— Ow!"

Julie slams herself up against the doorframe, a sharp pain ricocheting through her skull.

"Julie!" Aunt Rosa's voice is distant, fuzzy. The pain turns into a light behind Julie's eyes. She hears someone singing "Leader of the Pack."

"I'm fine." Julie rubs at her head. The world swims around, a maelstrom of wind and lightning. "They're going to the dance, right?"

"Of course."

Julie nods. The pain in her head is slowly disappearing. She has to come at Audrey sideways, she realizes. It's like Aldraa said. Audrey exists in a blind spot.

And she's taken Claire and Lawrence there with her.

"Okay. Thanks, Aunt Rosa." Julie gives her a kiss on the cheek. "If Lawrence calls, you tell him I'm looking for him, okay?"

"Of course." Aunt Rosa frowns. "Are you sure you're all right, hon?"

"I'm fine." Julie turns and bounds off the porch before Aunt Rosa can ask her any more questions. She slides into the driver's seat of the car and takes a deep breath. Aunt Rosa watches from the porch, and Julie gives her a smile and a wave, even though her heartbeat has picked up again, that wild drum-drum-drumming that echoes inside her own head.

A drop of rain lands on the windshield.

"Shit," she whispers, and she turns on the engine and jerks the car out of the driveway and then speeds through the pitch-black evening. The VFW hall is on the edge of town, a ten-minute drive from Aunt Rosa's house. Julie drives too fast, and she makes it there in six.

The parking lot is already crammed full of cars, and music thumps out of the building: Haddaway, Pet Shop Boys, DJ Jazzy Jeff. Thunder rumbles from the direction of the beach, a low and ominous sound that jars against the beat from the dance. Two women in feathery showgirl costumes cling to each other and race across the lot.

Julie steps out of the car. The door to the VFW swings open, revealing a fan of light, a swell of volume-distorted music. Claire runs across the lot. The rain is still sprinkling, but her skin prickles with electricity, and she knows the storm is coming. She knows she doesn't have much time.

"Stop, miss! Need your ticket."

It's a man dressed as a lobster. He waves one of his fabric claws at her. "Five-dollar entry fee."

"What?" Julie stares at him, not understanding.

The lobster taps a sign taped next to the door. *Tickets five dollars.* Of course. Julie pulls a wadded-up five out of her pocket and tosses it at him and then pushes through the door.

The inside of the VFW hall is a fever dream. Fog machines belt mist into the multicolored air, and the costumes catch the light and shine and sparkle. Everywhere Julie looks she sees cowboys and Terminators and Marge Simpsons and witches and sexy cats, all dancing together in the middle of the room.

Of course. It's a *masquerade*. They'll be wearing costumes. She should have asked Aunt Rosa how Lawrence is dressed, just to give her something to go on.

But then she remembers Claire asking to borrow the dress they found in her attic. Abigail's dress. She never explained why, just *asked* one day out of the blue.

A Victorian lady. Julie needs to look for a Victorian lady.

Julie slinks up against the wall. The music thumps against her head, bringing that sharp pain back to the fore. The costumes and the lights blur together. She can't see human faces anymore, only the costumes, bedazzled and surreal.

Everyone here looks like a monster.

No one looks like a Victorian woman.

No one looks like Abigail Sudek.

Abigail Sudek. Julie freezes next to the snack table. A boy in a Pinhead mask jostles up against her and shouts, "Hey!" but she ignores him.

Claire borrowed Abigail's dress. A dress from a hundred years ago.

The timelines are disrupted.

Thunder crashes outside the dance, louder than the music, and a cry of surprise erupts from the partygoers. Everyone looks up at the lights as if they're expecting them to go out.

A storm. A woman in a dress.

Just like the night a hundred years ago.

Julie paces away from the snack table, dodging a gang of zombies and a trio of girls from school dressed in red *Baywatch* swimsuits. Think.

Think. Think. A hundred years ago, a hurricane rolled in, dragging the monsters with it. They changed the timeline. They need it to stay changed. *Indianola* needs it to stay changed. And a hundred years ago, as part of that timeline, Julie's ancestor saved Claire's ancestor—

From a shack on the beach.

Julie has to go to the beach.

The astronaut is trying to change that night. She's using Claire to re-create it, to alter it, Julie's sure of it.

And what she's doing will wipe out the monsters and the town.

Julie hurries back outside. The lobster says something, but to Julie his voice is a blur. She races to the car. The trees in the parking lot thrash with the wind. The rain sounds like the chatter of insects.

She grabs hold of her car handle. Locked. Dammit. She fumbles for her keys, opens the door, starts the engine. She shakes with fear and anxiety, a sick dread that something has happened to Claire. *Is* happening to Claire. To Lawrence too. To everyone.

And she won't be able to stop it.

The rain falls harder and harder, splattering across the windshield. She pulls out of the parking lot, swerving to avoid hitting the stream of cars pouring in for the masquerade. After the pounding music of the dance, her hearing is fuzzy and distorted. The rain on the roof of the car sounds like buzzing. That can't be right.

Lightning shatters the sky into pieces.

Julie tightens her hands on the steering wheel. The wipers swish and click across the glass. Even in her panic she knows going to the beach in this weather is a terrible idea. But if Claire and Lawrence are out there...

Another flash of lightning. Julie jumps, nervous and frightened, even though she's never been afraid of lightning. But there's something ferocious about this lightning, like it's not electrons charging through the clouds but something else. Something no one on Earth has seen before.

"Hurry!" Julie whispers to herself, pressing her foot down on the gas. The car careens through downtown. Dunes rise up behind the buildings.

And then another flash of lightning arcs through the storm clouds. But this one doesn't flicker away. It etches lines all across the sky and hangs there. The sky looks like cracked porcelain.

Julie lets out a cry of horror. The engine roars and the car shoots forward, toward the silhouette of dunes at the end of a street. The rain falls harder, and the wipers can barely sluice it off. She feels a moment of clarity.

A hundred years ago, Javier saved Abigail. Now Julie is Javier. Claire is Abigail.

And Javier has to save Abigail again.

Julie's car bursts onto the beach, weaving through the dunes. Off in the Gulf the waves rise huge and towering. Over the constant, unnatural buzzing in her head, Julie think she hears something—a voice, muffled and far away. She slams on the brakes.

"Claire?" she shouts, whipping her head around. She can't see anything but falling rain. She climbs out of the car. The lightning lines still etch across the sky, although they're dimming. But then there's a riotous crash of thunder, and the lines infuse with light.

"No," she whispers. Then she spins around in place, ignoring the rain pounding down on her. "Claire!" she shouts. "It's Julie!"

"Julie?"

The voice again. It's not Claire's. Lawrence? It sounds closer now.

"Lawrence?" Julie shouts. "Hello? Where are you!?"

"Julie, is that you?"

It's hard to hear anything over the rain and the rushing waves. Julie stumbles over dune vines and lands hard in the wet sand.

"I think I can see you!" Definitely Lawrence. "Move a few feet forward."

Julie crawls, sand squeezing up between her fingers, rain beating down against her back. She lifts her head. Wet hair hangs in her eyes.

Lawrence sits in a chair at the top of the dune.

"What the hell are you doing?" Julie shouts. She scrambles to her feet. "Where's Claire? Is she with you?"

"Claire?" Lawrence shakes his head. "I don't know. She was in the car. That was the last—"

"The car?" Julie hangs back, suddenly cautious. Audrey's nowhere to be seen, but that doesn't mean anything. Especially with Lawrence acting so *weird*, sitting on a chair like he's the king of the beach. "What car? Where is she now?"

"Audrey's car. We were down near the water." Lawrence gazes at Julie through the sheeting rain. His eyes seem glassy and dark. "And then we were here on the dunes. I don't remember— She tied me to this chair?" He says it like a question, looking down at his lap.

"She *what*?" And suddenly, though the curtain of rain and the pale light fragmenting the sky, Julie can see the ropes cutting into Lawrence's arms. Some kind of stick or something is jammed into the ropes too. She darts forward and tugs at the knots behind the chair. Her fingers are slippery and the knots are tight, and her breath comes fast. "So you don't know where Claire is?"

"I told you, the car," Lawrence says. "I thought we were going to the dance. But then Audrey drove us here." His voice fades away. "I don't know where Audrey is."

"What the hell is with that cane?" Julie asks. "You didn't bring your gun, did you?"

"My gun?" Lawrence's head lolls. "No, why would I have my gun if I was going out with Audrey?"

"And Claire!" Julie shouts. "Is Claire still in Audrey's car? Is Audrey taking her somewhere?" Julie loosens his binds, digging her fingernails deep into the rope.

"No, I didn't bring my gun," Lawrence says, his voice far away. "This is my dad's cane. Part of my costume. We were supposed to be at the dance."

Thunder roars overhead. Julie gives a shriek of frustration—at the rope, at Lawrence, at everything. *Where is Claire?* she screams, one last time.

"In the car," he says dreamily. "We left her there."

Julie freezes, the knots half-undone beneath her fingers. She looks at Lawrence, dread coiling in her stomach. "What?" she whispers.

Lawrence meets her eye, rain streaming down his face. "Audrey locked her in the car on the beach," he says, a burst of clarity.

Julie attacks the rope with renewed fury, the ties dissolving in her hands, and it falls away. Lawrence's cane lands in Julie's lap. The carved wood is soft and soaked through, but the metal knob at the top has a name etched into it. A familiar one.

Emmert.

Julie stands up so quickly her head spins. Lawrence sits motionless, the ropes still wrapped around his torso.

"This," she says, shoving the cane at him. "Where did you get this?"

"We need to find Audrey," he says softly. "She's out there somewhere—"

"Stop talking about her! She's got you under some kind of spell!" Julie brandishes the cane. "I'm serious, Lawrence. Where did you get this?"

"My dad." Lawrence rubs his forehead. "Left it behind. It's always been in the family."

"Your dad's last name is Foster," Julie says, squeezing the cane tight. "Not Emmert."

"His great-grandfather was an Emmert." Lawrence stands up, the rope falling away, and a black cape flutters out behind him. In any other situation, Julie would find that funny. Not tonight. "You shouldn't be out here. This storm is dangerous. I need to find Audrey."

"Henry Emmert," Julie whispers. Of course. The third piece of the puzzle. An Alvarez, a Sudek, and an Emmert. The Emmert died, last time. But not tonight.

Tonight, a Sudek will die.

"I have to find Claire," Julie says. "Now."

"No," says Lawrence. "We have to find Audrey."

"Fuck Audrey!" Julie screams. "She's responsible for this, don't you understand? I need you to show me where Claire is!"

A Sudek will die, but not if an Alvarez saves her. The timelines have to be re-created.

"But Audrey—" Lawrence whimpers.

"Is responsible for all of this!" Julie grabs Lawrence's arm and tries to yank him toward the waves crashing in the storm. The rain thunders around them. Lawrence digs his feet into the sand.

"Please," Julie says, tears brimming at the edges of her eyes.

The air buzzes and hums, and the lines in the sky brighten. The waves are silver in the distance.

"To the left," Lawrence whispers.

He leads her out of the dunes, onto the open beach. The wind sweeps down the shore in violent, blustery gusts, and the waves crash off to the side, swelling bigger and bigger. The sky is lined with that weird lightning. It feels like the world is falling apart.

There are miles of beach in Indianola, Julie knows that, but she prays Lawrence knows where to find Claire even in his confused, jumbled-up state.

He halts abruptly. Julie runs into him. "Why'd you stop?"

"You said to find Claire," he says in a dull voice. The wind howls around them. "And there she is."

He points, and Julie looks into the darkness at a sphere of light growing out of the beach ahead of them.

Julie darts forward, but Lawrence grabs her by the arm and pulls her back.

"Audrey wouldn't want us to."

Julie hisses in disgust and throws off Lawrence's hand. "Who cares what Audrey wants?" She squints through the rain at the sphere of light. The storm is so loud, she can barely think.

"I can feel her in my head," Lawrence says. "She's telling me not—"

But Julie rushes forward, leaving him in the rain. She brings the cane with her. The light pulses in the darkness, slow and steady like a metronome. Julie feels that pulse boring into her brain. Numbing her.

She wipes water from her eyes. She won't let that light turn her numb. She has to see what's there. She has to see if Claire is in the car.

"Julie, she wants us to stop!" Lawrence's voice sounds far away. Julie ignores him.

The waves roar and crash against the sand. With each surge she moves closer to the ball of light, but slowly, she finds it harder and harder to move. The air is like sap, sticking to her limbs, holding her in place. The light hurts her eyes. She stares at it, terrified, not sure what's happening.

And then something moves inside the car. A shadow in the shape of a girl.

"Claire!" She tries to race forward, but there's a membrane between her and the light, and as hard as Julie pushes, she can't break free of it: She feels it sticking to her face, to her skin, tangling up in her hair. But she strains anyway, pushing toward that shadow in the light.

Inside the car, two fists appear in silhouette. Two fists, banging on the window. A noise rises out of the roar of the ocean, a sort of keening. It's coming from the direction of the light. It sounds like *eeeee*.

Julieee!

She hears her name in Claire's voice. It seems to drum up out of the rain.

Julie Julie Help me Julie

"I'm coming!" Julie screams, fighting against the thick membranous air. She shoves Lawrence's cane into the sand, using it as a lever to pull herself forward, her eyes never leaving the shadow. The rain has soaked through her clothes, and the waves are crashing closer and closer, their foam lapping up around her feet, but she has to get to that light. She has to save Claire.

Another crack of thunder. More lines appear in the sky, shattering it into pieces. The waves glow pink. Seawater swirls around Julie's ankles.

The molasses air is in her lungs now. It's getting harder to breathe. But the shadow keeps banging her fists against the car window and Julie thinks she can see features, Claire's features, all twisted up with fear.

"I'm coming!" she gasps, and then, with one last burst of strength, she hurls herself at the car.

It's enough: She breaks free of the thickness that was holding her back. The rain pounds down around her, but she can breathe more easily, and she doesn't feel so heavy. She's close enough to see Claire clearly inside.

Julie! Claire pounds on the window. Her mouth shapes Julie's name but Julie still only hears her voice in the rain. *Help! Help me!*

"I'm trying!" Julie rushes up to the door and grabs the handle. But the light sparks and shocks her and sends her stuttering back across the sand. Her head rings.

Eeee!

"I'm fine," she chokes out. She clambers up to her feet, coughing.

"I can't let you do that!"

Lawrence. Julie turns around, her muscles aching, and sees him lurching forward, still trapped in the membrane. His face is warped and strange in the light of the storm. His features almost look like Audrey's.

"Dammit!" she shouts. If he breaks through that membrane he's going to try to stop her.

Rainwater spills into her mouth, and the tide tugs on her each time it sucks back out into the Gulf. Claire stares at Julie through the window, her face ghostly in the pale light. Julie takes a deep breath.

There has to be some way of getting Claire out. After all, Javier saved Abigail from that shack. It's the same thing. They can reenact the timeline, set it back into place—ensure that the past remains unchanged, that Javier can go on to write the treaties, that the monsters can live alongside humans.

That their world is kept in place. And in peace.

Julie glances back at Lawrence. He howls something unintelligible at her, and then slams forward onto his knees in the storm surge, his cape floating out behind him.

"Stop moving!" she yells at him.

She splashes over to the back of the car. Claire follows her, pressing her hands against the windows. Her eyes are wide and bright with fear, and her mouth keeps moving, but Julie can only catch bits and pieces of what she says in the rush of the rain.

Trapped—Audrey drove—locked—inside—help!

"I'm trying!" Julie shouts. Her voice is ragged and she isn't sure if the water on her cheeks is from the rain or from tears.

She has no idea what to do.

She comes over to the driver's-side door and tries to open it again. This time, she braces herself for the light to shock her, and when it comes, rippling through her spine, at least she doesn't go stumbling over the sand.

Claire appears in the window, shaking her head.

"No?" Julie says. "What am I supposed to do? How do I get you out?"

Claire keeps shaking her head, and her mouth moves, and Julie hears *I don't know.*

A wave surges across the beach, the water splashing up around Julie's knees. She screams and falls forward and both her hands hit the car. The light sends shock waves running through her body, and she flies backward, landing on her back in the freezing seawater. She stares up at the sky, cracked and fragmented.

And she knows that the past is changing already. The treaties are dissolving. It's the end of her town.

The water surges, rushing over her. Something hits her hard on the side of her head. She sits up, gasping—it's Lawrence's cane. She grabs it.

"Julie! Stop this right now!" Lawrence's fingers claw through the air, leaving shreds of opalescent light in their wake. "Audrey says to stop you!"

The membrane. He's tearing through.

"Stay there!" Julie shouts.

"I'm ordering you to stop!" His face distorts with anger as the membrane rips around him. It's dissolving like the treaties, and she has to act fast.

Julie plunges forward toward the car, the cane's polished wood slippery in her grip. Claire stares out the window at her, and Julie remembers the first time she saw her, how scared she'd been of the monster in her grandmother's yard. The monster who was just trying to warn them.

"Julie! If you don't stop immediately I'm going to arrest you!" Lawrence's voice is distorted—doubled, as if Audrey's words are lurking behind his.

Julie squeezes the cane. The one weapon she has. Her one chance.

"I'm coming, Claire," she whispers, and then she pulls the cane back.

When the cane hits the glass it echoes like a gunshot. The sound tears through the storm, shining like lightning.

The light surrounding the car flares, bright as the sun, momentarily illuminating the water crashing along the beach. Aftershocks shoot up Julie's arm, jolts of searing, sizzling pain.

But the glass on the window is cracked.

Julie screams through her pain to swing the cane a second time. The crack deepens.

"Julie! It's working!"

It's Claire's voice, her actual voice. Julie's arms feel as if they're being crushed, but she lifts the cane a third time, swinging it with all of her strength.

The glass shatters.

She screams half in joy and half in disbelief, and drops the cane into the churning seawater, rushing forward. Claire's head appears. Not as a shadow, but as herself.

The back windshield is gone save for a ring of glass in the frame, spiderwebbed with tiny fractures. Claire peers out through this hole, gazing around in horror, her eyes wide with fear.

When she sees Julie, there's a moment like lightning, when everything falls into place.

"Julie," she gasps. "I thought I was going to die."

"I wasn't going to let that happen," Julie says. She holds out her hand. "We have to get out of here."

Shaking, Claire takes her hand, her touch a balm against the pain still reverberating through Julie's bones. She keeps her eyes fixed on Julie, her makeup streaked. She's wearing Abigail's dress, the gray silk turned black with rain, and as she climbs out of the car it catches on a piece of jagged glass and rips.

Then Claire's free, standing in the warm, frothy water with Julie. She's bleeding from a few places on her face, nothing major, and Julie tries to wipe the blood away. Claire catches her hand and smiles up at her.

"I'm sorry," she whispers.

Julie smiles back. Her heart is heavy with love—yes, she's certain of it, *love*. She reaches to smooth back a piece of hair that sticks to the side of Claire's forehead. The rain pounds around them both, and the water levels rise, and Claire wraps her arms around Julie's shoulders and kisses her.

The world falls away. Claire's kiss is shy, a little awkward, a little hesitant, but it's there, it's perfect, and Julie kisses back and her head swims and she thinks that she can drown right now in the ocean and everything will be okay.

"Julie!"

Lawrence's shout drags Julie back into the real world. She whips herself around, positioning her body in front of Claire's. She can feel Claire trembling against her.

"Back off," she says. "I'm serious. Arrest me if you want, I'm *not* letting you—"

"What are the hell are you doing?" Lawrence sways and stumbles, water splashing up around him. He staggers, his hair hanging in his eyes, that stupid cloak sloshing up around him.

"What the hell are we doing out here?" he screams.

And that's when Julie sees it. The rage in his face is gone. He looks exhausted and pale and terrified. His gaze sweeps around, taking in the car, the roaring ocean, the flooded beach.

And then his eyes settle on Claire, and a dark dawning realization crawls across his features.

"Oh my God," he says. "Audrey—" He reaches out to Julie. "She did something to me—"

"You were going to let me drown!" Claire shouts.

"I know." His face crumples. Is he crying? Julie can't tell, not with the rain streaming over them. "I know. I'm so sorry. Audrey—"

"Audrey did something to you," Julie says flatly. She looks back at Claire, who squeezes her arm again. "It's gone. I can tell. He's different."

"Yes." Lawrence's voice is ragged. "She did, she—I'm sorry, Claire." He splashes toward them. "I'm so sorry."

The water has risen almost to Julie's thighs. The undertow is more forceful now, trying to pull her out to sea. "We need to get past the sea-wall," she says, more to Claire than to Lawrence. "Him too. I really do think he's okay."

"I think he is too," Claire says softly.

"Come on," Julie says. "Time to peace out!"

She wraps her arm around Claire's waist and guides her forward. The weird lightning has disappeared out of the sky, and the glow is starting to diminish from the car. Reality doesn't feel so shaky anymore.

The undertow sucks at Julie's legs. She and Claire barely seem to be moving forward.

And then Claire tumbles and lands face-first in the water.

"No!" Julie shrieks as Claire is dragged past her, out toward the open ocean, her dress a streak of silver beneath the dark waves. Julie whirls around just in time to see Lawrence catch Claire and pull her up. She gasps and sputters, spitting out arcs of seawater.

"I'm not letting either of you drown now!" he shouts, sounding more like his old self. "Julie's right! Let's get to the dunes!"

Julie splashes over to them, digging her feet into the sand to keep her balance. Claire sucks in deep breaths of air and gives Julie a brave smile. Her hair is plastered to the side of her face, and her dress sticks to her legs.

"Yeah!" Claire shouts, over the rushing tide. "I want out of this water!"

"Grab on to me!" Lawrence gestures at Julie. "We're fighting against the current here!"

Julie loops her arm into Lawrence's, and the three of them plunge forward through the water.

The waves splash up around them, and Julie's feet slip once, and she crashes into Lawrence—but he and Claire have her by the arms, and they yank her back up to standing.

Together they form a chain strong enough to beat back the undertow.

When they finally make it to the shallows, Julie peels away from Lawrence and grabs Claire and squeezes her tight.

"Thank you for saving my life," Claire says breathlessly.

"What else was I going to do?" Julie smiles.

Together, they splash through the water up to the dunes as the tide recedes. The rain has slackened, and it doesn't have the terrifying ferocity of a hurricane anymore.

It's just a summertime rainstorm.

"Thank God." Lawrence looks at Claire and Julie in turn. "You're both okay?" He shakes his head. "I'm just so sorry, Claire, I don't…" He stops, looks out at the ocean. "What *was* she?"

The water laps at the sand a few feet away from them, shimmering like static from the raindrops. Julie knows the danger has passed. Something could have happened, but it didn't.

She stopped it.

"It's a long story," Julie says. "Hell, I'm not sure I even know."

Lawrence frowns, then begins making his way toward the street.

But Claire and Julie stay standing side by side, the water falling around them soft and gentle. The light is gone from the car now: It sits half-submerged in gray water, waves crashing around it.

Claire squeezes Julie's hand. Julie looks over at her, and Claire is smiling, her eyes shining.

"It seems like it shouldn't be real," she says.

"Why wouldn't it be?" Julie asks.

Claire shrugs. She looks down at her feet, her hair falling in her eyes. Julie leans over and kisses her on the cheek.

Of course it's real.

Everything is safe.

Twenty

CLAIRE

Kissing Julie is like waking up from a nightmare. The horror of being locked in the car, watching the Gulf draw closer and closer, drains away. Claire grabs both of Julie's hands and holds them tight.

"Thank you," she whispers. "Thank you for saving me."

Julie shrugs. Then she grins. "My pleasure."

Claire laughs. She throws her arms around Julie's neck and kisses her again. She doesn't care about the rain pounding around them, about the water sloshing up to the dunes, about Lawrence. All summer Claire has been working through her own confusion to come to this point, to this kiss. She used to want to kiss Josh, now she wants to kiss Julie. She can like both.

Lawrence coughs.

"This beach is still going to flood!" he shouts over the roar of the rain. "We need to get to higher ground."

Claire and Julie pull apart. Julie smiles. "Typical Lawrence," she says in a low voice, reassuringly. "When he gets freaked out he starts acting more like a cop than usual."

Claire laughs a little, but for the first time since crawling out of the car, she's aware that she's soaked through and shivering. Thunder rumbles overhead.

She grabs Julie's hand, and together they run toward the boardwalk, toward Lawrence standing with his arms crossed. He's still wearing that cape. Funny, how earlier it had made him seem all the more terrifying. Now he just looks ridiculous.

"Come on," he says brusquely, like he's an authority figure. Together the three of them walk through the dunes, Lawrence leading, Claire and Julie trailing, holding hands. Without the magic of the kiss, Claire slowly comes to terms with everything that happened.

Audrey put her in Abigail's dress.

She locked Claire in a car on the beach.

Claire almost died.

I almost died. The idea shudders around her head. She glances over at Julie, water-logged and smiling.

Nothing makes sense, except for Julie.

When they climb up over the seawall, they're standing on the edge of downtown. Half the streetlamps are out, but the Pirate's Den sign glows at the end of the block, casting eerie red light into the rain.

"We can call the station from there," Lawrence says, striding ahead with long, anxious steps. "Get out of the rain for a little while."

Julie glances over at Claire. "Sound okay?"

"Sounds perfect." Claire didn't realize how hungry she was until now. Her whole body is drained of energy.

They march through the downpour and file into the Pirate's Den. The arcade cabinets beep and chirp and let out light like a row of hearths. The man behind the counter gives a wave. Lawrence waves back like they know each other.

"Looks like you were caught in the storm," the man says. "Ever make it to the dance?"

"Not quite." Lawrence leans against the counter and runs his fingers through his hair. His hand is shaking, even if he's managing to keep his voice even. "Mind if I use your phone? I don't have any change on me."

The man chuckles. "Why don't you have something to eat? A large one-topping on the house. Looks like the three of you need it."

Lawrence glances over at Julie and Claire, frowning.

"We'll take it," Julie calls out. She looks at Claire. "What do you want? You're the lady of the hour."

Claire feels herself color. "Pepperoni, please. And thank you!"

"You heard the lady," Julie calls out. The man nods and bustles off to the back. Lawrence sighs, turns around to face them. Rainwater pools in a puddle beneath him. Beneath all of them.

"We need to report this to the committee immediately," he says, his voice strained. "They need to know there's a renegade monster—"

"Audrey's not a monster," Julie says quickly. "She's something else. The monsters are the ones who warned us about her."

Claire looks over at Julie, shocked. "*Really?*"

Julie nods. "Well, they tried, anyway. They aren't—they aren't good at dealing with humans."

"Well, we still need to tell the committee," Lawrence says. Then he looks at Claire, his gaze piercing and comforting at the same time. "I'm very sorry that I was—incapacitated. By whatever she is. I can't tell you how grateful I am that you're all right." He pauses. "I hope you'll forgive me."

Claire looks at him. When he's not with Audrey his eyes are brighter, his expression kinder. And she knows what it's like to be controlled by Audrey, doesn't she? "Of course I do."

Lawrence gives her a crooked, relieved smile.

"Go find us a table," he says. "I'm still going to call the station to let them know what happened. They'll be able to send out a notice to the committee."

"Yeah, yeah." Julie loops her arm in Claire's, which makes Claire glow. They walk to their usual table, dripping a trail of water behind them. Claire hopes the manager won't mind.

Something catches at the corner of her eye. She glances up.

Fear paralyzes her through to her core.

Julie tugs on her arm. "Claire, what is it, what's wr—"

She falls silent, and Claire knows she sees her too. Audrey, sitting at a table by herself, sipping a Coke through a straw. Her dress throws off dots of light. A half-eaten salad has been pushed to the side, a napkin crumpled on top of it. She finally looks up, catches Claire's eye. Claire swoons.

"Well," Audrey says. "This is unexpected."

The sound of her voice brings Claire back to the present. Anger rushes up through her system. "Why did you do that to me!" she shrieks, lunging at the table, not knowing what she plans to do. Audrey doesn't move, doesn't even blink. But Claire slams up against an invisible wall and lands sprawling on her back.

"Holy crap, are you okay?" Julie rushes to Claire and helps her sit up. Her touch is soft and warm, a respite against the harsh, crackling air.

Audrey doesn't move from the table.

"Why'd you do it?" Claire can hardly breathe. "What'd I ever do to you?"

Audrey sighs, crosses one leg over the other.

"What's going on here?" Lawrence's voice booms out behind them. "Claire, are you—" He freezes.

Audrey tilts her head at Lawrence. "Hi, boyfriend," she says.

Lawrence doesn't move. Claire and Julie both watch him from their place on the floor. Claire's breath is in her throat. She thinks about his blank expression in the car. His willingness to leave her to die in the car.

But then Lawrence shakes his head. "I'm—I'm taking you into custody." His voice shakes, though, and Claire suspects he knows that's an impossibility. "You did something to me. To us. I won't let you do that to anyone else."

"*You* were just supposed to watch," Audrey says.

Claire grabs Julie's hand without thinking. The air is still crackling. It reminds her of being trapped inside the car. Her heart beats too fast.

"What?" Lawrence says.

"The original trio, together at last." Audrey gestures with her Coke at Claire, Julie, and Lawrence, each in turn.

Claire shivers. She draws her knees up to her chest, the water-soaked fabric of her dress tangling around her legs.

No, not her dress. Abigail's dress.

"Yeah, I figured out all about that," Julie snaps. "That's why you made Lawrence bring that cane. And Claire wear this dress."

"I don't understand," says Claire, feeling dazed. "What are you both talking about?"

"I don't know." Lawrence looks pale.

"I'm Javier," Julie says. "You're Abigail." And then she points at Lawrence. "He's Emmert."

Claire stares at her. "*Him?*"

"Not like the Emmert a hundred years ago, that's for sure." Julie glares at Audrey. "No thanks to you."

Audrey laughs. "Congratulations, Lawrence. You're the first non-screw-up Emmert in years."

Lawrence's eyes narrow with anger, and he trembles in place.

Claire feels dizzy. Audrey was playing some kind of *game* with her, like all the games she played this summer—only so much more dangerous. Claire digs her hand into her forehead. She can feel the beginning of a migraine pounding beneath her skin.

Audrey brushes a strand of hair away from her face. She's completely dry, her hair fluffed and styled, none of her makeup streaked from the rain. "Anyway. Sorry. Nothing personal, like I said."

"Nothing personal?" Claire springs to her feet. Julie stands up with her, their hands connected. "You almost killed me."

Audrey doesn't say anything.

"Why?" Claire demands. The question cracks with tears. "Why would you do that to me?"

"The timelines," Julie says.

Everything in the Pirate's Den shuts down. The arcade cabinets fall dark and silent, and the overhead lights flutter away and are replaced by the dull yellow glow of the generators. Outside, the storm falls silent, the raindrops frozen on the windows.

When Claire glances back at the front counter, the cashier is frozen in place, his hand reaching toward a notepad on the counter.

She whips her head back, fear squeezing her throat shut.

"You were trying to disrupt the timelines," Julie says, her voice echoing. "Aldraa told me."

Audrey rolls her eyes. "Yes, Aldraa wasn't happy about my plans.

He and the rest of the *xenade* need Javier to be the town hero so he can go on to establish the treaties. It's the only reason they get to live here, you know. The good people of Indianola would have killed them off otherwise. That's another timeline." Audrey gives a satisfied nod. "But Aldraa's concerns weren't my problem."

"I don't understand what's going on." Lawrence looks back at Julie. "Do you? Can someone please explain?"

Julie shakes her head. "That's all I know."

Claire shivers, from the cold, the rain, her own confusion. "Why did you want to kill me?" she says. "What do I have to do with timelines?"

"I keep telling you, it wasn't personal. Changing the past is a tricky business. One I specialize in, but tricky." Audrey tosses her hair over her shoulder. "You fit the right cosmic profile. The only cosmic profile, for this particular *azojin*."

The last word hits Claire hard in the back of the head. She's heard it before, in the rough hissing voices of the monsters.

Every azojin, *something changes.*

"The only way to change the past," Audrey says, "is to re-create it in the present. Under the right circumstances, of course." She smiles. "I had to shape you a bit. Remember that game on the beach?"

Claire feels dizzy.

"You did well with it, really. Picked it up like a natural." Audrey sips her Coke. "'The music of Indianola,' that's how you put it. Poetic."

Claire gasps. "I never said that out loud!"

"Didn't have to. I can see right through you." Audrey grins. "Right through all of you. I'm operating on a different plane of existence." She pauses, one hand on her hip. "But yes, the music of Indianola, that's what all this was about. Changing the way those Indianolans of the past interacted with each other. That day on the beach was getting you ready. Wearing down the dimensional effluvium, so to speak. Cleaning you up for the *azojin*."

Claire takes deep breaths. The frozen Pirate's Den spins around her. She takes a step back, trying to get away from Audrey, and bangs up against one of the chairs. A hand on her arm. Julie. She pulls Claire in close, squeezes her.

"It's okay," she whispers, but Claire can't take her eyes off Audrey, who looks the same as she always did: blond and beautiful and normal. But she's not normal. She *manipulated* Claire somehow, twisted her own thoughts around inside of her. Claire trembles in Julie's embrace.

"What else did you do to me?" she asks. "What about that maze game at your house? Was that cleaning me up too?"

Audrey grins, but before she can answer, Julie interrupts.

"You were hiding her," Julie says. "From the monsters. They were trying to protect her."

Audrey nods. "Afraid so." She tilts her head and studies Julie for a moment. Claire wishes she would stop. The way she looks at Julie makes Claire think Julie's in danger. "You went snooping too. Found the family I created. Easier to build human models for when I need them than borrow a real family, you know?"

Claire thinks of Audrey's mother and father and brother, how blank they always seemed.

"I suppose I can thank the *xenade* for sending you my way. I underestimated them. I didn't think they'd go to a human for help." She shrugs. "They get desperate, those lost souls." Audrey stands and faces toward the exit.

"Stop right there." Lawrence's voice comes as a shock. Claire looks over at him; he's collapsed in a nearby booth, and he looks pale. "You put three people in danger, including an officer of the law. You don't get to just walk out of here."

Audrey turns her gaze to him. He seems to shrink back.

"First of all," she says, "you know perfectly well that I will in fact just walk out of here." She gives a dazzling smile. "And secondly, you're not in danger anymore. You fought against the constraints I put on you. Didn't call me down when Julie started swinging the cane." She shrugs. "For what it's worth, I'm impressed. With all of you, if I'm being honest."

Lawrence gapes at her.

"I'm leaving your dimension tonight. I just need to collect my last payment."

Claire feels like she's been punched in the face.

"Payment?" Julie repeats. Her voice sounds covered over by waves of static. "Someone *paid you* to kill Claire?"

"Yes. I was called here by a human. One of the *xenade* told her about me—a nasty business, if I understand correctly. She kept the poor thing chained up in her garage until it talked." She cocks her head. "All she said was that she was tired of this reality and wanted me to sculpt a new one."

Claire feels like she might throw up. "A new reality," she gasps. "One where I'm dead."

"Oh, sweetie." Audrey's face twists into a parody of sympathy. "Your death wasn't the goal. It was the means to an end. It's just poor luck that you turned out to be so cosmically significant."

"What was the goal?" Julie demands. Claire is grateful, because she can't bring herself to speak.

"She wanted a reality where Javier Alvarez never saved Abigail

Sudek, so I tried to set it up for her." Audrey's features shift around, become sharper, harsher, less human. Claire's stomach churns, and Lawrence gives a strangled gasp.

"Ah well." Audrey sighs. "I'll admit my heart wasn't completely in this one. Times have been tough, and I was sick of going hungry. So I took what I could get."

"Are you going to try to kill me again?" Claire's blood rushes. "Or have Lawrence kill me?"

"I'm not going to kill you," Lawrence says.

But Audrey just shrugs. "The *azojin*'s passed."

That word again.

"Won't work again for another hundred years. Everything had to fit together just so, and you lot screwed it up." She jabs her thumb at Julie. "Well, you and the *xenade*. That's really my employer's fault, though. She killed the one who talked, tossed the body out to sea. Can you imagine? The *xenade* were able to find it and draw out some of its history, so they knew that I was coming, but never who hired me." She picks up the Coke and takes one long drink. "Well, I'll be on my way. I'll miss these things, though. No other dimension has anything quite like them." She sets the can back down on the table and moves toward the door. Claire feels a rise of panic—she still doesn't know who wanted to kill her.

"Wait!"

Audrey stops and looks over at Claire. Her features have distorted even further, and her hair has turned to feathers the color of starlight.

"Who was it?" Claire spits out, choking back a wave of nausea. "Who wanted to change reality? *Who wanted to erase me?*"

Audrey hesitates. Something glows behind her eyes that's not human but isn't monstrous, either. A little lick of white flame.

"Tell me," Claire says, drawing up her strength.

Audrey looks at the door, where unmoving red raindrops decorate the glass. She turns back to Claire. The flame in her eyes brightens.

The air crackles. All the arcade cabinets turn back on at once. The raindrops turn to tributaries.

"I was on my way to collect my last payment," she says. "But I suppose I can let you speak to her first. It's only fair."

"Who is it?" Claire shrieks.

"Myrtle Sudek," Audrey says. "Your grammy."

She gives a hard smile, and then she blinks out like a broken lightbulb, a whiff of ozone in her wake.

The house is dark when Claire gets home. The storm has moved on, but night's fallen, a seamless transition of darkness.

Julie called Frank, the manager at the video store, and convinced him to let them borrow his car. Lawrence argued half-heartedly that they go to the sheriff's station, but he relented when Claire refused. She won't talk to anyone but Grammy. And the police aren't going to be able to help them anyway.

She wants answers. An explanation.

Frank sits at the curb, his car engine idling. Julie's a few feet away, standing with her hands on her hips. Lawrence is there too, scowling in his sopping wet suit and cape.

"I don't like this," he says. "We have no idea how dangerous she is."

Claire draws up her spine. "I told you, I don't want you there."

"I'm just worried about your safety. If what Audrey said is true—"

"I need to talk to my grandmother alone." Claire takes a deep breath. "Please, Lawrence. Let me do this alone."

He studies her, disapproval on his features.

Claire turns and looks at Grammy's house. Her clothes and hair are still wet, and a film of salt clings to her skin. Remnants of what happened.

Of what Grammy wanted to happen.

No—Claire can't think like that. She doesn't know for sure. Maybe Audrey is lying.

But at the same time, Claire keeps thinking of looks that passed between Grammy and Audrey, of the way Grammy forced her and Audrey together. She thinks about the little white pillbox containing nothing but aspirin. She thinks about Grammy's illness, the call to the doctor that proved she'd never gotten a diagnosis.

Payment, Claire thinks.

"Are you sure?" Julie whispers. "About going in there alone?"

Claire looks over at her. Julie gives a brave smile. Even with wet hair she's beautiful. As beautiful as Josh. More so.

"I think it'll be better if I do," Claire says.

"If there's any trouble *at all*," Lawrence says, shifting his weight, "you scream, do you understand?"

Claire nods. Julie says nothing, just takes Claire's hand. "I'll be out here," she says. "We both will. And if you aren't out in five minutes—"

"Fifteen minutes," Claire says. "Give me a chance to talk to her first."

"Ten minutes." Julie draws Claire into a hug. Claire buries her face in Julie's neck, breathes in the scent of rainwater and lavender. She never wants to let go.

She lets go.

"Ten minutes," Claire says.

Lawrence sighs, and Claire knows she probably has closer to five before he comes into the house with his badge and his gun, which he had insisted on picking up from his house before they came here. She takes a deep breath, turns around, cuts across the damp yard.

She goes inside.

Even though all the lights are out, the sound of the TV trickles in from the living room, the raucous laughter of some late-night talk show. Claire's heartbeat quickens. For a moment she leans up against the doorway, struggling to breathe.

She's my grandma. She wouldn't try to kill me. Would she?

Slowly, Claire moves into the living room. Grammy sits in the usual spot, although an ashtray rests on the table beside her, something Claire has never seen before. A trio of cigarette butts wallows in the ash.

Claire feels a low coil of dread at the sight of that ashtray.

"You're home." Grammy doesn't look away from the TV.

"Yes." Claire wants to be wrong. She wants Audrey to be lying. "Do you want to know how it went?"

Over on the TV, Jay Leno says something to make the audience roar with laughter. Claire shifts her weight. *Please answer*, she thinks. *Please please make none of this be true.*

Grammy keeps staring at the TV.

And then Claire sees something, a photograph lying on the end table. A Polaroid. It's facedown. With a trembling hand, Claire flips it over.

Neither she nor Audrey Duchesne is there. Claire has been replaced by the woman whose photograph she found in Grammy's closet. Abigail Sudek. It's not a costume. There's no trace of Claire in that photograph.

Audrey is a beam of silver light, bright feathers, a face with sharp predatory features.

Claire cries out. Tears brim against her lashes. She claps her hand over her mouth.

Grammy looks up. She seems tired. She looks at Claire, looks at the photograph in Claire's hand.

Then she turns back to the TV.

Claire throws the Polaroid back on the table. She can't stop trembling.

"If you won't ask," she says, "then I'll tell you. Audrey's plan didn't work. Julie Alvarez saved me. And her cousin Lawrence." She takes a deep, shuddering breath. "I'm guessing that's not what you wanted to happen."

Grammy picks up the remote and points it at the TV. Then, just as a commercial comes on, she switches it off.

"No," Grammy says. "That's not what I wanted to happen."

A sharp, violent paint shoots through the center of Claire's heart. She collapses down on the chair beside Grammy and stares at the blank TV.

It's real. Audrey wasn't lying.

A cold fear curls up inside her, weighted down with the heaviness of betrayal. She thinks of Julie and Lawrence standing out in the rain-soaked grass, listening for a scream, ready to come save her.

"How could you?" Claire whispers. Tears streak down her face. "I would have *died*, I would have—"

"Sometimes we have to make sacrifices." Grammy stands up abruptly. She walks over to the bookshelf full of old encyclopedias and pulls out the volumes *L* through *P*. Behind them sits the old photograph

311

of Julie's house. She pulls it out and stares down at it. "We lost this eighty years ago," she says, and holds it up for Claire to see.

Claire lets out a loud, gasping sob.

"Oh, it was lovely. My mother used to tell me all about it. The big atrium full of flowers and sunlight, the gardens…" Grammy's voice trails off, and she wipes a tear away from one of her eyes. Claire shakes. She almost died and her grandmother is crying over a house.

"All my life I thought it was just bad luck. Bad *history*. Unchangeable," Grammy goes on, still staring down at the photo. "But then a monster came to the backyard last winter, a talking monster. It said something about timelines, that they could be changed. Babbling, you know, the way they do. I took it for nonsense at first. But the idea wouldn't leave me alone." Grammy lifts her head. Her eyes shine with tears. "A hundred years ago Abigail Sudek was saved from drowning by Javier Alvarez. It destroyed this family. And you just let it happen again."

She throws the framed picture against the wall, a sudden violent movement. Claire recoils into her chair. She wonders if she should scream, if she should run out to Julie. But Grammy just shuffles back over to her chair and sits down.

"I spent weeks forcing that monster to tell me how to change the timelines," Grammy says in a calm, cold voice.

Revulsion crawls up the back of Claire's throat, thinking of Audrey's words at the Pirate's Den, about Grammy keeping a monster tied up in the garage and then killing it. She *can't* imagine it, but when she peers up at Grammy she can see a fire burning inside of her, so white hot, it's terrifying. Maybe Grammy was that desperate after all.

"It was hard work, but eventually it told me what I wanted: how the timelines worked, how to call that stupid alien here, how to make a deal she'd accept." Grammy looks over at Claire, and Claire freezes. It's like being caught in the stare of a poisonous snake.

"A Sudek, an Alvarez, and an Emmert," Grammy says in a singsong voice. "Tell me, how much of the story do you know?"

The question is sharp, scolding. Claire trembles. "Enough," she says.

"Oh, no, not a chance. Well, no harm in telling you now. It's too late anyway." Grammy stares at the TV. "Henry was supposed to help Abigail, Charlotte, and Javier get on a shipping boat. They were going to start their lives over down in Manzanillo, where Javier was born. But when Henry learned how much Abigail was worth, he kidnapped her instead, right from her bedroom. He figured he could get money from her husband *and* from Javier, who he'd blackmail about the affair—it would be worth so much more than whatever measly amount Javier had paid him for the tickets! But then the hurricane came through. Javier saved Abigail, and Henry died a crook." Grammy laughs and stares up at the ceiling. "It turns out Henry Emmert had done that sort of thing before, up in Kansas. Kidnapping. He was a wanted man. The cops gave Javier a big reward for turning in Henry Emmert dead. They did that sort of thing in those days."

"Why wasn't that in the paper?" Claire asks before she can stop herself.

Grammy's face turns cold. "You went investigating all of this?"

Claire tightens her fingers on the chair. She glances toward the hallway. She can run faster than Grammy. She can get out. Lawrence is waiting on the other side of the door.

"Of course you did. Your mother always said you were inquisitive. I don't know why it wasn't in the papers. The monsters coming through, it changed so much, it made people confused. That's what they do, you know. Confuse us."

Claire doesn't say anything. The monsters do confuse the people of the town. It's hard to look at them straight on. They erase your memory of them when you pass the city limits. But they're not the real danger. They never have been.

"Anyway, afterward, Javier became Indianola's big hero, people congratulating him everywhere he went." Grammy's eyes glitter. "That was the start of it. When the monsters started causing problems, where did the town turn? Who did they beg to help them?"

Claire doesn't say anything.

"Javier Alvarez." Grammy spits the name. "He sat down with the monsters, orchestrated the treaties. Gave them your great-great-grandfather's land. And I told you what happened then. Without the oilfields, the money dried up."

"That's not Javier's fault," Claire says in a trembling voice.

Rage flashes across Grammy's face. "Of course it is!" she bellows. "By then he and Abigail decided eloping was too risky, and he opened that goddamned hotel. Which did *shockingly* well for a nowhere place like Indianola."

Claire narrows her eyes.

Grammy makes a huff of annoyance. "I have to spell it out for you? Javier made some kind of deal with those monsters. Wouldn't surprise me a bit if he did a little timeline rearranging himself. He made the money while our family lost it. And we switched places."

Grammy looks over at Claire with her fierce glittering eyes. Claire can't breathe.

"Why wouldn't Javier have rearranged the timelines so he and

Abigail could be together?" Claire demands. "He didn't steal our family's money! It was just stupid luck!"

"Don't be a fool," Grammy mutters.

"You're the fool!" Anger surges up inside Claire's chest. "You would have killed me so you could—what? Reverse what happened? You think someone else wouldn't have given the Sudek land to the monsters?"

Grammy glowers, curling her fingers in. "Javier wanted to punish Gregory Garner," she snarls.

"Even so! That's worth killing me over?" Claire trembles. "You're *sick*. It's not like you could live your whole life over again—"

"I wouldn't have to," Gammy says, eyes flashing. "It would *be* my life. Don't you understand? At this point my life is nothing but memories. I wanted to die with good ones."

Claire stares at her. She's still shaking. Memories. "You wouldn't remember me," she says. "Or what you did to me."

There's a long and weighted silence.

"It was a sacrifice," Grammy says. "A small loss to compensate for the larger one a hundred years ago."

Claire lets out a shout of fear, of frustration.

"Don't be like that," Grammy snaps. "You weren't the only sacrifice. That alien wouldn't do it for free, you know. She was taking days of my life away from me. The energy that lets us live. It's what she eats, apparently." Grammy gives a harsh laugh. "She's going to kill me too, you understand, probably after you leave. Only before, I was to die with the memories of my new life, the life Javier Alvarez stole from me. I was to die in our ancestral home. Now I don't even get that."

Claire stares at her in horror, tears streaming down her face.

"And think of what it would have done for the rest of the

family!" Grammy says. "Your mother and aunt would have grown up in splendor—"

A fresh wave of terror washes over Claire. "Did Mom know?"

"What?"

"Is that why she sent me here? Did she know?"

Grammy frowns and settles back in her chair. "No," she says. "I knew she wouldn't understand. She's never been proud of the Sudek name."

Claire's sobs turn to the laughter of relief.

"You're just like her," Grammy whispers. "You don't understand either. It's lost now. Everything. This family will continue to slide into decline."

Claire stands up. She wipes the tears from her eyes, lets the last choking sobs die away. The house is suffocating her. She doesn't want to breathe the same still air as Grammy anymore. It's bad enough they share the same genes.

"The monsters aren't the monsters here," she says.

Grammy looks away.

"Audrey's coming, you know," Claire says. "To collect the rest of her payment."

"I know." Grammy taps her fingers against the arm of the chair. She never looks at Claire, just keeps staring at the wall, the dim lamp light flowing around her. "But don't play the hero, Claire. You won't be able to stop her."

Claire feels shaky. Her heart pounds in her ears.

"Go," Grammy says. "There's nothing here for you anymore."

Claire is crying again, and she doesn't know what she's crying for, if it's the horror of what Grammy did to her, or if it's the strange pain of Grammy's resignation.

"Go!" Grammy shouts. "I don't want you here when the alien arrives."

Claire stumbles out of the living room, into the hallway. Grammy keeps staring at the wall. The front door is a long way away. Claire turns. She walks toward it.

And then she runs toward it.

And then she bursts out into the damp night.

Julie paces back and forth across the driveway, her hands jammed in her pockets. Lawrence is standing alert in the yard and he strides forward when he sees Claire and calls out her name. "Claire! Are you all right?"

Claire nods. Julie stops pacing and lifts her head. Claire runs toward her, weeping so hard, the world looks as if it's underwater.

Julie doesn't say anything, only pulls her into an embrace. Claire presses up against her and cries. They stay like that for a long time, wrapped up together in the middle of the yard while the stars twinkle on unchanged above them.

Grammy's house stays dark. She never comes outside. There's no sign of Audrey, either. At least not yet.

"She wanted to kill me," Claire whispers. "All so she could be rich."

Claire tells the rest of the story, in fits and starts. Saying it aloud cements the hideousness of it all; she thinks back to the suffocating light of Audrey's car, the rain pounding against the roof, the waves washing up on shore.

Her own grandmother did that. She sacrificed herself, just to let Claire die.

"The monsters told me to save you, you know," Julie says suddenly. "After you—they told me I had to save you."

Claire peels away from Julie and blinks up at her through the veil of her tears. "They said if I saved you, then I saved Indianola." Julie runs her thumb down the side of Claire's face. "I think if her plan had worked, Mrs. Sudek wouldn't have gotten rich. I think the whole town would have just been undone."

Claire wonders what Grammy would say to that, if she'd believe it. Or if she'd ignore it all to restore the family name, to die with a lifetime's worth of new memories.

"C'mon," Julie says. "We should get you out of here. You can stay at my place. My parents won't mind."

She loops her arm around Claire's shoulder and pulls her close. They walk toward the driveway a few paces before Julie stops, sucking in her breath through her teeth.

Claire looks up and there's Audrey, illuminated by the yellow glow of the car's headlights. The world around them has frozen again. Audrey glides forward, her strange, inhuman bones shadowing beneath her skin.

"I'm not here for you," she says to Claire.

And then she brushes past Claire and Julie.

Claire turns around, her breath in her throat. Audrey steps onto the front porch of Grammy's house and pulls the door open and steps inside.

For a moment the world seems to hold its breath, and then the light burning in the living room window blinks out.

A blast of sea breeze blows Claire's hair into her face. She turns to Julie, who pulls her arm a little tighter around Claire's waist. "Are you okay?" she whispers as the wind picks up, bringing with it a strange metallic scent that Claire knows, somehow, is connected to Audrey.

She nods numbly. She doesn't know what to say.

Together they walk away from Grammy's house, toward the end of the driveway, into the future.

JULIE

The next morning, Julie wakes up to hot sunlight flooding her bedroom, as if the sun itself has been made brighter by last night's storm.

She lies for a moment in her early morning haze, but then the memory of everything that happened the night before comes rushing back. Claire. Claire almost died. Claire's grandmother was the one who wanted her dead.

And Claire is staying down in the hall, in the guest bedroom.

Julie flings the covers off the bed and slips out into the quiet house. The scent of coffee wafts up from the kitchen. The door to the guest bedroom is closed, and Julie pads over, knocks once.

No answer.

A cold fear seizes her—has Audrey come back?

She flings the door open and finds the room glowing with yellow sunlight, the bed neatly made, Abigail's gray dress hanging to dry over the back of a chair. It's been ruined, seawater stains set deep into the fabric.

A sheet of notebook paper sits in the middle of the bed. Her chest tight, her hands shaking a little, Julie picks it up—but it's a note from Claire. *Went for a walk along Sweetbriar Avenue. Come find me!*

Come find me. An invitation this time, not a rescue.

Julie darts back into her room and changes into the first clothes she can find: cut-off shorts and her Lunachicks shirt and her busted-up old Doc Martens. Then she bounds out into the morning's shimmering brightness.

It doesn't take her long to find Claire. She's at the playground at the end of Sweetbriar Avenue, sitting on the swing set in a sundress she borrowed from the back of Julie's closet. Julie's mom bought that sundress last year, and Julie always refused to wear it—but the tiny floral pattern suits Claire, her hair neat and shining in the lemony morning light, the sea breeze pushing it back away from her face. The air smells clean, the way it always does after a storm, as if the rain washed away all the old layers of salt from everything.

"Hey," Julie calls out, suddenly nervous.

Claire twists around in the swing and gives Julie a wave. Julie moves toward her, picking through the patches of muddy water left over from the storm last night.

"Hey," Claire says as Julie slides into the swing next to her.

They sit quietly for a moment. Claire leans her head against the chain of the swing, her gaze distant.

"How are you doing?" Julie asks.

Claire looks over at her. "I've been better." She laughs. "But I've been a lot worse too."

Julie isn't sure how to react, if it's okay for her to laugh at that.

"Everything still feels—" Claire knots the fabric of the dress up in her fist. "I don't know. I'm going to have to call my mom. Tell her something. I mean—" Claire looks up at the sky. "Audrey was going in there to—to take the rest of Grammy's *life* away. I don't—"

"We can send Lawrence over there," Julie says, pressing her hand against Claire's back. Claire looks up at her and smiles a little, and something flutters sweetly in Julie's stomach. "He can take care of all the official reports and stuff. He can call your mom. It'll probably just look like natural causes, you know?"

"And she was sick." Claire shakes her head. "I mean, Audrey had been—feeding off her for weeks."

Julie nods.

"I wish I could tell my mom the truth." Claire sighs. "But there's no way she'd believe it. I hardly believe it myself, you know?"

"Yeah." Julie squints out at the sun. "It feels like a bad dream."

And it does, especially in the buttery light of morning. Like it could all slip away, a memory undone.

But Julie knows she can't let that happen. She's going to have to sit down with her dad, with the entire council, and explain to them about Audrey and Mrs. Sudek. Lawrence will back her up. They have to know that the monsters aren't enemies. They saved the town. They saved everyone's entire existence.

Just like Javier saved Abigail, all those years ago. And just like Julie saved Claire.

Her cheeks burn a little, thinking about it.

"Thank you again," Claire says, looking down at her hands. "For everything. For letting me stay with you. It probably won't be for long, I'm sure my mom's going to make me go back to Houston."

Julie closes her eyes. She'd been trying not to think about that.

"I don't want to," Claire says quickly. "But—"

"Hey," Julie says. "We'll work it out. We can talk on the phone. You won't remember the monsters, but I'm sure you'll remember me." Julie isn't sure of that, though. She just doesn't want to think of the other possibility: that Claire will pass the city limits and disappear completely.

"I hope so. I mean—" She peers up at Julie, her eyes big and luminous, her cheeks pink from the morning heat. "You saved my life. I just—thank you. Thank you so much."

Claire looks so beautiful in that moment that Julie doesn't want to think about her leaving for Houston. She doesn't want to think about conversations with the council about monsters. She doesn't want to think about anything.

Julie can't help it: She leans forward in her swing and kisses Claire on the mouth.

And Claire kisses back without hesitation, just as she did last night after she was free. She touches Julie lightly on the arm—hesitantly, at first, but she pulls Julie closer, dragging her out of the swing.

"Ow!" Julie laughs, stumbling to her feet. Claire's blushing. Adorable.

"I'm sorry," she says.

"Hey, no worries." Julie grabs her hands and pulls her up to standing and they kiss again, properly this time, their bodies twining together. Claire pulls back, giggles nervously, then kisses Julie along her jawline, along her neck. Julie's whole body flushes with fever.

"Is this okay?" Claire whispers.

"More than okay," Julie says, her heart swelling.

And then something snaps in the shrubbery behind them.

Julie whips around, grabs Claire's hand—but it's just a monster, the one that looks like a small silken alligator. It stands up, unsteady on its hind legs. The red scarf wrapped around its neck flutters in the wind.

"You!" Julie says, surprised.

"Girl," says the monster, nodding at her. Then, to Claire: "Girl."

Julie glances sideways at Claire. She doesn't look afraid, the way she did the first time this monster came for a visit. The first time Julie ever saw her.

The monster drops forward on all fours and ambles toward them, its long thick tail swishing through the muddy grass. Claire squeezes Julie's hand.

"Girls," the monster says.

Julie smiles, glances at Claire. "That's about the whole of it, yeah."

The monster crawls closer, then rises up on its hind legs again. Claire stumbles back a little, but Julie holds firm, looking the monster in the eye. If there's another threat, she's going to stop it.

Instead, the monster drops back down to all fours and scurries away, vanishing into the grass.

"What was that about?" Claire says, a tremble in her voice. "Do you think Audrey—"

A tremor vibrates through the ground, rattling Julie's bones. The air takes on a heavy quality, thick and hard to breathe. Like the air inside the power plant.

And then a towering figure materializes, stepping out of nothing-ness like it's stepping through a doorway. It unfurls itself against the blue sky. Human-shaped, but not quite.

"Aldraa?" Julie gasps.

Aldraa bares his teeth in that way that's meant to be a smile.

"It's okay," Julie says to Claire, who's gaping up at him. "This is Aldraa. He's—" Julie looks over at him. "He's like the leader of the monsters."

"Not exactly." His voice booms out and the playground equipment rattles, clanking like chains. Claire slaps her hands over her ears.

"Forgive me," he says. "I don't often leave the power plant. I know my presence is disturbing to your kind." He bends down, lowering one of his long, strange arms. The gray monster jumps out of the grass and scurries up to Aldraa's shoulder, peering down at Julie and Claire with its bright eyes.

"But I have a gift," he says. "On behalf of all of the *xenade*."

And then he reaches out and presses the tip of one bony finger against Julie's forehead. Something sparks inside her brain, like all the synapses are firing at once. She yelps, reaches out to Claire just as Aldraa does the same thing to her. Claire jerks back, rubs her head.

"What kind of gift?" Julie asks slowly.

The wind picks up. Aldraa draws his hand back. "The council has freed you."

"Freed us?" Julie blinks. "From what?"

"From the cloudiness."

Julie looks over at Claire, who shakes her head a little.

"The cloudiness?" Julie calls out.

"When you leave this place," Aldraa says. "You will remember. You will remember us. You will remember the astronaut. And you will remember each other."

There is a swell of strange, staticky sounds, the wind and the cicadas and the ocean all rolled up together.

Claire is the first to speak. "Thank you," she says, her voice tight. "That's an amazing gift."

"Yeah, I agree. Thank you." Julie takes Claire's hand and smiles up at Aldraa. "That's really righteous of you."

Aldraa makes a low humming noise. "I have been too long outside the power plant," He says. "But I wished to deliver the gift myself." He steps backward, and the playground shudders again, and the strange sounds grows louder and the sun grows hotter and then Aldraa is gone.

Everything is still.

Julie looks over at Claire and feels a surge of electricity between them, then a sudden jolt in the air, and for a half second they are not on a playground in Indianola but standing in front of a coffee shop on a busy street, Claire with a backpack slung over one shoulder, Julie with a stack of flyers for a movie premier. Her movie, she knows. *Their* movie, that they made together.

And then the sound dampens. The world goes still. They're back in Indianola.

Claire's face is gleaming.

"Did you see that?" she whispers. "We were in Austin, I think."

Julie nods.

"The timeline." Aldraa's voice drifts on the wind, painless with distance. "This timeline. Folded for just a second. So you can see what you created."

Julie laughs. Claire throws her arms around her shoulders, startling her, and Julie buries her nose in Claire's hair, breathes in the scent of her flowery shampoo. Breathes in the scent of this timeline, shaped once again by a storm, by a night on the beach, by love.

A timeline where an Alvarez saves a Sudek, but this time, they leave Indianola.

Together.

*   *   *

ACKNOWLEDGMENTS

Five years ago I wrote the last word of the first draft of the book you're currently holding. It's been a long time coming, but I'm delighted that *Forget This Ever Happened* has finally found its way out into the world!

Thank you to my agent, Stacia Decker, for working to find this book a home, and to my editor, Mora Couch, for providing that home! Thanks to Mora as well for her spot-on editorial notes, including the excellent suggestion to set the story in the early '90s.

Thanks as always to my beloved writing community, who is always there to support me no matter what project I'm working on: Amanda Cole, Holly Walrath, Chun Lee, Kevin O'Neill, Michael Glazner, David Young, Bonnie Jo Stufflebeam, Stina Leicht, Elisabeth Commanday Swim, Lauren Dixon, the Writespace crew, and the many others I am probably forgetting to mention. Please forgive me!

And finally, thank you to my parents and to Aaron Holcomb, for all your love and support.